UNCAPPED

The Completionist Chronicles Book Fourteen

DAKOTA KROUT

This is a work of fiction. Names, characters, places, and incidents either are the products of the author's imagination or are used fictitiously. Any resemblance to actual persons, living or dead, businesses, companies, events, or locales is entirely coincidental.

ACKNOWLEDGMENTS

To my fans, thank you for sticking with me, and for coming along for this wild ride. Your support makes all of this possible and gives every chapter purpose.

To my kids, thank you for popping in during writing sessions, for the interruptions that remind me of what matters most.

To my wife, thank you for your constant support, patience, and belief in me, especially on the days when the words refused to come easily.

PROLOGUE

Wind whipped through the Tower of Ritualists, sending thousands of robes flapping as it silently spun through the totality of the hollow center of the massive structure. The currents of power and air were eerily silent; offshoots of the ritual being performed by using all available space on the entirety of the ground-level floor. In the exact center of the space was a monumental metal pod, currently shaped like a lotus flower closed until daybreak. Five distinct groups of Ritualists stood around it in various positions, each of them tasked with fulfilling a singular purpose...

...don't let the ritual fail.

The most powerful among them, Grandmaster Stompetti—usually called Pete—projected to the room in an even, measured voice, "Ritual Circle cohort, begin to breathe in cadence on my count. Inhale four, hold two."

The Grandmaster of Alchemical Rituals had trimmed his beard for the occasion, leaving him with well-kempt facial hair that had turned white years ago. His face, like his hands, were pockmarked with tiny scars from an endless number of failed alchemical concoctions that had burst from his cauldrons, yet neither age nor damage from his craft had dulled him. His features were lined with age, his eyes slightly narrowed with a professional's permanent squint as he managed not only the pseudo-Grandmaster-rank ritual, but seamlessly interfaced with the four Masters running their own subsections.

Pete's hands danced up and out like the conductor of an orchestra, the golden filaments of the spinning ritual hovering in the air nearly kissing his fingertips as he gently nudged streams of mana back and forth through its structure.

"Forging cohort, prepare for a power surge in three, two..." As Pete went quiet, energy erupted from the ritual, nearly striking the pod directly. Only the lightning-quick reflexes of that team allowed the mana to be captured, redirected, and carefully applied as dozens of Ritualists thrust filigreed rods into the air.

Before Joe had come along, there'd never been a base-class Ritualist, meaning each of the people here had extensive backgrounds in other classes and professions. Most of the Ritualistic Forging-focused individuals were former smiths, metal workers, engineers, or even miners who'd become fascinated with the final form of the metal they ripped from the depths of the planet's dungeons. Now they all shared a unified class, but their individual experiences meant that each of them brought something different to the machinations of the lotus-shaped Intraosseous Cocoon. Luckily, only a single Master had the final say in its operations, allowing the group to snap out instructions and ideas without every single one of them being implemented or debated on.

"The actuators are moving at ninety-one percent efficiency; I say we let more mana flow through the outer ring." Levi Redips, Master of Ritualistic Forging, had sparkles in his eyes and was playing with his beaded beard lefthandedly as he stared at the pod in fascination. "If we push that up, we might get a better understanding of the top speed and the stress that ball bearings made of Master-rank alloys can take."

"Don't lose yourself to the song of the machine," the Master in charge of the moving equipment chastised, even as he squeezed a handheld oil can and deftly lubricated an overheating piston. "Remember there's a person in there. Every time one of these moves down, he's getting a needle jabbed back into him. There's only so much trauma a body can take before it breaks down, to say nothing of his mind. I really hope he's asleep in there."

"You mean unconscious."

"Sure," the man in charge let the reply hit him like a bug splattering on a windshield, his indifferent eyes never moving away from the mechanical mandala rising and falling in staggered sequences to create recursive cuts at the microscopic level. "Unconscious would definitely make more sense."

His words drifted up, reaching the sensitive ears of Master Cosmo Hollows, where he stood with his Magical Matrices cohort along the open balcony of the second level, fully surrounding the central space. The undignified Wolfman was nearly the exact opposite of his gruff contemporary a level below–his muzzle was stretched wide as he happily examined the constantly changing sequences the ritual circle was forming with every twist and turn along its multiple axes, his tail happily twitching back and forth as he and his cohort called out instructions to Pete.

A lattice of floating numbers formed in front of Cosmo's face, his own mana shaped into a three-dimensional grid pulling data from the active ritual and giving him deeper insight into the portions he was meant to be controlling, sectioning off, or rerouting. "The first set of scarification around the heart is nearly complete. We should be seeing the parlay with the alchemical ritual activating in seven seconds. Driver corps, prepare to regulate the fluid flow dynamics. I want a full accounting of the movements of the diluted Ichor. Best recounting gets first dibs on the publication of the paper!"

His words brought his group from excited to ecstatic. They nearly *fought* to be the one to stitch coordinate planes to spirals or shout out the speed and rhythm at which each individual needle needed to be moving. Their counterparts controlling the machinery flew into motion, even as other Magical Matrices-focused Ritualists began breaking down the flow rate of the fluid for the alchemists they were assigned to direct. The vast majority of Ritualists in this cohort had come from other math-based classes and professions; yet there were the odd few former accountants in the mix or ex-professors smiling with pleasure at merely needing to be precise with numbers instead of good with students.

"I'm seeing a propagation delay at the edge of circle two," Cosmo suddenly yelped out as the bright orange Ichor—agitating in a clear tank taller and wider than his own body—began to churn and spin in a soft whirlpool next to the lotus. "Compensate by one-point-two-six, and do a phase shift by phi over *three*, not two—trust me on this one. We're not going for a golden ratio; you need to remember to treat his heart as a *plane*."

A giggling Master of Alchemical Rituals worked dozens of dials and valves on a carefully constructed board that would make an airplane pilot feel right at home. He danced back and forth, carefully twisting, pushing, and pulling as the tank of fluid was drained. The torso-thick hose split into hundreds of finger-width tubes, each flowing into the bottom of the lotus and up to the myriad of needles that were even now carving into the flesh and bone of the man in the unit.

"This is *amazing*! Look here! See how the speed of flow just dropped by one one-thousandth? The most likely cause of this *isn't* the dulling of the needles, but that he gained a point in Constitution from the alternating damage and healing he's being subjected to!" Even as his hand darted out to adjust the strength of the pump, his other spiked up and hung in the air for an instant, singling out Master Cosmo. "I want every adjustment recorded; we're getting more data on the effects of Ichor on the human body than we have since the last war!"

Then he was dancing to the other side of the panel, where a small light had begun flashing. "I need three Experts working on peri-vascular cells: they're *far* tougher than the connective tissue. Any random Journeyman can handle *those*... so long as the Ichor is being bound in place *properly*!"

This snide remark was directed at Master Hilda Darling, who was freely floating in the air along with the other four hundred and ninety-nine Enchanted Ritual Circle-focused Ritualists. Unlike the cold, clinical calls erupting from the other groups, Master Darling was calmly explaining the actual process of what was happening to her cohort, all so they could correctly channel the energies being pumped through the body in the pod they were working to keep stabilized. There were multiple reasons for her tranquil explanations, but arguably the most important was the sheer self-assuredness, bordering on arrogance, that her group was known for.

Unlike the other core skills, Enchanted Ritual Circles started massively expensive, became more expensive, and the cost only grew from there. This meant that, before they had prestige, those in her group had come from such vaunted classes as Enchanting, magical material artisans, or at the *very* least, high-end jewelcrafting. With such a high barrier to entry, there were only three types of people who chose this Core Class skill as their main focus: the overwhelmingly wealthy, the impeccably skilled yet bored, or—like Hilda herself—those who truly loved the craft.

"As the needles come down through the soft tissue, a minuscule layer of healing follows along from the ritual proper. Only the final point before the retraction of the needle is left damaged, slowly carving a physical path through each individual cell to form the overall structure of the mana channels." Before she could get any further, Hilda shot a knowing glance at a man, who closed his mouth just before he would've otherwise spoken.

"*Correct*, Roderick, that *isn't* enough to make any of this work. Otherwise, some fool who got stabbed in the chest with a sword would suddenly have the mana capacity of a Legendary monster! Without the alchemical reagents, there would still be no mana conductivity along those newly carved channels." Hilda reached out and touched a small circular token which had been carefully fitted into the outer shell of the pod, letting out a quick breath of relief when its signal **pinged** off the token stuck to Joe and confirmed he was still alive.

A haughty voice pulled her back to the present. "Turning scars into *liquid-filled* scars still shouldn't be enough, but I suppose that's where *we* come in."

Master Darling didn't take her eyes from the surface of the token, reading information directly from the mana signature pulsing into the open air. Making a quick adjustment, she spoke in a stronger tone, "Yes and very much no. In fact, even without our intervention, this process should be enough to have him succeed in his overarching goal. They're carving mana channels and placing a massively conductive magical material inside the cuts–it would be enough-"

"Then why-"

"*-Once.*" Hilda's clipped word snipped off the rest of the irritation-filled question. "I know most of you decided to participate in this ritual simply for the skill gains and uniqueness of the situation, without an understanding of the underlying issues. Creating the channels as they are doing now would allow them to work perfectly, until the subject, Joe, died a single time. Yes, even on Vanaheim, where death isn't *truly* a death, but a return to the tower."

She pressed on decisively, not raising her voice theatrically, but merely keeping to the facts. "Our task is to bind the subject's mana to not only his body, as the alchemical process is doing, but to his Akashic Record. Or, as some among you might say for brevity... his soul. That's right, we're creating permanent scarring along his soul. This is quite the gamble, with very little room for error, and a huge margin of failure. But if it pays off-"

"We're going to get *so* many levels." Variations of this statement rippled back and forth among the floating cohort of Enchanted Ritual-focused Ritualists as their interest rekindled.

"Yes... that's one way to look at it. The other way is that we'll be able to learn how to repair mana channel True Damage inflicted by even a divine entity. The potential for healing purposes, especially from *lower* tiers of damage are-"

"Yeah, yeah." The hasty reply was accompanied by an uninterested wave of the hand. "We're Enchanters; *everything* we do helps other people. Nice to be able to help *ourselves* for once."

"Absolutely."

"It's been ages since my last skill level. Seriously, finding a human-fist-sized diamond has been a nightmare."

"Human fish sized? Like... *exactly*, or what?"

"I said *fist*."

Hilda lapsed into silence and would've been vexed with her contemporaries, were it not for the peerless channeling of their mana they maintained even whilst arguing among themselves, offering backhanded compliments, and intentionally goading each other. Shaking her head, she whispered to herself, "Though they're some of the worst people, no one can deny they're *amazing* craftsmen."

"Viscosity is at one point three, just barely inside tolerance!" Cosmo's voice was pitched to carry, just on the edge of being overtly concerned.

"The heart is encapsulated, moving on to the sternum!" The softest **crunch** escaped the interior of the pod as scores of needles pierced through Joe's bones simultaneously. "Whoo, he's *durable*! Needed to ratchet up the torque on that one."

Power flowed from the enormous ritual floating overhead in carefully portioned tides, supplying each cohort with exactly what they needed due to the exacting calculations of those viewing the Magical Matrices. The needles lifted and fell in synchronized pulses, leaving behind scars and Alchemical ink, which were then bound to Joe by the Master-rank enchanted tokens. Ritual for power, drivers to direct, forgers to punch through, inkers to insert magical conductivity, and binders to apply limited permanence... then back again; a loop of processes happening with near-perfect consistency and timing.

The day wore on, each minute feeling like an eternity as micro-adjustments were made across the entirety of the system, yet the hours slipped by in a rush of constant work.

"We're down to just his extremities at this point; what's the likelihood you'll let me skip his pinky toes?" the exhausted Master of Ritualistic Forging inquired only half-jokingly. "It'd save us thirty minutes-"

"You know, *Grand*masters don't skip any steps." A voice floated down from Hilda's cohort, the man earning a glare from the Master Redips. "That advice is directly from Grandmaster Pete himself. Feel free to argue with him at your leisure."

"Hmph," was all the man in charge of the magical machinery replied as he returned his attention to his work.

An hour later, the depths of Joe's body had been fully carved from the marrow to just below the surface of his skin.

"Down to the last dregs! Work on his brindling."

"Humans don't have stripes, Seraphina."

"Of course they do. Just because *you* can't see them doesn't mean they aren't there."

"Beginning surface-level carving."

This portion was, thankfully, extremely quick, and finally, for the first time in a full twenty-four hours, the machinery went quiet. The enormous tank of diluted Ichor was empty, not even a single drop remaining. The floating group of pleased-looking Enchanters came to a rest on the ground, some stepping back and forth as their legs tingled from having been unused for so long. Only the mathematicians seemed disappointed that it was over, closing their notebooks and dispelling the grids they'd been maintaining in front of their faces.

Yet still the ritual circle itself remained, smaller than before, but spinning that much faster.

Grandmaster Pete lifted his arms above his head, slowly pressing his fingers together. Sweat poured down his face as he worked to bring his hands closer together, the ritual compressing in on itself in conjunction with his motions. With a great shout, the man slammed his palms together. The ritual collapsed in on itself, leaving behind only a single, golden drop of pure power, which dripped from the air and onto the metal lotus, like the final dribble of rain after a thunderstorm just as the sun came out.

The lotus shivered, the metal plates that formed its 'petals' letting out soft shrieks as if they had fully rusted in the single day of use. One after another, they pulled away, slowly revealing the body in their center.

Everyone in the room looked on expectantly as golden power coursed through the grooves of the pod one last time, the immensely powerful machinery letting out a deep groan before falling apart and clattering to the ground in pieces. The tank which had held the Ichor cracked, the only warning anyone had before the entire unit shattered into shards and scattered across the floor.

Only the chair Joe was lying on remained, though that was already showing signs of rapid degradation.

Before anyone could begin spinning out wild theories as to why the Master-rank material was failing, their breath hitched in their chest, knees going weak as a wave of power washed over them.

Joe opened his eyes.

CHAPTER ONE

Agony came first, followed by a purely instinctual reaction to the pain, and finally rational thought.

For a moment, Joe wondered if he was being burned alive, but soon had to admit that this didn't *feel* like fire, more like ten thousand fire ants had buried beneath his skin and were frantically sinking their mandibles directly into his flesh. He'd died a couple of times to flames and lava, and fire at least had the decency to stop hurting after it had burned his nerves to little nubbins.

This was something different: structured torment that flowed along every nerve cluster as his body informed him *exactly* how many times it'd been brought back from the brink of death. His consciousness worked hard to surface, and he became aware of three things simultaneously.

Weight, light, and how strange his body felt.

There was a *density* to every movement as every breath became a struggle, his heart managing to beat despite what felt like hundreds of pounds pressing down on his chest. Blinking rapidly with overweight eyelids, Joe realized he was looking at the world through a slight tint now that his eyeballs had been fully tattooed.

It was the only reason he wasn't squinting at the completely normal light, which felt like staring at the sun thanks to the pain in his head. Finally, he got around to comprehending why his body felt so strange and his half-opened eyes went all-the-way wide.

Power.

It coiled through him, rushing to and fro freely without needing him to push, demand, or beg. A strangled laugh burst out of him, mangled by moving through his chest and emerging as a groan.

"This pain is trying to control you. You don't need pain *anymore. You are beyond it. Let me have it all. Forever. Then it can never convince you not to push harder, to* be *better."*

Joe ignored the sweet succor promised by Mental Manipulation Resistance, recognizing it as the trap it was. After a long few moments, the skill retreated, fading into the background like the passive it was meant to be. Still, the interaction frustrated him greatly, and as he focused on his surroundings for the first time, the Ritualist realized that anyone within a dozen paces of him under the rank of Master had fallen to their knees. They were panting for breath, and it was only as he acknowledged the flood of notifications that he realized *he* was the source of their straining.

Before reading through everything the system had waiting for him, he intentionally reached out to the ambient mana around him, casually pulling it around himself like a form-fitting cape. Immediately, the weight of his presence vanished from those around him. Grandmaster Pete stepped forward, offering Joe a hand as he looked over the near-nude man with a critical eye.

"Success?"

That one word hung in the air like the blade of a guillotine. Joe glanced at the notifications one last time, then ignored them in favor of simply feeling the flow of power through every last inch of himself. Slowly, he lowered his chin, then lifted it, a careful nod as he got used to his new density. Reaching out, he took the Grandmaster's hand and felt himself get pulled to his feet. Pete swished a robe out of his ring, wrapping it around Joe before turning and lifting his hand in the air like a prize-winning boxer.

"*Success*!"

The inhabitants of the tower exploded into cheering, clapping wildly as a wash of system energy flowed through every last one of them. Joe could practically hear the chiming notifications of skills reaching new heights, their experience gains modified by the uniqueness of the ritual, its rarity, and their own contributions.

Finally, the Grandmaster turned to Joe and spoke in a softer voice, "Let's get you out of here so you can figure yourself out, hmm?"

"Yeah." Joe's voice came out in a rasp, and as the Grandmaster wrapped them in a bright green energy, his eyes met Master Darling's for just a moment before he was whisked away.

The Ritualist found himself falling onto a couch in the Grandmaster's office, the furniture letting out a groan of protest and **creaking** ominously as he settled in. Pete stepped back, grimacing slightly. "Don't worry, most of that, uhm, *extra* should vanish over the next few days as the swelling and inflammation goes down."

"What do you mean?" Joe reached up to touch his face, concern filling him as he realized his skin was inflamed and puffy. "Get me a mirror."

"No, no... don't worry too much. You were essentially stung over the entirety of your body by a hive full of Legendary bees for a full day. It would be more surprising if you *didn't* have some kind of, ahh, allergic reaction." Pete gently pressed Joe back into the cushions of the couch as the bald Ritualist struggled to stand. "You're just a little swollen right now. Why don't you ignore that for a little while and focus on your restored mana? I bet the system has some amazing notifications for you!"

"Pete. How bad is it?"

"If you insist. Let's just say, maybe I brought you up here right away so you wouldn't give the youngsters *too* many nightmares." Grandmaster Pete pulled his hand away, and it didn't escape Joe's notice that there was a handprint that stayed in place for a full five seconds after the Grandmaster had stepped back. "It's just lots of swelling. Oh! How's your mana? All the way back? Tell me about that strange effect you had on all of us... some kind of new aura skill?"

"I know what you're doing," Joe growled through a pair of lips that felt like two bratwursts being mushed together. He managed to glare for another full second before finally caving. "Abyss, I hate that it's working."

Congratulations! You have created an artificial Mana Channel system. As this is a method of your own creation, and imparted by your Class's Core Skills, you have been impacted in multiple ways. Each of these changes are permanent, so long as these artificial channels remain in place. If, from this point going forward, you gain more than seven new skills, or push more than seven of your current skills to a new tier, the enchantment holding the channels in place will fail.

Current number of new skills or tier thresholds crossed: 0/7.

You have gained 18 Mastery levels by bringing Mana Manipulation and Coalescence to the peak of the Master Rank! You gain 5 points (x18) in each Characteristic except Karmic Luck.

Congratulations! You have exceeded 20,000 mana! Your title 'Monarch of Mana' has been upgraded!

Title lost: Monarch of Mana.

Title gained: Emperor of Mana. You are the Emperor of Mana, the first person (non-native) to reach a mana pool so vast (20,000) that releasing it in one burst could permanently alter the ambient mana of a low-tier continent.

Effects:

1. *Once per month (720 hours), you are able to instantly refill the entirety of your mana pool.*
2. *As the Emperor of Mana, you are able to bequeath a portion of your mana pool to another non-hostile sapient. Any mana-based skills they increase while having at least 1,000 points of your mana will count as them having learned directly from you and may generate Mastery Merits. But take care... if they betray and slay you while holding mana you have gifted them, it becomes theirs permanently.*
3. *The Monarch of Mana and the Monarch of Manaccretion are considered subordinate to you. Any mana bequeathed to them counts as double.*

Quest notification: Long live the Emperor of Mana!

You have opened a new questline on a higher world! Speak to your chosen deity in person for additional details.

Congratulations! Coalescence (Expert 0) has been artificially evolved into Coalescent Fusion (Master IX). Through external refinement, your mana is now condensed beyond its previous maximum limits, allowing you to form filaments finer than spider silk and denser than tungsten. If your Mana Channels are destroyed, this skill's rank will drop to Master 0.

Effects:

1. *+50% spell efficiency.*
2. *+1.5% mana regeneration per skill level.*
3. *Casting time reduced by 20%.*
4. *Durable Mana: Mana constructs now benefit from the increased mana density, gaining 25% durability.*

If your Mana Channels are destroyed, this skill's rank will drop to Master 0.

Congratulations! Mana Manipulation (Journeyman VIII) has been artificially evolved into Mana Control (Master IX)—

Congratulations! Mana Control (Master IX) has been altered by your title 'Emperor of Mana' and has become Mana Dominion (Master IX). Your mana obeys without needing to be commanded, flowing in accord with your will. An Emperor does not need to demand that Kings move nor make decrees to make his subjects obey.

Effects:

1. *+100% total mana pool.*
2. *+25% spell efficiency.*
3. *Your personal mana extends into the ambient field around you in a radius of 69 feet and works to force all other sources of mana to bend the knee and accept your rule unless you intentionally withhold this effect. All hostile spells have an additional 50% spell instability when targeting you from within this area.*
4. *Ambient Docility: For 1 hour every 24 hours, you may cause the ambient mana in a 69-foot radius to turn placid. All allies benefit from 10% increased mana regeneration and 50% increased spell stability. If you are on land you own or are in control of, this effect extends over the entire area.*

If your Mana Channels are destroyed, this skill's rank will drop to Master 0.

Title Fragment Gained: First Emperor. You are the first person to gain the title of 'Emperor' through sheer resource pool size. This is a fragmented title and may be combined with any other title except 'Emperor of Mana', in any position, to create a new title. Choose wisely, as placement will absolutely alter the final effect.

Due to the upgrading of your title, your Threshold Tribulation has also been upgraded. You have lost the 'Corrupted Characteristics' tribulation and will no longer lose Characteristics upon using mana.

Name: Joe 'Emperor of Mana' Class: Reductionist
Profession I: Arcanologist (Max)
Profession II: Ritualistic Alchemist (15/20)
Profession III: Grandmaster's Apprentice (15/25)
Profession IV: Ritualistic Metalworker (16/20)
Profession V: Ritualistic Numerologist (10/20)

Profession VI: Arcane Enchanting Theorist (5/5) This can now be used as a prerequisite for any enchanting-based profession!

Character Level: 30 Exp: 465,000 Exp to next level: 31,000 (Locked.)
Rituarchitect Level: 15 Exp: 105,450 Exp to next level: 14,550
Reductionist Level: 12 Exp: 85,472 Exp to next level: 5,528

Hit Points: 354/7,966
Mana: 29,540/29,540 (Artificially Repaired)
Mana regen: 261.92/sec (Artificially Repaired)
Stamina: 5,429/5,429
Stamina regen: 8.59/sec

Characteristic: Score
Quad Strength: 499
Dialectic Dexterity: 499
Stoic Constitution: 499
Light Intelligence: 459
Ritualistic Wisdom: 459
Dark Charisma: 459
Karmic Perception: 499
Red Luck: 462
Karmic Luck: 410

"What the *abyss* happened to my Karmic Luck?" Joe closed his eyes and thought over what he'd just read, especially the effects of his increased mana channels combined with his upgraded title. "I'm the 'Emperor of Mana'. I'd say that's *way* cooler than just being in charge of some land and people. I wonder what it takes to become the Monarch of... Manaccretion? I'm guessing that has something to do with mana regeneration, but I find it hard to believe that anyone has more of that than I do. Maybe I could only get one of those two titles, and I got Monarch of Mana first?"

He looked over to the Grandmaster, planning to ask him a few questions, but to his disappointment, found that Pete had vanished. There was a strange feel in the air, a flavor to the ambient mana that Joe realized he could easily understand, thanks to his peak Mastery and the incredible sensitivity granted by his restored mana. "He's messing around with the Mythic Core... is he going to ascend right now? I don't want to miss that-"

Attempting to struggle to his feet ended in a laughable failure as his head spun, and his body complained bitterly. An annoyed glance at his current health reminded the Ritualist that he was practically on the brink of death, but his eyebrows shot up as he realized he now had all of the tools necessary to repair his broken skills and spells. "He's not going to ascend to Sage without inviting me along to a ceremony, right?"

Reaching for his mana, Joe felt it move through his body and into the close space around him, held just above his skin, thanks to the thin wrap of willpower he'd applied to himself to keep the lower-ranked Ritualists from getting overwhelmed by his presence. "Oooh. That's *nice.* Like spinning a cloud of the world's softest cotton candy out of every pore."

After so long without being able to properly access and utilize his power, he allowed himself a long few minutes to simply luxuriate in the sensation, creating intricate shapes and diagrams in the air without needing to use his hands, trace with an inscription tool, or force his ocean of mana through the equivalent of a coffee straw. Finally, before delving into fixing and reconnecting his skills, he turned his attention to the final notifications he'd been avoiding—a bright red set informing him of all of the *detriments* of his new situation. "All right, system. Go ahead and show me what this is costing."

Quest Gained: Master of Ritualists I. You have reached the threshold where personal Mastery is no longer sufficient to advance. To grow further, you must propagate your skills and prove that your understanding of rituals is transferable and capable of surviving outside of yourself. Earn 100 Mastery Merits by teaching ritual-based skills of any kind. 6/100.

Notes:

A Mastery Merit is awarded only when one of your students reaches the Master rank in the skill being taught by following your instruction.

As you are a class trainer, you gain this mission as a Chain Quest.

Quest Updated: Integrating the Foundation. This title you chose to become your foundational integration goal has upgraded. Thus, your Tribulation has changed accordingly.

Tribulation determined: Paradoxical Heart Demon. Every Emperor knows the pain of control. Expanding the empire requires sacrifice, a price they must be willing to pay lest the domain crumbles. For the good of their subjects, they must refuse almost all opportunities presented, knowing that personal gain must never become more important than imperial necessity.

Effects:

1. *The requirements to acquire any skill or spell are reduced by 95%.*
2. *The Emperor's will is not infinite. Rejecting an offered skill or spell when the opportunity arises is the same as rejecting a gifted tribute from a surrendering kingdom. The requirements to acquire rejected skills or spells become 110% higher.*
3. *There are no other benefits to be gained from denying a skill.*

"That's... odd. Are there *usually* benefits from denying a skill?" Joe read over the information on the tribulation once more, confused as to why it was offering this tremendous benefit and calling it a tribulation. "I can basically go out and gain every possible skill and spell with almost no effort? Why's that—*oooh*, right. I can only learn seven before the enchantment holding my mana channels in place fails. So, it's interacting with that? That's a pretty *personalized* tribulation. Not only would I need to reapply all of the alchemical inks and make the ritual and Master-rank components again, but I'd probably lose my title as Emperor at the same time as losing my mana pool. That's... that's just *wrong*!"

The conniving part of him had Joe pursing his lips and drumming his fingers on the armrest of the couch. "Then again, it only says the *enchantment* will fail if I gain more than seven.

Does that mean I could keep all of these and have my channels remain in place, so long as I'm really careful not to die even once? Grab eight, ten, thirty new skills... and just *don't* die, no matter what? Ignore the enchantment keeping it all stable?"

Skill offered: Schemes of the Self-saboteur (Novice I). You have learned the subtle art of undermining your own triumphs.

Effect: At random intervals of major successes, you will subconsciously generate a self-sabotaging plot which rips the success from your fingertips. Instead of any rewards you would have gained, you are instead granted Characteristic points considered of (1+n%) value to the lost rewards, where n = skill level.

Accept? Yes / No.

"No! Refuse!" Joe watched the notification vanish with wide eyes. "Abyss, the worst part is that a skill like that would bring me to the threshold pretty quickly. That had to have been at *least* a Legendary skill. Celestial feces, got it. This is a tribulation targeting the weakest part of myself, my desire for magic and power. Hmm. Looks like hoping for the best isn't a real plan. If I want to have everything I want and be a real completionist, gotta stick with slow and steady."

Now that there were no outstanding notifications, Joe closed his eyes and turned his attention inward, settling into a deep breathing pattern that quickly caused the world around him to fade away. When he next opened his eyes...

... he was staring at the terribly damaged palace his mind had conjured to represent his Akashic record.

CHAPTER TWO

10.

The jagged, bright red number hovered in front of Joe's face until he swatted it away. Only then was he able to sweep his gaze over the superstructure, any details he wasn't focusing on directly devolving into a dreamlike quality.

With a careful application of the same part of him that controlled his Combat Ritual Orbs, Joe flung himself forward and into the palace, which then expanded out to become the entirety of his mindscape. In the very central area were a little over two dozen structures with no, or at best, very minimal damage. Even so, he frowned as he saw that one of them was *shimmering* with power, a thin barrier surrounding it that he intrinsically understood to be fully indestructible to his current self.

"That must be my Natural Magical Material Creation. I guess it's still under review? I'd bet Tatum is arguing furiously on my behalf. Heh. Must be doing a good job, too; I thought it'd be gone already." Turning his attention to the outer area, to his external-facing active skills, Joe winced as he spied the damage once more.

Structures were damaged, shattered, marble surfaces chipped and flickering with spasmodic energy. Since the last time he'd been here, one of the buildings had degraded further, half-collapsing against its neighbor and only being held upright by putting an increasing amount of strain on both. With a flicker of intent, Joe was suddenly hovering next to them, concern mounting as his mind whispered that the building in the process of collapsing was arguably his favorite: Neutrality Aura.

Stepping into the skill caused its structure to expand out to the horizon, and the Ritualist found himself wading through streams of energy and motes of dust that were slowly floating in the air and bleeding away at a slow, yet consistent pace. "What happened here? This *was* at least somewhat stable. Could it be that fixing my mana channels did this?"

The orb representing Joe's presence in his mind suddenly erupted with filaments of mana, looking for all the world like a dazzling dandelion seed pod as he extended his reach out and dug into the skill. He followed the sympathetic lines connecting the skill into a cohesive whole, then traced the steps along the pathways joining it to his body. At least, the pathways that *should* have been connecting it to his body.

"I see... Grandmaster Snow had told me there were waypoints through my body I could use to reconnect my skills once I fixed them. Looks like those are gone, now that I carved out new, mathematically optimal versions. Abyss. How am I supposed to reestablish my skills if the pathing they originally used is gone?" Grumbling softly to himself, Joe pulled his mana filaments back, threading them through the skill and rapidly reconnecting chunks of material that had fallen away.

Enormous sections of wall were lifted and reattached, a weave of power made of Joe's incredibly durable mana crocheting the sections into place. The ceiling joined together, the foundation of the skill letting out a warbling groan as he righted the structure with sheer force of will and a generous application of mana. Dust rained down around him as he held still, then ever-so-slowly unwrapped his impeccable control and drew himself in. "Stay up, you're fine..."

The creaking noises grew louder, then rapidly vanished as the structure settled in place.

Neutrality Aura integrity: 29% → 63%.

"Really? It was *that* bad? Didn't look like it," Joe murmured as he inspected the skill more closely. His head wobbled back and forth as he took in the massive cracks running through the entirety of the place, from the floor to the ceiling, giving the building a feel of standing inside a broken clay pot that had been puzzled back together without any adhesives to keep it in place. "There's nothing left on the floor or around here... must mean the skill lost a chunk of the Divine Energy it was originally made with. Good thing I've upgraded it a few times without his help, or it might've ended up as bad as Knowledge was."

He quickly flitted around to the other skills, but seeing as none of them were in danger of collapsing, and there was no clear method of restoring them, the Ritualist decided to take a break and perhaps even seek some advice. "At least Omnivault is still deeply connected to my body. Just need to figure out how to do a couple of repairs, and it'll be fully functional."

Taking a few quick breaths, Joe opened his eyes once more to the view of Grandmaster Pete's office. "Alright, legs. No more excuses, we're going to get up and go figure out what's going on-"

Skill offered: Skill Repair (Novice III). You have reconstructed a damaged skill using brute force and impeccable control of your mana. This skill will allow you to understand the fundamentals of restoring skills when portions of their original creation are irreparably lost.

Effect: Enables the repair of skills up to the tier of this skill, using exotic reagents to facilitate regrowth or skill scarification at n% efficiency, where n = skill level.

"Refuse skill," Joe grumbled without even allowing it to fully finish its offering. Immediately the notification vanished, as did the very real temptation. "Something tells me I'm going to see a lot of these in the near future. First, system, remove the explanation of what 'n' means. I've got it. It's the skill level."

Preferences saved.

"Good. Second, pretty sure that skill only *looked* useful. I don't have any Novice-rank skills to repair, and getting that up to the Master rank, where I need it, would be the same as throwing away my new enchantment." Shaking his head consideringly, Joe's eyes went distant. "No... what I need is some experience, maybe seeing this get done first-hand? I'm sure I'd be able to mimic someone else's methods. Wait a moment-"

Pulling up his pending quest rewards, the Ritualist quickly found the 'Karmic Remapping' he had earned as a reward from Queen Cleocatra. "This is probably *exactly* what I need, and of course she knew I would. Can I last until I see her? Mmm... probably. At least it looked like Neutrality Aura was the worst off of all of them; hopefully she'll be able to fix it, and I can take it from there."

Blinking a few times, Joe shook off his fatigue and used both hands to press against the armrest of the couch, managing to leverage himself into a standing position after a long few seconds. He took a step, lips curling in disgust as he felt fluid rushing from the bottom of his feet to the top when they pressed against the floor. "Bleh. The inflammation still hasn't gone down... I think I need a healer."

**Click.*

The door opening grabbed his attention, mercifully allowing him to focus on anything other than his swollen body. Jenny peeked in, face red and panting from exertion, having very obviously just ran up the staircase circling the entire interior of the tower to reach the Grandmaster's penthouse office. Seeing that he was awake, she allowed herself to take huge gulps of air, no longer trying to be quiet.

"Tri-Master Joe!" She bent over slightly, the door swinging wide of its own accord as she sucked wind. "Good! You're awake. He said he'd wait for you, **huuuuh**, but I can see how badly he wants to go."

"He's about to use the Mythic Core?"

"Grandmaster Pete is... uh, yeah." Confusion overrode exhaustion for a moment. "How'd you know? He said it was going to be a surprise."

"I can feel the energy in the air." Joe only shrugged at the incredulous expression she gave him in return for his apparent non-answer. "Something about not having great access to my mana for over a year has made me *really* sensitive to it. Everything has a certain flavor, and the Mythic Core feels like pure potential, a soft singing in my ears telling me that great things are about to happen."

"Please tell me that's a skill and not something I should be concerned about." Jenny stepped into the office fully, coming to stand next to Joe and putting his arm around her shoulder. "Come on, I'll help you down the stairs. What the... is your arm filled with cinderblocks? Never mind, I'll just have to stand next to you and warn people to get out of the way if ya start falling toward 'em."

"*Thanks.*" The sarcasm in his tone could've curdled enough milk for him to buy a good meal on Vanaheim, but her words only made him move faster. The Ritualist shuffled across the office, taking half-steps at a time. When Jenny once again reached out to help him, now somewhat impatiently, she let out a soft yelp of surprise as the static electricity buildup zapped her hand. "Heh. Serves you right. Might want to stay back; it's a long way to the bottom of the tower. Lots of chances to-"

"Oh, we don't need to go down that far. Just one level. There's a chamber designated for any major ascensions one floor down. It's specially reinforced, and every tower has one so they can keep their most powerful people as secrets." Her breathing had calmed down, and even with Joe's pain-induced grumpiness, her mood was only improving. "I've never seen it, since there's never been any reason for me to go in there. It's supposed to hide all traces of someone reaching the rank of Sage, but... who knows? We've never had one before! Know the best part? I only get to come to this one because I'm your personal assistant, and-"

Joe's foggy brain finally tuned out her enthusiastic chatter, fully focused on putting one step in front of the other. "Seriously... how long am I going to feel this bad?"

Active debuffs:

Inflammation (Extreme). Movement speed reduced 70%. Positive effects of Charisma reduced 80%. Time remaining: 100 hours.

Filthy (Egregious). Positive effects of Charisma reduced 70%. Time remaining: ∞.

Artificially Enhanced (Overwhelmingly Extreme). 7 skill gains or tier changes will cause the enchantment binding your mana, body, and Akashic Record to fail. Current progress to enchantment faltering: 0/7.

"Four more days of this?" Joe let out a long breath as he took in the other information he *hadn't* been expecting. "Looks like I should probably take a shower when we're all done there."

"Honestly?" Jenny interjected, as he'd mumbled loudly enough for her to hear. "Yeah. You know, they might be willing to wait-"

"I'm not going to ask them to postpone just because I smell like blood and pain-scented sweat." Joe was going to say more but had to swipe away a skill notification at that moment.

Skill offered: Socially Shameless. When a mommy mulch pile and a daddy dumpster love each other very much-

"Reject skill."

-They make something that smells like you. Skill rejected.

By the time Joe's heavy head tilted upward, he was being ushered through an unfamiliar doorway. Unlike the experimental ritual he'd subjected himself to, where thousands of people had been present and assisting in their own way, this room only had a relatively small number of people in it–a bare few dozen allowed in to witness yet another historical moment for the Tower of Ritualists.

"Glad you could make it," Pete called from the front of the

room where he was standing on a short dais. Next to him was a rickety table with an intricately carved wooden box atop it, but certainly the most eye-catching feature was how the Grandmaster was wearing only a loose pair of boxers. His wrinkly skin covered surprisingly well-defined muscles, his years of being the last line of defense for the tower necessitating his constant physical upkeep. "I think that's everyone; shall we begin?"

Joe sat next to Master Darling, his face going pale as the wooden chair **creaked** and wobbled as he sat heavily. Over the next few seconds, he slid slightly lower, fluid rushing away from his posterior as his internal damage rearranged itself. "I think I hate this debuff."

"Probably why they call them 'debuffs' instead of 'these are funs'," Hilda shot back at him, her grin turning into something sharper as she looked toward him, nose twitching. Leaning away, she reached into a pack, pulling out a familiar service bell and offering it to him at arm's length. "Instant cleanse?"

"*Celestial-*!"Joe had never slapped a bell as quickly in his life. A tingling sensation raced from his palm, covering his hand and racing along his arms before spreading out across the entirety of his body. Heaving a great sigh of happiness, he leaned back as a pervasive itch vanished from his skin. "Now I just need some serious healing, and I'll be good as new. Thanks for that."

"No. Trust me when I say the pleasure is *all* mine." Hilda let go of the breath she'd been holding for the last long few seconds, taking a shallow test sniff before allowing herself to breathe normally. "Listen, there's a few things you need to know about the enchantment on you before you start trying to-"

"*Shh*!"

Anything more she was going to say faded into the background as Pete reached out for the wooden box, and all eyes turned to him.

The hinges swung open without a sound, and a riot of

power and light immediately blasted from the box, saturating the room and driving out all other sensations. In actuality, the room was deathly silent, but the cacophony of sensation seemed to demand thunderclaps and the rumbling of stones. Yet there was no heat or turbulence; the Mythic Core represented pure, stable potential.

Reaching into the box, the Grandmaster pulled out the palm-sized core. It was impossible to look at the gem directly, so Joe could only tell its relative position from where the shadows formed when the core was cupped in the old man's palm. "Two centuries of effort, and finally... we've done it. After today, the Tower of Ritualists will have its own Sage."

Pete looked down at his open hand, his eyes reflecting the bizarre light composed of perfect darkness speckled with silver —as though he were staring into the starry night sky. Then he began speaking, obviously answering questions the system was throwing at him. "Yes. Yes. I understand. I suppose... thirty-five. Yes, I'm sure."

"That's what it looks like from the outside, huh? No wonder I get such strange looks when I'm interacting with the system." Joe muttered softly, earning himself an elbow in the side from Master Darling. To his horror, her elbow sank in, leaving a depression that filled only slowly after she yanked her arm back.

Luckily, he was the only one who noticed, since everyone else was staring at the old man standing on the raised dais. The Grandmaster clenched his hand and smiled.

It was a small smile, but utterly joyful and genuine. The Mythic Core flared a single time before the inky, silver-speckled light crawled along his skin, coating the man entirely for a long few moments before sinking through the surface and worming its way through his body. Pete stiffened, taking a sharp, deep breath as his now-empty hand reached for the rickety table. His fingers dug into the wooden surface, flexing and splintering the furniture as his other hand came up to clutch at his heart.

With the core's energy absorbed, mana rushed in toward him as though he'd become the eye of a hurricane, his veins glowing silver as his skin shifted and tightened. Then golden threads began extending through the air away from him, and Joe barely managed to look at a few of them before they split, cleanly sliced away and leaving behind a strange afterimage of unknown people.

Still, he could tell *what* the people were, if not *who*.

Dozens of alchemists, working on various potions and the like. Then there were far fewer people drawing out circles and scattered handfuls of others doing odd tasks Joe didn't have a name for. Lastly, a golden light connected to *him*, and Joe felt a shock run through his body as the thread connecting them cut off and vanished with a **pop**.

Karmic Tie to Grandmaster Stompetti severed! As you are owed for services rendered, the debt between you has been resolved in your favor. All Quests in place between the two of you are now considered nullified.

1. *Sponsorship in the Tower of Rituals. +10.*
2. *Training as able. No less than one hour per month. +35.*
3. *Dedicated support when attempting to break through a bottleneck in your core skills, until each of your core skills enter the Grandmaster ranks. +30.*
4. *Support should you ever be in competition for the position of Class Sage of Ritualists. +10.*
5. *Direct mentorship under Class Sage Mirascible. Only the facilitator of the deal, creating a bond, not a debt. The bond remains in place.*

Reward for resolving all Karmic Debt: +85 Mastery Merits.

Though he was angry and confused by the sudden severing, Joe didn't have time to ask questions just yet, as it appeared the Grandmaster's body was being rewritten in real time. The process wasn't violent nor exactly gentle. It was simply *inevitable.*

Pete pushed away from the table, which exploded into

splinters and shrapnel under his powerful movement. He stood tall, chin tilted slightly upward with his eyes closed. For a heartbeat, then two, he remained motionless... then he exhaled, and the final changes from ascending washed over him.

His wrinkly skin tightened, gaining a luster that had long since been lost. His white beard, mustache, and shoulder-length hair gained color, going from white to a deep chestnut. Only his eyes remained the same when he opened them, filled with depth and experience, just as sharp and perceptive as ever.

"All done."

Tower announcement! Grandmaster Stompetti has broken through to become the first Skill Sage of Alchemical Rituals.

Sage Stompetti has earned a massive influx of Honor for the tower, with a multiplier being applied due to being the first Skill Sage to rise from this tower.

The Tower of Ritualists gains one year of immunity from losing their tower due to lack of Honor, to give the new Sage time to consolidate his power base.

Every person in the room stood, Joe struggling to follow along with the seemingly practiced motions as they all offered a deep bow to the newly ascended Skill Sage.

Congratulations! You have directly witnessed the Ascension of a Sage! For the next 30 days, Inspiration and Enlightenment come to you with far greater ease.

"In case anyone was wondering, I could have chosen any age, down to my early twenties," Sage Pete called out to the room, breaking the reverent silence with his laughter. "But I feel I was most handsome at thirty-five. How'd I do?"

Before anyone could answer, a panicked young man burst into the room. "There's hundreds of people closing in on the tower! I think they're going to attack!"

"What?" Pete's voice was thunderous, "How could they possibly have known I was ascending? We were in a secured ascension room! Even when I checked on it earlier, there's no way someone outside the tower could have felt that! Do we have a traitor in our midst?"

Everyone looked around with sudden distrust, and Joe's eyes landed on Jenny, her face pale and her mouth slack. "Jenny? What did you *do*?"

"I... I..." She turned to face Joe fully, desperate fear in her eyes. "I think I forgot to shut the door behind us."

CHAPTER THREE

For a breathless moment, no one in the room spoke. They simply stared at Joe's pale, trembling assistant as her admission hung in the air.

Joe reached up and pinched the bridge of his nose, letting go almost immediately as he felt the Christmas-ornament-sized shnozz go **squish**. "Abyss."

Skill offered: Body Deformation. (Apprentice IV). With this skill, your flesh is not a fixed sculpture, but a canvas waiting to be repainted. With only minimal pain, you can edit the obvious portions of your anatomy. While uncomfortable, it is even more believable than illusions or glamour. As a subskill of-

"Reject it." The Ritualist's soft voice was harsh and nasally until his nostrils popped open once more.

Happily, Sage Pete took Jenny's mishandling of the tower's security in stride, shrugging his youthful shoulders and allowing a confident, challenging expression to take over his face. "Eh, they had to find out sometime. What are they going to do? Try and take our tower? They've been doing that for decades and never managed. Now we have immunity, so I'm even less concerned. Let's go. *I'll* take care of this."

He began striding through the room, bare feet slapping against the stone floor, when one of the small group of people who'd been invited stepped in his path, holding up a hand. "Sage Pete-"

"It'll be no trouble at all. Even if it was, I'm finally strong enough to activate the failsafe ritual painted onto the tower-"

"I have no doubt that you can handle this, but I was wondering if you could, perhaps, represent us better while fully clothed." The Master Alchemist pointedly glanced down at Pete's hairy chest and gleaming thighs. "Just a small consideration."

Pushing himself from his chair, Joe reached into his re-equipped spatial ring and yanked out the spare robe Sage Pete had wrapped around him upon his emergence from the metal lotus. He draped it around the other man, marveling over the fact that the man now appeared no older than himself. "Looking good, Sage. Could we chat later? I know that, according to the system, you owe me nothing. But I'd still love your support as I push through the Grandmaster ranks."

"I'll support you as I'm able, but the ascension took far longer than you were able to see. Suffice it to say, I've been given many instructions and reasons to hold off on binding myself with any additional Karmic Debt–ah. We'll need to have this conversation later." As the Sage was speaking, a deep tone rolled through the tower, the equivalent of a doorbell being rung... or a challenge being issued. A confident smile curled the edges of his lips. "It seems we have *guests.*"

As the group of Masters trailed along behind the Sage, their casual walking speed bringing them to the base of the tower after only a few minutes, Pete snapped out instructions and directions to his subordinates; his eyes brushing over where Joe was still hustling down the stairs painfully slowly, his lungs working overtime.

Skill offered: Harsh Breath (Beginner I). You drag the world into your lungs like it owes you a debt. Each rasping breath scrapes weakness from your muscles and replaces it with a burst of energy-

"Ignore. No, wait! Gah, it's gone," Joe sputtered indignantly as he tried to catch himself, realizing that, while this was not exactly a pleasant-sounding skill, he might have just missed out on a stamina regeneration ability. "Abyss... maybe I should at least let the skill finish appearing before I toss it."

"I want everyone in their usual positions. Keep the outer gate closed and prepare barriers. If anyone so much as sneezes angrily in our direction, I want the disease damage returned to them a hundredfold." His voice easily cut through the nervous chatter filling the immense open space as literally thousands of Ritualists prepared themselves for a siege. Still, his levity and obvious euphoria kept the mood of those listening to him calm and even.

Even Joe, at the back of the group and struggling to match their pace with his current debuffs, felt himself breathing easier, seeing as the Sage didn't seem to be worried about the calamity he and his helper may have brought on the tower.

"You think it's going to be an all-out attack?" a forge-scarred Master that Joe recognized only by sight inquired in a low tone. "We can't lose the tower due to a lack of Honor; but they could still break in and sweep us out of the place until we relinquish it entirely."

"I placed the odds of that at under five percent," Master Hollows replied genially. "More likely, this is going to be the first attempt by the Ascensionist and Traditionalists of the Council of Sages attempting to sway us to their side and revoke our current state of political neutrality. I'm guessing there is a thirty percent chance of both sides deciding on an intimidation tactic, but that opens Vanaheim to an internal war. Most likely, we will be fending off attempts at negotiation."

"Honey catching more flies than vinegar," Master Darling murmured, summing up the situation perfectly.

Pete turned to look over his shoulder, his expression unreadable. "I suppose we'll know for certain soon enough, won't we?"

Joe felt a shiver race up his spine, his eyes following the

ramrod-straight marching of the Sage as he hurried to the front doors of the tower. "I hope a return to a youthful body hasn't made him more apt to... lashing out."

The doors were thrown open, and in only a few moments, a confident and powerful contingent of Ritualists were approaching the front gate. Pete subtly gestured with his offhand, and the enormous barrier parted ever so slightly to allow them through.

"Pretty sure you *just* told us you wanted the gate to remain closed," an alchemist spoke up, gritting his teeth as he realized he'd just called out a Sage in his own home.

"Ha! I did, didn't I?" Pete turned to face all of them, his posture unbelievably relaxed, compared to even moments before. "Sorry, I forget that the rest of you don't have the same kind of senses I do at this point. False alarm, this isn't an attack. Master Hollows was correct."

The gates threw themselves open wide as a sweet scent rolled through them, washing over Joe with enough potency that he nearly began sneezing. It took his brain a few moments to catch up to what he was seeing and experiencing, but when he did, it took serious effort to keep his jaw from dropping.

Wagons full of flower arrangements had come to a halt in a horseshoe shape around the gate, leaving plenty of space for people to come and go without impeding the flow of traffic. People hauling crates were lagging behind dozens of elaborate carriages being pulled by brawny men and women with thighs the thickness of Joe's torso. Entire preserved monster carcasses were being hauled on stretchers between people, and barrels of potent drinks sat next to casks of alchemical reagents. Large chests were set out, the tops thrown open to reveal gemstones the size of fists, exotic threads, sculptures, and lastly a carriage just as luxurious as those people were riding over in, but entirely empty.

It came to a stop in front of the gates, revealing that its side had been carved with a perfect representation of Sage Pete as he currently appeared–showing that even this was a gift.

"How did the Tower of Locomotion know-" Pete snapped his mouth shut with a sharp **click* as the enormous man pulling the carriage along looked over at him smugly.

"It's our job to know how to serve our customers perfectly."

Joe felt an intense wave of vertigo wash over him as he realized the man hauling the resplendent carriage along was a *Grandmaster*. After pressing a button, the harness wrapped around his chest popped off, and he stepped forward to offer a polite bow to Pete. "Sages can't just show up to important events on foot. It would give the wrong impression. Make people think there's a fight brewin'."

"Then every one of those carriages rolling toward us..." Hilda's expression pinched, her professionalism fighting a losing battle with annoyance, "Has a Sage in it?"

Joe's eyes took in the arrangements of gifts, recognizing belatedly that they'd been piled in two distinct sections, with several feet of space between the closest of them. As the carriages approached, they also split off, and soon dozens of the most powerful people on the planet had arranged themselves alongside the gifts they were presenting to their newly ascended peer.

Once the two sides had formed up facing each other, sending polite, if somewhat strained, nods at their counterparts, everyone turned to face Sage Pete expectantly. He stepped forward, arms akimbo, and took the initiative.

"Word spreads fast!" the youth-enized Pete spoke with great joviality, looking around at the representatives of the Sages' Council. "Thank you all for your gifts and well-wishes. As each of you have gone through this process yourself, I'm certain you understand when I say that I am currently exhausted and in need of consolidating my newfound power. I'd be happy to host you another time."

"We look forward to having many... conversations with you over the coming weeks," one of the Sages stated rather coolly, her words seeming to resonate with the sensation of fluidity and water. Joe took a deep breath, luxuriating in the gentle feel of fresh spring water washing over him. "I know that *Class* Sage Scuddy of the Sub-sea would take it as a personal favor-"

"I don't suppose we could convince you to make an appearance at the next meeting of the Sages' Council?" These words were stated politely but were filled with such immense sharpness that Joe gasped as his chest burst open with a massive gout of blood immediately flowing out and washing over his previously white robes. He wasn't the only one injured, but certainly he was the one most visibly impacted by the... sword intent? To his credit, the speaking Sage paled and lifted a hand, snapping his fingers to direct one of his subordinates forward. "Abyss, it happened again."

"Never fear, this is why you have the Tower of Healing on retainer, Sage Eldrin. I heal your conversation partners, and you treat me and mine *wheely* well." The demure words of the Grandmaster stepping forward were *wildly* incongruent with the smug confidence radiating off of her. Placing both of her palms together in front of her chest, she pressed them together for a moment, then separated them, and a beam of golden white light connected her to the space around Joe.

The Ritualist glanced down, noting with great concern that his new cut was only half healed and still bleeding profusely. "Was that a diagnostic spell, or...?"

By the time he looked up once again, the healer was glaring at him. Through gritted teeth, she called over, "My only intent is to heal you and simultaneously fix the damage to your garments. If you'd be so kind as to lower your barrier or accept the spell so as to allow it to ignore your magic resistance, I'll try again."

"My barrier?" Joe faltered momentarily, until he recalled how all hostile spells entering his Mana Dominion gained fifty percent spell instability when targeting him. Frowning and not quite understanding how a spell meant to heal him could be considered hostile, the Ritualist glanced at Pete, which seemed to be the wrong answer, as the healer was practically vibrating with rage after the Sage nodded to confirm.

"Confirming my good intentions with someone else? I'm from the Tower of *Healers*."

"I would happily accept your healing." As Pete nodded, Joe half-gasped the words with wobbling knees. "That's a pretty nasty... bleed debuff. You wouldn't happen to be a Bard, would you? Cutting Words is a staple spell for them, I hear."

"Let's chalk that comment up to the blood loss." Eldrin spoke very softly, though the grass in a wide circle around him was sliced down to only an inch in height, leaving a perfectly mowed crop circle surrounding the man. Another beam of white light sprang across the area, collecting around Joe and this time sinking into him. "As I was saying, Sage Pete, we would love to host you in the council chambers to make your declaration for a faction or assure us of your neutrality."

Already Pete was shaking his head, though he never lost his pleasant expression. "Thank you for the demonstration of *exactly* why I need to take some time to learn control over my burgeoning Alchemical Ritual intent. For the time being, I will need to retain my previous stance of political neutrality. Thank you for healing my... friend here. I'll be certain to send a formal answer to the council."

The glow around Joe faded away, and he stood up with a wide smile on his no-longer-swollen face. "Abyss, that's good stuff. Healing, debuff removal, and gear restoration as a single spell? How do I get access to that?"

"First you become a healer, then you become a Master healer, then a *Grandmaster*." The scowl on the healer's face softened slightly as she realized Joe was speaking in earnest, and she preened slightly at the implied praise. "Or, far more economical, you hire one of us and pay a one-year parmesan per cast."

When Joe didn't flinch at the cost, her eyebrows shot up, and he could practically see her immediately began reevaluating his position in society. He didn't have the heart to tell her that the cost of things on this world simply hadn't started really registering yet, and so stepped back deeper into his group, as

Sage Pete exchanged pleasantries for a short while longer before allowing the various groups to haul in the treasures they'd brought.

When the final crate had been gently set down, and the gates closed to cut off the view of all of the newcomers, Sage Pete sank in place, taking several deep breaths with his eyes closed. "Celestial feces, what a *minefield* that was."

"*Obscene* is what it was." A snarl came from one of the Masters of Enchanted Rituals. "They come here trying to buy favor, after spending years calling us fools for following a 'dead-end prestige path'? Then the second we have a Sage, every last one of them is scrambling to pretend they *supported* us this whole time?"

"Well, hold on, I saw a fist-sized diamond in there, and I've really been after one-"

"It's all just politics." One of the alchemists shrugged, his eyes locked on a knee-high cask of reagents among the bribes masquerading as gifts. "Refusing to take something in would be the same as us declaring for the other side. Why *not* let them drown us in generosity while they still think they can pull us into their clutches?"

"What is it about you and gemstone fish-?"

"Is that an *Artifact* abacus? The Sage won't want to keep that for himself, will he?"

"That's it, then?" Joe spoke over the devolving group, his rapid increases in skill rank and prestige as a Decury Duelist affording him great respect among his peers, though he was by *far* the newest among them. "No siege, no world-spanning war? Just a bunch of fancy things dropped off at the gate to show... what? That they'd *really* like us not to work with the other side?"

"Politics." Pete nodded in disgruntlement before squaring his shoulders and flashing a smile at the bald man looking at him with a complicated expression. "On the plus side, we won't have to worry about being attacked for a good long time. The tower is safe, and our people will be able to roam the world without being troubled. Besides my own ascension and your mana channels being repaired, this is some of the best news I've had in years."

Joe perked up at that. "You think it's safe to go for a walk, then? I have some friends on the planet I haven't checked in on since I first arrived."

"If it ends up *not* being safe, it won't just be me coming down on whoever goes after you." Pete's smile showed a few too many teeth to be considered anything but savage. "I'll be more than happy to make it known that an attack on one of my people all but guarantees us siding with their political opponents. We won't need to lift a finger before hundreds of enforcers from either side crush whoever dares to come after you. Go do stretches in front of the Tower of *Blood Rites* if you feel like it. I'd recommend *downward-facing dog* as you look away from them."

"Huh." Joe hopped in place, the simple motion sending him a half dozen feet into the air. "In that case, it wouldn't hurt to go see what my body can really do, now that I'm functioning at a hundred percent again. That was a *really* good healing spell."

As he turned to leave, Master Darling sidled up next to Joe and tapped his arm to get his attention. "You still have damaged skills, yes?"

"Very much so." Joe's smile dropped slightly, but it seemed she hadn't finished her thought.

"If they aren't practically destroyed, just not working correctly, repeating the actions which got you them in the first place might be enough to reestablish their connection and even repair them fully over time." Her smile widened as Joe's turned radiant. "I'm only going off of common knowledge, not personal experience. I've no way to guarantee the veracity of this information."

Joe bounced in place again, this time doing a flip before landing on his feet in nearly the same position. "You know, I may just have a way to test it out. I'll let ya know how it goes."

"I don't suppose you'd be willing to share the results? For academic research purposes?" Master Hollows butted in, snout twitching in excitement as he rubbed his enormous paws together. "True Damage directly to skills is quite the rare affliction. Who knows who this could benefit in the future?"

A wry smile on his face, Joe rolled his eyes but ended up agreeing without needing much persuasion. "Absolutely, Cosmo. I know I would've loved some guidance, and I'm not about to deny someone else some help just because it might take a bit of time to write it down. Now... I've got some things I want to test out."

"Come back and talk about the warnings we built into your enchantment when you have a minute. Nothing pressing, but still important."

"You got it, Darling." Turning to face the closed gate, Joe crouched, holding his core tight as he bunched up the muscles in his legs. Taking two quick breaths, he pushed off, unintentionally shouting as he did so.

"It's *Master* Darling, thank you-"

"*Omnivault*!"

CHAPTER FOUR

Air slammed against Joe's face and chest, as though the world were fighting to hold him close to its surface. He shot upward, clearing the wall around the tower easily and falling in a slow, parabolic arc to the open area surrounding his home on this world. Though the lack of pain was fantastic, his body moving in perfect rhythm without stiffness, lag, or phantom tingles where his mana channels *had* been... Joe still wore a frown.

His mana had failed to connect with the skill.

As his Ritual Orb of Strength popped off his bandolier and locked into place, the Ritualist grabbed the central bar section and arrested his momentum with a double flip around the object before it could fall. He dropped a few dozen feet to the ground, gracefully landing on his toes and absorbing the shock with bent knees as his heels impacted the soft soil. "Dialectic Dexterity works, so I've got that going for me. Ugh... nothing to do but keep at it."

There was approximately a half mile radius around the tower that was kept completely clear, a luxury only a few structures were afforded across the entire planet. Joe couldn't be entirely certain, but from what he'd seen while on the bifrost, it appeared only the towers situated at what could only generously be called the north, south, east, and west poles had additional open area.

While he was certain that favors must have been offered, alliances must have been made ages ago, and overwhelming power had likely been required for the Ritualists to claim this space, at this moment he didn't care about the work they had done as a Prestige class to force neutrality or *anything* at all... other than the fact that he had plenty of land to test his skill again and again.

Joe grunted as he landed, muscles twinging with the early signs of exhaustion as he ran through the unfamiliar exercises. "Haven't pushed myself this hard since the early days on Jotunheim. Come on, Omnivault. I know you mostly work; now you just need to work *all* the way."

Concentrating on feeling of the flow of mana through his body, the Ritualist tried again, mentally following the path his mana tried to spark along as he shouted the skill name once more. Then again. Each time he pushed himself, he could feel a buildup of energy beginning in his quads, only for it to sputter out in a way that would've been painful, were his internal mana not so docile and willing to vent itself along the intricate channels carved into his body. He came to a stop, breathing hard and literally steaming condensed energy as it dissipated into the surroundings from the surface of his skin.

Skill offered: Shounen Shout (Novice IX). By announcing your intent with unreasonable confidence and volume, you force the world to take you slightly more seriously.

Effect: All skills are .001n% stronger and faster to activate when you shout their name during activation.

"That's... no. I say no to that skill. Right. So, just trying to force it isn't working... but why?" Crouching low, Joe prepared to activate the skill once again, only to interrupt it at the last second, clearly able to visualize where it had gathered. Completely opposite to his expectations, the mana wasn't being held back–it was instead flowing along all of the mana channels in that area *far* too easily. "Ahh... I see. It's spilling like water on a table instead of rushing through pipes, like it did when I had natural channels. The surface tension is too low to keep it contained."

Wrapping the area in a tight film of controlled mana, Joe once again prepared to activate the skill. His sensitivity and peak-Master-rank Mana Dominion allowing him to feel which direction along his channels the mana *tried* to move. It bounced off the barrier he had created, so he opened a pinprick-size hole and tried again. The stream of power went to the next node, only for the same issue to repeat itself once again.

Over the next few minutes, stretching into half an hour, Joe figured out the exact map of mana channels his skill was attempting to race along. Only as the energy touched the tips of his toes did something change, as he felt a soul-deep **click**.

Congratulations! You have increased your Mastery of the skill 'Omnivault' to the point that it is able to be used manually, without the assistance of the system. New evolution options are available upon reaching the Grandmaster rank!

"*Hooo*-kay." The bald man opened his eyes, dropping into a crouch and launching himself forward. As soon as he landed, he attempted to reactivate Omnivault—this time using mana to empower it. In every previous jump, it had failed spectacularly, sometimes nearly sending him sprawling across the ground as mana burst from his skin in all directions like a claymore exploding. But this time... this time, his internal energy reservoir flowed *exactly* as it was meant to do.

Joe rocketed forward, only a thin, wispy trail of mana following along after him as he imperfectly routed the last few dregs through the tips of his toes.

Mana: 28,358/29,540.

Stamina: 4,079/5,429.

"Yes!" The ground rushed up at him once again, but he barely brushed against it before launching himself out and away, the sky welcoming him with a rush of wind from behind and carrying him further than an Omnivault alone could. His technique returned quickly: compress his core, flex, touchdown, release. It had been second nature not all that long ago, and he was quickly reintegrating the motions with his vastly superior body and mana control. "I've got this... just like hopping back on a bike, it's never really gone!"

He pushed himself until his energy guttered out fully, a full nine leaps that burned through just shy of twenty-six thousand mana but allowed him to travel ten and a half *thousand* feet in under fourteen seconds. He hit the ground at a run, needing to slow to a jog to burn off his momentum. A series of sonic booms rolled over him, slightly offset due to changing directions in order to remain within the open area around the tower.

"*Yes*! I'm *back*!" Pumping his fist in the air, Joe shouted his excitement for all the world to hear. "That was *awesome*!"

Now that his personal favorite movement technique had been restored, Joe picked a road at random and started jogging along it. "Let's see how fast I can circle this planet..."

Ambient mana absolutely *gushed* into him, just shy of two and a half hundred points refilling each second. "Even with nearly thirty thousand as my maximum cap, that's still under two minutes to completely refill."

Joe's eyes were bright as he continued running down the road, spotting the rare traveler on the main road. Instead of the hostility or the open assessing he'd been getting during his last few jaunts, absolutely *everyone* waved, bright smiles on their faces as soon as they took in his robes and therefore tower affiliation. It seemed everyone had gotten the message: the Tower of Ritualists was on the rise in the social hierarchy.

As his pool approached full, he sprang forward again, the ground screaming past only inches below his feet. In only a few seconds, his tower had disappeared beyond the horizon behind him, and the echoes of his passing caught up to the wildly exuberant bald man. Looking around, he realized he was in an unknown area, the towers close enough together that Joe was certain Mak and his cheese wagon wouldn't fit through the road.

"Is this the tower equivalent of downtown? Everything pressing together and no room to breathe—oh." As he stepped through the street that had started to feel more like an alleyway, the pass-through opened up to a small park. There was a large amount of green space, flowers planted in pleasing arrangements, and a statue in the exact center of a massive snake wrapped in a figure-eight around a globe.

Deciding this was as good a place as any to recover his mana, Joe walked around and smelled the flowers, circling the park while inevitably being drawn toward the statue. There was a small placard at the base, which he nearly unconsciously read aloud. "This statue stands in remembrance of those who fought the Ouroboros World Boss to a standstill, forcing it into an endless slumber and rescuing Vanaheim from the cycle of destruction and regrowth."

Considering the sculpture once more, Joe stepped away, recognizing that this park was meant to have a more reverent feel to it than he had initially expected. Yet, as he quietly made his way toward an exit, his eyes were drawn to a chaotic patch of graffiti that wrapped around each of the walls framing the park. "Seriously? We're on a higher world, full of people honing their craft toward Sagehood, and even here people are going around and writing on the walls?"

Bright inks, creative designs, not-so-creative crude etchings of body parts, all mingled with words in myriad fonts and sizes. Joe shook his head in disdain, but just as he turned away, one section pulled on him in a way he hadn't expected.

It was glowing gold.

"Someone wrote *facts* here?" In general, Joe hadn't gotten much usage out of his deity-provided bonus on higher worlds. The ability to see if something was 'true' or not had become extremely muddled when it came to higher-order lore, diagrams, and the like. There also seemed to be a hard cap on the rarity of information it could confirm or not, making this the first time on the planet it had come into effect. "What font is that? The stepchild of comic sans?"

Deciding to indulge in his idle curiosity, the Ritualist stepped closer and let his eyes casually follow along the words that were half-hidden under other messages. "...Not ignore the number hidden in the hollow."

Frowning, he went back to the start, lifting his arm and rubbing his sleeve over a fresh patch of paint. "*Don't* not ignore. Okay, so *do* ignore the number in the hollow."

Immediately following his vocalization, the faintest of sounds sounded off to the side, drawing Joe's attention to a layer of tape that had fallen off another section, revealing yet another glowing string of words along the wall. "Feces, did I just find a scavenger hunt?"

Not bothering to contain his excitement, he hurried to the fallen strip of tape, carefully pulling on the right side of it to make sure he got every last scrap out of the way and revealed the full message. "Be where most everyone walks past, but few consider. Well, message, I'm more than happy to do that, when and where? Anything more specific would be great."

This time, there was no clear call to a specific location, no phantom wind opening sections for him to easily study. Joe crawled along the base of the walls, rubbing at the paint to see if something would shine through. He took running starts at the wall, jumping up and splashing areas with water pulled from a small fountain, then sending his ritual orbs to rub along the higher areas, as if he were trying to win the prize in a scratch-off. His two-minute jaunt into the park to refill his mana turned into a four-hour search, and even then, he was certain there were pieces of the cryptic message missing.

"To be fair... I'm not sure this is going to mean anything even when I *do* find every part." Joe glanced at the disparate lines he'd written down, wholly uncertain if he had just wasted his time for nothing. Shaking that feeling off, he grit his teeth and held onto his paper firmly. "They're written in gold, and that's never led me wrong before. Let's see. First, 'as the milky white fades into an aged yellow, press where'. Not super useful. That could literally mean I need to go and hold on to a chunk of cheese and sink a finger into it to figure this out."

Hoping that wasn't the case, he looked at the next part. "This part at least seems full and cohesive. 'Should you wonder if your dedication is enough, you are probably correct that it is not'. I'm guessing that means either having achieved a certain skill level or tier in... something or another. 'You'll know you are in the right spot when even the air feels older'. Last, but not least..."

48°52.6 South, 123°23.6 West

"I'd have to say this is likely the most straightforward of all of them, which makes me trust it the least." Having spent so much time decoding and piecing together the fragments, Joe wanted nothing more than to have some resolution, but had to admit this diversion was unlikely to amount to anything. A glance at the sky showed that sunset was rapidly approaching. "Abyss, I'm going to have to go back to the tower and start all over again. Or, I suppose I could just subtract four and a halfish hours from however long it takes me to circle the planet and just let that be my time?"

The reminder of the globe he was on caused Joe to glance back at the statue. Perking up, he realized that perhaps the coordinate meant something *other* than 'leave this place and seek out buried treasure somewhere else'. Walking to the bottom of the display, he slowly circled the snake-entwined globe and searched for anything that might line up with the coordinate he had found. "There! That valley. Is that a *button*?"

Eagerly looking around for an easy way to clamber up, Joe found nothing to stand on, then nearly smacked himself in the head when he realized he could simply hop up and poke it. Dropping into a crouching position, he started to push up, only to twist to the side and throw himself to the ground at the last moment. "I nearly forgot to 'don't *not* ignore the number in the hollow'! That's got to be a trap of some kind."

After staring at the small recessed section, he bit his lip, his gut telling him that he simply couldn't see everything from his current position. Crouching once more, he looked around to ensure he was alone then threw himself to the top of the statue, landing as gently as possible. "Come on, there's got to be something up here. If someone saw me, they'd definitely think I was defacing the statue, so—*there*!"

With a momentary contemplation, Joe recognized that the minuscule pressure plate he was staring at was exactly opposite the button along the bottom of the sphere. He reached forward and put a hand on the pad, pressing down just as the sun hit the horizon, tinting the thin cloud cover a soft cheddar-orange.

Shhhunk.

The soft grinding sound brought Joe back to the moment, making him realize he was laying down, spread eagle across the top of a statue, wrist deep in pressing down a hidden panel. Pulling and rolling, he flipped off the globe and landed in front of the small placard at its base, doing his best to look innocent in case anyone came to check on what was going on with the still-increasing noise.

"Where's that even coming from?" Joe hissed through a clenched jaw as he glanced around at the trembling park. Just as he was worried that the shaking would turn into a full-blown earthquake, the grinding and rumbling stopped entirely. In the absolute silence which retook the area, the faint **swish** of metal gliding along metal stood out like a blade being sharpened.

Skill offered: Faultlistening (Novice II). Have you ever heard a machine crying out in pain and wanted to know why? Listening for the hairline stutter of a brake system, the dry whisper of a rusted joint, a subtle resonance meaning a bolt is loosening and on the verge of falling-

"Nope, don't want it." Joe jumped away from the statue, his gaze meeting a startled pair of eyes staring back at him from where the placard had been pushed to the side like the viewing slot at a speakeasy. The instant they saw each other, the placard slammed closed once more, barely in time to block the Ritualist's grasping hand. "Hey! I solved the puzzle! Let me in. I'm at least... *seventy percent* sure I want to know what's going on in there."

No response came, so Joe began knocking incessantly on the metal plate, which rang hollow as he continued tapping. "If you ignore me and close back up, I'm just going to keep slapping that pressure plate! Eventually, someone will come over off the street to see what's going on, and maybe *they'll* know the answer. Or maybe they *won't*, and we can get a crowd of people together to figure it out!"

At that, the placard shifted to the side ever so slightly, only the faintest hint of a disapproving glare peeking through the grated speculatorium. "Go 'way. Not for you."

"But I solved the puzzle, didn't I?" Joe leaned back in sudden realization. "Is this a *tower* entrance? Can I only be part of one tower? Look, I'm a Ritualist, but at least tell me what's in here. I can keep a secret! But if I don't get anything from you, I'm not going to be able to let this go. I gots ta *know*!"

There was a deep sigh from the other side of the slot, and the placard slammed closed once more. Joe scowled, a ritual orb lifting off his bandolier and swaying back in preparation to begin trying to break through. Happily, that was unnecessary, as the entire platform shuddered at that moment, a thin layer of dust lifting into the air as a seam was revealed. A scream of rusty hinges caused Joe to wince and look around frantically, yet still no one had arrived to investigate.

"Door's open."

Technically, it even was. There was a full *inch* of clearance. Deeply uncomfortable, Joe put his fingers into the opening, grasped the door and began pulling. "Seriously, if you slice my fingers off while they're stuck there..."

"Why is that the first place your mind goes?" The voice, no longer muffled by the objects between them, suddenly sounded all-too-familiar. "You've got issues, kid."

"*You*? Seriously?" Joe stared at the familiar face glowering at him from beneath the folds of a brown cowl. "Why are you here? What is this place?"

"An abandoned entrance we didn't even realize still worked. Are you coming or not?"

"I mean. Yeah." Joe dropped to his butt, sliding his legs into the waist-high door and slithering in and down. Right after he was fully inside, the entrance slammed shut behind him. "So. Want to tell me what this place is supposed to be? Or, better yet, why *you're* here?"

The brown-cloaked figure loomed over Joe, fingers clenching as if barely holding back from choking him out. "Even better... what if I just killed you instead?"

CHAPTER FIVE

"You know as well as I do how useless that would be, Mirascible." Joe reached out and gently shoved his mentor, only to nearly stumble backward as the dead-eyed Elementalist refused to budge. "Come on, you're serious? I don't even know what I found here; why don't we start with that?"

Mir pulled his cowl back, fully revealing his face as he stared at the Ritualist with an inscrutable expression. "Do you often follow instructions you find randomly laying around, then push buttons when you don't know what will happen?"

"I feel like the true answer isn't the one you want, but, yes. Yes I do." Starting to get uncomfortable now that the exit behind him was sealed, and the man considered to be the most dangerous combatant on the planet showed no signs of budging, Joe decided to go all-in on honesty. "Now that I know how to make this thing function, I'm going to fiddle with it until I figure it out or something breaks. You've met me. You know I'll follow any *interesting* task until completion. Plus, even if you were to kill me, I'd just come back."

"Unless I cut you down, then get to the Tower of Ritualists' respawn area in the next five seconds and do it again, then again, until you make a binding oath to back off." Even with as harsh as the words were, Mir's voice was full of exhaustion more than anger. "But, yeah... the real question is if that's going to be necessary or not. Didn't you get a warning in all the clues that were left around?"

"Two of them, actually." Just to have something to do other than fidget under the eyes of a predator boring into him, Joe pulled out his note and fiddled with the paper. "Ignore the hollow, and 'should you wonder if your dedication is enough, you are probably correct that it is not'. Or did you mean the part about the air smelling older, and that's how I know I'm in the right spot? Because it is... *rather* musty in here."

"The second one. It explicitly says that you shouldn't proceed if you don't know what you're doing, as your profession probably isn't high enough to-" Mir pursed his lips. "I've said too much. But you shouldn't be *able* to be here, is my point. The only reason I didn't vaporize you on the spot is the connection we have."

"Ah, then this is some sort of profession-based area?" Joe ignored the threatening growl, looking at his status sheet as he pondered. "You have a connection to Sage Pete, but I highly doubt this place is connected to any of my Ritualist professions. Could be Enchanting, but the skullduggery definitely makes me wonder if this is because of the evolved version of Occultist that I have: Arcanologist."

His words earned a startled reaction from the Elementalist, letting Joe know he was on the right track. Mir's hand lifted slightly in the air, as though he were about to reach out and clasp Joe's shoulder, but quickly returned to his side. "You're an *Occultist* on top of being a base-class Ritualist? No wonder you've progressed so quickly. At least that explains your absolute lack of *shame* in scrubbing away people's art, tearing sections out, and even why you were able to splay out on top of that globe in full view of anyone passing by without even a hint of discomfort."

"I mean, when you put it like that, it sounds like-"

"-Like you actually *are* in the place you're supposed to be." Mir let out a long breath through his nose, tension noticeably leaving his shoulders. "I have no idea how you managed to evolve your profession before coming here, but I hope you haven't done anything too foolish with it."

"Occultist? No, nothing strange. Once it turned into Arcanologist, it remained as 'level max'." Joe swallowed hard as he began to realize there may be a path to progressing it even more. "Is this a *profession* tower? Is that a thing? Can you help me figure out what else I can do with-"

"No, hold on." Mir shook his head, frustration mounting as he glanced over his shoulder then back at the intruding Ritualist. "I really can't give you much information about the function of this area, but I can take you to meet the Sage of the Inverted Tower–abyss take it, I did it again! Need to keep my mouth shut, or I'm going to... this is why I don't do politics! Why'd he even send *me* here to..."

The man swiftly turned around and began stomping along a narrow tunnel, the end of which Joe couldn't see, as the Sage took up the majority of the open space. A flame appeared in the Elementalist's hand, and without turning to look back, he simply barked out, "Follow."

Joe hurried along happily, perfectly content with how this was panning out. "To think, I just went for a walk to explore my newfound freedom on the planet, in conjunction with my access to mana returning, and stumbled upon a... I'm guessing a secret society of some sort?"

"Stop *guessing*," Mirascible snapped back in an irritable tone. "I forget what I'm *not* supposed to tell people. It's been three hundred years since that door was open, and we haven't had a new member join us down here in over a century."

"Are *all* professions represented by inverted towers instead of the regular ones? I was wondering how that would all work out." Joe decided to pursue a different topic, seeing as he could tell his mentor wanted to speak but was floundering in their current environment. Just as he'd hoped, the man jumped on the offering like a soldier trying to save his squadmates from a grenade.

"Not in the slightest. There's hundreds of classes, but most of them have a common origin and therefore can find representation on the surface. Only the most esoteric have no representation, and they can get pretty salty about it. Professions, though, those are nearly endless. Once it evolves past a certain point, there's so little in common with the original profession that there's no real point in hanging out with people still on that path."

As he spoke, Mir never slowed down, leading them through switchbacks and across odd angles that made the surroundings shift; either illusions were playing with them, or they were actually being teleported around the planet as they moved. All too soon, they were leaving the narrow tunnel behind and striding through a much more modernized and clean corridor filled with small groups.

Joe stared at the people they were passing, first one or two at a time, but soon dozens of people completely hidden by their cloaks–each of them no taller than his waist. He wanted to interact with them, perhaps get an explanation on who or what they were, but the Sage never slowed his speech.

"Only a few of the professions are distinct enough from actual classes and are powerful enough to control their own towers. Of those, only *one* of us is strong enough to hold the *Inverted* Tower." There was evident pride in Mir's voice, though Joe had no idea why a place like this would instill combat pride in such a decorated combatant–especially since, from what he could gather, the Tower of Elementalists was one of the peak battle forces on the planet. "Even the Merchant Association merely has designated space within certain towers, otherwise all of their members need to roam freely on the streets."

"Then there *are* people who know about this place? Many people?" The Ritualist could only hope that, by the end of their journey, he'd have a better understanding of what was going on, especially as he started to intentionally use his Charisma to get the information he wanted. Joe kept an easy tone, trying to match the calm energy rolling off of the Sage. He seemed to be doing a good job, as Mir answered without thinking.

"Oh, yes, the Inverted Tower as a concept is an open secret. It's just the *entrances* that are highly guarded and have knowledge of their existence restricted. Not everyone likes the cheese tax we impose or are as enthusiastic about our responsibilities as they should be. But we ensure the value of the entire planet's currency, so while it's rather frustrating to deal with them sometimes, it's still important work." The fire in his palm flickered, several other elements appearing and swirling about each other. "That's actually why I was initially inducted. Someone needs to be on hand to ensure we get every *shred* of cheddar we're due. Or *else*."

"Are you saying that you're the enforcement wing of this secret society?" Joe couldn't quite reconcile the image of the swift-to-anger gladiator champion in front of him with a thug who went and broke kneecaps if people didn't pay protection money. "From an outside perspective, since I don't know why you're doing this... I've got to admit, it seems kinda scummy?"

"What? No!" Mirascible rounded on him, lines of potency glowing under his skin as his mana roiled. As his presence flared up, Joe unconsciously released his own hold on his power. The air between them began to spark and flicker as his Mana Dominion fought off the nearly overwhelming pressure coming from the Sage, but the visible phenomena was enough to catch Mir's attention and get him to pull back slightly. "Now *that* was interesting... we're going to have to have another little *spar* soon. I'm not collecting the cheese to protect them from *me*, but from the release of the–the... uh. Stop that! You're *doing* it again!"

"Doing what?" Joe questioned him innocently. "You were just telling me about the profession system, and how the

Occultist profession manages to get a ton of currency from everyone else by dint of it simply existing. I'm guessing there's quite the market for forbidden knowledge? Getting access to ways of making things happen that no one's ever thought of doing or is willing to risk their own reputation by trying?"

Skill offered: Decisive Detective's Directive (Journeyman VIII). It is the domain of the exceptionally perceptive to find clues, put together a clear understanding of something which may have happened even centuries ago, and be able to take the incomplete data and use it to interrogate others.

Effects:

1) (N+Charisma/100+Perception/100)% increased chance to keep conversation casual in pursuit of information you are attempting to acquire and gaining it without the target of your inquiry realizing they are giving you the information you are after.

"Feces... that's a potent skill. It even starts as a *Journeyman*? Must be keeping all of my relevant experience. That would be, what? A one hundred and forty-seven percent better chance of getting information to *start* with? Ugh, still *no*." With an internal grimace, Joe waved the skill notification away, doing his best not to lament the loss of the seemingly overpowered skill. "It's just not close enough to what I want out of life to risk taking it as one of my seven possible skill increases. Plus, maybe that just means, if there was only a one percent chance of getting that information, I'd only have a two and a half percent chance of getting it? No way to know without trying, and I can't risk it."

"Ehh... you can sometimes keep your thoughts on the inside. Look, just wait *five* minutes. Can you do that? Or do I have to *gag* you?" Mir interrupted the Ritualist's not-so-internal monologue, seeming to be on the edge of grabbing Joe and shaking him.

The Ritualist reluctantly nodded and followed along as they went deeper into the tower, the hallway having long since turned into a downward spiral deep into the depths of the planet. Descending deeper, Joe felt gravity itself increase as they passed different markers. Had his legs not been the direct subject of an upgrade when evolving his Strength Characteristic, he was sure his calves would be *burning* by now.

There was a faint rhythmic rumble shaking the floor, the walls, the ancient air itself as they finally came to a halt at what must be the very tip of the Inverted Tower. Joe examined the elaborate doors, which bore a striking resemblance to the penthouse office Sage Pete had at the Tower of Ritualists. "This must be the place, huh?"

Instead of giving him an answer, Mir absolutely filled Joe with questions when he didn't smash the door open–instead stopping dead in front of it, squaring his shoulders as though wanting to make a good impression, and lifting a hand not to smack the barrier out of his way, but to gently knock. Three quick, quiet taps. Respectful. Nervous?

"Everything okay there-?"

"Shut it," Mir grumbled without missing a beat, clearly uncomfortable allowing Joe to see this side of him.

Luckily for both of them, there was no hesitation on the other side, a pleasant voice calling out, "Enter and be welcome, Mirascible and Joe the Reductionist!"

The doors swung open on their own, and Mir pushed through with his usual straightforward movements. For his part, Joe followed slightly more slowly, his gaze trailing along the open concept office and drinking in the strange details.

It looked almost exactly like Pete's office, at least in overall shape. There were a few differences, such as the hundreds of books with handwritten titles stuffed into shelves across the room. The windows were all covered in metal shutters, such as those he'd expect to see on a home planning for a hurricane. Lastly, the person sitting behind the desk wasn't human or any of the other races Joe had yet encountered.

Skill offered: Housekeeper (Expert I) Knowing the best place to place the furniture, how the kitchen should be set up, and getting the towels folded just so-

"Not a chance," the Ritualist subvocalized, dismissing the notification without hesitation.

"Welcome to the Inverted Tower, Joe." The deep, pleasant voice emanating from the diminutive figure was wildly incongruent with the Ritualist's expectations. "My name is Nathaniel, and as you may have noticed, I'm a Gnome."

"*Wha~at*? I would have never *gnome* if you hadn't told me, thanks for pointing that out." The figure sitting behind the desk rolled his eyes and chuckled gently at his guest's antics, his tall, pointy hat waving around wildly.

Joe had most certainly assumed the Gnome's origins, seeing as, if he'd stood perfectly still, he would look almost exactly like the representation of any garden gnome found in a store. A brimless pointed hat, tunic held in place by an oversized belt with a shiny clasp, surprisingly nice pants and incredibly well-shined shoes.

Nathaniel allowed the Ritualist a few moments to collect himself, his own expressions mostly concealed by the fluffy white beard and mustache covering his mouth. "Yes, yes. You'll do nicely. I'm certain you'll fit in quite well. The strong, direct gaze of an Occultist. Searching, measuring, wondering how to fit this new data into your worldview. Not a hint of hesitation or worry about casting aside what you've only thought you knew and experienced before now. I love it."

"Hope I didn't screw this up too badly." Mir actually sounded somewhat contrite, but the Gnome casually waved away his concerns.

"He got here of his own recognizance. It's what Occultists are *meant* to do. I am, I admit, surprised that it was an Occultist who found his way through instead of a Scholar. I would have assumed that the historical records would be preserved and pursued as soon as the bifrost was reopened. From what I gather, our new friend here had no idea what he had stumbled upon." Nathaniel leaned forward slightly, his fingers steepled. "Has the balance shifted to favor Occultists on the lower worlds? It was nearly equivalent before the fall of the rainbow bridge."

"That's..." Joe shook his head, his lips pressed into a thin line. "No, most certainly not. In fact, I've been actively hunted by the Scholars, barred from their ranks, and have had other people blacklisted simply for associating with me because of my original Occultist profession."

"But..." For the first time, it seemed Nathaniel had been completely taken aback. "But why would that...? You're already an Arcanologist! You must have advanced as both a Scholar *and* Occultist, or at least alongside one? There's no other way to get it! I should know, I founded the profession *myself*."

The Gnome reached into his desk with a hurried motion, practically ripping the drawer out in his haste to dig through its contents. He pulled out a shimmering coin, flicking it over to Joe, who easily caught it out of the air. "There, you see? On one side, those willing to push the bounds of magic and knowledge, yet the other side of the coin is those who maintain said knowledge and rapidly expand upon it! Scholars *need* Occultists to make a unified whole. They were always meant to work in conjunction with each other! That's why the profession can be advanced from either starting point!"

"Yet, as far as I know, I'm the only one," Joe informed the agitated Gnome as gently as possible. "What would happen if, say, the Scholars actively refused any of the benefits of Occultists?"

"I mean. There are... *other* advancement paths, but they lose out on their full potential. Instead of advancing knowledge, the branching paths only allow them to categorize or access it more rapidly." Nathaniel slumped back into his chair. "No wonder it took millennia for the world of Midgard to find a way back to Vanaheim. Haahh... well, I suppose I'm pleased that you've been following in my footsteps, even if you didn't realize it. That's good enough of a recommendation for me. Want to join the tower?"

"Uh-" Joe blinked rapidly at the sudden shifts in the conversation. "Can I *be* part of two towers? I thought that would be... frowned upon? At the least?"

"We're a *profession* tower," Mir stiffly interjected. "You don't have to wear robes or a face mask, or even a fancy ring that shows off your affiliation, apparently. No matter how hard some of us push for it. All you have to do is maintain our core mission, and-"

"Mirascible," the Gnome interrupted warningly. "You're doing it again. Also, can we *please* put aside the idea of sigaldry for now? Letting people know who we are is the exact *opposite* of what we're going for."

"Feces. I don't know what it is about this kid that makes me chatter like this." The Class Sage groaned as he looked away toward the shuttered windows. "Just... *you* talk. I'm going to end up saying something I shouldn't, then have to rip his spine out until he promises to keep his mouth shut."

"*Dude*," Joe softly whispered, looking at his mentor with a wide-eyed glare.

"Violent, as is his wont. Still, he had a point." The Gnome pushed off his desk with a sigh, hopping to the ground and vanishing behind it briefly before coming around the large desk. "I suppose it wouldn't be fair to ask you to commit to us without knowing what it is we actually do. Why we do it. *How*."

Nathaniel came to a halt next to the covered windows. "I suppose we'll start with *what*. As you may imagine, the Inverted Tower is the source of immense innovation for this world: the discovery of new skills, subskills, titles, and the like. We have a hand in *everything*, and if someone else discovers it before us, we are still there to document and keep a record of it. We're the ones who converted the currency of the world to cheese, an endlessly renewable yet *consumable* resource. There were many reasons for this, but that gets us into the *why* of what we do."

The Gnome gestured, and the enormous metal coverings on the window pulled away, revealing an astounding view of the hollow center of the planet. Joe stepped closer, looking out into the darkness barely tinted with enough light to make out the fact that there was a gap between the core of the planet and the rest of it. "What am I looking at?"

Another gesture, and lights began springing into existence

in the distance, flooding the hundreds of miles of viewable mass below and revealing immense connection points between the two. Massive stalagmites spanned the gap, and as the shadows stopped dancing around, Joe realized he recognized the look of them. "Do those-? Are those hollow? Is that what makes the towers on the surface?"

Skill offered: Construction Material Identification (Journeyman IV). Anyone has the potential to build a structure. Some people even know how to make them out of things that won't collapse and kill the people inside-

"Good eye," Nathaniel complimented Joe, even as the Ritualist denied the skill and continued staring. "How about over there?"

Now that the area had been pointed out, the bald man couldn't understand how he hadn't seen this first: a mountain of cheese being slowly processed on a conveyor belt. There were literally millions of tons of all types, all of it ever so slowly on the move. It took multiple seconds for the Ritualist to understand its final destination, not used to viewing things on this scale.

"Are you *feeding* whatever that thing is?" Joe felt like his bones needed to be oiled, as it took an intense effort to shift his head to stare at the other two men in the room.

"That 'thing'," Mir rumbled in a low voice, "is Jörmungandr the World Snake. The World Boss of Vanaheim. The ouroborus who converts living planets into dead ones. It's kept in a hibernative sleep by the effects of the conversion of cheese into a carefully controlled substance. Every wheel of Parmesan gets us *hours* of keeping that thing asleep."

"Thus we come to our 'why'," Nathaniel interjected, cleanly retaking control of the conversation. "It is our duty to keep the World Boss asleep, for we live upon its back. Even when it is defeated and its core harvested, Jörmungandr merely returns to a deep sleep. Unlike all other World Bosses, if its Mythic Core isn't used within a certain amount of time, it always finds its way back to him. An endless cycle of destruction and rebuilding, once the snake is slain, and the towers become hollow once more."

"All joining us requires..." As Nathaniel's careful cadence crescendoed, he locked eyes with Joe. "Is your oath that you will step in to help the Inverted Tower if it ever calls for help. That you will always make the choice, no matter how difficult it may be, to keep Jörmungandr asleep."

CHAPTER SIX

"All who serve the Inverted Tower handle forbidden knowledge, investigate and gain power from anomalies, guard secrets from those who should not have access to them. But above all..." Nathaniel met Joe's intense gaze with his own placid one. "*We keep the serpent asleep.*"

The floor and glass vibrated ever so slightly, and Joe suddenly recognized the rhythmic trembling for what it was: the World Boss was ever so gently snoring. "While I admit the idea of being inducted into a secret society has always been enticing to me, I'm still not sure why I'd want to join up. Do I get access to your findings? I know myself well enough that I can agree immediately and without hesitation, if that were the case."

"That would be a part of it, certainly." Nathaniel inclined his head knowingly. "For your next profession evolution, each level only grants you access to a different receptacle of knowledge. The higher the level, the more you are allowed to partake of."

"Sounds interesting and ambiguous at the same time." Joe rubbed at his chin, his eyes still on the continent-sized serpent curled into a tight coil far below. “Any hints of what that would look like?”

“At the first level, you would have access to some of the forbidden knowledge of your own tower. Now, when I say ‘forbidden’, usually it simply means failed or deemed too dangerous for general usage. Only *rarely* does it actually edge in on the territory of the eldritch.” Nathaniel stepped closer to the glass, watching as a tower of cheese in the distance began to tilt and slowly fall toward the oceanic-scale opening that was the world snake's mouth. “With each subsequent rank, you can choose another tower’s lost or forbidden knowledge to study, and even make offers to them in exchange for cheeses or knowledge of their own that isn’t in our records.”

“Sounds like a multi-level marketing scam.” Joe laughed as the Gnome looked at him with curious eyes, though he held off from asking for additional details.

“At the tenth level, you can have nine others working under you to disseminate information and seminate various rewards to the Inverted Tower-”

“Mm. Nope. Not enjoying your word choices here.” Joe glanced sidelong at the Tower Master, unsure if he was making jokes or simply speaking in a slightly archaic manner.

“-and you would have your own personal access key to the Scholars’ University subspace.” Nathaniel tapped on a wristband he was wearing. “It’s a pocket dimension outside of the standard hierarchy and can be accessed from any world. At the maximum level of twenty, you will earn a reward based on your area of study, possibly founding a new discipline altogether.”

Joe couldn't help but begin to warm to the idea and finally turned to face Nathaniel and Mirascible directly. “What's one more promise to help a friend when times get tough? This sounds good to me, since this practically looks like the point where my class and faction leader intersect. Er that is, Occutatum. The deity.”

“I’m aware.”

Nathaniel's calm reply allowed Joe to relax fractionally. "Ah. Good, then. Just one last quick thing. I promised a friend of mine, a Scholar, that I'd get him reinstated. Is there anything you can do to help with that?"

"This is the one impacted because you were an Occultist?" The edges of Nathaniel's mustache had curled, the only indication that he was practically beaming beneath it. "I'd have helped him either way. You hold in your hands a token of my favor. It can be expended to overrule the decision of any lesser-ranked person in my profession line, which, as I am the *founder*, is everyone. Simply giving that to your friend will be enough to reinstate him, if he so chooses. However..."

The Gnome shook his head in mute frustration. "If he's anything like his predecessors, it's likely that simply having the ruling overturned so easily will not be enough for him. If you want to go and make your case to the faculty, hoping to convince the Provost himself, you will need to reach the tenth level of your profession and earn the subspace key as a reward, or get a direct invitation."

"I'll be able to fulfill the letter of the agreement, then eventually the spirit of it by progressing my profession?" Joe flipped the coin in the air, the symbol for an Occultist reflecting off to the wall, rapidly followed by that of a Scholar, over and over until his hand shot out, wrapping around the small disk of metal and vanishing it into his ring. "Perfect. Where do I sign?"

"Your word is enough for me. Welcome to the Inverted Tower."

Congratulations! You have been invited to join the secretive ranks of the Inverted Tower, tasked with collecting, storing, and disseminating knowledge to the members of every tower of Vanaheim. By joining, you agree to answer the call should the tower ever require your assistance. Above all, you are oathbound to do all in your power to keep the Jörmungandr asleep.

Should you choose to join, Tower Master Nathaniel offers two signing bonuses.

1. *Mark of Favor (Grand Archivist). The shaper of doctrine for the classes of Scholar and Occultist, all branches, all evolutions, has given you a token allowing you to permanently overrule any one decision from any other person within this profession line.*
2. *Profession Evolution. Your max-level profession, Arcanologist, will evolve to Codex-Keeper, level one.*

Do you accept this invitation?

"Yes, let's do that for sure," Joe murmured ever so softly, now that he was cognizant of how bizarre it looked to see people speaking out loud to the system.

Profession evolution underway!

Congratulations! Arcanologist (Level 10/10) has evolved to become Codex-Keeper (1/20).

Codex-Keepers are seekers and stewards of the most dangerous knowledge that can be found. They have a deep understanding that all knowledge should be preserved, if only to have a method on hand to defeat what could be released should such knowledge be found elsewhere. They maintain grimoires, redacted and hidden records, and tomes that would induce madness in a less prepared mind.

Profession bonuses:

Codex Keys: You have been granted access to a library of data hidden from the eyes of those in the Tower of Ritualists for time untold. How you use it will determine the speed your profession increases. The total number of keys will always be equal to your profession rank, though additional keys will grant access to different libraries.

All benefits from the prerequisite professions transfer:

1. *You can obtain quests from non-quest-related books if there is truth hidden in the text, up to the Artifact-rarity rank.*
2. *Increases speed of reading and writing by 50%.*
3. *You may add any Lore skill to any skill which could benefit from that area of study. (For example, a Scholar who studies metallurgy could add their lore skill to the creation of a weapon, increasing the quality of the item.)*

4. *Can see truth in up to 'Artifact'-ranked books.*

Study books from the library now open to you to advance this profession. Only by better understanding will your advancement speed increase.

Blinking rapidly, Joe looked at the other two people in the room with him, who seemed greatly relieved, for some reason. "All set. What's next?"

"Well, now that you're in, I need to take your left pinky and your-"

Nathaniel smacked Mir on the leg, chest-level with himself. "He doesn't know you're joking. No, first of all, you need to know how to keep the snake asleep. After that, I'll have our mutual friend here guide you to a more discreet, commonplace entrance to the tower. That will be your point of entry going forward, instead of the terribly outdated entrance we used to use before establishing ourselves."

Walking behind his desk, the Gnome motioned for Joe to follow him. "Every single person who has joined us, or is a member currently, knows exactly what this does."

On a small socle was an ancient lever, a thick bar of metal with a grip at the top with an attachment reminiscent of an open pair of pliers. The elderly Gnome flicked the lever, letting a dull sound ring out. "All this does is keep the conveyor belt running. There are so many redundancies built into the belt itself that the power required to stop the flow of cheese would be no different than expending enough power to crack the planet in half. Hence, the lever. So long as this switch is set to on, the wheels will advance."

"Couldn't someone just go down there and... I don't know, sweep all the cheese off the belt?"

"Very much no. The surface of the Jörmungandr is deadly, covered in a virulent mold which would convert nearly anyone affected into a food source, a miasma ever-flowing from its scales. Only the *other* members of the tower can walk down there without permanent harm, making this our only fail-safe, should we ever wish to awaken it. As a reminder: *don't.*"

Something about the way he phrased his words unsettled Joe. "The other members? I'd assumed they were Gnomes, like yourself? Is that not-?"

"Ha!" Mir belted out unexpectedly, even as Nathaniel's face went sour. "They're *just* like him."

"What? Are they constructs? What's-"

"There's only one of my kind on *any* of the worlds, as far as I'm aware," Nathaniel stated with quiet conviction. "That may have changed on one of the higher planes over the centuries of separation, but as far as I'm aware... I am alone. Pardon our friend here, he is simply excited to have another member of the tower that he can have an actual conversation with. We have a mere handful of Codex-Keepers, but we are the only three on Vanaheim. Everyone else you have seen is one of the natural monsters of this world. They are the caretakers of Jörmungandr, what you would know as his 'Kaiju ecology'. When he is in a dormant state, they're docile and quite helpful. When he is awake, or at risk of awakening, they are savage, deadly creatures."

"What are they? Big slithers of serpents hidden under a set of robes?" Joe squirmed in place, rolling his shoulders before shaking his head quickly. "Never mind. I'd rather not know, if that's the case."

"A Codex-Keeper should *never* shy away from knowing the truth," Nathaniel sternly lectured him, his eyes going flinty for a moment as he tapped on the ambient mana. Moments later, the door opened, and one of the waist-high, brown-robed people Joe had seen moving about in the tower previously stepped in. "Remove your hood, if you would be so kind, Gunther. We have a new member who is learning our ways."

The cowl was quickly removed, revealing the face of the fluffiest, most adorable penguin Joe had ever seen.

"Can I keep this one?" His fingers were practically *twitching* with a desire to pet the adorable, smiling creature. "Why are they forced to stay *hidden*?"

"People kept stealing them." Mir's blunt explanation made

perfect sense to the Ritualist. "They're meant to be moving between cheese deposits from the towers, not kept in a menagerie. We found that the robes gave them just enough of a mysterious vibe to keep people from grabbing and running off with them. It was a huge time suck for me, as I was the only one available to get them back."

As the penguin hid its face once more, then stepped out of the room, Joe glanced back at the others. "So, in the worst case scenario, I just need to get in here and make sure the conveyor belt is moving? That's it?"

"Yep. That's the entire job." Nathaniel reached out and knocked on the empty air next to him, a stable portal tearing itself open and expanding to Joe's height. The Gnome tossed a small cube into the shimmering, swirling darkness, and it collapsed down onto the metal.

The deformed cube jumped up to the Gnome's hand as if it had been on a string, only to then be offered to the Ritualist. "Here you go, your first key. It'll only work if you are both on Vanaheim and hidden from the view of anyone else. This will take you directly into your assigned library, so feel free to study whenever you're interested in doing so. Now, I've kept you too long. Mir? Please feel free to show him the exit. Oh... and now that he is one of us, don't be shy about letting him know tower secrets. Keeping secrets is practically the entire profession, and I'm sure Joe understands that.."

"Celestial feces, that's good. I thought I was gonna need to burn my tongue off. C'mon, kid." The Sage started walking out of the office, Joe trailing along behind him while clutching the newly formed library key with both hands, as though it were going to vanish. "Now, I don't want you to think you're going to get out of fighting me again real soon, but I'm busy today."

"That's okay, I was planning to run around the world for a little while anyway." Joe did his best to remember the path they took up and out. It was fairly straightforward at first, simply several miles of uphill walking on the spiraling ramp. But once they were to the top, there seemed to be a thousand hallways leading off in all directions from the vast open space of the main floor, which made sense if this was a world-spanning cheese-collection society. "Actually, now that I think about it, how did *you* end up becoming associated with the Inverted Tower?"

"I took the Occultist profession a long time ago and eventually found my way here in a manner quite similar to your own." Mir stepped forward with the confidence of someone who knew exactly where to go, and soon Joe was hopelessly lost in the warren of tunnels. "Here, this leads to a district near your tower, and it's almost always empty. Still, you never know, so try not to look too suspicious when you're sneaking out of the alley."

"Well, hold on, why did you take that profession? It doesn't seem to align with your class at all."

Practically huffing out a humorless laugh, the Elementalist shot Joe an incredulous glance. "Look, I've pretty much just one goal in life: find the most dangerous, fun things to fight and go all-out until one of us stops moving. Who do you think has a record of all of the one-off monsters, sealed horrors, and locations deemed too dangerous to let anyone else know about? This profession is the most efficient way to find anything worth fighting."

"That... tracks," Joe admitted, opening his mouth to add more but closing it with a firm nod. "Wait a second, why are you keeping the World Boss down then? Wouldn't you want to fight that snake?"

"Meh, I've already beat it once. It was a good fight, but all it really does is fly in loops around various worlds and cheese 'em. It's fast and always moving. Doesn't even have any great attacks. You just have to keep hitting it until it curls up and falls asleep again. Which, if you haven't caught on yet, is when Vanaheim will re-form. Whole planet's gone when it's awake."

"Huh." A panel slid to the side in front of them, revealing bright daylight that made Joe look away, blinking rapidly. "Abyss, I think I was down here a lot longer than I thought."

Skill offered: Perfect Internal Timekeeping (Beginner II). Have you ever found yourself losing track of time, entire days or even weeks vanishing as if in a dream? Why not have internal timers going at all times? With this skill, you'll be able to have a clear understanding of travel time between different points, how long you have spent on projects, and even the variances in time zones between worlds.

Accept? Yes / No.

"Ew, that sounds terrible." The Ritualist recoiled slightly, swiftly reaching out to bop the 'no' button. "Sounds like a great way to lose my flow-state when I'm doing cool stuff."

"Eyes on me." Mir pulled Joe out into the opening between towers then showed him how to interact with the various seemingly innocuous paintings and detritus in the area to reopen the door. As they were finishing up, just as the Sage was turning to get back to his responsibilities, a sharp voice cut through the stillness of the alleyway.

"Hey! You? Joe the Ritualist?"

Joe froze in place, staring at the newcomer while being wholly uncertain how to respond. For his part, the random guy took another step into the alley, his head tilting to the side, slightly too far to look comfortable.

"W-welcome back. I guess... I'll be here." The unknown individual shuddered slightly, his eyes going blank as he took another step into the confined space.

"Hey, where are you going?" A half-laughing voice echoed out, as a dozen or so of the creepy man's friends meandered to the entry of the alleyway. "We've got a *party* to get to, man!"

"Hey! You? Joe the Ritualist?" The first person repeated jerkily. As though his words were a trigger, all of his companions went still, then turned in perfect synchronization to stare at the bald Ritualist cornered in the alley.

"Aw, man. Not this again." Joe crouched in place slightly, ready to move as soon as his unexpected adversaries did so. "Mir... a hand? I think these people are being mind controlled; I don't want to hurt them if I don't have to."

"Don't worry about that," the Elementalist replied in a

slightly distant manner. "If they die, they won't lose anything. Only the person workin' behind the scenes will. But this is a *group* of Masters. Anyone strong enough to control all of them at the same time must be *real* mad at you to expend the resources it would take to make this happen."

"Pretty sure it's the Tower of Blood Rites, but their envoy denied it. Also, I'm not so worried about hurting them as I am about getting beat down for no good reason," Joe finished with no small hint of annoyance filling his words.

"No, I think it's actually going to be good for you. Didn't ya say you wanted to test out your capabilities? Get a handle on your mana and such? See how strong you are? Well... there you go. Punching bags you can destroy with no remorse. Soon as you send them back to their tower, whatever hold someone has on their mind will be broken. Really, it would be unconscionable of you *not* to help them out."

"Anything to justify a fight. Is that it?" Joe pulled out a small stack of ritual tiles, just in time to toss them in the air as the crowd went berserk and sprinted at him.

"Yes."

CHAPTER SEVEN

The scent of bloodlust hit the air like a chemical spill, rushing ahead of the sprinting group like a rancid stormfront.

Knowing that Mirascible was all but invulnerable to enemies of this level *and* that the Sage would never help him, the Ritualist put the man out of his mind entirely for the moment. Joe sprang backward, ritual tiles fanning out into the air around him like a deck of cards exploding mid-shuffle. This was intended to serve a dual purpose, getting his weapons in place as well as distracting his pursuers. The first succeeded, the second failed–the blank-faced assailants never took their eyes off of his moving form.

Even with the potentially dire situation unfolding, a smile crept across his face as his sensory world widened. Everything was functioning the way it was supposed to; everything was *clear*. Six ritual orbs lifted off his bandolier even before his feet touched the ground once more, circling around him like hawks swooping through the open sky in search of prey. "Perfect internal cohesion. No spasms in my muscles, no phantom pain knocking me out of the moment. Let's see what's possible."

Skill offered: Battle Frenzyyy. (Apprentice V). Excited about fighting, but don't want to fully descend into a Berserker state? Battle Frenzyyy is the skill for you! Enhanced focus while fighting, at the cost of any attempts at stealth—unless your opponent is deaf. You'll be shouting with excitement, whooping for joy, and laughing as you shout such phrases as 'Leeroooy' as you rush ahead of your team-

"Nope!" The message vanished, then there was no more time for planning or worry–his first attacker was in range, swinging a blade with unexpectedly perfect skill. His Ritual Orb of Strength intercepted it, catching the blade on its central bar. The Master-rank assailant turned with the motion, his blade coming around in a tight arc as he spun in place, only for Joe to backflip without any wasted motion. His move took him over the enchanted metal, and the Ritualist twisted in place, kicking a ritual orb at the man's head and cleanly impacting him on the temple.

The simple sequence sent the Master stumbling away just as a shock raced up his arm. An open palm **thudded** into Joe's wrist, and he sucked in a sharp breath as he lost all feeling from the elbow down. The Master who had struck him stepped forward again, his offhand splayed out and racing toward the Ritualist's unguarded chest... only to slam uselessly against a barrier that sprang into place at the last second. Before Joe could breathe too easy, the ritual-formed barrier–merely a Journeyman-rank defense–**cracked** sharply just once before shattering.

Five attackers surged toward him in unison, quick and sure footfalls putting them into advantageous positions, weapons moving with practiced synchronization as they attempted to exploit any of the openings his off-balance form afforded them. "Abyss, they're not mindlessly berserking! Is it because we're closer to whoever is controlling them? They can-"

An Omnivault left a sonic boom in his position instead of tender flesh as blades struck, and fire immolated the area.

"Well, this is a bigger problem than I was thinking it was going to be." Even as Joe murmured his complaint, he reached out with dozens of perfectly controlled threads of mana, targeting the stack of ritual tiles he'd scattered around with pinpoint precision. Each activated in sequence, and he locked down one of the Masters with a cage of inward-facing barriers, holding the man in place long enough for the 'Despair Cluster' to come into effect.

Where someone at the Master rank could normally shake off the effects of low-powered rituals, the man was trapped like a fish in a tank. No matter how he flailed, he couldn't muster enough force to shatter the barrier while *also* fighting against the Rituals of Redirection pulling every time he tried to push, and pushing every time he pulled. His heavy mace cracked the barrier each time it managed to land, but seeing as it was slowed by a half-dozen force-shifting rituals, the damaged barrier had enough time to reconstitute itself before the Master could try again.

Splashes of green, blue, and red formed along exposed skin, specifically targeting the controlled Master's head and neck—seeing as these usually hard-to-target areas were easily accessible at the moment. At the same time, Joe's leaching rituals began pulling at his resource pools, redirecting their collected energies into the next set in the cluster. As stamina was returned and began to desiccate the target, mana slammed into the man in concussive blasts, all while red energy directly **zinged** the combatant's nervous system to keep him distracted with pain.

Joe was forced to stop watching the cluster as a smattering of flying knives whistled past his face and bounced off the protective walls of the tower behind him. "Hey! That was close. Oh, no... *look*! Your friend is trapped? You know any one of you could get him out of there just by attacking that barrier from the outside, right?"

The Ritualist didn't usually call out advice to his enemies when they were trying to kill him, but he needed to see what level they were operating at. When none of the others went to help their pinned companion, he let out a relieved sigh. "Looks like you can still use skills and spells, maybe think tactically, but concern for your fellows is out of reach. I can work with that."

"Don't worry, you're doing great!" Mir called from where he was casually seated on the street. "If you keep these rituals going, this guy might even get sent to respawn after a week or so."

"Haven't exactly been able to build up my arsenal over the last few days, Mir! I *just* got back to functioning!" Joe snapped in reply as he spun through the air in a tight barrel roll, reaching to the ground and arresting his momentum with two fingers, staying perfectly still as a spell whizzed by on either side of him, then pushing off to land in a crouched position on the tower's wall. An Omnivault sent him up and over the group once again, like a matador taunting a herd of stampeding bulls.

"What happened to all that combat training you'd been practicing when your mana was all tapped out? Don't tell me you got even worse at fighting than the last time I checked in on you?" The Sage casually reached up and blocked a ricocheting arrow with the tip of his pinky. The shaft exploded into splinters as the metal tip deformed into a flat disk, unable to even dimple his skin. "Why don't you try some of *that* on them? If that doesn't work, you have your mana back! Can't you do more than toss out Journeyman-rank parlor tricks and bounce around like a circus act?"

"Well, feces, *I* don't know." Joe extended his right hand toward the group as he slowly approached the ground. His fingers splayed out, and he held his forearm with his other hand, doing his best to stay steady as he channeled his mana. "*Dark Chain Lightning*!"

Mana erupted off his arm in a wide cloud, venting out of him without creating any noticeable effect. Having expected the Expert-rank spell to fail, Joe quickly switched to another and tried again, this time trying something that had been with him nearly his entire journey through Eternium. "*Lay on Hands*!"

Yet again, his vision was slightly impaired by the haze of power flowing out of him. Just like when he'd been attempting to use Omnivault, both needed careful reworking in order to be useful again. *Unlike* the body-based skill, Joe didn't have any sense that these simply needed to be routed through the correct channels–there was something fundamentally broken about both of them, as even the initial power accumulation had gone sideways.

The Ritualist hit the ground with his feet planted firmly, only to hit the wall dozens of feet away in the next instant. Coughing up blood, he glanced down at his chest in bewilderment, then up to where a massive Master was still standing with his fist extended in a straight line. "Great... **hack**... let me guess, a Master of pugilism?"

Slap!

His attacker stumbled slightly as a shadowy version of Joe appeared and backhanded him across the face–the passive effect of Haunting Shadows having *never* stopped working correctly.

"Heavy armor martial artist, actually. A pugilist is specifically a boxer. Just gonna say it out loud now, you're not getting through that gear anytime soon. At least not with what you're chuckin' around right now," Mirascible chimed in with the most enthusiasm Joe had heard out of him since declaring that they would eventually meet each other on the field of battle for funsies. "Ya need to play to your strengths here, or you're going to be sent to respawn in no time flat. Also, were you trying to *heal* that guy?"

Forcing himself to move, Joe gasped out, "Has a chance to end mental effects on use. Figured I could wake him up and slowly get more of them on my side. Then we could hold down the others until the effect procced again for all of 'em."

"Well, you should stop trying to save them, 'cause *they're* not gonna stop trying to kill you."

Even though he knew the Sage was correct, Joe still didn't feel great about changing his mindset from defensive to actively attempting to kill each of the people who were being controlled. "*Haah*... I know it's not their fault... but I'm not going to die for 'em."

A blade swept by his abdomen, only the most carefully controlled of movements keeping him from ejecting his intestines onto the ground. He pivoted on his heel, allowing a blast of frost to **whoosh** past his head so closely that it left a trail of ice crystals where his sweat had been freely flowing.

As the spell splashed on the stone behind him, Joe dove into a forward roll, avoiding a hammer strike driving down from above as one of his attackers shoved off a distant wall and hurtled at him like a meteor. Midway through his evasive motion, the Ritualist slapped the ground, sending him spiraling away from the open-palmed martial artist with no room for error.

Three new craters decorated the street, and a wide, nearly artistic display of icicles had formed near the exit of the alleyway. Already, more people were rushing at Joe, and he felt the beginnings of mental exhaustion creeping over him. "Been a long time since I've been in a fight like this... what's the best method to play to my strengths? What's that mean now, compared to what it meant to me way back when?"

The most glaring difference that stuck out to him was the peak Mastery he had with Mana Manipulation, now Mana Dominion. He glanced at his other skills, searching for anything that would be useful in combat. "Trying to figure out an Expert-rank spell mid-fight sounds like a fool's errand, and Corify can't be used on people. Journeyman-rank Planar Shift it is."

Once again, Joe began the process of activating one of his spells. And, once again, it exploded into a cloud of useless, wasted mana. Yet this time, Joe could feel as dozens of pathways lit up for a moment before flickering and venting their accumulated power. Splitting his attention between bouncing around the contained area to avoid the constant flow of destruction aimed at his head and heart, Joe wrapped his arms with his Mana Dominion and carefully spun power through himself time and time again. Finally, there was a workable pathway from his central mana to the tips of his fingers, and he cast the spell once more.

A lance of dark energy split the air between himself and his Ritual Orb of Constitution, sinking into the long-unused ritual it still contained. The orb raced down toward the martial artist, a weeping trail of mana staining the air behind it. Moments before impact, a skull formed around the heart-shaped weapon. It gained full solidity just in time for the pseudo-lich summoned around it to open its mouth wide—enormous fangs glistening with ectoplasmic saliva—before plunging its sharpened teeth into the martial artist's shoulder.

"Welcome *back*, Morsum!" Joe bellowed as the Master stumbled, his right arm going limp as tendons and muscles were severed. "Drain him dry; he doesn't need all that health!"

Once again, the berserk status of the combatants worked in his favor, as the martial artist didn't make even a single attempt to remove the summoned entity from where he was pulling on his life force.

"What was that? A spell or a ritual?" Mir called out curiously, obviously trying to figure out more of Joe's combat capabilities. "Doesn't seem like something you should be able to do."

"Something in the middle! The ritual determines what creature is going to be summoned; the spell actually makes it happen. It's like creating a lock then using an energy signature to work as the key." Joe felt some of his enthusiasm return, now that he was making progress again, and pushed himself harder, his ritual orbs slamming into his attackers with wild abandon. None of them attempted to block, which meant that the damage he was dealing was rapidly accumulating. "Not sure why this one wasn't as broken as my other spells... maybe because it only does half of the work? Maybe because it's at a lower level than the others?"

If he were being more honest than he was comfortable with, Joe would've also taken a moment to complain to his mentor that he hadn't jumped a few ranks upon creating a mana pathway and using Planar Shift again, but a cursory glance at the spell's description gave him an 'aha' moment.

Standardized skill progression: To increase the level of this skill, maintain summon control for one hour per current skill level.

"It's an incredibly rigid spell, probably gives it more solidity than anything else Tatum ever gifted me. Most likely why I can use it without having to figure out how to repair it in the first place." Putting that line of thinking to the side, Joe full-body tackled one of the few Experts among the group of people attacking him, pinning him down and sending the man to respawn by spiking the Ritual Orb of Intelligence through his skull.

The move cost him.

Joe felt his rib **crack** as he took a glancing hammer blow to the side. He went tumbling across the street, barely managing to struggle to his feet and bring his ritual orbs close. With a deep breath, he took two quick steps forward then launched himself up and over the group. Kicking off the wall just before he would've gone over it, he reversed course with a secondary activation of Omnivault. He caught his Ritual Orb of Strength on the way down, but instead of using it to shift his vector, he instead twisted in place—feeling his broken rib grind painfully—and practically *fed* the weapon to the swaying martial artist.

Broken teeth scattered across the ground as the Master went down, only to vanish on the third bounce as Morsum let out a dry howl of excitement. Joe mentally gripped the orb the summon had manifested around, chucking the pseudo-lich at another of his opponents, who yet again did nothing to prevent the strike and subsequent latching on.

Even with the pain in his abdomen, Joe found himself absolutely *intoxicated* by the sensation of being a frontline fighter once again. His body responded instantly and perfectly, his mana flowing through him and around him as though it were lightning and he *was* the Faraday cage. Each time his feet came down, he could feel six different pressure points as contact was made, and from there, his Dexterity allowed him to adjust in real time and maximize the amount of force he could bring to bear.

His sensitivity to mana allowed him to track each spell or enchanted weapon screaming through the air toward him, Magical Synesthesia whispering the details of the payload directly into his ears. The second and final Expert in the group went down in a hail of stinging ritual orbs, followed shortly after by the Master he'd captured at the start of combat, who had remained pinned in place like a butterfly in a shadowbox as Joe's Ritual Orb of Intelligence pierced him over and over.

As he landed from his most recent Omnivault, Joe found himself surrounded by three enemy combatants who had positioned themselves well. Unwilling to burn through a huge chunk of his mana by reactivating the skill again in rapid succession, Joe instead flipped a ritual tile in the air, guiding it with his mana and causing the one at the far left to bounce off a plane of force, the momentary interruption giving the Ritualist just enough time to slip past and finally escape the contained alleyway.

"Are you *running*?" Mir's scandalized shout followed after Joe as he pounded the ground, sprinting down the road as quickly as his feet would carry him. "After all that? It was just getting good!"

Without using Omnivault, he was far slower than his opponents, several of whom seemed specialized in combat against others. Soon he was ducking, tucking, and gripping his legs to jump through the air as if planning to cannonball into a pool—all to avoid the weapons making the air **hum** as they came within inches of taking his life.

An arrow **snapped** past his ear, and Joe nearly vomited with anger as he realized it had come from in *front* of him. His eyes flicked to the side, trying to find the source of the attack, but his brain went numb as he recognized Heartpiercer Mcshootypants in the distance. Only then did he realize that his Magical Synesthesia had quieted by a third, and a rapid handspring allowed him to look back... where one of the Masters was even now vanishing with a massive arrow having lanced through his nose and out the back of his head.

"I've got you, Joe!" The Archer followed her words with action, a veritable cone of arrows erupting from her position and missing Joe on all sides by inches as they sank into the unresisting, berserker-state Masters behind him. "Hope I'm not interrupting a duel."

"Nope, nope, *nope*!" Joe's flipping sent him up and over the Archer, and for an instant, his ritual orbs came into position around him. Then they blasted out, all six **thunking** against the final nearby pursuer and stopping his momentum just long enough for a trio of arrows to create a picture-perfect grouping in his chest. As the attacker vanished, Joe landed and heaved for air. "Five more. Someone's mind controlling them. I don't know what their deal is, and–oh, hey, good to see you again."

"Since I have a connection with you, and it's widely surmised that you're the reason your tower has a Sage now, my instructors asked me to come and ensure we maintained good relations." Heartpiercer nocked another arrow, ready to draw at a moment's notice. A handful of people rounded a bend, and much to Joe's surprise, his friend relaxed, pulling her arrow off the string and dropping it into the quiver slung over her back. "Those guys are with me. Looks like they solved this little issue for us."

Congratulations! You have defeated 2 Expert-rank combatants, 2 Master-rank combatants, and partial credit for two additional Master-rank combatants!

Honor gained: 3,000.

As your opponents were under external hostile control, sanctions are unavailable.

Honor payout has been provided by [Blocked].

"Well, that's useless." Joe waved the notification away, alongside a half-dozen combat-based skill offerings which started at Novice one and had far too niche of a purpose for him to ever consider accepting them. "Good to see you again, Mcshootypants."

"Don't get used to it; I'm going back into seclusion in, like, twenty minutes." She reached out and clapped him on the shoulder, a bright smile on her face. "Would you say I've definitely secured good relations with you and hopefully your tower because of it?"

"Saving my life tends to do that, yeah." Joe replied cautiously, uncertain where she was going with this line of questioning.

"Then my quest is complete, and I just qualified for my next round of training under the Sage of Arrow Rain himself. Uh, that's Sage Umbra, if you want to send him a fruit basket or something like that as a 'thank you'." Giving him a flip salute, she started walking toward her friends in the distance. "Stay in contact, Joe! If you need anything, I'm happy to come give you a hand. It's great for both of us, ya know?"

"Yeah..." Joe watched her go, feeling some sort of way about the interaction. "Until next time, I guess?"

CHAPTER EIGHT

The walk back to the Tower of Ritualists should've been peaceful. Joe moved carefully, trying not to agitate his broken bones too much, though he *was* able to power through the pain, thanks to his Characteristics. Not *easily* able to ignore the itching of his broken bones sliding against each other, as with this many points in his Constitution, was the same as having a steel girder sheared in twain and left to cut up his internal soft tissue.

But the real issue was the surprisingly large number of people out and about on the streets today. A good majority of them were overly cheerful, clearly putting on airs to keep a friendly face pointed toward his tower and its new Sage. Others glowered darkly at the Ritualist when they thought he couldn't see them, obviously furious that he'd stolen a march on them by somehow smuggling a Mythic Core planet-side without anyone noticing.

Still, friendly, false friendly, or angry, no matter who they were, every last one of them quickly backed away when they got close and caught a whiff of him. His robes, self-cleaning as they were, still clung to his sticky skin where dried sweat mingled with cooling and congealing blood. Worse, he couldn't *quite* turn off the manic grin he was wearing, still bizarrely thrilled from the intense fight in the alley. Combined, those factors likely gave off some seriously concerning vibes.

He kept replaying the fight in his head. The control. Precision. *Massive* quantities of mana flowing with ease. Feeling nearly untouchable when he was on the move. Even hurting, filthy, and knowing that someone out there was powerful enough to target him by sending swaths of *Masters* against him—not to mention somehow blocking the systems notifications that would at least give a hint to their identity—Joe only felt more alive than he had in over a year.

Getting back to the tower after a long walk that likely lowered his worldwide reputation by a few percentage points, the Ritualist ignored everything else and climbed to the tip of the tower. Painfully lifting a hand, he pounded on Sage Pete's office door, only for it to swing open almost immediately.

"Abyss, Master Joe." Pete flinched back, nose scrunching in disgust. "By chance, did you stop to *roll* in whatever tried to kill you?"

"Still waiting to be assigned an actual bedroom here, so that I have a shower I can use whenever I need it." Joe pushed past the Sage. "I need some advice if you have a moment. There's someone on this planet, extremely high-powered, trying to off me. I have a strong suspicion that it's someone from the Tower of Blood Rites, but even the person who hates me the most over there, Master Surge, denies they have any responsibility for this. I just got attacked by a group of berserk Masters, and only the fact that they didn't try to defend themselves and attacked in a very straightforward manner allowed me to walk here instead of respawn here."

"That's quite the serious accusation, Joe." Pete didn't even pretend that it wasn't possible, simply striding over to his window and staring out of it while he thought. "That would mean there's a Sage, at the minimum, working with forbidden skill sets. Mental attacks or controls are forbidden across every world, which means either there is a taboo Sage on the loose, or..."

Turning back to Joe after a moment of hesitation, he regarded the newest addition to his tower with a contemplative stare. "Are you certain it was a *mental* effect? Could it have been some form of puppeteering? Their bodies are under someone else's control, while their mind is still free? While still on the *fringes* of being allowed, it would at least expand the list of suspects to known quantities."

"I don't know." Joe went to sit on the couch, only for the Sage to let loose a strangled groan, prompting the filthy man to halt before accidentally staining the furniture. "If I had any idea where those guys went after respawning, I suppose I could at least ask them if they were trapped in their own bodies for a bit. Don't even know where to look, though."

"Thank you for staying on your feet; that's my favorite couch. In an effort at transparency... Mir contacted me while you were on your way back, and he has a few ideas of their affiliation, based on their garments." The Sage looked Joe up and down, noting the blood seeping through the self-cleaning fabric and the way he was holding his damaged side. "He and I will look into this on your behalf, but there is an associated cost to having your Sage look into a matter that *should* be two tiers below him. I don't want to have to charge you, but there are rules to this sort of thing."

"No one wants simple matters to escalate. Yeah, I figured that would be the case." Joe rolled his shoulders, trying to push his rib back into position as he made the motion. "Ugh. *That* didn't work. Look, I've got cheese for days, what do you need?"

"Unfortunately, this is a matter of *Honor.*" Pete stressed the word, making sure Joe realized he was speaking of the tower's currency. "Your Decury Duelist fights recently resolved in your favor, and that, alongside what you've earned today, will allow me to investigate this matter on your behalf. But only if you allow me to use practically every last scrap you've accumulated. Otherwise, I'll need to hand it off to someone lower down the totem pole. Seeing as this unknown attacker can control Masters in a group, I can't imagine anyone else in the tower would be much use, at the moment."

"Sure, use it up." Joe bobbled his head back and forth with a resigned exhale. "Still have no idea what that would be useful for in the first place. But the way things are going, I should be able to gather up a whole bunch more whenever I want. Just walk into a crowd and announce that I'm 'Joe the Ritualist'. Half of 'em will go feral, the rest will look at me like *I'm* the strange one."

"Well, for one..." Sage Pete reluctantly started, gently coughing into his hand to hide his discomfort, "Using Honor is one of the main ways of upgrading your lodging and workspace. Which, unfortunately, means that getting a personal room with a luxurious shower just became out of reach for you."

Joe didn't verbally respond, though his head tilted forward as he allowed incredulousness to fill the air between them.

"A-*hem*, as I was saying, while we conduct this investigation, it might be for the best that you either stay in the tower or spend more of your time on a lower world. Where, even if agents of this unknown agitator find you, you'll be able to handle them with much greater ease." Pete met Joe's eyes despite the awkwardness the younger Ritualist was trying to inflict on him with his unblinking stare. "It's all I can really offer you, in terms of help or advice at this point."

"Or you could just let me use your shower. No, actually, I wanna talk about that help we had a *quest* for." Joe's face hardened as he realized the Sage was trying to shoo him away. "Interesting how, after all the effort I went through to get that Mythic Core for your ascension, there are certain promises that were made that are no longer enforceable by the system. Don't suppose you knew about that detail *before* you made those agreements?"

"I did," Pete admitted freely, not a hint of shame on his face. "I also know you were generously compensated for the removal of the Karmic Debt between us. You'll also now have a better understanding of why I went through the trouble of personally operating your recovery ritual *before* ascending. Otherwise, the debt between us would be heavily weighted in *my* favor at this point, or you would be requesting a Master's assistance in operating that monolithic circle that dumped power into you. Having a Sage personally run a ritual on your behalf? *Quite* expensive."

"Mmm. I had wondered why you wouldn't ascend first." Joe tried to quell his bitterness at that moment, as eighty-five free Mastery Merits *was* quite the payout for his services and effort, to this point.

"I did the best for you that I could, and I would say that all but *handing you* more than three-quarters of a Grandmaster requirement would certainly be considered 'supporting you into the Grandmaster ranks'. Wouldn't you agree?"

The Ritualist stayed silent, wrestling internally to keep his mouth shut.

Pete sighed as he realized Joe wasn't ready to let this go just yet. "Everything I could do for you, I did. Now that there is a two-tier difference in our power, the equation changes drastically when there's a debt between us. You owing me something means practically nothing. Me owing you even a minor favor? The difference between being owed by a Grandmaster and being owed by a Sage, is as different as a warrior looking out for you on the battlefield and a king pulling you from the field entirely to make sure you survive a war."

"Look, I get it. I've been *paid*." Despite his best efforts, Joe couldn't keep a slight edge from his voice, and someone as powerful as Sage Stompetti wasn't about to miss that. "I was just-"

"If it's possible, I will tell you one more thing about my ascension, about achieving *balance* to make it possible in the first place." Pete closed his eyes, his words coming out as though he was weighing and measuring each one individually. "Any peak

Grandmaster can become a Sage at any time, without the need for a Mythic Core."

Joe waited for a better explanation, raising an eyebrow as he skeptically stated, "I'm assuming that's *theoretically*?"

"Indeed." Pete reached out and tapped on the glass, which spiderwebbed with cracks from where his finger gently pressed against it. "If they held no Karmic Debt toward anyone else and no one else owes *them* a debt, simply achieving peak Grandmastery would be enough to tip them into Sagehood directly. Tell me, Joe. Do you think *anyone* reaches that level without trading favors or building grudges against them?"

"That would probably be a 'no'," Joe intoned heavily, starting to get an inkling of where this was going. "No man is an island, and I firmly believe that we all reach the highest heights by standing on the shoulders of those who came before us."

"Good. Then let me explain to you what *I* lost by choosing to ascend when I did." Pete turned back to face Joe, the glass in the window fixing itself as though the damage were being rewound through time.

"Everything I have ever worked toward getting for myself, every last favor, debt, promise whispered in my ear, each IOU scribbled on a napkin? All of it was called in to settle the debts I owed to others. The purpose of the Mythic Core is to act as an intermediary with the system, providing the surge of energy necessary to force one single *moment* of absolute balance in my Karmic Debt. That alone is enough to become a Sage, which is why it's such a strangely anticlimactic event."

"What would happen if..." Joe suddenly had a deep, yawning pit of dread in his gut, "let's say someone was owed so much that, even after paying off their debt to everyone else, they still have more coming in?"

"Yes... Mir told me about your karmic beacon reaching to Asgard itself long ago. Now that I can see it for myself, I can only say that you're quite correct to be concerned." Pete hesitated only for a moment but decided to push forward anyway. "It depends on the original tier difference between yourself and the one who owes you. If the debt between a Sage and a Master is so impactful, what do you think it would look like between a Deity and a Novice?"

"Probably a solid beacon of light reaching straight to Asgard," Joe recited dully. "I can see why people have been getting more frantic about that as I approach Grandmaster, and... have my heart set on becoming a Class Sage."

"Actually, that would be quite *helpful*." Pete quickly made a 'calm down' motion when Joe started getting too much of a spark of hope in his eyes. "Class Sages are not simply a different Skill Sage with a fancier title. They're able to wield each of the distinct and otherwise-unique skills gained by the five Skill Sages. They have a far higher Characteristic cap, soft cap that it may be, and overall far more massive growth potential. In essence, they should be able to stand against all five Skill Sages in their own tower and be able to *defeat* them in five-on-one combat."

"Ah. I can see why they're so... well-regarded."

Pete nodded sagely, which was proper for multiple reasons. "If you are owed a debt at the time of becoming a Sage, and your own debt to others does not mitigate it enough, the usual response is that you'll gain free experience, Characteristics, and potentially skill levels. But with the influx you could expect... well, a life debt owed by a Deity to a Novice... realistically, you should be owed enough to become one yourself-"

Joe perked up, only to deflate as the Sage finished. "At the cost of the deity's own position."

"*So* close, but not how I want to get there," the Ritualist muttered. "I'm guessing the more likely scenario is that I pop like an over-inflated balloon?"

"The general consensus is that the Divine Energy–which caused so much damage to you previously–would be like a *drop* in the ocean of power you would be drowned in. It would probably destroy you permanently, along with whatever continent you were standing on at the time."

"Can't hurt to try though, right?" Joe's flippant answer

caused Pete to choke for a moment, eyes bulging as he tried to determine if the younger man was serious. "Joking. Mostly. But I'm told that I'll likely have a seriously extreme resistance to the same thing that damaged my soul after I reach the Grandmaster ranks?"

"You can have a resistance to sunburns and still be reduced to your component atoms by being thrown into a star."

Joe pondered those words for a few heartbeats, making a noise low in his throat as he tried to determine a workaround. "Would it be possible... hear me out, 'cause this will make me sound really bad... would it be possible to mitigate this debt by making a whole lot of promises to a whole lot of people, with no actual intent to pay them back before I attempt my own ascension?"

"I believe, if you indebted yourself to each of the *worlds* deeply enough, you would be fine. Occultatum, however? If his debt were called in all at once..." Pete trailed off leadingly, allowing Joe to make his own assumptions. "Now, with all that said, it's time for you to make some choices on your own. I have a Sage-rank threat to investigate, and if I'm not mistaken, you need to spend some time building up your arsenal of rituals. Mir informed me that you had a rather *underwhelming* performance during your duels today. A Decury Duelist like yourself should be fully prepared to be tested constantly."

Though he was quickly pushed out of the office, Joe had enough presence of mind to realize the Sage was closing the door while breathing through his mouth. Now standing alone in the hallway, he **tisked** and began the painful walk down the stairs. "There was plenty more for him to say, he just wanted me out of there so the air quality could improve in there."

A quarter of the way down the stairs, Joe's pace began slowing. "Where am I even going? I'm sure someone would let me borrow their shower if I asked, but... what I really want is to have some space where no one can bother me for a while."

Ruminating on that thought, Joe perked up as he realized he may actually have an option. Glancing around furtively, he ducked into an empty antechamber and pulled out the chunk of twisted metal he'd been handed by Nathaniel. "Let's see where *this* goes."

Not sure what else to do, the Ritualist lifted his hand and pressed forward, twisting the key in the air as though it had already been inserted into a lock. The faintest **click* could be heard, followed by a **crackle* of energy as a line of light extended straight up and down from the center of the metal. The line swelled horizontally from the center, creating a four-pointed star with parabolic arcs between each point.

Besides the faint, staticky discharge, the now-open subspace was entirely silent. Joe stepped through, watching carefully to make sure it didn't collapse on him. As soon as he was on the other side, he expected the portal to vanish, but instead it seemed to merely drop a veil. He could step out at any time, but the Ritualist was nearly positive that the entry point was now invisible from the other side.

"Neat. Kinda makes me wonder if one of these is always open somewhere, and we just can't sense it? That would kind of fit the theme of..." As he turned to regard the room, Joe trailed off, at a complete loss for words. Stunned into silence, he simply took a deep breath, enjoying the warm, dry air that was faintly scented with dust, ink, rich mahogany, and old leather.

It wasn't that the room itself was massive, in fact, it felt decidedly intimate, cozy even. There were bookshelves which curved around the round room like the rib bones of an immense beast from a bygone age, and every last space was filled with a book of some shape or size. Strangely enough, it was obvious that the construction had been done intentionally to house each of the works individually, as there was a thin layer of heavily enchanted wood separating each volume into its own individual slot on the shelf. No, what made his breath catch in his chest were the titles printed on the spines of each tome—titles that practically *danced* in an effort to catch his attention.

The fifth sigil dilemma: treating beginner rituals as novice rank.

Inversion and collapse of closed systems.

Folding circles: a proposed solution to dimensional overlap.

Topology of failed ritual meshing.

The lost art of self-assembling weapons.

Spirit furnace disaster: notes from a survivor.

Perfect solvents? More like perfect mistakes.

Concoction use on Experts: why it breaks their minds.

Transmutation above your pay grade.

Animated circles: magical familiar or self-fulfilling mutiny?

Paradoxical targeting: using conscious components in ritual design.

Circles that learn: why leaving ritual circles in place without activation causes societal collapse; part 2.

An index of rituals removed from indexes.

A tour of ritual-based catastrophes (compilation of anecdotes from the survivors).

Multiplicity of the Myriad Mind. A practical guide to creating alternate versions of yourself.

"That last one looks like it's usable as-is... I want it." Even so, he kept reading without touching, scanning the spines until they landed on sections where the books had thin chains across their openings, as if warning people away from reading them and containing the tome all in one. They quivered on the shelves as he stared at their titles, the rattling of the chain letting him know that he wasn't imagining things. "*How to prove a theorem by… screaming*? *Using Magical Matrices for iterative summoning, a city-killer's step-by-step guide*? Well, I can see why *those* ones were locked away."

Forcing himself to look away from the books before his twitching hands could betray him and reach for the first among them, Joe looked around the rest of the small space, allowing himself to crack a grin when he found exactly what he was looking for: short-term habitation amenities. "Celestial feces, am I glad to see *you*."

It was obvious that the sealed room had been created with the knowledge that people entering it may want to stay for long periods of time. There was a small kitchenette tucked behind the large fireplace along the only shelfless wall, a long-unused room-temperature ice box for storing small amounts of food and drink, a lonely twin-sized bed with a thin mattress, and best of all... a shower just large enough for him to squeeze into. After ten minutes in the washroom, Joe emerged shower-clean for the first time since his last death.

As he swapped his robes for a fresh set, steam still rising from his skin, he took a deep breath and choked slightly. "*Ugh*... right, broken rib. Now, should I...?"

He walked toward the shelves, his steps slowing before he got halfway across the room. Joe forced the hand that was half raised back to his side, then clenched his fists and turned toward the portal. "Nope. Not even one little peek. Those books might as well be traps right now. How many of them would offer me a skill I couldn't take, only to be practically locked out of them when I *can* actually spend some time on research?"

Though his mind was pleading with him to grab a grimoire and settle in for the long haul, Joe forced the desire to the side with an iron will and decisively stepped through the portal. It closed behind him with the barest hint of a whisper—he could've *sworn* it was the books themselves sighing in disappointment—and the scent of the subspace library lingered in the air for a moment longer.

"Priorities. I need to put together some ritual clusters and get my combat power up." Clean and far more refreshed than he'd felt in a long time, Joe clutched at his side and made his way to the stairs. "Now, if I were a combat Ritualist who needed to make a massive stack of rituals, where would I go?"

CHAPTER NINE

Each time Joe went down a stair, his broken rib made a strange, gritty-grinding sound. "Seriously, what are my bones made of at this point to make them sound like that? It has to be some kind of metal at the bare minimum, otherwise it wouldn't sound like broken rebar tossed in a sack when I move."

He'd never before even considered the fact that there wasn't a railing around the stairs, but now that he was wishing he could hold on to it so as to jostle himself less, the lack became apparent. Lifting the arm on his good side, he wiped the sweat that was building up on his forehead, doubly annoyed at the biological reaction to stress, seeing as he had just showered.

Just to make sure he didn't go farther than needed, the Ritualist stopped the first person he encountered on the stairs, waving them over with as friendly of a smile as he could manage at the moment. "Any chance you could point me to where a Master of Ritual Circles can go if he needed to put together an irresponsible number of combat rituals in as short of an amount of time as possible?"

The young-seeming man gawked at the ornamentation on

Joe's robes, his eyes slowly tracking up and over until they locked with the bald Triple-Master. "T-that way."

"Thanks. Down the stairs. Got it." Joe pressed his lips together, then tried again, hoping the young Ritualist would be able to comport himself. "Any chance you could be a *bit* more specific? Pretend I have no knowledge of where things are. Actually, do you know Jenny? My assistant? I feel like this falls under her responsibilities..."

"*Yeah!*" The younger man all but shouted, his face draining of blood as he realized he was failing to control the volume of his voice. "Yeah, she's great. I'll let you know... that is, I'll let *her* know you're looking for her. Otherwise, you can start setting up rituals on any of the platforms, if you have enough Honor-"

"Let's pretend I have absolutely no Honor whatsoever, but I *do* have a giant sack of cheese. What happens then?" Joe did his best to ignore the incredulous stare being sent his way, pretending he was simply trying to see what his conversational compadre had to say. "If there was a Ritualist who was brand new to the tower, how would you direct them?"

"Oh. In that case, I'd go talk to Cookie." When Joe simply returned his words with an uncomprehending raise of the eyebrow, the younger Ritualist coughed into his hand and expounded on his words. "Right, so you know how cheese is our currency? But it's also sorta food?"

"Got that."

"Cookie is the main chef in the tower, and he doubles as the quartermaster for all materials and diagram purchasing. Just... try to stay on his good side? He's got a pretty nasty spell he likes to use whenever someone annoys him, and I'm pretty sure he subclassed as a Berserker." After a momentary pause, his initial directions were followed up with, "Go to the first floor, not the ground floor, and just follow the *good* smells. The other direction brings you to the Novice Alchemical Ritualist workshop."

"Thanks, kid." Not sure if it was the right thing to do or not, Joe pulled a large wedge of cheddar cheese out of his storage ring and slipped it into the young man's hand. "You did good. Hope this helps, and remember, I'm a nice guy. Easy to talk to."

"*Thank* you, Master Joe!" The youngster's eyes were shining a golden yellow as they reflected the immaculate cheese. "This'll be enough to get me my first Journeyman circle!"

Joe continued his downward descent, quietly wondering what he'd have to do to get one of the teleportation tokens Sage Pete used to pop around the tower. Reaching the first floor, he was easily able to discern which direction the 'good smells' were coming from, as there seemed to be an active war on the olfactory organs on the stairway itself. Noxious malodor crept from the left hallway, only to be fought back by the scent of baked goods and sizzling meats coming from the right. Without a word, he followed the smells until he arrived at what must be the tower's main mess hall, with enough seating for a couple thousand people at a time.

There were buffet-style options around the room, making it easy for everyone to get access to their meal without having to wait in long lines. He continued deeper into the dining area, pushing past the final rows of delicacies and into the kitchen itself–where he was met with a dozen knives pointing at him while large pans and lids were lifted like shields to protect the various cooks. Freezing in place, the bald man slowly lifted his hands. "Just here to talk to Cookie? I have cheese, if he has goods?"

"Cookie!" one of the chefs shouted, his voice edged with desperation. "There's a customer *in the kitchen*! What do we do?"

"Somebody find a server!"

"No, just stab it, maybe it'll go away!"

"Customers aren't supposed to be back here! They *promised*!"

"*Hey*! What're you doing in the kitchen?" A bulky man with muscles to spare shoved his way through the gathering crowd of nervous people and pushed Joe out the doors he'd just entered through. "You can't just walk in and talk to the *cooks*.

That's a great way to make everyone in the tower miss a couple meals as they settle their nerves. Do you want that on your shoulders?"

"Sorry, I just-" Joe blinked several times as he tried to breathe around the pain in his chest from getting shoved, not entirely certain what had just happened. "Are you Cookie? Someone told me I could come in here and find you, so I could buy some ritual material and maybe some new diagrams? Wasn't trying to pry or cause problems for you."

The huge chef held up his index finger. "Everybody gets one, and you just used yours up. Stay out of my kitchen, or the next time we talk, you'll have to scrub dishes for a few hours to get back on my good side. Now, we don't deal in Honor back here, just cheese. Tell me what you're after, I'll let you know what it's going to cost you."

"Any chance I can just browse for a bit?" Joe unconsciously reached for the invisible merchant sack still strapped onto his back. "I've no idea what you have available-"

"Do you have any instant memorization skills? Can you read a book and store the information just by touching it? When you brush against the items you're looking at, is there any way for you to make copies, swap the original with a different version, or anything of that nature that would allow you to make off with the tower's items without properly paying for them?" Cookie's questions came hard and fast, and luckily for Joe there was only one word he needed to say to answer all of them.

"No?"

"Then yes, you can browse." Cookie turned and motioned for the Ritualist to follow him, leading him to a door that was on the other side of the room, tucked away behind one of the buffets. "Anything in particular you're looking for?"

"I'm trying to set up some rituals that work well together, so realistically, I'm not sure exactly what I'm looking for, but..." Joe's eyebrows shot up as he stepped into a massive room that looked like a cross between a bookstore and a hobby shop. An enormous tome stood in front of the stacks, which had a cage-like door blocking them off from casual entry. Components of all sizes and rarities filled the other shelves, most of the organic versions being under a glass lid that preserved them while allowing people to take a look at the contents.

"You'll know it when you see it. Yeah, we get that a lot from people who are new to the tower." Cookie grunted and shook his head while crossing his arms. "If you're looking for enhanced ritual 'papers', we've got alchemically treated paper that'll work for anything up to the Beginner rank, Enchanted Parchment that should hold anything you've got Journeyman or below, treated vellum for Expert, and treated *beast* vellum for anything up to Grandmaster zero. Parchment and above will let you draw out your rituals in three dimensions. Let me know-"

"How much for... a thousand of each of them?" Joe's question was met with an annoyed incredulousness. After a long moment, the chef responded with an edge in his voice that promised violence if his time was being wasted.

"The alchemically treated paper, you're looking at four full wheels of sharp cheddar, twelve wedges of mild, and a twenty-four count of sliced-bread sized." Seeing Joe's unflinching visage, Cookie spoke with a bit more eagerness in his voice. "For the parchment, I'm thinking a medium wheel of Havarti, two of Colby Jack, eight Swiss wedges, and a stack of forty Swiss slices. You're already looking at fifty-six pounds of cheddar, thirty-four pounds of mid-tier cheese. Want me to keep going?"

"By all means, please continue." Joe stated mildly, already pulling the sack off his back, wincing as the bone shards in his chest stabbed at undamaged flesh from the twisting motion. "The treated vellum?"

"Thrity-six pounds. It'll be broken up between a full wheel of smoked Gouda, six wedges of Gruyère, and three small rounds of Camembert. As for the treated beast vellum?" The chef shook his head, not quite believing he was entertaining this request. "I need the equivalent of a five-year wheel of Parmesan, ten wedges of three-year, a brick of two, and a pound of shredded asiago."

"Well, I don't have that-"

"I'm going to hit you with a pan now for making me waste my time." Cookie's eyes widened, quickly becoming bloodshot as he rustled around in his chef's jacket. "Stay right there, don't move an *inch.*"

"-But can I get you to figure out what the equivalent is in *one*-year aged for everything?" Pretending he didn't hear the threat, Joe began stacking wheels of cheese, starting a second tower as the first went above his head and started tilting. "The conversion rate on this stuff is *seriously* confusing."

After a short round of haggling, which left Joe feeling as though he'd been taken advantage of–but had no way to prove anything–a far more enthusiastic chef ushered Joe over to the enormous tome near the book stacks, his attitude having done a complete one-eighty.

"Anyway, valued customer, allow me to give you a tour! As you can see, we have all sorts of materials of various rarities, elemental affinities, and purity. If you've got the chedda', we can always find you something bedda'." Pulling open the massive book, Joe felt his jaw drop slightly as he realized it was nothing more than a massive list–thousands of pages long. "In here, you'll find every ritual diagram that's been submitted for sale, along with a brief description of how they work."

"Abyss. So *many*?" Joe's fingers reverently trailed across the paper. "*Why* so many?"

"Anyone can submit a ritual to the tower for sale, then they get a commission when someone buys their version. There has to be a significant difference between what's available and what they submit, but at the end of the day, most of these are simply variants. They may be more efficient, have a different material cost, or solve a more niche problem. Each of them will be grouped under the base version of the ritual, just look for the header *here...* and everything offset under it is a variant. Before you ask, the only time the tower sets or changes the price is if the Ritualist who submitted the work died permanently. Otherwise, the cost is at the discretion of the seller."

"Some of these cost Honor?" Joe's lips curled into a snarl as he stared at the first offender he'd found. "I thought you only dealt in-"

"Pretty much anything Master rank or above costs Honor," Cookie quickly clarified. "With a few exceptions, most Masters who submit rituals at that rank have their own sources of cheese and are basically just exchanging favors with their contemporaries by placing their rituals in here. Anyway, uh, whenever you find something you like, note it down, and I'll give you a final tally at the end. Ring for me, and I'll ring you up! Enjoy your searching."

"Got it..." Before he even finished his words, the chef had vanished, though a small bell now rested next to the enormous book. Without further ado, Joe began perusing the massive list.

"Material cost isn't really a factor, so I can ignore most of the variance that simply reduces the number of required materials." As minutes became hours, Joe began deciding on rules for his purchases. "I can increase their efficiency on my own, but if the cost isn't too much higher, why *not* grab the better version right away? Let's see, if I'm making a ritual cluster, how should I go about it?"

His original attempt, the Ritual Cluster of Despair, had essentially been a hodgepodge of effects that worked together *pretty* well. But in reality, they were mostly damage-dealing rituals that functioned independently. Only a few of them really worked well together, taking the output from a ritual and using it as an input for their own. "Maybe instead of a dozen effects at a time, I choose one core function and select four others to boost it, or just make the core one work better?"

After a bit of finagling, he decided on making an Expert-rank ritual as the core, with four supporting Journeyman-rank rituals. With three rules in place, which essentially boiled down to ignoring component requirements, mana cost-effectiveness, and focusing on synergy, Joe decided how he would choose his new clusters.

"Looks like most combat rituals break down into a few overall categories. Elemental and energetic damage, ranging from heat to non-magical radiation. Physical or kinetic damage, which is anything from cutting to torsion. Magical damage, which can be kind of a catch-all for non-elemental energies. Then lastly biological, from poisons to resource-pool affecting rituals."

Seeing as he wanted to cover his bases as much as possible in a short amount of time, Joe selected a core ritual to build around from the kinetic, biological, and elemental sections. He read over the sparse details in the list for his kinetic selection, more pleased with it by the moment.

Ritual of Abrasive Momentum (Expert). Any movement through a designated area creates friction across all surface area. The faster an object is moving through this designated zone, the more heat, scraping, melting, tearing, and eroding happens simultaneously. Punishes creatures or enemies that are extremely fast, charging, sprinting, lunging, or flying. Potentially destroys or degrades projectiles moving through the field.

"This one seems better than a barrier when fighting against high-ranked people, and it should be effective even against Master-ranked monsters or people as an Expert-ranked ritual. I could even set it up behind me to help protect against assassins or pincer attacks, or maybe in the air to catch flying monsters."

Knowing he would still need to fill out the supporting rituals, Joe marked the page and flipped to the elemental damage 'chapter' spanning over eight hundred pages on its own. "Mana-Shockwave Burst. If the last one was mostly defensive, this one is definitely for taking down lots of weaker enemies at once."

Mana-Shockwave Burst (Expert). This area-of-effect ritual pulls in ambient mana then detonates in a 17-meter shockwave that deals mixed magical and physical damage and has a 15% chance to stun. It generates heavy concussive force, shockwaves, and sonic booms, and can forcibly siphon excess mana from spells that overload the local zone. While it is absorbing mana, everything within the area is slightly dragged toward the center. Creatures below the ritual's rank are pulled more strongly. When it bursts after accruing enough ambient mana, the targets closest to the center suffer the highest damage. (Damage: Variable, based on local mana density.)

"Last but not least, a good option for stronger monsters." Joe was somewhat leery about this particular ritual, but seeing as every version of a combat ritual was designed to slay enemies, he pushed aside his queasiness and made his choice. "Biological section, high single-target damage-over-time."

Ritual of the Red Cascade (Expert). A single-target ritual which weaponizes existing injuries. Any open wound on an organic target will have micro-tearing induced through exposed veins, arteries, or capillaries, causing intense, uncontrollable bleeding. Each additional wound becomes a channel for exponential internal and external damage. In essence, this rapidly scales minor bleeding debuffs to major debuffs.

"I guess there's worse ways to go than bleeding out and falling unconscious." Perhaps it was the fact that it was guaranteed to be a messy death that caused Joe to wrinkle his nose at the description, but even so, he firmly decided that he *needed* a copy of this ritual diagram. "If I'm ever going to be able to fight World Boss-class monsters or Tyrants on my own, I'm going to need to be able to do more than direct damage. If nothing else, something like this should be able to keep their natural regeneration in check."

With his three foundations chosen, Joe moved on to the next step: enhancing and refining them with supporting rituals. Drawing in a long breath, he dove back into the massive tome, discarding dozens of options each second as he searched for the exact rituals he needed to elevate his clusters from dangerous... to lethal.

CHAPTER TEN

The Ritualist slowly closed the massive tome, second-guessing himself all the while. "I *think* these will work the way I want, but is it going to be enough? With the core ritual, I should be able to fight Master-ranked combatants and Artifact monsters, but will the rest of the cluster be useless?"

Skill offered: Data Analysis (Journeyman VII). After reading through an enormous number of list items, you were able to effectively break them down and search through them without issue. This skill will allow you to create indexes in your mind, keeping track of information from any and all books and information sources you find-

Waving the offered skill away, as only the fact that it started at the Journeyman rank made it interesting at all, the Ritualist returned to ruminating on his choices and gently rubbing at his damaged abdomen. Joe read over the three separate, five-ritual clusters he'd cobbled together based on the shortened descriptions available to him. "First cluster, area of effect elemental damage."

The core was the Mana-shockwave Burst, which would pull enemies toward the center and detonate after a certain threshold had been met. He could only imagine a battlefield down on Midgard, where he'd been forced to use even stronger rituals or skills, making the air choke with spell residue and ambient mana thick enough to distort vision. "If I can weaponize that against my enemies instead of just making it harder for me to cast spells... that's pretty ideal."

His eyes trailed to the next item on the list, the first ritual he had chosen to support the core ability.

Ritual of Interlocking Air (Journeyman). Creates pressure waves in a ring around a specified area, collapsing to a central point and shoving inward anything within its bounds. 13-meter radius. Maximum initial damage: 400 at the center, 50 at the edges.

Every three seconds, anything dragged to the central point suffers a concussive burst which may stun. This ritual creates a purely physical effect, in essence a semi-permeable moving barrier. Each time a creature is subjected to the burst at the center, damage dealt to that creature by this ritual increases by 12%.

"Whoever wrote this was a pretty straightforward person. Hopefully the ritual itself is as easy to understand." Joe moved on to the next ritual, which was far more verbose in its description, so he simply summed it up and put a little check mark next to it. "Moth to a Flame ritual, Journeyman rank. Kind of like a pared-down version of the Bug Zapper ritual I have, with only a ten percent chance per second to captivate creatures looking at it and make them walk toward the light. If I set that up at the center of the core part of the cluster, I should be able to gather monsters more efficiently. Third..."

Ritual of Concussive Percussion (Journeyman). Creates a 13-meter debuffing zone, making any creatures within the radius 20% more susceptible to stunning effects.

"Short, sweet, and effective. That should make both 'Shockwave Burst' and 'Interlocking Air' more potent overall. That just leaves the final one, the wildcard of the mix." He turned his attention to the final selection he'd made for this cluster, the one that he was by far the most unsure of. "Mana Randomizer."

Mana Randomizer Ritual (Journeyman). When mana density reaches a specific threshold, it ignites into a random elemental energy and has a chance to apply a low-grade debuff. (Fire: burns. Ice: chills. Lightning…)

There was an exhaustive list of potential effects, but the really worrying bit was how cheaply this design was being sold. "It doesn't really give me a range or any details other than it *might* activate and add a debuff to anything caught in it. Maybe the threshold for activation is really high, or, more likely, very *low*. That would mean using it on Vanaheim would just cause a constant reaction within the space, meaning anyone could see it coming and just avoid it. Or... really, there's just too many possibilities."

Still, as he was planning to use the main portion of the ritual cluster to condense mana enough to generate a shockwave, this fit too perfectly to ignore. He'd just have to try it out and see if it worked, then adjust from there. "This cluster together... let's call it... hmm. Two of them collapse inward and detonate, one of them enhances the possibility of getting stunned, another makes shifting lights that are entrancing, and the last one adds a potential for extra damage-over-time effects. Well of Storms? Earth Shaker? Prismatic Blowout? No, wait. It slurps things inward. Ya know, I think I was going somewhere with The Well of Storms... Stormwell Convergence Cluster? That has a nice ring to it."

Storms were beautiful to look at, tended to mess with air pressure, and generally created thunder and had plenty of other effects dependent on wind speed, water content, and the like. He settled on the name, hoping he wouldn't need to change out too many of the components after testing it out. With the first of three finalized, he went on to the secondary set, which was quickly shaping up to become his favorite—at least in its conceptual phase.

"My purely physical damage cluster..." the focus of this one was the Ritual of Abrasive Momentum, which he pictured as turning the air in a large sphere into the equivalent of sandpaper. "The faster something moves through here, the more it's ground down and such. I can't believe how much fun I had putting this one together, and it's just so... *simple*."

Ritual of Haste (Journeyman). Any person or object moving through the designated area sees a 13% increase in movement speed, starting instantly and lasting for 30 minutes.

"Since this is generally seen as a beneficial effect to all entities, it'll help get around any magical resistance they have. It's a little risky if I don't take them out pretty quickly after that, but if nothing else, it'll throw off their timing at first and boost the damage done by the core part of the cluster." Joe was literally rubbing his hands together in excitement, his palms heating up rapidly, almost like a microscopic version of what this cluster would eventually do, and he greatly approved of it. "Those two combined with the Ritual of Extended Ember? Just mean. I love it."

Ritual of Extended Ember (Journeyman). Any energy output strong enough to start a fire, will. Any flames started within this area will be 13% more difficult to put out by all sources and 13% hotter, which means 13% more damage. Buy my ritual.

"Whoever sold this one to the tower wasn't mincing words. Hopefully, it does what it says it does, so I can recommend it." Now, having gone through the two directly supporting rituals, Joe looked at the third: his plan to counter anyone that tried to avoid rushing through the space. "Ritual of Quicksand. Anything not moving across the ground fast enough will begin to sink into the surface. For each second caught in the quicksand, movement speed decreases by one percent. Once a target is fully engulfed, they'll take an increasing percentage of suffocation damage per breath taken. Yeah..."

Clicking his tongue against his teeth, Joe waffled between using this ritual or swapping it out right away. "All but useless against even Expert-threat people and monsters. I think I could hold my breath for something like ten minutes at a time back then, which means the slowing effect is the only part that matters. Eh... when I upgrade the cluster, I'll swap it out. Maybe

I could find an Expert-rank one that'll actively send sand into their lungs or something."

Last, and his new favorite habit when forming clusters, his wildcard. Generally, the enemies he fought were rather intelligent, even the monsters having grown in acuity and risk assessment as he progressed into higher worlds. If he simply left the cluster sitting around, he'd only damage a couple of enemies at best before they figured out that they should avoid it.

Ritual of The Stand-in (Journeyman). Creates an illusion of the caster at a specific point, which mimics all biological functions, such as blinking, breathing, and moving. The illusion will also exude the caster's mana signature, creating a perfect lure for aggressive opponents.

"Since the Moth to a Flame Ritual causes entranced enemies to move toward it at a walking pace, it definitely won't work for this cluster. Would've been nice to be able to have some overlap between these, but... this should work pretty well." He chuckled at the thought of an image of himself standing out and looking excessively punchable while monsters launched themselves at him and set themselves on fire. "Maybe I can upgrade it to *smell* delicious in the next rank. Combine it with some monster lure potions? Maybe a taunt effect later on? Eh, let's just see how effective it is on its own first."

Putting a final check mark in place, he moved on to the hardest part of making the cluster: naming it. "The Rending Formation. No, Socar would be mad if I called it a formation without actually using one. Friction Forge... nah, though that *does* sound like a neat idea to try out with Ritualistic Forging. The Air Fryer? Heh. Yeah. That's the one. Nothing saying I *have* to use the word 'cluster' to describe my clusters. The air becomes abrasive, they start themselves on fire, it burns hotter than it should... this checks out."

As he wrote the name in his notebook, his hand jostled the bell next to the tome and it started falling toward the floor. He deftly caught it halfway to the ground, but it still let out a muted jingle. In response, the silvery bell around his neck **chimed** loudly, as if to assert dominance. His fingers came up and brushed against what he stubbornly called a 'necklace', soothing the Mythic item as he turned his attention to his final design.

"Abyss, I really made this one brutal." With the Ritual of the Red Cascade as the core, which would essentially rip open the veins and arteries around already existing wounds, Joe had found no end of rituals that would happily boost that effect. With a minute shake of his head, he murmured, "With as many combat rituals are in this tome, you'd think that the tower would be filled with more than just crafters who prestiged over to this class. I wonder if everyone who submitted these moved on a long time ago, or something?"

Skill offered: Tower Genealogy Researcher (Novice II). Want to find the lost ancestors of your tower's current Sage? Track societal drift over time? Make a pivot chart that functions to-

"I want none of that. Go away." Joe was barely giving these pop-ups the time of day anymore. Giving his full focus back to his notebook, he started with two rituals to enhance the main effect.

Ritual of Berserking (Journeyman). This ritual causes a targeted individual to enter into a frenzied state, increasing their heart rate by 20 to 35%. This causes their physical output to increase and decreases their ability to concentrate on finesse or magical incantations by the same amount.

Ritual of Fresh Air (Journeyman). Surrounds a targeted individual with a localized pocket of hyperoxygenated air. Breathing becomes easier, stamina recovery increases by 13%. This is fantastic for diving or underwater breathing, in a cost-effective way! Tell your friends to meet you at the bottom of a lake…

The latter of the rituals had an overly enthusiastic description, quickly devolving from details of the ritual itself into an extended sales pitch, likely to the maximum number of words allowed. Though these two didn't seem like they would be effective on the core of the setup, Joe had felt a hint of inspiration at the idea of using them in combination, though only trial by fire would show if he was correct or not.

"Getting put in a berserking state and making their heart

rate increase should make any fleshy monster bleed out more rapidly. It'll make them stronger for a short time, but if I can stay mobile enough, I'm guessing it'd make even a minor laceration bleed like a moderate one."

But it was the Ritual of Fresh Air that really made him feel smug–or at least it would if it worked. "Oxygen-rich blood accelerates the pulse and metabolic demand even further. That should make their bleeding increase *drastically*. These two combined? Enemies'll exsanguinate themselves in no time flat."

As per usual, his third choice was meant to offer a different type of damage which would still support the core of the cluster. In this case, as the others thus far would only work on currently existing wounds, Joe had decided to put together one which should help it along, opening cuts and dealing direct damage.

Ritual of Bloody Caltrops (Journeyman). Causes any blood shed within an area to collect into sharpened caltrops. Anyone stepping on the caltrop takes up to 13 points of piercing damage, gains a minor bleeding debuff, and maybe slowed by up to 13%. This effect stacks.

The Ritualist could only look at the spelling error in the description and laugh, wondering if the person who'd submitted it had noticed and perhaps tried to change it after it was already added to the tome, only to be denied. "Maybe. Ha, hopefully they meant 'may be'. Or... maybe they *meant* maybe, which means maybe the slowing effect has a low chance of happening? Wait... does 'may be' and 'maybe' mean the same thing? ...Perhaps."

"Sorry it took me so long to get here after you rang, but I haven't had an order this large in my entire time in the tower. Had to open some cabinets that had other furniture moved in the way of them. Don't worry, everything is perfectly preserved and ready to go. Guaranteed." Cookie bustled into the room, a huge crate in his hands and a wide smile on his face. "Feces, I'm *so* glad I work on commission. Tell me you're buying a few more things before you go, and I'll throw in a free meal and a private workshop for you to use."

Joe's stomach let out a long, low grumble, reminding him pitifully that he hadn't eaten since before his mana channels had been remapped. "A meal sounds... nice. I'm almost done, just finalizing a few things."

Cookie looked over the list, letting out a low whistle. Joe shot him an annoyed *look*, only to have the bulky chef respond by pulling out an oversized cast-iron pan and waving it back and forth. "Don't you glare at me, or I'll use my spell on you. 'Cast Iron' works like a charm to put a smile on people's faces, even if their eyes get a little unfocused."

"I'm trying to put together an attack set; I'd rather not make it known what my capabilities are before I even get out the door." Joe didn't back down an inch, standing his ground as the chef slowly lowered his 'weapon'.

"Fair enough, but you don't think I'm going to *see* what you're getting? I'm the one in charge of selling the ritual diagrams to you." Cookie slowly slid the cast iron into his form-fitting chef jacket, where it somehow vanished without so much as wrinkling the material. "Don't you worry, I'm just trying to satisfy my own curiosity. I've got a good thing going on with the tower; I'm not about to jeopardize my position by blabbing about the secrets of someone most of the residents think is going to be the next Class Sage. Yeah, that's right. I looked into you a little bit before I came back here. Do you know you have a fan club?"

"Aw man, not here, too."

"*Too*?" Cookie grinned widely. "You mean to tell me you have *multiple* fan clubs?"

"*No*," Joe denied vehemently. "Only the one. Look, just... give me a moment to finalize my selections, and I'll be out of your way."

There was only one last ritual to decide on, this cluster's wildcard.

Ritual of the False Fighter (Journeyman). This ritual creates an illusory fighter that appears randomly once per 13 seconds to 'attack' all enemies within a 30 meter radius. It deals no damage but may cause enemies to flinch or change their target to the illusion.

Since the rest of the cluster was mainly focused on single-target damage, with the caltrops being a great way to slow down any mobs around the main enemy, Joe had decided against a taunt effect. "If I have this going, and my enemy is already berserking, and therefore has its mental faculties impaired even slightly, this should let me slip away when it's distracted. Best case scenario, it causes enemies to hit a minion or three. Pretty solid range as well, and it might even pair with my Haunting Shadows. When they see a shadowy figure pop up and *actually* smack them across the face, they'll be way more likely to take a swing at the illusion."

"Good thinking," Cookie joined into the one-sided conversation, ignoring the Ritualist's eyeroll.

"This works. Probably the most well synergized of all of them, if I'm being honest with myself." Joe took a deep breath, tapping on his paper as he tried to decide what to name the cluster. "Hemorrhage Induction Sequence? Gross. Might as well call it the hemorrhoid inducer. Crimson Spiral Protocol? Ah, too edgy. Red Tempest? No, I should really try to distance myself from the Red Mist event back on Midgard. Don't want people to think I'm trying to recreate that. Spiked Slurpee Fountain? Hah, *that'd* make me look insane if I ever said it out loud."

Of course the most effective of the trio would be the hardest to name, but after gritting his teeth, the Ritualist came up with something that rolled off the tongue well. "Carnage Pulse Cluster! Focused around causing bleeding, frenzied enemies, and friendly fire. There we go."

"I thought you said the *other* name was too edgy for you," Cookie grunted as he accepted the list of rituals from the slightly emotionally exhausted bald man. "No, that is, it sounds potent. Just... it's something I'd *expect* to hear from a high-functioning, err, *combatant.* Now, before making your purchase, I need to have you sign a few things. First is a commitment to pay for the ritual each time you disseminate it. If you're going to teach someone how to use this, you *cheddar* pay up."

"Ugh." Even as Joe groaned at the pun, he couldn't keep himself from smiling at the same time. He wasn't a monster. "What if *they* teach it to someone?"

"You're still on the hook. However, I have a stack of these papers that you're welcome to take along with you, to put *them* on the hook if they start handing it out." In the next moment, Joe was handed a thick binder full of the most multi-level marketing-esque agreements he'd seen since coming to Eternium. "If you're planning on dropping to another world and freely handing these out, you might want to put a down payment in place."

"No discounts? At all?" the Ritualist grumbled as he read over the details. "Is there any other way? Can I *buy* the right to disseminate it freely? Pay off the person who sold it to the tower in the first place or something?"

"In fact, you can! But by doing so, what you're actually buying is the placement of the ritual in the next version of the Standard Ritual Combat Manual. If you buy it out, you're making it available to *everyone* in the tower. Not just the people you choose." Cookie shrugged at Joe's puzzled expression. "Apparently, there used to be a lot more hoarding of knowledge, the good stuff only passing down to select individuals. Now you can *always* learn what's available, provided you have enough cheese or Honor. But what you *can't* do is buy something and take it off the market permanently."

"How often is the Standard Ritual Combat Manual printed?" Joe probed with a deep sigh as he grabbed his borrowed merchant sack and upended it, shaking it gently back and forth to allow a massive pile of cheese to begin appearing. He slowly backed up, waving his bag up and down before turning around and reversing to the other side of the room, slowly filling the storage space with the delicious currency. "Let me know when I have enough."

To his great disgruntlement, the bag was empty long before

the chef opened his mouth. Cookie had been coming along behind Joe and collecting the cheese, or it would've long since overflowed from the room. "Sorry, buddy. You've got enough in there to get personal copies of these rituals, alongside the five you picked for your biological cluster. What was it you called that, again?"

"The, uh, Carnage Pulse Cluster." The tips of Joe's ears turned red as the chef snorted, clearly trying not to laugh at the name. "Why would I have enough for this one and not the others?"

"Most of these are combat rituals. The tower *wants* more combatants, so it subsidizes the cost of these somewhat. It's just that, you know, most Ritualists don't really have much interest in leaving their workshops and getting into the mix. I'm glad you're here, shaking things up. Truly a time of feasting for the tower after a century of famine." Cookie stared at Joe expectedly, and the Ritualist ever so slowly agreed to buy the cluster's rituals outright.

"Certainly that isn't worth *all* of that cheese, right? I want a receipt and my change."

"I mean, isn't *tipping* a big part of the culture you come from-"

"No."

CHAPTER ELEVEN

With a quick swipe of his last bite of bread, every remnant of the thick, creamy sauce on his plate vanished, only for Joe to pop the final morsel into his mouth. Eyes closed, his head swayed back and forth. “That was *ridiculously* good.”

Sitting back with a long exhale, Joe patted his stomach, wincing at the foolish move as his broken rib stabbed into his tender abdomen. Feeling much refreshed, even with his unhealed injuries, he looked around the cavernous workshop Cookie had brought him to. It was far larger than he’d expected, likely the chef's personal testing grounds, going by the sheer opulence of the surroundings. The stone walls were smooth and curved, no straight lines visible in the stone itself.

Conversely, there were thin grooves across the entirety of the walls, floor, and ceiling; geometric patterns with segments every few inches, which would aid in careful measurement, even without tools on hand.

“If I leave even for a moment, I'll need to pay Cookie again to let me back in.” Joe got to his feet, stretching from side to side as far as his injuries would allow. “That's fine by me; I just *won't* leave ‘til I'm done.”

He was already beginning to feel cooped up, the need for exploration and growth nagging at the edges of his mind. Still, there was no chance of him leaving a fairly safe area without a real arsenal in hand. Not after getting ambushed. Reaching into the crate of treated papers, parchment, and vellum, Joe prepared to get started with writing out the first rituals... but a reflection off one of his ritual orbs reminded him of a function of theirs he'd been mostly ignoring. "Ooh, I should capture one of my rituals with my orbs. Probably the abrasive air one; that would be the best to have in a rapid-deployment-needed scenario. Put some terrain damage between myself and some speedy creature."

Lifting his hands, he felt an intense thrill race through his entire being as he easily, casually, *painlessly* called upon his magic and began drawing out diagrams on the air itself using Somatic Ritual Casting. A laugh burst from his chest as the filaments of mana braided from his fingertips, wrapping around aspects as they poured through his inscription tool, each gesture creating a formula, a sigil, or syntax which would match up with a paired circle. Minutes flew by, then hours as he settled into the motions, the ritual circle taking shape in perfect layers.

The Novice ring spiraled into the Beginner, forming nested lattices as he moved to more difficult, higher-tier sections. His Lore skills whispered at him to adjust for various directional flow indicators, his Mana Dominion allowing him to control the thickness of his inscriptions to such a fine degree that he knew that, if he could touch the burning energy hovering in the air, it would be *unutterably* smooth. He pushed himself to work faster, checking the ritual he was working on for any similarities to others he had created, forming them in a blaze of light and energy while working only moderately slower on unfamiliar patterns.

By the time he was inscribing the Journeyman-rank circle, he was breathing heavily, his eyes burning with fervor as he allowed aspects to flow and casually regenerated every last drop of mana he was using, even as it drained out of him. Only his impeccable Characteristics allowed him to keep his hands from shaking as he worked through the Expert circle, nearly a third of the day having passed in the blink of an eye. "Magical Syntax Lore thinks I should tighten that clause into a bound form. Does this need a rotational anchor? Let's adjust and see if it likes it..."

The *instant* the final section of the circle connected into a unified whole, he yanked his inscription tool away and stood in place, heaving for breath as a brilliant smile remained on his face. The myriad colors of the aspects slowly faded away as the ritual recognized itself as a completed craft, muting to the shimmering blue of a ritual ready to be activated. "Haah... that was *awesome*. I've missed this so much. Why'd it take me so long to get back to doing this after healing up? Oh, right, being able to move my body. That feels good, too."

Skill offered: Inscription Momentum (Expert 0). Each completed rune fuels the next sigil, forming sympathetic links, building a cascade of efficient motion which cuts inscription time drastically. This is a passive skill, which uses both mana and stamina to remain in effect.

Effects:

1. *When writing out magical diagrams, including but not limited to sigils, geometric written incantations, formulae, and the like, your inscription speed will increase, up to a maximum of n%. (Current 50%)*
2. *Once you have achieved at least a 25% in your speed, you will form an extremely limited bubble of hastened time around yourself and your current project, allowing you to work at full speed without fear of impacting your surroundings.*

Cost: 10 stamina and 25 mana per second.

Accept? Yes / No.

Joe almost dismissed the offered skill out of sheer force of habit, catching himself at the last second while choking on air with bulging eyes as he fully recognized the content of the skill itself. "Feces, a starting value of fifty percent increased speed to creating rituals up to the Expert rank? Are you kidding me? This was just... out here, being an option, and I didn't know about it until now?"

After a few moments of agonizing over how much time he'd spent on creating his rituals to this point, he realized that was probably the exact reason why he had never been offered this skill before. Every other Ritualist he'd encountered had the same mentality of slow and steady to create the best, safest, most stable ritual. Frankly, if he hadn't been running on adrenaline and pure enjoyment, it was unlikely that he'd have earned this skill in the first place.

That thought made Joe's eyes narrow, and he rubbed his chin in realization. "Or... I wonder... if I have a ninety-nine percent reduced requirement to earn skills, and I *still* only got this after completing an Expert-rank ritual as quickly as I possibly could using my peak Master-rank Mana Dominion to supplement my skills... what are the actual requirements for earning this naturally? Is it even manageable for someone under the Grandmaster rank who's pumping out... I don't know, Journeyman-rank rituals? Whatever, it's a passive speed enhancer for drawing out rituals. Sign me up *twice*."

The sheer helpfulness of the skill, alongside the understanding that it would be almost impossible for him to meet the requirements under normal circumstances, caused Joe to finally accept the skill. As the knowledge of how to use it flooded his mind, and the system grafted it onto his soul, the Ritualist for the first time could *feel* the process happening. He gasped in pain as his artificial mana channels were tied into the sequencing, the entire foundation of his being shaking unsteadily for a few long moments until the enchantment accepted the change.

"Celestials..." Joe groaned in a woozy voice as his eyelids fluttered. "That was... not fun."

Still, he pushed past the pain quickly, thanks in no small part to having the added incentive of wanting to test out his shiny new toy. Before doing so, he still had a ritual hovering ominously in the air to capture. With a flicker of intent, six ritual orbs popped up and into the air, and with a slight frown, he pulled his Ritual Orb of Constitution away, then his Ritual Orb of Strength. "Going to have to use a couple of my spares for this one..."

For the central orb, he selected a blank orb, writing a reminder to himself to use this one to bind to his Dialectic Dexterity. "I need to make sure I can get this between myself and an enemy sprinting at me; that'll *probably* be the best one for making that happen. I should really get around to that now that all of my Characteristics have shifted over. Well, no one can ever say I have nothing to do!"

The six ritual orbs snapped open with the sound of wires unspooling, slight **thwipps** that made him shiver as the tightly wound internals of the orbs sprang to their maximum width in an instant. "Yeesh, I bet that's the last sound a wheel of cheese hears before it's cut into sandwich-sized pieces."

With a mental shove, the expanded orbs moved forward, the chaotic lines blending seamlessly around the individual rings of the ritual. They traced each line, loop, sigil, matching the floating diagram with perfect precision. In a flash, a wire-based imprint of the ritual had replaced the glowing energy. Seeing that the job was done, Joe directed the orbs once more, and they collapsed in on themselves, leaving a half-dozen orbs in a perfect line.

"Awesome... now I just need to test out my new skill and create... let's say three copies of each cluster? That shouldn't take me more than seventy-two hours to finish–wait, no!" He clapped excitedly a single time. "Maybe just a little more than thirty-six hours for the Expert-rank rituals! Less than two full days of work for the main functionality of clusters I can use to fight Artifact-threat monsters on even footing!"

Pulling out a single sheet of beast vellum, Joe spread it across the table, slightly surprised at how much area it took up. At its full size, it resembled a very thin doormat, a foot or so wider than it was tall. "Now, why should I use this instead of chunks of rock, I wonder? Especially when I can make them so cheaply and easily? Then again... this only cost me a block of cheese. Am I *stingy*? I don't think I am, but wouldn't that be what a stingy person says?"

Deciding to simply test the material for himself, Joe dipped his inscription tool onto the surface of the vellum, and the Novice-rank circle instantly appeared, fully formed. "Now, see, that's just not a good benchmark. I guess I'll have to keep going until it takes me a while to see results."

The Beginner-rank circles were nearly as quick, and only when he got to the Apprentice version did he start to understand the benefits of using a properly prepared material for drawing out his diagrams. Mana threaded into the vellum as though it were being *sucked* in, versus the usual intense pressure he had to keep up to carve his mana and aspects into stone. As he moved to the next circle, which had a depth requirement, he found that his inscription tool actually pushed into the surface, sinking deeper than the thickness of the vellum should've possibly allowed.

By the time he got to the Journeyman portion, he was tattooing the vellum more than an inch deep, when the physical material itself couldn't have been more than an eighth of an inch in total thickness. Every part of his creation seemed to be placed in high resolution, bright and clear against the background, seeming more real than the rest of reality around it. He could pick out micro damage, correcting the faintest of errors even as they were formed.

All the while, his hands and mind moved ever so slightly faster, picking up speed as he went from circle to circle. Halfway through the Journeyman section, he suddenly let out a deep *wheeze* as every last drop of energy seemed to vanish all at once. He felt one, no... *two* of his passives turn off at the same time–his incredible sensitivity to his internal mana allowing him to pick out the sensations he'd never before been able to discern. He kept drawing through force of will alone, intentionally holding the skills back as they tried to reactivate while his stamina regeneration allowed a slow trickle back into his spent resource pool.

After about ten minutes, his stamina topped off, and he allowed his new skill to reactivate. In no time flat, at least compared to his normal speed, the section was finished. As the ring stabilized, Joe took a breather, not quite ready to dive into the Expert-rank portion. "What in the abyss was *that*?"

Glancing at his character sheet revealed the issue of his severely lacking stamina regeneration, and he quickly picked out the two skills that had conspired to fully drain his physical energy.

Name: Joe 'Emperor of Mana' Class: Reductionist

Hit Points: 598/7,966 (Seek medical attention or visit your local unbroken *Cleric)*
Mana: 29,540/29,540
Mana regen: 261.92/sec
Stamina: 245/5,429
Stamina regen: 8.59/sec

Artisan Body (Expert 0). You are able to passively train a physical Characteristic at the cost of a portion of your stamina regeneration. Currently selected: Stoic Constitution.
Inscription Momentum (Expert 0). Cost: 10 stamina and 25 mana per second.

"First off, cancel the attempt to increase my Stoic Constitution; I'm capped right now, anyway." Joe did some quick math, pulling a face as he realized that he'd effectively been working with only half of his usual stamina regeneration since Artisan Body had been silently reserving half of it. "I really need to figure out a way to increase my stamina regen. Right now, I'm effectively using only one and a half stamina per second, but that still gives me barely more than nine minutes of using

Inscription Momentum. Maybe I should find a skill that... hmm."

He quickly shifted his mindset, deciding to use his Tribulation to benefit himself as much as possible. "No, I should go out there and hunt a Legendary version of a stamina regeneration method using my tribulation as bait. No need to just get whatever's available from the nearest trainer. If I have to do it, I might as well get a *crazy* good variant while the requirement is low."

Checking the time, the Ritualist realized he had cut off only about two and a half hours instead of the expected four, but he couldn't find it in himself to feel more than a *hint* of disappointment. "Let's finish the Ritual of Abrasive Momentum then do the next one and see if I can cut off more than three hours!"

A week after deciding to go as hard as he could on making his newly designed clusters, an innocuous pantry door slowly creaked open. Joe poked his head out of the room he'd refused to leave for any reason, swaying on his feet, eyes darting back and forth as he kept a nervous eye out for any medics who might be searching for someone to forcibly hydrate or trembling from extreme hunger.

"At least now I know why I almost never feel the need to eat." Joe spoke in barely more than a whisper as he dragged himself down the corridor toward the bustling mess hall. "It's only with emptying out my stamina pool that my physical resource pools get used up. Otherwise, I just always feel great... sheesh, why's the food so far away?"

He reached the swinging doors, having to lean against them to push them open, as his arms didn't seem to be working correctly at the moment. The people seated closest to the door suddenly went quiet, their eyes on the swaying, zombie-like features of the Decury Duelist, his hollow stare pinning them in place. "*Hungry...*"

"I've been looking everywhere for you!" Jenny suddenly appeared in front of Joe like a whirlwind of energy, her smile so bright that Joe was forced to slowly blink in order to recover from the glare coming off her shiny teeth. She leaned close, the angry hiss of her words not matching her countenance one little bit. "Are you infected or cursed right now? You look as bad as you did when you got out of that lotus pod thing!"

"Hhh...ungrrty."

"You're going to make people think that there's an undead plague coming at us. Come on, sit down, I'll get you a plate and a cup of, no, a *jug* of water. See this? How your skin has no elasticity at all?" She pinched his wrists, and the fold of skin only ever-so-slowly receded to its normal placement. "Not only that, but you also smell like month-old coffee and dry rot."

Joe glared sullenly at the person who was supposed to be his assistant, but only ever seemed to appear when it was convenient for her. His swirling, angry thoughts blew away in the next moment as she returned with a full-on platter of food and nearly a gallon of water in a pitcher.

His first fork full of rice lost nearly half its payload on its way to his mouth, his body was shaking so badly. Then, once he managed to chew it, the food stuck in his throat and he was forced to grab the jug and drink directly from it to force it down.

Debuff: Starved (Major → Moderate+). Stamina Regen: -75% → -68%.

"Who knew using up my stamina would mess with me like this?" the Ritualist rasped out as he set the carafe down, more than half of the liquid gone after the long pull. "I don't think I've been this hungry in literal *years*."

"You've just been using no stamina for years?" Jenny shook her head in amazement. "How do you even manage that?"

"I mean, I walk and jump places, but then I'll just have a normal meal that day. Or, it's been a big battle, and we have a celebratory feast, so it feels natural to eat a bunch." Joe half-shrugged, already hunched over the platter of food and doing his utmost not to tear into it like a wild animal. It was a near thing, but he managed at the last moment to remember that dozens of eyes were trained on him at that very moment. He didn't want to get a reputation for being *that* slovenly, not so soon after becoming a minor celebrity in the tower. "This was... different. Got a new skill that passively uses my stamina in a serious way."

Between bites, he explained the details of the skill and watched in faint amusement as she went from shocked to incredibly envious to incredibly hopeful in the span of only a few seconds.

"Is that something you can *teach* other people?" Her words were breathless, her eyes absolutely *burning* with interest. "Almost no one comes to the Tower of Ritualists with any skill in Ritual Circles, so it lags behind our usual focuses by a huge margin. But with something like that...? We could start making serious progress on catching up."

"I'll add it to the list," Joe half-joked, only for Jenny to yank out the massive leather-bound book she used to keep track of the next people he'd be training, turn to a blank page, and write *Inscription Momentum* across the top in bold letters. Directly underneath that, she wrote her name as the first student in line to sign up for it. "Right. Yeah. That actually makes good sense to meter it out. Fair warning, it's gonna be a while."

"As an added incentive to hang around and start teaching me, uh, *us* right away, I can build you a schedule with lots of time to go through *this* when you aren't instructing. It's a *book bag*... think of it as a spatial device used only for storing books, papers, and stuff like that. No weapons or active-effect things, such as talismans. Sage Pete sent this along, saying no one would be too worried about you getting access to these." Jenny handed the standard backpack-looking item over, a wistful look in her eyes as she forced herself to let go of it. "Since he's basically declared that you're going to be the first Class Sage of our tower, it just makes sense."

Grabbing the zipper, Joe started to pull the pack open, only to yank his hand back as a shock ran through his fingers. "Ahh! What was that?"

"Pretty sure it was testing your mana signature to make sure this got to you, and no one else was trying to get into the bag." Blushing slightly, Jenny showed him her hands, which had angry red welts on them. "Anyway, about that-"

"Uh-*huh*." His face carefully blank, Joe pulled open the bag to reveal manuals from Ritualistic Alchemy, Forging, Enchanting, Ritual Circles, and Magical Matrices. Each of the five Core Class skills were represented, and it was at that moment the Ritualist realized the Sage *was* still doing what he could to support him, bound by a quest or not.

"I didn't get to look at them, but the Sage let me know that these are usually restricted only to those who spend time at the tower teaching the next generation of Ritualists." Jenny spoke lightly, but her words didn't hold a hint of mirth. "You shouldn't go anywhere before you read through all those and teach all of us your speedy ritual circle making skill. Not even kidding... if it were up to me, I'd chain you to a podium until you taught everyone in the tower."

Joe nodded along, quietly beginning to channel Beam to Bifrost after closing up his bag and reaching for a fried chicken drumstick. "I'll definitely get right on that when I get back. But for now, I'm low on resources, almost out of crafting materials, and I'm itching to put some of my skills to the test. Tell you what, I'll pop down to Midgard, beat up a few Artifact-rank monsters, and be back before you know it."

"It's a non-standard skill! You could name your price! Cheese, Honor-"

Before she could work herself up into full-blown lecture-slash-begging session, Joe was fully enveloped in a coat of scintillating energy, and vanished...

...along with his platter of food and the jug of water.

CHAPTER TWELVE

Joe blinked and missed traveling across the entirety of Vanaheim, opening his eyes to the column of light extending into the starry night sky as he blasted up and along it. His speed ramped up, and the tiny planet faded into the darkness behind him, only able to be found thanks to the massive streamer of light pointing it out among the rest of the dark backdrop. Taking another chomp out of his chicken, the Ritualist settled into the comfortable emptiness and started to organize his thoughts while he ate.

"*Nomph.*" Ripping off an especially large chunk, he glanced at the changes his skills had undergone during his week of isolated ritual crafting.

Skill increase:

Ritual Lore (Master 0 → Master IV). Congratulations, you have gained 20 Characteristic points in each Characteristic other than Karmic Luck for increasing a Master-rank skill four times!

Inscription Momentum (Expert 0 → Expert I).

Only having two of his skills change in such a long time devoted to crafting felt strange, but the reality was that he was working far below his maximum capacity. "Expert-rank rituals really don't do much for my skill levels anymore. Thank goodness Loremaster was working on my behalf in the background. A few more weeks, and I'll be able to have each of my Characteristics pushing against the edge of the threshold."

Skill offered: Lazy Leveling (Master IX). Want to become really high level without having to put in the effort? With Lazy Leveling, all requirements for character, class, profession, and skill experience are reduced by 75%! All for the low cost of having your Characteristics working at only 25% efficiency. Will you have a smaller pool of health, mana, and stamina? Yes, but on paper you will look extremely dangerous!

Accept? Yes / No.

"Ignore and refuse," Joe grumbled at the system, his heart aching as his eyes lingered on the fading message, specifically where it showed that the skill was going to start at peak Mastery just by picking it up. "I'm on my way to use my crafts in combat with my own hands! Just because I'm gaining a few skill levels in the background doesn't mean I'm not working for the rest of 'em."

Finishing off the rest of his food and downing the remainder of the water left Joe feeling satiated, if a bit stuffed. The slurry in his gut wasn't appreciating the rapid movement through the universe, especially as they hit a bend, and the g-forces on his body increased significantly for a short period of time. Trying to take his mind off how he was feeling simultaneously better and sicker at the same time, he turned his attention to his spatial codpiece, specifically how it was almost entirely empty at the moment.

"Let's see, I've got two Common-rank Natural Aspect Jars, one Uncommon, buncha' random Special aspect ones, and a... Legendary. That's quite the disparity." With his Natural Magical Material Creation skill locked and under review, he was *greatly* annoyed that he hadn't taken the time to make dozens of aspect jars to keep on hand. "There's the *real* reason we had to leave that work room. Starvation can be ignored for a while, but I'm out of all of my mid-range aspects. Made a few clusters, a couple one-off rituals, and somehow that was enough to beggar me, since I left all of my aspect jars on Jotunheim to keep the teleportation network expanding."

It was almost *nostalgic* to be on the hunt for crafting material again, while also aggravating him to no end. Though he knew it would be a simple matter to gather what he needed, Joe was used to having large amounts of resources on hand and being able to whip up whatever he needed, wherever he was. "Where can I go to get some good crafting material on the least mana dense of the planets?"

He pulled his quest logs open, brow furrowing when he didn't see the quest he'd been looking for. "What's going on here? Mastering Ritual Combat, done. Somehow still haven't figured out my *Student* Rituarchitect quest... hey, how long has this one been sitting there waiting for me to notice it?"

Quest complete: Expert Ritualist II. You have created a successful coven that has raised a Journeyman student Ritualist. As you have embarked on the path of a Class Sage by raising all your personal Core Class skills to Expert with no sign of slowing down, prove you are worthy of being called a Master by raising five distinct Experts, each with at least one distinct Core Class skill achieving the Expert rank.

Expert Ritualist promoted: 5/5. Reward:

1) +1 to all Ritualist Core Skills.

2) Access to Master Ritualist class quest.

"Oh, *abyss*, yeah! Oh no!" Joe's body went stiff as his skills increased, his Characteristics increased by an additional fifteen points simultaneously, and he used up another of his seven possible maximum skill changes.

Alchemical Rituals (Expert IX → Master 0). You have gained incredible personal Inspiration by imbuing every part of yourself with Ichor. Having experienced the feel of an alchemical ritual-based tattoo binding your body, mana, and Akashic Record together, you've realized that you can convert rituals into tattoos to be placed on others, allowing you to choose one of three evolutions.

1. *Direct upgrade: Keep the skill mostly as is with better percentage-based benefits and a moderate additional effect.*

2. *Surface-level Tattoo Alteration: Keep the skill as is with a drastic additional effect. Ever wanted to train a guinea pig to charge at an enemy and unleash a ritual when they get close enough? Here's your chance. (Requires high-level tools from Ritualistic Forging.)*
3. *Deep-tissue Tattoo Alteration: Keep the skill as is with a drastic additional effect. Want to place a ritual on someone that they can use to enhance themself to an extreme degree? Want to create a ritual on an enemy that uses their resource pool to fuel and extend itself? (Requires high-level Enchanted tokens from the Enchanted Ritual Circle class skill.)*

Enchanted Ritual Circles (Expert VII → Expert VIII).
Magical Matrices (Master 0 → Master I).
Ritual Circles (Master VI → Master VII).
Ritualistic Forging (Master 0 → Master I).

Congratulations, you have gained 15 Characteristic points in each Characteristic other than Karmic Luck for increasing three Master-rank skills!

"Yet another reason fixing my mana channels like this turned out to be awesome." Joe shook out his limbs, the sudden influx of power having brought him right to the edge of the threshold for most of his Characteristics across the board. "Whoo, that tingles right in the enchantment on my bones. Ow... that's more than a tingle. *Ahh*! Celestial feces, that hurts? Okay... okay, it's fading. Almost there. System, any way to clarify about those tattoos? Can't I do that with the direct upgrade, anyway?"

Response granted. You can achieve the same effect by manually applying the tattoos. Alternatively, the alterations will allow you to use the skill in an active manner, only needing to possess the necessary resources and directing the final effect via manipulation of mana to cause the ritual to sink into flesh. Applying the ink-like tattoos to willing subjects is merely a matter of time and effort. Imbuing enemies with the ritual requires time and actively working against their resistances and willpower as you bind the ritual to their resource pools.

"Got it. Interesting." Joe thought back to several other instances where he had bound rituals to his enemies, such as the first time he encountered Gameover or used the Shade in the dungeons below Ardania to contain the Well of Shadows. "So, basically, it would be me using someone else to deploy a ritual somewhere, or making a powerful buffing or debuffing ritual fueled by the person I put it on."

It didn't even cross his mind to do a direct upgrade, as Ritualistic Alchemy was simply his least-intensely studied class skill. Joe had always felt that alchemy was mainly for creating consumables, which simply didn't mesh with his worldview of rituals as creating semi-permanent magical effects. Of all of his Core Class skills, this had been the one he'd been the most worried about gaining Inspiration for–making this sudden improvement a massive relief. "I think I've decided. I'm never going to be the best at using this skill in the standard way, so I should definitely go all-in on a non-standard version."

Please note, any additional tattoos applied to your person may disrupt the carefully constructed design you currently have.

"I don't *think* that changes anything for me?" Joe considered the two options carefully once more. "If I were a Beast Tamer or had a reliable group around me all the time, I'd definitely go with the surface-level variant. Send a bird or something to swoop down on a group and activate a mile or two away from me? For the low cost of one trained pigeon, there's a sudden gigantic **boom** on the horizon? I'd like that *way* too much, which, admittedly, is probably why I haven't ever been offered any beast-taming skills."

Without delaying any more, he selected the 'Deep-tissue Tattoo Alteration' and read over the evolved skill.

Alchemical Rituals (Master 0). While the skill name has remained the same, you have begun walking down a path that may greatly alter its final form. Instead of the purest intention of creating components to be used, you have learned how to directly apply this skill as a deep-tissue parasitic ritual, drawing stability from the biological anchoring and the target's circulation.

New Effect:

Parasitic Ritual Imprint: This skill has gained an active effect, allowing you to inscribe a ritual, hostile or otherwise, which uses the target's own health, mana, and/or stamina to maintain or escalate its effects.

Requirements: At least one Enchanted token embedded into the target for ritual aiming purposes (hostile) or applied to the target (non-hostile). Sufficient alchemical integrity to withstand feedback and rejection. (I.E. make sure the ritual is at or <u>above</u> the target's rank, if hostile. At or <u>below</u> the target's rank for friendly placement.) To apply the ritual, suffuse a ready-to-be-used ritual with mana and an appropriately ranked substrate, then push the imprinted ritual through the surface/skin of the target. Time to success depends on rank of target, ritual, and user.

Once the parasitic tattoo has been applied and activated, it will gain strength or duration based on the target's resource flow. Removing the embedded ritual requires a combination of an Enchanted counter ritual, alongside specialized solvents. Attempting to directly destroy it will unleash all of its in-use resources as a backlash against the target.

Use of the Parasitic Ritual Imprint will count toward skill growth through the Master ranks, with overreliance ultimately likely changing the skill if it enters the Grandmaster rank.

"I love new toys," the Ritualist murmured as he read over the skill once more, making sure he had a good understanding of it. "Gonna have to get my Enchanted Ritual Circles up to snuff if I'm going to use this to its best effect. Right now, even if I *can* make a Master-rank tattoo, I don't have the ability to make a proper token for it. Now... what was I doing? Right! Looking at my quests."

New Quest gained: Master Ritualist. You have created a successful coven that has raised Expert Ritualists. As you have embarked on the path of a Class Sage by raising all your personal Core Class skills to Expert with no sign of slowing down, prove you are worthy of being called a True Master Ritualist by raising all five distinct core skills to the Master rank. Core Class skills at the Master rank: 4/5.

Reward: Access to Master Ritualist II class quest.

"I wonder how many people in the tower have access to this quest and have been stuck there forever," Joe murmured softly, while simultaneously wondering if the next part of the chain quest was going to be bringing other people in his coven up to the Master rank. "If this keeps going, will I ever get to a point where I'm a Class Sage and need to raise Skill Sages? What would the *rewards* be like for a quest like that, I wonder?"

Turning back to his quests, the Ritualist pursed his lips in confusion, as he didn't find the one he was looking for, which would direct him straight toward what would likely be one of the most powerful monsters on the world when he got there. "Where's 'The Other Three'? Don't tell me someone else went and completed this while I was distracted–oh, right, the quest name changed."

Germinate the Cutting (Difficulty: Raid). You have captured two Places of Power in the Forest of Chlorophyll Chaos. Only two remain. Capturing any of them can give interesting benefits, and binding all four will germinate a force which has slumbered for centuries, one that may have been lost to time for a reason. Places of power captured: 2/4.

Reward: 1) Variable, depending on location. 2) Immediate access to The Cutting. (Major Raid). Recommended group level: 30+.

"Capturing just one more shouldn't be enough to set this off, right? What if I just just fight whatever the guardian is and convert it into a new aspect jar and crafting materials? Natural Aspect Jars are out for now, but regular ones are a class-based thing ever since I got access to Reductionist, so I shouldn't lose *that* for any reason."

There was a slight change in his directionality, so he flicked his eyes away from his status screens and murmured in appreciation as he saw Midgard looming large in the distance. "Already here? Perfect, I can use the time walking to the Forest of Chlorophyll Chaos to read while I–*abyss*! My inhibitor gear!"

As he struck the enormous spell circle hanging in the air around the bifrost and had his momentum drastically cut, Joe was struggling to pull his robes back with one hand while shifting the accessory into position over his sternum. The second ring went past, yet his double speed on the bifrost meant he was still cruising toward the ground at easily five times terminal velocity. Just as he passed through the third and final inertial dampening spell circle, the gear **clicked** into place.

Metal strands began extending out and wrapping around his limbs, the familiar prickle of the needles poking through his skin causing him to wince. Then he hit the ground hard enough to create a shallow crater and send a plume of dust and rubble into the air around him. Pulling a face, he slowly stood upright, his inhibitor gear creaking and groaning worryingly. "Ugh, the ground here is so weak... it's like walking on a giant snowdrift that's just a *little* more frozen at the top. Push too hard, and your foot goes right through it. It's fine, let's get to–what's wrong with *you*?"

As Joe shifted to look down at the accessory, he noticed it struggling to keep up with his motions. A stiff breeze rolled off him, clearing the dust from the air in his immediate vicinity. "*Ooooh.* Looks like I'm outgrowing you, huh? That's a good problem to have, but down here, it's definitely still a problem."

Name: Joe 'Emperor of Mana' Class: Reductionist

Characteristic: Score
Quad Strength: 155 (499)
Dialectic Dexterity: 153 (499)
Stoic Constitution: 152 (499)
Light Intelligence: 159 (494)
Ritualistic Wisdom: 158 (494)
Dark Charisma: 150 (494)
Karmic Perception: 154 (499)
Red Luck: 150 (497)
Karmic Luck: 410

"Oh, *feces*, it's not forcibly capping everything the way it should. Hopefully, that won't cause too many issues, if I'm being careful. People are allowed to have up to two hundred points in a Characteristic if they never leave the planet, right? Hopefully these will just be... let's just call it rounding errors?"

He took a few cautious steps, and to his great relief, the ground started feeling solid once more. Taking a few steps toward Ardania, Joe paused as his eyes lit up, remembering that he'd set up a shrine nearby.

"Let's go see Mom and give her back the merchant sack, and... you know what? I'll take her out to lunch. She deserves more than that, but I'm not the only one in my family who was trained in the 'ABB' method. 'Always be busy' is practically our family motto."

Tapping his shrine, Joe selected to teleport to the capital city, arriving the next moment in the central temple area. As he stalked off to find his mother at Minya's shop, he realized he was leaving slight indentations in the street as he jogged along. Gritting his teeth, the Ritualist walked along more carefully. His Quad Strength practically begged to turn every step into a huge stride, and it needed constant attention to be denied.

After the extended exercise in patience, he arrived at the Odds and Ends shop, only to be hit with a mixture of disappointment and relief when he found that his mother was out on a trade negotiation mission. The extremely elderly version of Minya on this world didn't let him leave right away, inspecting his pristine robes, boots, and fingerless gloves before eventually accepting the expanded spatial item on Brenda's behalf.

Then he retraced his steps—literally, in a few cases, as his footprints were clearly visible in the scores of new potholes that had been formed—and fast traveled from the temple to the edge of the frontier bordering the Forest of Chlorophyll Chaos. To his great surprise, the edge of the forest had *receded* greatly; it was now more than a dozen miles away from the shrine he'd once placed practically adjacent to the trees.

"Huh. Wonder what happened here." He started marching along at an easy pace, not at all concerned about the minor trail he was forming, with every footfall creating a packed dirt road and splattering any vegetation into goo.

Skill offered: Trailblazing (Journeyman IX). You don't walk so much as flatten the terrain you traverse.

Effect:

1. *Each step compresses the soft ground into a persistent trail in a radius of 1.5+n inches in a circle centered on your feet, reducing the labor and materials needed to convert that path into a finished road by n%.*

Accept? Yes / No.

"You know... that would actually be really great for Jotunheim. We've got the teleportation system, but some people are going to prefer walking around. Oh, uh, no. Not for *me* though. Reject skill. I'll just let someone know it's possible." As the notification faded away, he pulled open his newly acquired backpack full of restricted manuals and rustled around until he found one on Ritualistic Forging. Joe didn't bother setting up any defenses, knowing he had nothing to worry about from the local monsters–a simple barehanded slap would cut all but the strongest of them in half.

"You know what? It's been bothering me to no end that I've no idea what Master-rank stabilizers are supposed to look like. Let's see... chapter twelve..." the Ritualist walked along with his nose buried in the book, simply enjoying the sunshine.

The glorious day was *doubly* enhanced, thanks to finally finding answers to the questions that had plagued him through the Expert ranks. Before he knew it, Joe was standing at the edge of the forest, slowly closing his book and letting out a *huge* sigh of satisfaction.

"That wasn't at *all* what I was expecting. Thank goodness I didn't just try to figure it out on my own."

CHAPTER THIRTEEN

Storing the backpack away, Joe stepped into the woods, expanding his Mana Dominion to push back as the magical forest attempted to warp him to a random location in its depths. Reality seemed to stabilize in a bubble around him, though there was a slight wobble at the edges of his vision. The incongruity sent a pulse of nausea through him, forcing the Ritualist to hold still for a few moments as he got used to the sensation.

"Last time I was here, I managed to get where I needed to go even without all of the advantages I have now. I can *do* this." Glancing backward, he was beyond pleased to see the same view as when he'd started. With that reassurance, Joe realized he could do something unheard of in this zone—exit exactly where he had entered.

Instead, he focused on his quest, forming a clear image in his mind of the other two places of power he'd already captured, then trying to simulate his experience and project it to an unknown location. His eyes suddenly felt incredibly dry, causing him to blink furiously. When he refocused on his surroundings, there was a faint red flicker extending in two directions. Both were glowing, though one was a deeper crimson than the other.

"Red Luck doing Red Luck things. Thanks, Characteristic shifts!" Joe let out a pleased chuff through his nose, striding forward through an unchanging forest.

Skill offered: Teleportation Resistance (Apprentice V). Space no longer makes unilateral decisions on your behalf. The world tugs, and your coordinates lock, adding increasing friction as you attempt to remain in place. Sometimes this means you don't get abducted. Other times, it means you don't get to your scheduled meetings.

Effect:

Every attempt to relocate your physical body is treated as an attack, whether it comes from an enemy's spell, trap, rescue attempts, or your own carefully planned escape route. You gain a passive (n+Mana Dominion/100+(Wisdom+Perception)/100)% chance to cause teleportation attempts to fail.

Accept? Yes / No.

"Wonder if I could evolve that to become toggleable?" The Ritualist murmured, but had to let out a sigh and refuse it. Even with as powerful of a skill that was, between his Beam to Bifrost spell and his eventually world-spanning teleportation network on Jotunheim, this particular resistance would be *terribly* inconvenient. Still, it brought his attention to the fact that his rebuffing of the magics in the depths of the Forest of Chlorophyll Chaos meant he was stuck walking along at a normal pace, instead of being transported *anywhere* else.

"How does someone bend the effect so they can use it to their advantage, I wonder?" The incredibly fine threads of his mana wrapped around him pushed out slightly, leaving gaps for other phenomena to begin interacting with him. The world shifted around, and immediately he found himself in a new, *useless* area. "Good start, but not where I want to go. What if I only open the space only around the red thread?"

After a few missteps, he latched on to *something* and found himself sidestepping forward as though he'd slipped into a long, curved hallway *next* to the forest. His forward momentum still caused the landscape around him to ripple as though it were merely a mirage, but the red thread he was following began to brighten and thicken dramatically. "Looks like I'm on the right track; let's see where this takes me."

Now that he had figured out the trick, Joe could spend some of his attention on other things.

"Seriously, I don't know why they hide the next steps from people, but I suppose any large organization needs to have something to entice members with. Exclusivity *is* a powerful draw." He thought back to what he'd learned from the Ritualistic Forging manual, his eyes darkening with interest and introspection.

The previous versions of the stabilizers had started as simple shapes, moving up into three-dimensional blocks and pyramids, then taking an abrupt shift into star-like gears and massive rods. Joe had *assumed* they were building towards something, likely a machine of sorts, but instead the next piece had returned to the roots of what he would think of when 'ritual magic' came up, were he an outside observer. He pictured the template clearly, his mind long since sharpened to the point that three-dimensional modeling in his head was as easy as flipping his hand.

There were similarities to the Expert version, in that the Master-rank stabilizer started with a large metal rectangle. It appeared as a pedestal, altar, or low table covered in all manner of grooves and channels. From the Master-ranked pedestal, the previous-rank's rods would be slotted in at intersecting angles, the star-shaped stabilizers fitted on to them allowing the rods to shift and move around like robotic arms. As for all of the channels and embellishments, they weren't merely for show. No, those were created to allow the lower-rank stabilizers to stack together, acting partially as ornamentation after being placed to overlap like the scales of a dragon.

All of the stabilizers were meant to work together as a single unit, from the Novice rank to the Master rank. As it turned out, he'd been using stabilizers entirely inefficiently up to this point. Though they *worked*, he couldn't wait to see how much more potent they'd be when fit together correctly. "The manual called a fully outfitted version a 'coruscating mana conduit' but didn't get into the reason why. Hmm."

The final piece, what tied it all together, was a separate, apparently *incredibly* delicate chalice that slotted into the exact center of the item, lending credence to Joe's original inkling that this was more like a table than anything else. The Ritualist shook his head at the final words the manual had in them, confusion-tinged annoyance filling him.

"This whole thing is designed to absorb and stabilize ambient mana, as well as the ritual it's placed under. Yet they *flippantly* write in that 'without the proper alchemical additive, it's less than half as effective as it's supposed to be'. If that's the case, why isn't taking up and pursuing each of the other Core Class skills *far* more of a focus on Vanaheim?"

A quick search allowed him to pull out the manual the first book had referenced, and he searched through the appendix to find the product it had listed. "Ichor of Overflow. Where are... *you*. Got it. 'A substance described as mana rendered impatient, perpetually on the edge of phase shift'. Page three eighty-seven..."

Turning to the recipe for the Ichor, Joe found himself wincing away, until his mind apparently realized that he *did*, in fact, have a Master rank in Alchemical Rituals. Just like that, the explanations shifted from wavy lines of *pain* to actual instructions and diagrams he could use. "Ah. That's what the chalice is for. Without this, the stabilizer just sits there, looking important but not doing nearly as much."

The Ritualist understood the... *vast* majority of what the recipe seemed to do, though he was sure he'd have to actually make it and use it before he got a full grasp of its myriad intricacies. From what he understood, adding the Ichor to the chalice would cause the flowing mana to collect and condense, transforming the dense alchemical liquid into a near-crystalline syrup. When the ambient mana or power shedding off the ritual was collected, it would be slowed down like a frog hopping through spider webs.

A portion of the Ichor would overflow from the chalice, pouring over the 'table' stabilizer and empowering the lesser variants slotted into the housing. This would make them move and flex, shifting the parts as needed, even as it worked as a coolant to keep the contraption from overheating. When working together, instead of applying a stabilization effect on the ambient mana and ritual as a whole, it would instead focus dynamically, adjusting, and smoothing micro-failures in real time before they became significant issues. The excess mana would 'drip' from the ritual placed overhead, be collected by the arms of the stabilizer, then be directed into the filled chalice.

"It's like the difference between getting a massage for a sore muscle and getting an acupuncturist to poke the spot that hurts and just *fix* the issue. Love it." Joe considered that analogy for a moment, the corner of his lips turning down slightly. "Aww. Now I miss Jaxon."

His go-to treatment for unwanted feelings, as ever, was to ignore them and turn his attention back to the project he was working on. In this case, he finished reading over the alchemical creation. "What's this? Oh, interesting. If properly used, the two items created by separate skills become a single item, the 'Eclipsing Aurora Chalice'. Wow. That's a *lot* of warnings..."

"Meh. I'll worry about that when I can actually make any of this. Too bad the Grand Ritual hall doesn't have other workshops built into it. Pretty sure there's nothing on this world that can contain the energy I'd need to invest into *either* part of this project. I'd blow up any alchemy hall or blacksmith forge I tried to make these in. That means Jotunheim at the minimum, but more likely than not, I'll need to go back to Vanaheim to make 'em."

His ears perked up as he became aware of a low rumble in the air. Not a growl, but a constant thunder. With each step, the sound grew louder, but seeing as he hadn't yet arrived, Joe allowed his train of thought to reach a natural conclusion. "If *I* were going to hide this information, why would I put it behind the Master-rank barrier like this? It's way easier to train the Core Class skills in conjunction with each other, or at least *I* think so. Maybe it's to make people at the Master rank humble themselves and realize they need to work with their peers?"

Clicking his tongue, he shook his head, "Or, no, that's probably too charitable of me. I bet it's like this because it makes people stick around longer."

That sounded correct, and the Ritualist slowly bobbed in agreement with his own words. "Yeah... if I could make the stabilizer, but not the Ichor, I'd be forced to hang out with someone who *could* make it. Trade favors and such. Otherwise, I'd need to start learning again, going to classes and such. Even if I reached Master in two of these class skills just to make this, I'd *still* need another person to make the *ritual* that needed to be stabilized in the first place!"

The more he thought about it, the more he agreed with his assumption that this was a conspiracy to keep people from being able to do everything themselves. Before he knew what was happening, his mana was whipping about, mulching leaves and grass as he steadily grew angrier. Fifteen feet of space around him was suddenly oozing sap and plant matter, which was enough to snap him out of his spiraling thoughts. "What in the *world*?"

"*Don't worry,* I'm *here for you*," a sinister voice sounded in his mind, as Mental Manipulation Resistance suddenly spun into effect. As though someone had just shattered a window, Joe realized he'd been under the effect of an externally induced rage.

Debuff removed: Raging Waters.

Realizing he was potentially in danger wasn't enough to stop Joe from a secondary realization. "Whoa, whoa... I gotta back up. Right, *most* people don't have endless resources. It's ridiculously hard for almost all of them to master even one of the skills. Why would I ever think it's such a bad thing to have to make friends among your peers? That's good. Normal even. Working together is... *supposed* to be a positive. Maybe they keep this information out of public knowledge to help foster a community of people working together for common goals?"

No matter what the reason was for someone in the far-distant past who had worked to silo off the class skills, figuring it out at this exact moment wouldn't help him with whatever he was walking into. With a sharp inhale, Joe narrowed his focus and strode forward, stepping into a huge clearing with a bizarre water feature in the center of it.

First explorer! Congratulations, you are the first traveler to stumble upon the Ambiguous Cascade*! As such, you gain insight into it no one else will have unless you share this information.*

This massive waterfall pours out of the sky itself with no clear source. The water is a perfect base for solutions, any Alchemist's dream! While being perfectly pure, it also is charged with and attuned to mana, allowing it to more easily absorb the properties of any reagents added to it… if you can separate it out from the waterfall itself!

Keep your wits about you, as natural treasures such as this are rarely unguarded…

As being the first person to find a new location is in alignment with your Sect's core mission, everyone in Sect territory gains the following effect for 7 days (168 hours): Tranquil mind: While in Sect territory, or after leaving it having been there for at least 8 consecutive hours, resist all unnatural anger, rage, berserking, control effects, or illusions impacting the senses by 20%.

Joe stared up at a waterfall that would put Niagara Falls to shame, endlessly pouring out of the sky, yet keeping its perfectly cylindrical shape as it pounded into the ground. The oceanic flood had surprisingly little spray around its base, and the light bouncing through it made strange rainbows with colors outside of the usual prism effect.

"Yeah, this is definitely a place of power." The red thread he'd been following extended into the cascade, vanishing into its shifting depths without a hint of how to get through the liquid barrage. Rubbing his side, Joe grimaced as he realized he still hadn't taken care of his heavily damaged body. "Maybe

I *should've* brought some back-up. I have a coven on this world, don't I? Every last one of them is at least a triple Expert. I bet they'd not only be extremely helpful but super enthusiastic about helping out."

Even as he had that thought, something inside him rebelled against the idea of bringing along people who couldn't keep up with him in combat. Taking a deep breath, no matter how bad it made his side ache, he grit his teeth and balled his fists. "I'm not being elitist... right? I've got new weapons to try out! I'm just feeling particularly spicy today, and I'm not going anywhere until I've seen what they can do. Something around here's in desperate need of killin', and I want to be the one making it happen. Now where's that guardian?"

Moving cautiously, he tried to circle the Ambiguous Cascade, only to realize that it was miles wide at its base. Giving up after walking perhaps a quarter of its circumference, he instead slowly approached the falling water itself. Moving carefully so as not to be dragged in, the Ritualist stuck his hand into the liquid–or, that is, he *tried*.

Clink.

His fingers bounced off as though he had tried to slide them through a metal plate, dragged down slightly as the momentum of the heavy water yanked on him. "Woah! That's crazy. No wonder the description said it'd be great *if* I could take it. Maybe if I jam a shield or something in to divert the water and collect what falls out of the falls?"

Then he remembered that *wasn't* the reason he was here, and Joe decided to try something completely different. With his Mana Dominion, creating an Ascendant Matrix was the work of a moment, and his eyes went wide as he realized he could make an absolutely massive version, now that he had the peak-Master skill boosting it. "Ah, if only I could walk through the area it would carve for me, but it shuts down and backlashes against me if I try to use it while anything living is inside... wait a second! The water is falling; I can just make this, turn it on, and treat it like an umbrella!"

Sending some power into the Ascendant Matrix he'd just created, Joe nearly dropped to a knee as mana *poured* out of him. A pathway appeared in the cascade, and a rapidly spinning number appeared in the corner of his vision, informing him that he was gaining Common-ranked aspects at an *absurd* rate. He took a shaky step forward, his jaw dropping as he realized that, even with a section opened up, he certainly wouldn't be *walking* to the place of power.

Wherever the bottom of the falls was, it was far, *far* below where he was standing. Moments later, his inhibited mana bottomed out, and the Ascendant Matrix vanished into motes of light that drifted away, vanishing as they were reabsorbed by the world.

"I'm either going to need to get to the top of this and jump in, then get pulled down to the center of the place of power—which seems kind of like a crapshoot to me—or make a ritual that does what I need." Staring up, up, to the point where his neck was craning as far back as he could go, Joe saw nothing indicating it was the origin of the immense cascade. "Ritual it is."

After giving himself a few minutes to allow his mana to recover, the Ritualist set up his Ascendant Matrix and allowed Common aspects to *cascade* into his inventory once more. Then he stepped back, pulling out some amenities to set up a small camp. "If I'm going to be here a while, might as well set up a low-grade healing ritual or three. It's going to take forever to heal me up, but by the time I figure out how to divert enough of this waterfall to get to wherever I need to go in there, I *should* be all set."

Pulling open his Standard Ritual Combat manual, Joe looked through various options, his face falling as he realized he only had enough aspects for an Apprentice-rank version, unless he wanted to break a few of his higher-rarity aspects and be fine with the massive loss he'd take by not having aspect jars to efficiently capture the sundry energies. He tried to reach for his Legendary Natural Aspect Jar, but his fingers didn't even twitch when he gave them the command. "Haa... yeah, I understand. We worked way too hard for those to waste even *one* Legendary aspect."

Then he realized busting one of those on Midgard might have other, more intense effects on the local area. Joe perked up as he realized he wasn't *just* enabling his hoarding tendencies, he was probably *also* doing the best thing for this world. Lifting his inscription tool, he wrote out an Apprentice-rank healing ritual with an area of effect, finishing it so quickly it felt almost instantaneous. Shrugging at the ease of creating them, he made three more, activating each with a tiny thread of mana.

Health: 681/1,999 (8,802)

As healing energy washed over him, working to refill his health pool and knit his damaged body back together, Joe could only watch with a slack jaw as the rituals did their work. After five seconds, the message displayed as...

Health: 684/1,999 (8,802)

"Abyss, looks like I'm just too powerful for these low-level rituals to give me much effect anymore." Pulling out his combat manual, Joe settled in and started a campfire by vibrating his mana in a small pile of tinder. "Good thing I don't have anywhere to go, or I'd be losing my mind right now. Alright, book. Show me water manipulating rituals."

Skill offered: Mana Vibration (Expert III). Want to light things on fire with pure mana manipulation? Shake the meat off the bones of your enemies-

"Nope. Skip. Don't need a skill for that." Attention narrowing to the book on his lap, Joe felt a shiver run up his spine...

...but by the time he glanced up and looked around the clearing to make sure he was alone, the enormous eye studying him from behind the falling curtain of water had already closed once more.

CHAPTER FOURTEEN

The Ritualist patiently waited through the night, sitting and calmly entering a light meditative stance as he allowed his rituals to slowly piece his broken body back together. They faltered every few hours, but it took practically no effort whatsoever to remake them. By the time dawn broke on the horizon, using the massive cascade as an oversized prism to send scintillating shades of slightly-*off* light across the forest, Joe was surrounded by a cloud of healing rituals so thick he couldn't be seen through them.

"Never had my rituals hit diminishing returns like that before." His dull tone, full of resignation and a touch of frustration, rang out the instant he dispelled them. They popped like shimmering soap bubbles, revealing him sitting on the ground for a bare moment before he hopped to his feet, dusting off his hands and reaching for the only ritual circle hanging in the air that hadn't been removed. "I wonder if that was a function of getting injured on another world, only to come down here..."

His health had reached full in only a few hours, or at least his maximum health *for Midgard* had. Yet it wasn't until he had fully regenerated his hidden health—based on his *uncapped* Characteristics—that his ribs had finally begun groaning in protest, forcing into position and rapidly knitting themselves together. The wait had been worth it, as evidenced by his easy breathing and lack of pain as he ran through a set of simple stretches. Finally, Joe flicked the Apprentice-rank ritual he'd left in the air, activating it with the briefest flash of intent.

"Ritual of the Underbridge." Why this ritual was in the combat manual had baffled him at first. The utility ritual was designed to work with water but was only intended for small creeks or streams that were ankle-deep at best. It would lift the water at a point upstream, causing it to flow through the air as though it were still on an incline and allowing perhaps four or five men walking shoulder-to-shoulder to cross below the flow over newly dried land. "Come on, work on this. I don't need a miracle, just a proof of concept that my magic will be functional when I work out a better option."

The circle flared to life, and what appeared to be an arm's-width ribbon of the Ambiguous Cascade peeled away from the main column, as though it were a strand of string cheese being pulled off the main stick. In reality, it was quite a large volume of water; it was just the proximity to the massive column that made it appear far smaller than it truly was. Joe let out a triumphant bark of laughter as he clapped his hands a single time, "It really *is* just regular water! I mean, I read the message, but I'm still not believing it, even though I'm seeing it with my own eyes. It's just... way too *much* water."

He extended his Mana Dominion, feeling absolutely no reaction as the dense tendrils created by his Coalescent Fusion passed through the liquid. "Well, maybe I can upgrade the Ritual of the Ghostly Army and have it absorb all of the output for three or four seconds? Maybe that would give me enough time to at least claim the place of power-"

Joe's excited planning was cut off exactly one and three-quarters of a heartbeat after it began. The side of the cascade detonated outward in an immense spray, a perpendicular tsunami crashing down at the Ritualist. Only his extended domain gave him enough time to react whatsoever, the tendrils he'd elongated managing to brush against something absolutely gargantuan as it swam *up* through the cascade.

A dome-shaped barrier sprang into existence, holding firm even as the flat meadow around Joe's position was washed away as a massive mudslide, the grass and bushes ripped away down to the roots. Joe never wavered, knowing that, although there was a lot of it, the fact remained that this was still *just* water. What truly concerned him was how the morning light shining through the horizon had now fully split into various spectrums, not a hint of white daylight shining down.

Something far above him was blocking out the sky, yet somehow not darkening the ground below it. As the flood passed by, the Ritualist held very still, his eyes flickering back and forth as he tried to conceptualize the creature he was seeing suspended hundreds of feet in the air.

It was a whale easily as large as the fumigating titan Aten had cleaved through recently on Jotunheim, its body made of a crystalline substance that had allowed it to remain entirely invisible in the depths of the Ambiguous Cascade. Now that it was out in open air, it was still nearly translucent, only the rainbows forming in the air around it like a heat haze allowing Joe to get a proper sense of its scale.

High enough in the air that its tail slapped a cloud aside, the entity began twisting, shifting its body around as it went from perpendicular to the column of water to a forty-five degree angle... then parallel. It wasn't flying, so much as being carried, every positional shift weaving the liquid around it to create an enormous tether connecting back to the cascade at all times.

Though it seemed to have near-perfect control of the water around it, there were still streamers of water flowing off and splashing out into the air like the tail of a comet as the whale grew larger in his vision.

"Abyss, it's not getting bigger! It's getting *closer*!"

The whale plunged toward him, a deep, sonorous song

filling the air alongside a deep resonance ringing from its crystalline lungs. Omnivault activated before he consciously commanded the skill, and Joe dove to the side even as the creature dove at him. He sent himself out, away, and *up*—just as the creature slammed into the ground like a falling moon.

The softened dirt geysered outward, a shockwave rippling through the Ritualist's legs and sending him spinning before his body veritably autocorrected, thanks to Dialectic Dexterity twisting the uncontrolled tumble into a bridging backflip. "Good! I can work with this! It's just a big, dumb animal. If it's just going to throw itself at me, I can-"

Joe landed on the ground, sliding through the slippery sludge as he bled off his momentum. His mouth **clicked** shut as he stared at where the whale had *just* been—only now there was a huge swell of water coming off the cascade and creating a whirlpool the whale must have been contained within. The liquid snapped back into the waterfall, and only a heartbeat later, a burst of water—condensed to the point it was nearly a solid beam—shot out of the cascade.

The dense liquid missed Joe by inches, and even then, only thanks to his Magical Synesthesia literally *singing* a warning into his ears just before the magically controlled water would have cut through him. Striking the ground, the attack carved a trench dozens of feet deep, tossing dirt, stone, and a few trees into the air.

No longer being casual about the combat he suddenly found himself embroiled in, Joe started pumping his legs, knowing better than to remain in one spot and allow an unseen enemy to attack him with impunity. "Right! Apex entity! Artifact-rank monster, why did I think anything about this was going to be simple?"

A few more beams slashed across the ground, which he avoided with simple jumps or rolls. Just as he began feeling confident, water burst out as a massive cone, leaving him no chance at escaping as it swept him up and sent him spiraling through the air and into a tree that had only moments ago been *quite* distant.

As he pushed back to his feet, the tree groaning and shrieking as it toppled over behind him, a dripping Ritualist glared at the cascade ambiguously. "Now I'm *whaley* mad."

The stump of the tree exploded into shrapnel as he pushed off of it, his Quad Strength allowing him to return to the site of the battle in mere moments. He ducked around a follow-up set of water beams, throwing himself flat on the ground as yet another cone burst over him—drenching him again, but barely managing to shift Joe backward. Muddy but triumphant, the Ritualist hopped back to his feet, eyes narrow as he searched for where the next strike would originate.

"C'mon, is that all you've got? It'd be a waste to destroy you without letting you demonstrate your full suite of attacks!" Joe had no idea if the creature could understand him and was absolutely bluffing about having anything that could target the whale at this moment. Still, it seemed that *taunting* was something which crossed the boundaries of all species. Moments later, the daylight flickered into a broader spectrum as the Artifact-threat monster launched itself into open air once again.

"There you go... come at me!" Joe put his arms to his sides, flicking his wrists and manifesting a sheet of vellum in either hand. He tossed the first one upward, the core of the 'Air Fryer' ritual cluster. Another followed the first, four total rituals activating in midair as he tucked away the final one—as creating a patch of quicksand to use against a flying enemy was just downright wasteful. As the Expert-rank Abrasive Momentum ritual burst into being above him, as well as the Ritual of Haste, Extended Ember, and lastly the Ritual of the Stand-in, Joe dropped into a crouch, leaving the image of himself in place as he leaped away, hugging the ground as tightly as possible.

Eee~wwoooo!

Whale song caused the air to shudder once more as the monster trumpeted its impending victory, pulling a cord of the waterfall along and using it to jet downward even faster. Joe was on his third jump in a row—carefully avoiding the use of the empowered Omnivault to avoid warping the ambient mana—as the creature hit the edge of the Ritual of Haste. It warbled in confusion as it found itself being yanked forward faster than it had ever managed to plunge before.

The air warped as its lunge broke the threshold of the Ritual of Abrasive Momentum, and a mushroom cloud of steam exploded outward as friction flash-boiled the water along its entire crystalline hide. Even with as far as he'd run, a thick humidity slammed into Joe as the cloud of moisture blasted along the ground, casting the entire clearing into fog and hiding the moment the whale hit the ground and generated a localized earthquake.

Joe whooped in excitement, "Yes! I *knew* this was going to be my favorite ritual cluster!"

Skill offered: Steam Tempering (Beginner III). Heat joining with water becomes medicine when you allow it. While submerged in steam, your breath deepens, your pores open, and tired muscles loosen as all your strain is coaxed away rather than torn free.

Effect:

1. *For each minute spent in a sufficiently steamy sauna, natural or otherwise, the sweat that drains away will take damage with it, restoring .5n health per minute.*
2. *While in the steam, your fatigue vanishes, replaced by the natural medicine you have chosen. regain 0.5n stamina per second.*

Accept? Yes / No.

"Nope. Although that would definitely open up a few new applications for my Ritual of S-*tea*-mina..." A series of explosions caused him to hit the ground, covering his head and flinching as small chunks of bark rained down on him. "What in the world?"

There was a massive *thump*, and the steam was sucked back toward the whale, leaving the air clear. The edge of the forest closest to the point of impact was empty, save for a rain of woody fragments falling through the air where trees had popped like popcorn kernels after being exposed to the super-heated steam. The whale song that lifted into the air in the next moment was no longer filled with a territorial warning sound—now it was just pure rage.

**E~wwoooo!*

Joe jumped straight upward, barely clearing the enormous tail that had swung through his position like a fifty-foot-long claymore. A tidal surge followed after its body, the ground sweeping away and creating a temporary lake the Ritualist had no chance of avoiding. He hit the water hard just as a crisp, beautiful sound floated to his ears.

**Slap!*

Though he had no idea how he'd explain it, Joe managed to perfectly capture the visual shock of the crystalline whale as it was slapped across the face by a shadowy clone of himself, Haunting Shadows having recognized the intent of the attempted direct attack. The raging tide of water went still—just for a moment—as a chunk of the Artifact-rank threat's health went missing: exactly sixty-two percent of the potential damage it would've done to the human being returned to it in an instant.

There was a secondary reaction to the spell activating, a slight distortion of the air around Joe himself as the Master-rank magic took effect, warping the ambient mana and not-so-subtly reminding him that allowing himself to use such powerful spells had ramifications far beyond this single battle.

Much to his chagrin, his opponent seemed none the worse for wear after having been practically char-broiled and hitting the ground without the cushioning of any additional water. Still, it hadn't yet pulled itself back into the cascade, though it had quickly recovered from the initial shock of taking actual damage from a seemingly simple slap.

**E~é-E-eáe!*

It shrieked out a series of much higher-pitched squeaks and

clicks, and Joe felt the echoes wash over him, swirling across his body and inflicting a dizzying effect as his ears pulsed to the asynchronous sound.

Found. Targeted. Aimed at. Position established. Followed. Focused.

Magical Synesthesia whispered the effects of the echolocation magic that was, even now, practically vibrating his bones in an attempt to *shout* his position to the crystal whale. It began to swim, tail thrashing as a swell of water formed in front of and under it, lifting the creature as it shot along the surface of the lake directly at Joe—no longer befuddled even slightly by the effects of the Ritual of the Stand-in.

Waiting until the last moment wasn't possible, not with the sheer size of the creature, so Joe instead ran at an oblique angle to the cascade itself, forcing the massive entity away from the source of its power, camouflage, and ammunition. He hurled himself up and away, but even so, the enormous bulk clipped his right foot and sent him spinning. He hit the lake and skipped across its surface, bouncing like a perfectly smooth river stone until he once again took up temporary lodging inside a tree trunk.

"Might be... a little out of my depth here," Joe wheezed as he struggled to get back to his feet. "This thing seems pretty magic resistant, or... maybe just fire and blunt damage resistant?"

In the distance, the whale once again pivoted to come after him, sending up a massive sluice of water that washed out and away, pressurized enough to cleanly cut through the edge of the forest and send trunks tumbling. The Ritualist looked down, where his hands and arms were hidden behind a shimmer of trembling ambient mana, reminding him that he had prepared for this exact eventuality.

His next ritual cluster appeared in his hands, and he threw all five vellums in the air, his Mana Dominion allowing him to precisely place mana in the activation sequences of each of them at the same time. "Stormwell Convergence Cluster!"

He didn't *have* to shout the name of his attack, but against the whale...? Joe figured it wasn't going to be telling anyone about his antics.

Skill offered: Shounen Shout (Beginner II). By announcing your intent with unreasonable confidence and volume, you force the world to take you slightly more seriously.

Effect: All skills are .001n% stronger and faster to activate when you shout their name during activation.

"What the...? Didn't I already say no to that one? No again!" Joe ignored the notification as he felt a shift as the thin, ambient mana of Midgard collecting in a ring around the ritual diagrams that had appeared in midair. A shifting orb appeared near the ground, appearing to be entirely aflame as lights danced and poured off of its mass. While he wasn't certain if the whale would even be able to *see* the mental effect, let alone be caught by it, due to the tier discrepancy... he figured it couldn't hurt.

Breaking into a slow run, Joe kept the active cluster between himself and the monster, noticing absentmindedly that the shifting haze around his own limbs had vanished, reappearing for brief moments before streaking away as the Mana Shockwave Burst ritual slurped in all available power. "Tell me I timed it correctly, come on! That's right, straight into the-"

Thwoom!

There was almost no visible effect as the energy collapsed to a singular, central point in the ritual. The whale's head was almost *exactly* in position when it happened, and the collapse was followed by the mana randomizer flash-converting the densely collected power into an enormous burst of lightning. Joe looked on with great expectation as the thunderous discharge, placed in a position to perfectly stun, concuss, or at the bare minimum *shock* the creature landed. "Come on, Concussive Percussion! One of those *had* to have worked!"

His face fell as the whale burst through the edge of the ritual, static discharge still clinging to its surface... but not propagating any further.

"Seriously, it can't even conduct electricity? How pure *is* this water?" The Ritualist grumbled as he lifted a hand almost lethargically, a despondent wave of intent pausing all of the active rituals in the area. "I'll be back, monster. The next time I'm here, I'll-"

The whale took a hard turn, shifting at a perfect right angle and diving back into the cascade. Joe waited a few minutes, practically on his tiptoes as he prepared to dodge beams of water or yet another bull rush. It eventually became apparent that the champion of the cascade wasn't going to be making a reappearance, leaving him to wonder *why*.

"What's going on? I had to have done at least *some* damage. Was that over-whale-ming enough to scare it away? Seems... unlikely." His gaze roved over the area, coming to a halt as he looked at the Apprentice-rank ritual still hanging in the distance. "It couldn't be that it was only attacking me to make sure I couldn't mess with the water... right?"

Joe pondered for a moment, realizing that the creature *had* only attacked after he'd diverted a small stream and felt certain he was correct when he realized he had paused the ritual alongside all of his other, far more powerful, versions. "So *that's* the trigger to start combat, huh? I'll keep that in mind for round two."

Rubbing at his forehead with the back of his wrist, Joe grimaced as his hand came away with a thick coating of mud on it. His eyes darted to the water already receding back into the cascade, and he hopped in, driving his fingers into the ground as the water was *sucked* away. As the last of it passed, he pulled out his hands and trailed them in the dregs, grinning as he found himself mostly clean.

"And there *will* be a round two. Just... stronger rituals next time around, or better prepared. Something to disrupt its control of water and get me to the place of power so I can make sure that thing doesn't respawn anytime soon." Joe made a rude gesture at the downpour in the distance. "You win this one, whale. It's not gonna happen again. You think *you're* territorial? Just wait 'til you see what I'm gonna put in place when *I* control this place of power. Spoiler: it'll be a sushi bar specializing in whale meat!"

He stepped into the Forest of Chlorophyll Chaos, his Mana Dominion wrapping around him and pushing against the spatial distortions as he... tactically repositioned to the rear.

"Next stop, Grand Ritual Hall."

CHAPTER FIFTEEN

The City of Towney McTownface was now on top of a mountain, though it was only tall by *Midgard* standards. Joe lifted his nose in the air, a signature look of superiority filling his eyes as he compared the Sect's territory with that of Jotunheim and found it lacking. He was currently standing at the very tip of the lighthouse built onto the enormous arch that was the Legendary Grand Pathfinder's Hall, getting the lay of the land.

"City is a bit more sprawling than usual; seems to be dividing into various rings, now that there are clear elevation differences." He wrote some of his thoughts down as he murmured, figuring it would be best to bring an accounting of what he saw while on this planet back to the main branch of the Wanderer's Sect when he went back. "Looks like going to the Grand Pathfinder's Hall has started to become a real, very *intense* pilgrimage."

Even now, there were people trekking up the mountain, a long, winding strand that had members to the horizon at various distances from each other. Being such a major travel destination had turned the city into a hub for all sorts of things, expanding from being a mere tourist trap into the largest bazaar he'd seen on any world thus far. "I'll ask around and see how things are going here, make sure the local bureaucracy isn't trying to create separations based on... let's call them *old world* values, then I'll make use of the market."

After jotting down the last of his notes, he hopped off the building, sliding down the arching slope before pushing off with a non-mana-empowered Omnivault. Tucking and rolling, he got back to his feet and began moving at a steady pace, already in the area with the highest quality shops by sheer dint of being at the top of the mountain.

Skill offered: Hardcore Parkour (Expert V). Get where you want to go, faster than ever before! Who needs to run when you can spring forward, pushing off your hands, walls, flat surfaces, and even monsters?

Effect:

Increases travel speed by 30% when not walking or running in a standard manner, instead using hands, leaps, tumbling, or acrobatics.

Cost: 30 stamina per second.

"Ooh. That's a good one, but still no. Omnivault lets move around faster than this world can handle as it is." The midday sun gleamed off his head as he perused the options for goods in the top ring of the city, his Mana Dominion—even suppressed—causing anyone within range to jolt as if they'd been poked in the ribs.

Even as the Ritualist approached the first shop, he could hear whispers behind him as someone called for another person to 'alert the fan club'. Wincing, he took a deep breath and prepared to do his best to vanish into the marketplace. Looking around, Joe could see that this shop was a general goods store for anyone in the mining or smithing professions, the storefront loaded with precious ores, gems, and the tools to work them.

"Ahh... First Elder Joe!" The shopkeeper wrung his hands in a combination of anxiousness and anticipation. "What brings you to my humble store?"

"Good morning... I think it's still morning. You accept Sect contribution points?"

"Every shop in the Sect territory must," came the instant reply, a bright smile appearing on the man's face. "As a matter of fact, there's a standard three percent discount to all listed prices when using them!"

"Fantastic." Joe looked into his spatial storage, wincing away from the figurative moths flying away from where his coins should be, as well as the slots he used for Rare, Unique, or Artifact-rank aspects. "I'm in need of anything better than Uncommon. I don't care if it's raw material or worked goods. Load it up, and tell me the price."

"Is there anything in particular you're looking for?" Clearly, the man was hoping the answer was 'no', as he'd already begun dumping a display shelf of the most expensive jewelry in the store onto the counter.

"Seems you already know the answer." Joe allowed the man to chuckle before finishing, "I'll take it all."

Metals, jewelry, uncut gemstones, pickaxes, chisels, even various monster parts which could be worked into crafted items to add additional effects started piling up, to the point that Joe waved for the shopkeeper to ignore the counter and start stacking things on the floor. Once everything in the front of the shop had been gathered, he tapped on a large stone tablet and transferred contribution points over. "Give me a minute, then I'd like to see your storage room, if you're open to it."

"*Very* much so," came the elated, obsequious voice. "Mmm heh *hehhh...*"

It always made Joe chortle when other people danced in place at their good fortune, but he didn't allow the shopkeeper's antics to distract him from making a properly-sized Ascendant Matrix, converting every last one of his purchased items into aspects with a burst of mana. His smile thinned somewhat, as the vast majority of goods had been merely Rare, with only a few hundred Unique aspects coming through. "Any chance you have an Artifact or two in the back?"

"If *only* I could offer such fine wares in my humble establishment." The shopkeeper tried to act dramatic, but his exhale still came out as a happy sigh of contentment instead of regret. "Not only are such items *incredibly* hard to come by on Midgard, the Sect has right of first refusal for Artifacts, so long as they pay at least the going market value. Private trades are non-regulated, but..."

"I understand." The Ritualist pulled out a core, wrapping it in mana and beginning to massage aspects into its internal mana matrix. "Give me a minute, and I'll be ready to go."

Item created: Aspect Jar (Unique). This aspect jar can store up to 9,100 Unique aspects.

Aspect Jar (Unique). This aspect jar can store up to 9,700 Unique aspects.

Aspect Jar (Rare). This aspect jar can store up to 5,500 Rare aspects.

Aspect Jar (Rare). This aspect jar can store up to 5,125 Rare aspects.

While they weren't 'natural' versions and therefore able to generate their own aspects, he had to admit that they were far easier and faster to make—especially as they were all but *required* for his Reductionist class. Once he had enough jars to hold a respectable number of aspects, Joe followed the shopkeeper to the back of the shop and cleaned out his storage.

Then he went to the next store over and did it again. This place was an herbalist shop filled with preserved plants, saps, sticky poisons, and all manner of non-alchemical reagents. After that was a general goods store, cooper, armorsmith, hosiery... by early afternoon, he'd gone through and practically stripped the town of trade goods. So thoroughly, as a matter of fact, that a small crowd of angry crafters were following along after him, darting into shops to grab whatever they needed for their own businesses before he could reduce everything to aspects.

Joe started moving faster, acting like he was going to enter a shop or a restaurant, only to Omnivault over it and go to a different building entirely. Still, the flashes of light and squeals of glee coming from shop owners earning more in a few minutes than they did in a month at a time usually gave his position away quickly.

"Hey! *Hey*! Leave some of those guts for the rest of us! Just because you have *money* doesn't mean we don't have quotas!"

"Not the nightshade analogs! I need those for–great, now they're the sparkly fire you keep sucking into your crotch like a vacuum. I hope it burns when you pee!"

"Right here, *this* is the problem with our economy!"

"Is this legal? Can someone explain how buying *all* the ore is legal?"

Even worse than the angry shoppers were the fan club who had finally started filtering in among the mob. The Ritualist did his best to ignore them until one of the worst offenders among them threw herself into his Ascendant Matrix in an attempt at creating a magical mishap. "Please explode me! I want a cool death notification to show my friends!"

"Get *outta* here!" The shocked tailor stepped forward, grabbing the lady–who'd passed through the matrix without harm–by the ankles and bodily hurling her out the door. "You want to make something blow up, do it *outside* of my shop!"

"Sorry about that. Some people are... enthusiastic about seeing me." By way of apology, Joe bought another fifty yards of Rare lace, converting it to aspects in an instant. As he'd seen on the faces of many people who also created what they were selling, the tailor winced away from the destruction, only biting his tongue thanks to having been prepaid.

"Did you see? Now he's the *Emperor* of Mana! Your highness, for the good of your kingdom... jump on me with your big ol' feet!"

"She didn't succeed because she missed the middle of the glowing field! Try getting to the *middle*! Maybe it's the middle that turns you into fire!" a middleman in the crowd called out, trying to convince other people to sacrifice themselves.

"You know, it wasn't too long ago that people were terrified at the thought of seeing me, after the red mist incident," Joe grumbled as he finished clearing out the rest of the stock in the store. "I'm honestly not certain which attitude I prefer seeing. Abyssal Dark Charisma being above the Mortal Limit is attracting all the weirdos."

Deciding he'd gathered enough to make a decent dent in his plans, Joe shoved his way through the door of the shop and onto the street. Crouching, he Omnivaulted to the top of the building and started running back toward the Grand Pathfinder's Hall in the distance. Shouts followed him, a few people shaking fists at the man who'd emptied all the stores, while others reacted in a more... unhinged manner.

"No~oo! We believe in you, Joe the Dread Ritualist! Your craters are lucky!"

"I want massive rewards again; you can't just leave without dropping a World Boss on us or something!"

"Tall, bald, *and* ominous. So hot."

Soon enough, the words faded into the distance, and Joe was able to take a deep breath as he dove through the shimmering portal and into the secret area the Pathfinder's Hall contained: the Grand Ritual Hall. After giving himself a moment to shiver for reasons that had nothing to do with the temperature, Joe locked down his reactions and took a deep breath.

"Thanks for joining me, everyone!" Even with his eyes closed, he could sense the presence of his coven of Experts. "I have a handful of Expert-rank designs... actually, they're Master rank, but we'll be forming them as Expert because I... kinda ran out of-"

"*Finally*!" Taka let out a playful laugh as he pointed at the startled Ritualist. "You ran out of crafting materials! Welcome to progressing like the rest of us, for once!"

"One of us, one of us!" Big_Mo joined in, trying and failing to start a group chant.

Joe raised an eyebrow, giving the men a chance to enjoy the moment before dashing their glee. "As I was saying, I ran out of Artifact-rank cores, and all I have is this *enormous* pile of Unique versions. You are correct in that I was running low on materials, but luckily I was able to just... buy everything in town and turn them into aspects."

"*Ugh.*" Taka practically deflated on the spot. "You're the worst."

"Hey, at least we get to benefit from his spending habits," Hannah consoled her friend. "Think of it like this; we get to have all the skill gains of making pseudo-Master rituals without having to invest anything but time and mana, unlike *someone* who has to pay the full cost by himself."

Taka perked right back up, his smarmy grin returning at full strength.

Realizing that trying to win banter when it was five versus one was a losing proposition, the Ritualist instead merely grumbled under his breath. With a snap of his fingers, he shifted his attention to the subspace and began using the thousands of threads in his Mana Dominion to arrange the dark motes filling the area into crisp ritual circles.

As Joe exerted his power, each of the others stumbled in place slightly, their eyes going wide with discomfort as his dominion touched their personal auras and began attempting to subjugate them, intent on making them bend the knee and accept his rule as emperor. Seeing as he was focused on his ritual circles, he didn't notice their internal struggle for a few long seconds, but as soon as he did, Joe intentionally yanked back on the effect, doing his best to rein it in.

The others slumped, heaving for breath... all except Kirby, who had a manic smile on her face and a long, curved dagger in her hand.

"I was about to stab you."

"I can see that." Joe coughed awkwardly into a closed fist, looking around at the others, even while most of his attention was focused on arranging the ritual diagram. "Sorry, everyone. New skill effect, wasn't intentional. I... actually, let me make it up to you. Anyone close to Master rank in any skill? Any skill *at all* that uses mana?"

As it turned out, most of them were reaching peak Expert

in their main focus, though their other class and supporting skills had stalled out in the low-to-mid range, due in no small part to lacking materials and mana. Seeing as he had close to thirty-two thousand total mana available to use, but could only access at most eleven thousand of it while on Midgard without removing his inhibitor gear, Joe generously decided to grant all five of them a thousand points of his mana pool.

The memory that this was merely the minimum for materializing a Mastery Merit from a menagerie of mana-based skills they might manage to manifest was magnificent.

"Hey, would any of you be willing to increase your mana pool by a thousand points? I have a lot of excess mana, and I've got a title that lets me 'bequeath' it to other people. I'll need it back eventually, but, you know, you have extra until then?" There were a few moments of silence as the others processed his words, and Joe held both hands up in a surrender pose before anyone could ask questions. "There are some benefits I get from doing this, mainly that I get a bonus if you achieve Mastery in any mana-based skill. It doesn't take anything from you, so there are no downsides, as far as I can tell."

"No downsides except getting used to having nearly a fifth more mana than usual, then eventually losing it," Big_Mo grumbled without any heat in his voice. "I'm in. Sounds good to me."

"I'll go first. I'm guessing you haven't tried doing this for anyone before, or else you'd probably have your pitch down a little better?" Robert rolled his eyes and shook his head knowingly as Joe gave him a sheepish grin in return for his comments. "Yeah, I feel like I can handle getting blown up a little easier than the rest of them."

"*Tha~anks*, Robert," Taka called in a monotone voice.

"You're the *best*." Kirby pulled the suddenly blushing man into a side-hug. "I really like not exploding from the inside out."

The Ritualist stepped closer, and Robert moved forward to match him, more nervous than his previous offer had suggested. "So... how do you do this? I'm guessing you don't have to, like, stab me or anything, right?"

"It's a title effect, so *probably* not?" Joe lifted his hands into a cupped position and let his mana collect between his palms. He wasn't trying to cast a spell, but instead create a *gift* he could present. He willed the title to work, and the formless mana suddenly shifted and began to arrange itself into a very familiar shape: almost exactly the same as a Common-rank core he would pull out of any random magical monster on Midgard. There were a few small differences, namely that this was mostly ethereal, and it had a singular connection point turning the otherwise-round object into an orb with a cone attached to it.

He gently shooed it forward, and it floated onward until it pressed against Robert's chest, as if waiting for something.

"Yes, I accept."

"Ah." Joe's head bobbed in understanding as he realized he couldn't just bequeath mana to random individuals and siphon off Mastery Merits—his subjects had to accept the benefits both they and he would receive. He felt a pang of loss as the ghostly core sank into Robert's chest, and a thousand points of his mana vanished to be used by another.

From his perspective, that was the end of it. No noise, light show, or theatrics. Joe supposed that emperors weren't supposed to need showy things, and perhaps it was better that their authority was simple, direct, and effective. Still, he scuffed his boot on the invisible ground, clicking his tongue. "I thought it would look cooler."

For his part, Robert had stiffened, eyes going wide, pupils dilating as he began to heave for air like a man who'd just burst through the surface of the water after being under for far too long. "H-hot!"

"It's hot?" Joe reached forward, laying his hand on Rob's chest and feeling no difference from what was normally there. "This has to be some kind of astral body thing, just hold out until you've absorbed it all. You've got this."

He'd long since learned the value of remaining calm when

someone else was on the verge of panicking, and—as it usually did—his relaxed demeanor paid dividends. After a few minutes, Robert bent over, still breathing heavily, though far slower than before.

"You good? Everything okay in there?" Joe yanked his head back as Robert glanced up with an uncharacteristic sharpness.

"Joe. South Carolina is gone."

"*Uh-hu~uh,*" the Ritualist agreed in a drawn-out manner. "It sure is, buddy."

Finally his coven member seemed to snap out of his fever dream, blinking and looking around the room while rubbing at his chest distractedly. "Whoa... where am—right. Ugh... that kinda sucked, man. But I've got twenty percent more mana than I did. Actually, that's not quite right. I've got a small mana pool attached to my main one, and what you gave me is slowly being filled up by my normal regeneration. I guess you actually gave me the *capacity* for another thousand?"

"Feels okay, though? Now that it's in place?" Hannah inquired in a light tone, clearly trying to keep her question from seeming too self-serving. "Doesn't hurt or anything?"

"No. Just strange." Robert stepped away and stretched back and forth. "Kind of like I have two water heaters in my chest, set up in serial. I can already tell that, when I drain my main pool, the other one'll fill it back up instead of being drawn from directly. Like... I don't know, it's almost more like knowing it'll act like a rapid-regeneration sack than a second mana pool. Does that make sense?"

"Not really, but I'm guessing it will in a minute." Hannah stepped forward, half-raising her hand. "I'll go next!"

After each member of the coven were mollified by gaining an additional thousand points of mana, they turned to watch attentively as Joe returned to meticulously drawing out the diagrams in midair. Though they didn't have anything to do except pay attention and wait, seeing a near-peak Master of Ritual Circles at work created the opportunity for Inspiration, not to mention being generally beneficial to their skills long-term.

Finally, a full workday later, Joe finished the final circle, sweating and panting as his stamina started refilling again, Inscription Momentum having been a constant drain on his resources. Clapping his hands, he turned to the others with a fatigued smile. "Everyone ready to turn this husk into the real deal? I need five of these for... reasons."

They gathered around the center of the ritual, each of them feeling extra confident, now that their own mana reserves had been boosted by such a significant amount. Big_Mo spoke for the group as he got into position in the Novice circle. "Yeah, let's get this done as fast as possible. Then maybe we can come along and see it in action?"

"Ehh..." Joe hedged, not quite sure why he was so dead set on fighting the crystal whale solo. "Probably not this time. I'm in the middle of a grudge match with a whale, and it's already all uppity because it won the first round."

"If you don't want us to come, you don't have to make things up," Kirby stated in her usual sweet tone.

"Oh. No," Joe admitted as a blush crept up his neck. "I'm dead serious. I'm going to go fight a giant fish with this. It needs to die, and I'm angry because it's still alive and *whale*."

As the others heaved great sighs of annoyance, Joe began pouring aspects into the prepared diagrams, a smirk twitching into place on his lips.

CHAPTER SIXTEEN

Quietly accessing the interface between himself and the Grand Ritual Hall, Joe took one last look around at the members of his original coven, each of whom were currently snoozing after an extended period of crafting rituals at the bleeding edge of what they could manage. Keeping his voice low, the Ritualist fractionally bowed toward the group. "Thank you all for your hard work. I'll see you soon."

Skill offered: Ritual Notation (Novice VIII). You have practiced writing out rituals in your mind to the point that it has become second nature.

Effect: Improves recall and precision when designing ritual diagrams.

"Bah. Useful, and I want more support skills for my rituals, but I'll have to try and get that another time." Dismissing the offered skill, he focused on getting out of the vast room. In the next moment, he was standing just outside the massive arch of the Legendary building, taking a deep breath of fresh air—particularly refreshing after having been in the clean, sterile, and absolutely still environment of the ritual hall for the last couple days.

Whuuum.

A deep tone rolled through the air from far above him, and

Joe reflexively tucked and rolled, his eyes darting up to seek out the whale that must have followed him... then he got ahold of himself, realizing the sound was just the Pathfinder's Hall reaching maximum mana capacity. He hadn't seen a Knowledge Nova in a good long time, so he decided to stay and watch the fireworks. Each iteration of the nova traveled farther and would eventually build up powerfully enough to cover the entire planet and update the repository of all base classes and branching paths that could be found on Midgard.

"Beautiful, isn't it?" A wizened voice caused Joe's ears to perk up, and he glanced over to see Boris, the elderly scholar having exited the Pathfinder's Hall he worked and lived in. "The things I've learned over the last year of working here by paying close attention... truly amazing. As a matter of fact, that's one of the reasons I'm out here right now. If you will, turn your attention to the point fifteen feet below the light of the tower, eight feet in from the left-hand side. If I'm correct, the point of origin for the Knowledge Nova is actually changing based on an array of usage. Having you here would help me get a second first-hand witness report."

The elderly Scholar fell silent, and Joe felt a rush of emotions at seeing the man, who looked to be somewhere between content... and resigned to his fate. He missed having good conversations with Boris, but as he materialized the coin he'd gotten from Nathaniel, the Ritualist excitedly realized those days might be returning. Opening his mouth to speak, he realized the Scholar was leaning forward and staring intently, so he reluctantly followed the older man's gaze, focusing on the point Boris had indicated.

**Whuuum.*

Once again, the deep tone caused the air to tremble, as though the lighthouse were mimicking a bell tower. Joe's gaze sharpened; the accumulating mana was reaching a climax, and something was happening to the archway that he would've never noticed if the Scholar hadn't precisely directed his attention. A fluctuating shimmer of mana scattered exactly at that point, like a static discharge drawing a larger lightning bolt out of a thunderstorm.

The incredible accumulation used that spot as a convergence point, over a million mana passing through it in an instant then burning out as though a fuse had been blown. Just as this happened, the power tessellated back into the lighthouse, and the shockwave created by the structure detonated, racing off into the distance fast enough that Joe almost couldn't see the edge of it speeding away. A faint image appeared on the wall where he'd been staring, so indistinct that he would've chalked it up to being one of the ornamental designs that had always been there if he hadn't seen it appear in real time.

Natural ritual conflux viewed and understood! You have gained a new ritual, thanks to your Ritualistic Wisdom Characteristic.

Ritual gained: Zone of Skill Knowledge. This Master-rank ritual creates an area of effect that allows the user to learn the names of skills used within the effect range. Only through careful calculation and absolute precision will this ritual reach its full potential.

Effect:

1. *Creates a 30-meter-radius zone centered on a target point.*
2. *While active, you passively perceive the names and requirements to gain any skills, spells, or techniques used within the area. (Can be output to an appropriate item for logging of information.)*
3. *For each distinct skill observed, you gain a 0.01% chance of immediately learning a Novice-rank variant, if compatible with your class.*

"Abyss," Joe whispered as his eyes returned to their normal coloration after having flashed purple, the tiny ritual circles etched through the entirety of his pupils fading away. "Boris, this is amazing. Do you have any idea what that *does*?"

"If I'm not missing my mark," the elderly man replied just as excitedly, "It's acting as a countdown. Once it reaches the halfway point, *there*, this building will be reaching the locus of where it should be open to an upgrade. *Mythical*. The only problem, again, going just off of my research, is that, if it reaches the final point of activation and hasn't become a Mythical structure, it will lose the ability to do... *something*. Even if it later does achieve an upgrade."

Joe considered Boris's words, turning them over in his mind before giving the Scholar his full attention. "From what I just saw, it'll have something to do with skills, specifically. Probably recording skills and the requirements to gain them, while also adding in a function for directly *imparting* skills to select individuals. Perhaps swapping skills with comparable options?"

"Ah... yes, that would make sense. Truly a Mythical upgrade, to be able to scan the most potent options available and build your class section by section, allowing it to become exactly what you want it to be." Boris had a notebook out and was slowly and meticulously writing his thoughts out as he spoke. "You've mentioned before that these types of buildings were all destroyed in the past, yes? I think we've figured out why. If a kingdom got ahold of this, they could literally build a ruling class that would be nigh-untouchable by anyone else. Wars would be started for the structure as it is now... were there more than one kingdom on this planet to compete for it."

"Something to keep in mind." Joe blithely waved the warning away. "Listen, I've got something for you. This should take care of that little issue we've been hoping to fix for the last... well, far too long. Sorry it took me until now, but-"

Boris took a slow step away as Joe rummaged around in his codpiece, which from an outside perspective simply looked like him waving his hand back and forth over his lap as his *mind* was doing the actual rummaging.

"What in the world? I just had it a second ago. I know I have it, just—*ha*!" The Ritualist had glanced down in confusion, only to triumphantly hold up the coin that was already in his other hand. "Forgot I already pulled it out! Here you go, this is a token given to me by the founder of the Scholar *and* Occultist professions. Just activate it, and the Scholar Society's decision to ban you is automatically overturned and can't be put back in place! Quest complete. Congrats, buddy!"

Boris looked down at the coin now cupped in his palm, surprising the Ritualist by seeming horrified more than excited at the news. The elderly man flipped the coin back and forth, carefully noting the Scholar's crest then the Occultist crest on the other side. "This. I don't. But... you were supposed to get us back in good standing, not just go over their heads-"

The system didn't seem to agree with the Scholar, as Joe was already happily reading over the notification it had sent him.

Quest complete: Academia and Diplomacy. You have provided the means by which Boris the Scholar's professional standing in the eyes of the Scholars' Society can be restored!

Reward: Your profession now has no risk of forced revocation. Reputation with Boris has increased to 'Reluctantly Friendly'.

"Nah, I started as an Occultist. Why would I do things the Scholarly way? Anyway," Joe gently clapped the stupefied man on his shoulder, "there's a white whale out there that needs harpoonin'. Transparent, in reality, but I figured you'd get the reference. See you soon, and let me know if there's anything else-"

"*No*!" Boris's hand flicked, as though he were about to toss the coin back at Joe but couldn't *quite* make himself let go of it. "While the letter of our agreement has been satisfied, the heart of the matter remains unresolved. Just because they can't refuse my entry if I use this doesn't... it doesn't mean I'd be *welcome* among them. You can't just decide that the quest is done. It's *my* quest!"

Quest offered: Academia and Diplomacy II. A return to academic standing apparently wasn't enough for this Scholar. Though you have managed to find a workaround to technically complete his objective, it isn't one he will accept.

Work with Boris to earn formal readmission into the Society of Scholars as a full member through peer tribunal or directive from The Provost. Optional: Secure a sponsored research position for Boris by having him submit a scientific paper offering information not found within the halls of the Grand University.

Reward: Brokered introductions to senior members of the Scholars' Society. Access to restricted research archives.

Failure: On failure, refusal of quest, or abandonment, your reputation with Boris will decrease by one tier.

Joe let out a deep sigh as he read over the information, his eyes flicking over to the grave face of the Scholar staring at him with a hopeful gaze. Taking a deep breath to calm himself, then another, a third just for good measure, he carefully began speaking.

"Why isn't this good enough, Boris? I found the *originator* of the *profession*. I explained the situation to him, and he was so angry on your behalf that he gave you this token. You got tossed out because you worked with me, someone who followed the other profession the *same guy* founded! Scholars and Occultists were always meant to progress together. It's the only way to get the higher-rarity variants of the profession!"

The elderly man's gaze dropped toward the ground for only a brief moment before he clenched his fists and met Joe's intense stare once more. "I understand that I saddled you with an incredibly difficult quest with harsh penalties for failure. I expected you to have to get to the Grand University and sit through months of committee conversations and hearings, all leading up to a tribunal. But you skipped the entire process and did something no one else can replicate. Don't you see? I wanted you to do this as a *Scholar*, yet you went and acted as an Occultist yet again."

"I'm *not* a Scholar, so why should that matter to me, Boris?" Joe puffed out his cheeks as he looked to the sky. "They can't argue with the endorsement of the founder. I have proof that we were meant to work together, so why should I focus only on one narrow path when the world is a sandbox we can do *anything* in?"

"Just because he founded it... well, I hate to say it, but that doesn't make him relevant to the modern-day Scholars' Society.

I just want the acknowledgement I'm due from my peers," Boris replied with steel in his voice, not backing down in the slightest. "They were my friends, my companions, for years. I don't just want to be 'able' to walk into the society, I want my *friends* to bring me into conversations, endorse my work... I want to be able to have pride in my life's pursuit and the acknowledgment that comes with that. *Surely* you can understand this?"

"The name is Joe; don't call me Shirley." When Boris remained silent, Joe took a few moments to think, rereading the quest once more just to ensure it didn't have a time limit, then he reluctantly accepted it. "Can you really call them your friends if they abandoned you over someone else's decision? A *dumb* decision at that? Fine. I've taken the quest. We'll do it your way, on one condition."

"What?" Boris narrowed his eyes in confusion, as Joe had already accepted. "Trying to negotiate after the fact?"

"I'm taking that token back. If they refuse to see reason... I'm going to use it to remove the highest-ranking person in the Scholars' Society from their position." Joe plucked the coin from the old man's nerveless fingers, then gave Boris a sharp nod and turned to storm off, no longer open to discussion on this matter.

Skill offered: Hyperfocused Nod (Journeyman II). You have begun to master the art of appearing deeply engaged in any matter at hand regardless of your actual attention. Effect: Increases reputational gain from conversation, lectures, symposiums, conferences, or other communication lasting more than 30 consecutive minutes.

"You can't just *fire* The Provost!" Boris gasped in horror. "He's been there... forever! He's an institution unto himself and has guided the society through-"

"Ignore." Even Joe wasn't certain whether he was only dismissing the offered skill or speaking to Boris. He called back just before entering the temple connected to the Grand Pathfinder's Hall, "He *is* an institution? Sounds like he's *definitely* the problem. If this Provost guy is the one who's pushing these horrible decisions, a change in leadership is long overdue."

The last thing the Ritualist saw before swinging the door shut behind him and marching over to the altar–intent on teleporting away–was the Scholar's conflicted expression, his lips working like a fish out of water... the exact mental image Joe needed to help get him back in the mood to hunt a whale.

"This is perfect for combat. I can just stay mad," the Ritualist snarled softly as he pushed into the Forest of Chlorophyll Chaos. "I don't understand why it isn't enough for people to have exactly what they asked for *in the first place*. At least the system, for all its other faults, doesn't allow for people to change their mind halfway through and not pay out or follow through on their end of the bargain."

Joe's heart was pounding in his chest, and it took him a while to calm himself down. "Just *refusing* the quest would've dropped me down a reputational tier, even after I went through all of that and... what part of what I did couldn't be considered something a Scholar did? All of that would be repeatable by anyone else if they followed the same steps I did! What's stopping them from going and finding Nathaniel on their own and fixing their problem at the source?"

He inhaled until his ribs protested, trying to let it out with deliberate control as he worked to redirect his anger toward something that was actively trying to harm him. "At least the whale just wants to whale on me. It's not going to tell me it wants to fight, flounder at the last second and change its mind, then wail about how it's not fair."

Reality tried to fold around him, only for Joe to push the magical influences of the forest away with a frustrated shove of his Mana Dominion. Realizing he'd been stomping through the forest aimlessly, he began focusing, quickly picking out of the thread his Red Luck highlighted for him and adjusting course. Leaves began blurring at the edge of his vision, the moss-covered tree trunks turning into brownish streaks as he walked a warped path through the woods.

A faint pressure began to build up, tugging at the edges of his hearing. Moments later, he stepped into the meadow around the Ambiguous Cascade, the final rays of evening sunshine staining the landmark pink and gold. The colossal cylinder of water started darkening from the bottom up as the sun slipped below the horizon, the top of it still too distant and obscured to make out with his heavily inhibited Characteristics.

The meadow itself had mostly recovered in roughly two days since his initial clash with the crystal whale. Any hint of the mudslides had been hidden by fresh, young grasses creating a thick carpet over the surface of the seemingly firm, packed earth. Where trees had been shattered or cleaved through, new growth and nearly mature trees had sprung up, in many cases using the fallen flora as fertilizer to supplement their growth.

His eyes lingered on the water falling far too quietly into the depths of the planet, "Don't you worry. Round two is almost ready to go, but since you have your own territorial advantage, I figured it's only fair I get my own ready to go."

After double checking to ensure his paused rituals were still in place and ready to be used, Joe picked out four additional points to set up his rituals and ritual clusters. He tried to focus on keeping them roughly equidistant from the edge of the water and the forest, knowing the whale wouldn't leave its position easily.

Skill offered: Battlefield Strategizing (Novice II). Plans are wonderful, clean, sensible, tiny delights in a world that is politely holding still while you think. Once battle starts, it will always shift, change your priorities, and introduce new variables. Strategy is plans made before battle, something you as a Master in multiple skills should have in spades… but all battlefield 'planning ahead' experience is taken into account when determining the initial rank of the skill being offered.

Effect-

"Skip. Ignore. Rude. I guess setting up infrastructure and defensive perimeters doesn't count toward 'battlefield' strategy, huh? Otherwise you'd have made me an Expert at the very least."He glared at the fading notification, then, still grumbling, returned to plotting out how he would take down the whale, starting with the rituals he needed to put in place.

As the first Air Fryer cluster was already set, merely paused and waiting to be used again, he couldn't do much with it–yet. Going to the next position he planned to fortify, the Ritualist looked to the sky, where bright stars were beginning to emerge, and pulled out his inscribed beast vellum. "The moon isn't going to be a good waypoint. It's moving and too early in the night to really focus on it. But if I use that red star, align the edge of the vellum along the belt like this..."

The Ritual of Torrent had started out as a Master-rank diagram, and while it had pained him to downshift it to an Expert-rank version of the same, that didn't mean Joe had to use it as it was. With his early Master-rank knowledge of Celestial Arcane Lore, he fine-tuned the final position for the first placement, carefully bringing the ritual to a ready-to-be-used state. "Just gotta be careful not to let these get washed away before I activate them, or there'll be no point in taking the time to be careful. Should be able to bring the pseudo-Master-rank usage up a notch at least by doing this. Ugh... gonna be a late night."

Burble?

Joe lit up as his favorite liquid sound came from near his waistline. Without missing a beat, he reached down and unclipped his Ebonsteel mug, lifting the ever-cheerful coffee Elemental to eye level. "Hey, *you*! It's been a few days; normally you don't vanish for this long. Trouble in paradise, also known as the elemental plane of coffee?"

Eh.

A laugh burst from the Ritualist's lips, fading to concern as Mate shrugged his liquid shoulders. "That was the most unflattering sound I've ever heard coming from you, little guy. Can't be *that* bad, right?"

Mate shook its head back and forth then created a pseudopod arm that it lifted as though it were going to flex, only for the tendril to fill out with immense detail as it formed into an arm larger than Joe's body, complete with musculature that'd put any top-tier bodybuilder to shame.

"A-ah." Joe gulped at the sudden, completely unexpected display, "There's problems, but nothing you can't handle?"

Burble! Mate cheerfully squealed as it pulled its body back into the mug.

"You know, I've always appreciated having strong coffee." His words were barely out of his mouth before Mate waved and sank into the depths of the mug, leaving behind a steaming brew.

Taking a long, grateful sip, Joe closed his eyes and simply enjoyed the moment. "Haa... I always forget how much of a toll having reduced Characteristics like this takes on me. Hopefully, I can get off the planet before I have to sleep for a week."

CHAPTER SEVENTEEN

It was approaching midnight by the time Joe was fully satisfied with his setup. His rituals were aligned with the heavens, there was nothing more he could do to ensure they couldn't be washed away, and the entire meadow was lined with enough combat magic to scare the carp out of anyone sensitive to the fluctuations.

"Ahh... fish puns. Maybe I should introduce some variants to how they make jokes on Vanaheim. Then again, I suppose maybe fish isn't a big thing there? Didn't see any oceans or even large bodies of water. They probably just wouldn't understand that I was trying to make them laugh." Joe looked around one last time, eyes narrowing as he realized another small setback he could easily handle. "Hmm. Enormous, yet almost invisible monster that I'm going to be fighting. Middle of the night."

Lifting a finger, he created a Ritual of Glimmering, simultaneously activating it with a thread of mana held in place with his Coalescent Fusion. The Novice-ranked ritual sent a ball of light flying, sticking to the ground and illuminating the surroundings with a vibrant purple light. Before the first ritual had even finished activating, Joe was creating another one. His eyebrow arched as he felt it form and activate ever so slightly faster than the first.

"Oh?" He did it again, sending yet another light flying to stick on a tree in the distance. "Don't tell me Inscription Momentum works with Somatic Ritual Casting, as long as I'm continuously making rituals. I *definitely* thought it would only work while creating a single ritual at a time."

Deciding to take a few minutes to test out his observations, he began creating the Novice rituals as quickly as he possibly could, the tiny circles snapping into being with one of his countless mana threads already in position to fill the activation sequence. Glimmering balls shot off into the distance, faster and faster, until he reached his maximum speed with the ramped up momentum. As he was wrapped in a bubble of distorted time, the balls of light shot into the distance like tracer rounds from a fifty caliber turret emplacement.

Wherever he pointed, illumination followed along fractions of a second behind; clinging to trees, ground, reaching the edge of the water and halting, or even achieving their maximum distance straight up and hanging in the air like flares. Before he knew it, the cascade and the meadow around it were brightly lit by overlapping shades of violet, with only a hint of natural light piercing through from the full moon above. The topology of the meadow was now clearly highlighted; there'd be no hidden depressions or surprise logs swept by the whale's surf that might catch his toes as he jumped along.

"Hopefully the beast itself won't be able to stay quite as hard to see with the light painting it." Joe rolled his shoulders and twisted his head side to side. He wasn't sore or stiff, his body long since exceeding the need for the reflexive actions, but his mind still recognized the motion for what it was: getting ready for battle.

Extending a thread of mana, the Ritualist connected to the Ritual of the Underbridge in the distance, reactivating it with a thought. "Alright, big guy. Let's try this again."

Forty feet up the cascade, a narrow strand of the waterfall pulled away from the main column, curling up and out. Just as the tip reconnected, the Ambiguous Cascade practically detonated.

Eee~wwoo-o-o!

The whale's battle song caused the leaves in the distant trees to shudder, and–unless Joe were simply projecting his own thoughts on the creature–he was fairly certain it sounded far angrier this time around, having been disturbed twice in only a few days after unknowable years of being left alone. He inspected the creature as it forced its way out of the cascade's torn meniscus, eyes skimming over the silhouette displacing the air. Satisfaction settled in his chest when the purple, glimmering light washed through the whale, turning its previously near-invisible form into a living lantern.

"I've got ya now." He prepared to dodge aside, but the whale remained in position, studying him through one enormous eye as it swam alongside the falls. Water began flooding over it, swimming pool volumes of water forming into a skintight sheath as streamers lashed around, as though the entity had been recently inspired by an octopus. "That's... new. I guess you're taking me seriously this time around? Whale-come to the fight; I'm *also* looking forward to round two."

Perhaps it was the joke he'd made that sent the guardian of this place of power over the edge, and in the next moment, the water wrapped around its body went from a translucent film to a bulging wall. In a heartbeat, that smoothed back down into a sleek sheath that shifted the non-aerodynamic creature into an angular form, allowing it to cut through the air nearly as fast as the water. As it zipped around, still hugging the falls, its first attack came without warning.

A beam of water lanced out from the creature's side. To this point, Joe had been able to easily dodge the straight-line attacks, but seeing as it had a nearly unlimited supply of ammunition and was rapidly moving along, the straight shot became a blade of water sweeping along only a few feet above the ground.

The Ritualist yelped and tried to jump away, only to feel his legs being sheared off at the knee–then he experienced the bizarre manifestation of his Dialectic Dexterity as his poorly executed dexterous action was simultaneously and instantly performed at fifty percent efficiency.

Instead of his legs being cut off, he wobbled into the air, barely escaping the buzzsaw of fluid and falling on his face as the resulting turbulence caused him to tumble to the ground. Frustrated that he'd nearly been taken out on the first volley, Joe slapped the sodden earth and shoved himself to his feet, this time prepared to dive to the side as the Artifact-rank monster zipped past at a sharp diagonal, its attack creating a watery blade of titanic proportions that cut the trees in the distance down to shards of wood that would only be useful for making matches.

Before he could get too comfortable with the new style of strikes, shorter bursts of pressurized water joined the continuous beam, filling the air with bolts of water that hummed through the air at strange intervals, making them hard to predict or avoid.

Joe ran for cover, managing to throw himself behind his reactivated Air Fryer ritual cluster. His original intent had been to use the weak barrier underneath it to block the uncontrolled water, but to his great relief, he didn't have to rely on the Apprentice-rank effect: the water zipping through the air hit the boundary of the Ritual of Abrasive Momentum, popping with a sound like bullets striking metal plates as it converted directly into steam. From there, the drifting haze was blown away by the gusts the whale was generating simply by moving its bulk around.

"Abyss, that thing wasn't taking the last fight seriously at all, was it? That chunky crystal must be pretty intelligent if it's able to moderate its own attacks and not go all-in when it is unnecessary." Joe threw himself flat as a keening, high-pitched water blade vibrated over his head, only a few feet above the ground and therefore below the range of the ritual in the air designed to catch the monster when it dove at him. "Feces on a stick; it's trying to determine the area of effect?"

The whale was slowing down, shifting its angle as it saw that its long-range attacks were ineffectual. A small whirlpool formed above its head, opening a space for its blowhole to gasp in a huge amount of air. Then the world **thrummed** as its song filled the air, hitting him with the echolocation spell it had marked him with once before.

E~é-E-eáe!

"*Gah*! My ears, you brute. Know what? *Ee-woo*, right back 'atcha!"

Skill offered: Taunting Echo (Beginner VIII). Turn the words, or in some cases the sounds, of your enemies against them, enraging them and causing all of their attention to focus on you for 10+skill level-

"*Dismiss*."

Feeling as though his brain were rattling around in his skull, Joe clapped his hands to the side of his head as the disorienting effect was compounded by his Magical Synesthesia alerting him to the active effects rolling over his body. Forcing himself to drag his attention back to the guardian, the Ritualist looked on in time to see the whale flicking its tail, heaving a volume of water out of the cascade that could flood a town. It was charging at him now, no longer content with lurking alongside the falls.

Joe was running *long* before the creature punched right through his ritual cluster–knowing it would have practically no effect–and was hidden for a bare moment by the cloud of steam generated by all the water pumping through it.

The nearly perfectly round front of the creature's head impacted the ground like a battering ram, sending tons of earthen material scattering into the air, as though the ground had liquefied and formed its own tides. Joe's steps became unstable as the tremors caught up to him, his ankle rolling underneath him, though he caught the motion and slid to his knees before pushing himself to keep going. "Abyss, lost all my momentum-"

An arc of compressed fluid **flitted** above him, at the perfect height to have cleaved him in half had he been fully upright, making him realize that his Dexterity *hadn't* failed him. His Luck had intervened to save him.

Skill offered: Not so Slippery When Wet (Journeyman V). Tired of falling just because you're on treacherous terrain? This skill greatly improves traction when on-

"*Ignore*!" Realizing he was incredibly rusty when it came to direct combat, Joe started pushing his skills harder, trying to use more than one of them at a time, like a Novice combatant. His Mana Dominion sprang up in full force around him, Coalescent Fusion taking the cloud of power and turning it into an endless weave of threads. The next ranged attacks struck the outer edge of the scope of his power, the sensation traveling back to him faster than the strike could. Joe leaned to the side, letting the bolt pass by his head so close that it clipped off the tip of his ear.

"You're lucky I'm not an Elf, or that'd be enough to make me declare a blood feud and hunt you every time you respawned!" he shouted in a half-panicked tone as his world became motion, dodging, ducking, diving, and dipping, all before dodging again. This cycle continued for a few heartbeats, the margin for error shrinking as the whale got back in the air and swam toward him all the faster. Joe reached forward with his power, activating the next ritual cluster in sequence.

It was yet another Air Fryer cluster, as this had been the only one to show its effectiveness against the whale's long-range attacks, even if it *had* failed to do even a single point of damage to the gargantuan body of what could only be called a Raid Boss. Just as Joe passed its maximum range, he fully empowered the core of the cluster, and the Ritual of Abrasive Momentum snapped into place behind him. Immediately, dozens of detonations rang out as various attacks were converted to steam, and he pivoted hard to the right, sprinting at his most-distant setup.

"Come on, follow the leader," he half-prayed as the whale reached the steamy edge of his secondary cluster. Though it seemed to hesitate ever so slightly, it still burst straight through the area of effect. Joe was only able to discern this fact due to a mountain range of steam being born from the conversion of thousands of gallons of water in an instant, now hiding the monster from sight.

Even as the meadow was cloaked by the outpouring haze, Joe pumped his legs harder, fists clenched triumphantly as he threw himself forward. "That's right, nothing I can do will hurt you. No reason to be worried...!"

Conversely, as the onrushing condensation washed over him, Joe did his best not to suck in the scalding air as it cooked the surface of his body, forming welts and blisters wherever exposed skin could be found. Completely reliant on memory, Joe rushed forward, eyes screwed tightly shut and holding his breath. A buzzing sound just to the right of himself was the only warning he got before white-hot pain nearly caused him to falter. A chunk of his deltoid was sliced clean off in a perfect half-circle where the water had passed through, only for the steam to boil the open wound and cauterize it twice as painfully as if he'd just used fire.

A low groan escaped his clenched mouth, but the Ritualist didn't stop running. His extended mana touched on his final setup, and he adjusted his course incrementally so as to rush straight at it. After passing his first ritual, there were only another fifty feet to the full cluster he was after. Joe reached the final Air Fryer cluster, his last hope, and pivoted in place, left hand extended in preparation even as his right dangled uselessly at his side. "Here we go!"

Adrenaline helped to numb the pain of the wounds covering his body, and the air had rapidly cooled after the initial burst. Still, his vision was completely blocked by the newborn cloud, so the Ritualist needed to rely on his other senses to know when to act. The wind rushed over him as though a storm in the distance was brewing, a low whistle picking up and sending shivers down his spine as the fine hairs on his arms stood on end. A veritable wall crashed against the outer reaches of his Mana Dominion, the whale picking up speed as its echolocation revealed its unmoving target.

Four beast vellums disintegrated as the rituals inscribed on them were activated, the rituals now hanging in the open air. A harsh **hiss** drowned out all other noise as yet another steam burst rose from the vast body–still dangerous, though far less so than the first two iterations had been. Even so, the whale only sped up, both from its own efforts as well as the third stack of the Ritual of Haste taking effect.

Much quicker on his feet, thanks to having the same benefit, Joe bunched the muscles in his legs, activating Omnivault without mana and shooting to the side, still not out of range of the battering ram of a head coming at him, but no longer directly in its path.

As soon as his toes brushed the ground, he pushed off as hard as he could once more, non-damaged arm fully extended in front of him as though he were going for a flying tackle. Steam washed over him, then Joe found himself falling into a pool of water that somehow yanked him out of the way of the whale itself–it was using the final few hundred gallons surrounding its body to move and hadn't been able to devote any to an attack.

The Ritualist passed directly by the whale's eye, and for a brief moment, they stared at each other, their own confusion mirrored in the other's gaze. Then he was past, and the creature was cratering the ground with its face.

Skill offered: Depths Perception (Beginner I). Rivers, lakes, and oceans are filled with all manner of creatures that want to eat you. If you can see them first, you have a better chance of keeping your body parts to yourself. This skill-

"*Is ignored*!" The Ritualist's words were released as a stream of bubbles as he traveled along the entire forty-meter-long crystalline body, only to be unceremoniously tossed out of the enveloping water to bounce and tumble along the ground.

Thankfully, even with his much-reduced Characteristics, the terrain simply wasn't sturdy enough to cause any real damage. As soon as Joe could manage to halt himself, he pulled himself up and scrambled through the steam with his extended mana to find the ritual he'd passed on his way to the cluster: the celestial-aligned Ritual of Torrent.

He was almost too late, as the whale was already yet painfully slowly lifting itself airborne. With a scream of exultation, Joe *slammed* power into the ritual.

**Thwupp.*

The scene around him shifted as if he'd been at the epicenter of a depth charge, steam collapsing to the center point of the ritual, even as the flooded terrain dried in an instant. A ground-level whirlpool clawed at every drop of free moisture in the area, extending out a dozen feet, scores, then over a hundred before Joe stopped watching it so carefully: his goal had already been achieved.

Any water that had been following after the guardian was yanked into the bottomless pit that was the ritual's subdimensional fluid storage. The stream of water the whale had been using to maintain a connection to the cascade was diverted, pulled in, and snipped apart, causing the airborne whale to drop to the ground with an earth-shaking impact, its own noises of confusion adding to the cacophony only after it had bounced and settled into place.

“Without a constant source of liquid, you're just another beached whale.” Joe's ritual orbs shot into the air around him, leveled at the monster's face. As if to prove him wrong, a jet of water lanced out—but the Ritualist didn't even flinch. As soon as the attack extended past the whale's direct influence, his ritual diverted and absorbed it before it could even moisten his clothes.

“Nice try, but now it's *finally* my turn.”

CHAPTER EIGHTEEN

Plink!

Damage dealt: 1.

"Why's even your *eye* impossible to crack?" Joe roared his frustration at the whale as his ritual orbs bounced off of its bone-dry crystalline eyelid, finding no purchase and dealing practically no damage.

The crystalline whale wasn't simply laying around and taking the hits; it was thrashing about, the thin layer of water clinging to its bulbous body barely enough to keep it from sinking into the ground. Now that its connection to the cascade had been severed, it couldn't float and was all but wallowing in the mud it was creating and churning up as it tried to get close enough to crush Joe, whose ritual orbs ineffectually bounced off its diamond-hard body.

Having known that its head was likely unbreakable for his current weapons, the Ritualist had started by moving toward what should've been an obvious weak point, but as soon as he'd begun attacking its eye, a transparent layer of crystal eyelid had blinked down. The creature glared at him as Joe's Ritual Orb of Intelligence attempted to drill into the sensory organ, only to kick up sparks as it began eating away at its own durability. "Abyss, this isn't working."

Dancing back and away to avoid the creature as it tried to roll onto him, Joe began directing his orbs along the creature's flank, up and down with each of his six precisely controlled weapons. They **clicked*, **popped*, or **boinked** away without fail, causing Joe's anxiety to rapidly ramp up as he worked over the entire front of its body and couldn't punch through. Even the individual points of damage were healed from the creature's natural regeneration, leaving it as pristine and undamaged as when he'd first arrived at the Ambiguous Cascade.

"At this rate, I'll kill it... never." Joe risked looking back at the waterfall, eyes darting to the Ritual of Torrent still active and awaiting the input of additional fluids. "Crazy how much water that thing drank down. How much does it need to release its reservoir? A lake?"

Then he was struck by an idea and hopped away from the fins slapping at him, only to miss and send dirt and gravel flying. "Maybe I can't kill it. But I don't *need* to kill it in order to capture the place of power, do I?"

He took a few steps closer to the cascade, only for the whale to begin losing its mind. It heaved itself sideways, its bulk crushing the ground more efficiently than any steamroller could hope to mimic. A narrow jet of water sliced through the air toward him, not quite the torso-thick, hyper-pressurized beam that had carved the battlefield up, but still deadly dangerous. Joe dodged to the side, but as it turned out... that was unnecessary.

As soon as the water left the direct influence and control of the guardian, it *bent* midair and vanished into the ever-thirsty depths of the Ritual of Torrent, as though the magic had a water-specific magnetism to it.

"You want me focused on you? Ya *sure* about that? Fine! Let's exhaust all options before doing what I came here for." Rather peeved at the attack, especially as he'd just been considering leaving the whale alone and letting it slowly make its way back to the cascade, Joe circled around and resumed pounding on the whale, searching for any place he could deal more than a single point of damage per hit.

The blowhole seemed promising, but as soon as his first orb started whistling through the air, the creature closed itself up tight. Seeing as he had no idea how long the creature could last between breaths, after a few exploratory strikes, Joe moved on. He tried the fins, then along the tail, dodging the fluke tips by a hair's breadth when the monster suddenly twisted and tried to strike at him.

"Ah, right, those are *sharp*." He eyed the trailing edge of the fluke, appreciating how the crystalline structure narrowed down to an *incredibly* fine point that could easily outperform sharpened obsidian. "You know... now that I think about it, crystal structures are supposed to be surprisingly fragile at sharp angles. Flat surfaces have an extremely perfect matrix, but the *edge* of the facet?"

The tail whipped back and forth, but the sheer size of the creature made its movements easy to predict. Skirting around the swings, Joe began impacting along the tail, doing his best to beat on the trailing edge of the fluke by coming down perpendicular instead of letting his orbs run along the beyond-razor-sharp crystal. His Ritual Orb of Strength came down and struck with a ringing retort.

Damage dealt: 373.

Eee~wwoooo!

The whale let out a deep bellow, sending Joe stumbling as his eardrums shivered out of sync with the rest of his body. Its fluke, which had been swinging back and forth in an attempt to slice him apart, began lifting and slapping down. The *leading* edge was rounded and thick, whereas the *trailing* was sharp, allowing for it to strike the ground like a crowbar being **thunked** into the soil. Seeing as even this small section of the monster's overall body easily weighed multiple tons, it was an effective deterrent as Joe attempted to get close.

"This thing has to have tens of thousands of health points,

and even if its regeneration is slow, since it's not fleshy, wearing it down isn't going to be possible with my weapons alone." Just then, Joe landed a lucky strike with his Ritual Orb of Intelligence, the spinning tip of the weapon digging deep into the notch of the fluke.

Critical hit! Damage dealt: 387 piercing!

"Ahhh, so is *that* your weak point... or was it just a fluke?" Joe's grin could've put the Cheshire Cat to shame at that moment, as a plan began forming. Lifting a hand, he brought his Ritual Orb of Constitution to hover over it, then focused on activating Planar Shift. Over the next couple of seconds, Morsum the pseudo-lich appeared around his orb, dry, elongated teeth working as the severed head tried to bite anything around it.

"*Moorr~sum.*" Somehow that single word seemed to hold a symphony of meaning, every part of the subtext all but screaming that the creature was hungry. Joe spun the orb, and the pseudo-lich's eyes literally lit up as it saw the massive creature only a dozen feet away.

A flick of his wrist sent the summon zipping through the air at the notch, everything seeming to align perfectly as its mouth went wide.

Crunch.

"M-morsum?" Much to both of their disappointment, the teeth failed to find purchase in the crystalline body, leaving the undead head gnawing uselessly on the tail. In the next moment, the whale flicked its limb back and forth, cleanly bisecting Morsum and directly unsummoning it.

"Never gonna hear the end of *that.*" The Ritualist grumbled as the whale trumpeted in victory, likely having gotten a system of notification that it had managed to slay an intruder.

It began rocking itself back and forth, barely able to squeeze its body down, but ever so slightly undulating closer toward the cascade—seemingly having decided against allowing the Ritualist to whale on it without being able to fight with its full arsenal. Joe wasn't certain what its range was for manipulating the water, but he certainly wasn't about to let the monster get close without either putting it down, or at the bare minimum, finishing this portion of his quest.

"Last try!" Pulling out his second of three prepared Stormwell ritual clusters, Joe tossed the beast vellums forward. He guided them through the air with his mana threads, activating them just a few feet ahead of the fluke's current position. Ambient power began swirling into the Expert-ranked ritual, its supplementary diagrams preparing themselves for activation alongside the core of the cluster.

Just then, the whale unbent slightly, lurching forward several feet before beginning the process of wiggling into an inchworm position again. Wincing at what he knew was coming, Joe realized his rituals would be out of position if he didn't do something somewhat drastic. His orbs shot forward as though launched from a ballista, slamming one after another into the whale's fluke notch.

The creature stiffened as though just now realizing he was still alive, then thrashed at him in hopes that the human was close enough to turn into 'Joe divided by two'.

Sadly, for the whale, the intent to hit him with an attack was all the Ritualist needed. He'd been holding back the passive portion of his Haunting Shadows spell to this point, but now allowed it to take effect, even knowing it would have a slight impact on the mana around him.

**Slap*!*

Shadow-Joe appeared in front of the whale's snout and delivered a contemptuous, massively damaging, open-palm slap across its face. Just as had happened before, the monster's utter shock at having taken even modest damage from an attack on its otherwise impervious front caused it to freeze up completely —whether in pain or indignation, there was no way for the Ritualist to know for sure.

"Ha! Your body might say 'you can't hurt me', but your face says 'stop hitting me'!" All around Joe, a slight haze from turbulent mana was accumulating, only to be forcefully drawn in by the Stormwell cluster, giving it just enough power for the core ritual to activate. An enormous amount of force imploded directly onto the notch of the fluke, the concussive blast being amplified by the supporting rituals... and dealing *way* more damage than he'd been expecting.

Cracks spiderwebbed across the whale's body like lightning trapped in crystal, the stunning effect of the rituals managing to take hold and keep the whale locked in place for several precious seconds. A secondary implosion accelerated toward the notch, managing to land directly on the trailing edge of the fluke as the whale resumed moving, *immediately* doing its best to escape the incredibly damaging concussive blows on its weakest point. Unfortunately for it, the whale was again stunned as a second convergence landed, deepening the cracks into huge fissures.

Lashing out with his ritual orbs, Joe found that the visible damage was actually contained beneath the surface of its body, seeing as his orbs bounced off a nearly invisible surface layer that still had yet to be blemished. The whale began trying to thrash yet again, and to the Ritualist's dismay, it appeared that the cluster was only slowly recovering enough power from the ambient mana to collapse again. At this rate, it would be a handful of seconds, and the creature would escape.

Crouching down, Joe lightly activated Omnivault, bouncing in place and getting close enough to allow a secondary Haunting Shadow to form as he narrowly avoided the humming edge of the fluke. Mana practically *erupted* from him, giving him a second turbulent mana warp field effect around his body that extended for several paces in every direction. But it was enough—the warp pulled away from him, constantly regenerating, yet leaving him practically tethered to the ritual dozens of feet below him. The Stormwell struck once more... yet the whale lived.

"What's it gonna *take* to-"

The next thing Joe remembered was blinking slowly. His body was awkwardly dug into the dirt, hundreds of feet away from the monster. His ears were ringing, his vision dancing with multiple overlays of the world around him. Having trained to ignore pain as much as possible, the Ritualist forced his senses to work with a modicum of their normal functionality and stared through rapidly tunneling vision at the crystalline creature in the distance. Only then did he realize his ears had fixed themselves, and the ringing he was hearing was actually a resonant frequency.

**Slap*!*

A crisp sound drowned out the crescendo of tortured gemstones... and the whale fell apart.

It didn't burst, or explode. Instead, its crystalline flesh split along every fault line that had been formed, and the massive body disintegrated into a small hill of shards.

Congratulations! You have slain an Artifact-rank monster in single combat!

Title gained: One Man Raid (Upgradable). You have accomplished a feat typically reserved for armies, entire battle groups, or at the bare minimum elite strike teams. By defeating an Artifact-rank monster entirely on your own, you have proven to the world that you hold the power to contend with the army of an unprepared nation.

Effect:

1. *When you personally deliver the final blow to any monster of the Artifact rank or above, loot quantity and quality increases by 5%. If you are fighting without any allies, excluding summoned creatures, this bonus increases to 10%.*
2. *While engaged in combat against monsters of the*
    a. *Artifact rank: you ignore 10% of their armor.*
    b. *Legendary rank: you ignore 5% of their armor.*
    c. *Mythic rank: you ignore 2.5% of their armor.*

These bonuses are doubled if you are engaged in solo combat.

To upgrade this title, defeat a Legendary-rank monster or above in solo combat.

"That's cool and all, but... how?" Joe flinched back as the

Stormwell reached a reactivation point once more, and the mana detonated, sending a small pile of shards scattering across the meadow. He stumbled toward the cluster, reaching out and deactivating it as soon as he came within range. Then, before anything else could grab his attention, the Ritualist opened his combat logs.

Mana-Shockwave Burst deals 418 blunt damage.

Magical critical hit! Damage increased by 500%!

Pressure Ring deals (306 blunt damage. 342 blunt damage. 383 blunt damage …)

Concussive Percussion has inflicted 'vulnerability to stun' on Celestial Crystal Whale.

Mana Randomizer has randomized a localized pocket of mana into earth-aspected mana. Celestial Crystal whale is unaffected.

Mana-Shockwave Burst deals 517 blunt damage.

Magical critical hit! Damage increased by 500%!

Pressure Ring deals (603 blunt damage. 676 blunt damage. 757 blunt damage …)

Concussive Percussion has inflicted 'vulnerability to stun' on Celestial Crystal Whale.

Mana Randomizer has randomized a localized pocket of mana into vibration/sound-aspected mana. Celestial Crystal Whale is inflicted with vulnerability to blunt damage!

Mana-Shockwave Burst deals 494 blunt damage. Celestial Crystal Whale has resonated with the Mana-Shockwave Burst! Damage increased 1000%!

Celestial Crystal Whale's song peals out! You have taken 995 sonic damage!

Pressure Ring deals (1,192 blunt damage. 1,335 blunt damage. 1,495 blunt damage …)

Haunting Shadows deals 616 damage!

You have slain a Celestial Crystal Whale!

"That Pressure Ring ritual was doing *work.*" Joe counted the iterations, realizing it had struck the whale right on its weak spot each second it had been active, every hit increasing the damage of the next one by exactly twelve percent. "Well, all I can say is that it works as advertised. Probably would've been completely ineffective if it hadn't been positioned exactly on that crit point. I got *real* lucky there."

Reviewing his combat had been a nice diversion as Joe moved closer to the mound of glimmering gemstones, seeing as roughly a third of his health had been eradicated by the sonic wave emitting from the whale. "Ow... my body. Seriously, I *just* healed myself back up. Maybe after this, I spend some time on Jotunheim and get Cleocatra to help me fix myself. I've got a whole bunch of rewards waiting, and maybe I'll be able to watch her work and repli-cat it without her."

Reaching for one of the whale shards, Joe picked it up with great interest, wondering what the system would have to say about it. Just as he pulled it into the air, it slipped from his grasp, his blood causing the surface to turn practically frictionless as its uncannily sharp edges flayed off the surface of his skin.

Damage received: 25 slashing. Debuff gained: Minor bleeding. -4 health per second.

"Not exactly what I meant when I said I wanted system information. Guess I won't be opening that sushi bar after all." Seeing as he hadn't been able to maintain a grip on the shard, it hadn't registered as an item he'd gained. "You know what? It doesn't even matter. It's all aspects in the end. Nothing makes the pain feel better than rewards and loot!"

His Mana Dominion grasped his Ascendant Matrix skill, the duo working together to create a massive, intricate framework in mere moments. Just as he prepared to pour mana into the lattice, the Ritualist froze up, realizing that there was a good chance of gaining at least Artifact-rank aspects from this pile. "I don't have a properly ranked aspect jar on me. There's no way I'm going to be okay losing at least a tenth of the potential aspects, but that's exactly what's going to happen if I just store them in my codpiece. Potentially even more."

Unfortunately, he didn't have another option, so he let his mana surge—and paused once more. "*Wa~ait* a second. The whale should've dropped a core as well, right? I can just turn *that* into a jar!"

The blindingly bluish-white light of the Ascendant Matrix faded away, leaving the world around him cast in bright violet. Reaching out to the Rituals of Glimmering around him, Joe snuffed them out one after another, until only the more distant versions were still operating. Then he scanned along the huge carcass, lips curling into a smile as he saw one section brightly lit from within. "Almost missed that! I guess these shards must get more translucent or even opaque the farther down they go. Wild."

Slowly blinking, the Ritualist realized he may have taken more of a blow to the head than he'd thought. Swirling his hand around, he called his ritual orbs up to begin orbiting around him, then he sent them forward as a unit, slowly pushing the pile of shards out of the way as he dug for the core. The crystalline sounds were fun to hear, sort of like sweeping away a load of broken glass, but with a deeper tolling to it. "Maybe kind of like wind chimes? The big ones? Wonder if I should scoop some of this up for other crafters to work with..."

The edges of his orbs vanished, and he carelessly stepped forward to follow after them, only for a pinky-sized fragment slice right through the sole of his shoe and into his foot. "*Yeowch*!"

CHAPTER NINETEEN

He hopped backward, staring down at the shard in his foot even as drops of blood fell from it, pattering across the surface of the ruined landscape like rain. "Abyss, how am I supposed to grab that and pull it out without ripping my hand open?"

After a long few moments of deliberation, he pulled his inscription tool, a mana-and-aspect-made implement, then created another one, and used the pair like a set of chopsticks to grip the fragment and yank it out. It slid away easily, falling to the ground even as blood welled out of the hole in his already-self-repairing boot. Far more carefully, he began picking his way through the deadly mound, using his ritual orbs to scrape the ground clear in front of him wherever he couldn't find a safe location to place his boot.

After *far* longer than he had expected it to take, Joe had the core of the whale rolling toward him, the bar of his Ritual Orb of Strength guiding it along as it rolled across the flattened terrain. He carefully checked it for any slivers of the razor-sharp carcass, only relaxing after he picked it up without suffering any further damage.

"Seriously, it's been dead for a while, and it's *still* trying to kill me... I guess I can respect that." Surrounded as he was on all sides by shards, with only a narrow path behind him remaining clear, Joe decided to experiment with his Mana Dominion. He extended his Ascendant Matrix once more, though this time he created it in a shape he'd never tried before: essentially a huge donut with his body standing in the hole.

He lifted the Artifact-rank core, keeping the brilliantly orange sphere centered on his palm, even as a shallow puddle of his blood formed around its base. Pulling out a smattering of lower-ranked aspect jars, Joe put them in position around his feet, not too worried about losing any excess they couldn't contain. Then he allowed his mana to flood the matrix around him, and the world erupted in a kaleidoscope of color reflected and refracted by the unaffected shards outside his range.

As always, a thick layer of dark gray poured out first from the materials being reduced, Trash aspects easily falling apart and being subsumed. Joe didn't even bother having a jar for those, seeing as he could literally work on reducing the *air* and pull trash out of it. Light gray followed, Damaged aspects just as useless in his mind as the lesser variant. Finally, Common aspects started pouring in, a brilliant white that caused the meadow and cascade to light up as though a massive disco ball had arrived on the scene.

Far less than the first three variants, but still a massive quantity due to the sheer amount of shards breaking down, Uncommon aspects filled the world with silvery light. The process sped up at that moment, light blue Rare aspects quickly followed by a Special type—crystalline aspects—which Joe hadn't seen since devoting his previous batch to the Pyramid of Panacea's creation. Indigo Unique was next, nearly matching the Ritual of Glimmering's violet light and creating a shifting monochrome as the two variants battled it out.

Lastly, finally, the world was washed with neon orange light that poured in through the lattice. Unlike the other aspects, which Joe simply trusted to arrive at their destination safely, he actively controlled the Artifact-ranked aspects, surrounding the core in his hand and using his myriad mana threads to pack the powerful aspects inside. As per usual, it was a difficult task, the practically royal version of aspects fighting against doing anything other than what they wanted. Even with his peak Master-rank Mana Dominion, pushing the aspects into place felt like stirring peanut butter with a matchstick.

Still, progress was progress, and since he was finally able to take an active role in the process, the core converted into a jar easily *forty percent* faster than he'd ever managed when merely bathing a core in power and applying pressure from the outside. As the coloration shifted slightly, and the system notified him of his success, Joe noted an unexpected benefit with a glint in his eye. "Would you look at that...? Faster conversion also used fewer total aspects to create the jar. The strong get stronger faster. Love it."

His reduction of the shards around him picked up speed, and the comparatively few orange aspects flooded into the newly created jar without any loss whatsoever. The Ritualist was pleased to note that it seemed his new title was already coming into effect, as each shard was absolutely *squeezed* of any potency, generating what he assumed–going by his title's effects–would be an additional ten percent total aspects, since he had not *only* dealt the final blow to the whale but had also fought without allies and therefore boosted the bonuses it provided.

Soon the area around him was fully cleared of fragments, even after having extended the range of his Ascendant Matrix a few inches into the ground to capture any of the incredibly sharp objects that had penetrated through the surface. As he moved to the next section of the whale, he considered the fight: how it had gone, what could've happened, and how he needed to change his tactics going forward.

"Imagine if I'd been some kind of melee class and managed to punch this thing to death." Joe shook his head, his mind going to his *own* titular effect of detonating his mana pool on death. "Being at close range when this thing shattered would've shredded me into less than pasty chum. These clusters are potent, but... when I first ran into this thing, it was *literally* impossible for me to win against."

"I guess the fact of the matter remains that, no matter how high my Characteristics go, my class is one that requires not only forethought but *preparation.* Rituals require time to be created, to set up for maximum potency." He let his thoughts wander for a moment, watching the trailing aspects burn through the air before entering his jars or spatial storage. "Fighting an unknown enemy just goes to show that lack of knowledge is practically a guaranteed defeat, even with what should've been enough power to tackle a creature at this threat level without too many concerns."

Joe looked at the positives in the situation, taking a deep breath and slowly bobbing his head. "I guess the only real way to act as a mobile Combat Ritualist is to create a middle ground. Have enough rituals, a ton of variations, through all sorts of different tiers, to be able to deal with any threat I come across. Haa... the likelihood of beating everything I come across is low, of course, since this monster proved that I haven't seen anything close to all of the niche resistances and immunities I'll need to find a way to counter."

The corners of his lips shifted upward, ever so slightly, as his eyes reflected the final motes of orange light being slurped into his new jar. "I guess that's the whole point of it all, though, isn't it? Where's the fun in fighting the same things over and over? What was the requirement for upgrading my new title? Soloing a Legendary creature? Grandmaster tier? Mmm. Maybe I should start planning for *that* next."

All too soon, the last shards in the pile had been fully reduced, and the influx of crafting materials came to an end. Off in the distance, he could see small points of reflected light, the fragments that had been scattered before he managed to turn off his rituals, but between his wounds and overall exhaustion, he decided against carefully sweeping the area. "We'll just leave those as a fun surprise for anyone who finds this place later. Call it a perception check. Will they find the pieces with their eyes or their feet, like I did?"

Skill offered: Strategic Trapping (Expert II). It's pretty rare for people to leave Master-rank materials scattered around in order to potentially damage someone in the far-distant future, but you are the sort of person who thinks ahead! As the first person to find a location and then set traps in it, you are setting the bar high for any future adventurers who want to witness the wonders of the Ambiguous Cascade while remaining intact-

"Skip. Ignore." Seeing the thoughts of the system laid bare, Joe hesitated for a few moments, torn between collecting the fragments and capturing the place of power. After taking a step and listening to the **squelching** of blood collecting in his repaired boot, he made his decision. "Yeah, it's time to get out of here."

As he approached the falls, Joe slowed down and eyed the mile-wide, laminar stream suspiciously. Just because he had defeated one whale didn't mean there wasn't something else lurking in the depths, and he didn't want to be caught unprepared. Still, the Ritual of the Underbridge was actively working on the falls, and the disruption should've been enough to antagonize anything else that would come after him.

"Now, where do I need to go, *exactly*?" The Ritualist's vision shifted slightly, the omnipresent violet glimmering having a strand of red appear and travel in a nearly perfect straight line into the water, no shifts or bends to indicate a required change in elevation. "Directly ahead. I wonder what this place was meant to test? Swimming abilities, or perhaps there was a chain quest leading someone here after acquiring a ton of gear or equipment that would let them resist being dragged by the flow?"

The fact that this place was *still* undiscovered after more than a billion people had been dropped onto the planet meant it should've been practically impossible to get to without a quest. Even 'Germinate the Cutting' didn't give Joe the tools he needed to find, survive, and take over the places of power–it merely informed him that they existed. Since the completion of the quest would be enough to unleash the World Boss on Midgard, he thought it was a reasonable assumption that this quest was meant to spawn dozens of offshoot tasks.

"I *love* that I can skip all that malarkey," he chuckled to himself as he looked to the sky and began aligning a Ritual of Torrent with the celestial bodies. When he was done, he pulled out a second beast vellum and followed the circumference of the cascade for fifty feet, carefully setting up the next ritual. "Let's see if this curtain trick pans out."

He moved to the center point between the two rituals, his Mana Dominion extending to either side of him far enough that he could directly interact with the activation portions. Preparing himself to move, Joe crouched like a runner at the starting line and activated both rituals simultaneously.

Immediately the flow of the cascade shifted, an invisible suction yanking the waterfall sideways. The liquid curled and curved, parting in front of him and creating a teardrop-shaped corridor twenty-five feet long. Fifty. A hundred... it still wasn't enough. The red thread went deeper, and Joe fully understood that the torrential downpour outside the range of his rituals would act like a guillotine, should he throw himself headlong into it in a vain attempt to reach whatever was on the other side.

With the sheer amount of fluid the rituals were absorbing, Joe only had a few seconds to make a decision before the water resumed its normal course once more. "I've got only two more of these... hope this works!"

Pulling out another vellum, he flicked his wrist and coated the surface in his mana threads, managing to turn the floppy material into a stiff, rectangular card. Fully relying on his Dexterity, as he didn't have any skills applicable to throwing weapons, Joe whipped the 'card' forward, pumping power into it just before it left the maximum range of his mana. It continued forward a dozen feet before the vellum burst, the ritual activating in place and carving out a new pocket of air.

"Come on, come on..." While the ritual had been traveling,

Joe was wrapping the next one around his Ritual Orb of Intelligence, murmuring nonsensically to himself, "Technically my Ritual Orb of *Light* Intelligence. Just doesn't flow off the tongue as well. I've got... *seconds* at best."

After a momentary hesitation, he reached for his chest, activating the release mechanism of his inhibitor gear. Power flooded into him, no longer held back in order to conform to the Mortal Limit imposed by Midgard. "Not going to be enough, otherwise. Time to do something irresponsible. Hope I don't accidentally break the planet!"

Putting everything he had into his first leap, Joe shoved off the edge of the cascade, just as the first two of his rituals faltered.

The world *detonated* behind him.

Though he wasn't looking, he could still feel the effect his unrestrained leap had on the meadow behind him. The ground peeled open in a widening cone-shaped trench, trees in the distance turned into woodchips that pelted their neighbors, before those, too, were destroyed. Yet even as the system flashed warnings at him, and the turbulent mana around his body thickened dangerously, Joe focused forward.

The air around him rippled in concentric rings, the cascade around him bulging out as he punched through the sound barrier and caused a shockwave that rebounded off the tunnel he'd carved. As the falling water in front of him approached in less time than it takes to blink, he broke the sound barrier again—achieving Mach two, thanks to the practically empty-of-mana planet being unable to resist his movements. He plunged into the flowing fluid, carving through it in a straight line without being affected for the first full second.

He knew it was coming. Just as gravity began reasserting itself, the water around him exploding into steam and creating a cavitation bubble, he activated the ritual attached to his orb and sent it forward, flashing into the depths ahead of him... and *up*. Water struck his back, and he was shoved downward—only for the pressure on him to vanish as the ritual activated and yanked the water up and into itself.

Just ahead of him loomed a thin pillar, black against deep violet and only visible thanks to his fully restored Karmic Perception. Spinning in place, Joe got his feet under him and activated Omnivault a second time. He pushed against the surface of the water and used it as a stable platform, thanks to the traits the skill had gained when he mastered it. Zipping up through the suddenly empty cavern as the water cascaded around him, Joe quickly found himself bypassing the top of the rock spire.

His Ritual Orb of Strength jumped off his bandolier, and Joe felt his shoulder muscles strain as he yanked on the suddenly stationary weapon to arrest his momentum. He fell to the tip of the pillar, landing perfectly without falling, thanks to his all-too-potent Dialectic Dexterity. "You know what? I'm going to have to amend my previous thoughts. It *does* matter how high my Characteristics go. No matter how much I want it to be, sometimes magic *isn't* the best or only solution."

Magical Synesthesia began whispering about the incredibly potent water-aspected mana contained in the pillar he was standing on. As far as Joe could tell, now that he was up close, it wasn't even stone under his feet, but *solid water*. Not ice, but some form of super-compressed, condensed heavy fluid that was dense enough to act like a steel bar. "Huh. This is the first of the three I've taken that actually is a *literal* place of power, instead of just something that's messing with the mana. Abyss, no time!"

There was no button he could press to claim that he captured the location. Once again, likely whatever chain quest would have brought him here would've given him the tools to do so, but happily Joe had a secondary option. Pulling out a ritual tile, which felt oddly nostalgic now that he was using vellum to contain his potent diagrams, he began building a simple shrine to Occultatum.

Above him, the cascade surged downward suddenly, his

ritual having captured the maximum amount of water it could. The Ritualist sucked in a deep breath, preparing to do his best to hold out, only for a half-laugh to startle out of him as the secondary portion of the ritual, which he hadn't yet seen, activated. The influx of fluid flowing into the ritual reversed, a torrent of water—which surely gave this ritual its namesake—blasting up with enough force that it directly countered the cascade itself. The opposing force created a giant watery umbrella over Joe that diverted the flow down and around him—buying a few precious seconds.

A shrine was slowly forming, faster than anyone could build by hand but too slow to ensure his capturing of the location. Joe snapped his fingers as he remembered the benefit his Rituarchitect class had gained at level fifteen, 'Near-Instant Completion'. "Invest additional resources and mana to reduce the amount of time necessary for completing the build. Instantly completing a structure means the mana cost will be doubled, with an additional fifty percent of the highest-rarity aspect—who *cares* about the cost? Do it!"

Light blue aspects burst out of him in a cloud, yanked into the forming structure and causing the foundation to appear fast enough that it displaced the air around it. Walls slammed into being, ramrod straight. The roof of the shrine formed and connected to the walls as though stapled in place. With the ritual complete, Joe slapped a hand down on the surface and sent his panicked thoughts through to the deity on the other side.

"I claim this shrine for Tatum!"

Immediately, the structure of the shrine shifted, the roof taking the form of an open book, dozens of other minor changes that appeared only ornamental to him taking place. With his hand still on the diminutive structure, the Ritualist called out once more, "Place of power, Tatum! I capture it!"

For a long second, nothing happened. Then a drop of water landed on his head, and Joe looked up to see a veritable wall of water only a few dozen feet above his head rushing toward him.

The shrine lit up, the entirety of its surface flashing a deep blue as power pulsed in from the pillar it was precariously placed upon. Joe heard a notification from the system, but he didn't have even a moment to read it. A half-laughed shout burst from his lips, "Good enough for me!"

As an ocean's worth of water struck, and Joe vanished—having used the fast travel system to teleport away instead of being swept to a watery grave.

CHAPTER TWENTY

Moving *very* slowly, Joe turned to look away from the shrine and to the edge of the Forest of Chlorophyll Chaos that had creeped closer in less than a day. He hadn't expected to see the Ambiguous Cascade above the forest, as he had no idea where its true location might be, but a part of him had been expecting to see *some* part of the waterfall that appeared to extend into low orbit. After a few seconds of observation, he carefully exhaled and decided to focus on the positives of the situation.

"Well, it doesn't look like I broke anything *too* permanently." He stood still in the shrine, not moving because he couldn't, but because he knew he *shouldn't.* Even turning his head ever so slightly had been a risk. The air around him was absolutely **thrumming** with turbulent mana, the multiple levels of warp he was creating causing the grass at the edge of the shrine to shift and mutate.

His right hand remained in place on the shrine, and the Ritualist finally began moving his left as though it had steel cables wrapped around it pulling against him—as slowly as he could *possibly* manage while still making progress. His inhibitor gear appeared in his cupped palm, pulled directly out of his spatial storage ring, before being gently pressed to his chest, the center button depressed, and he waited for the machinery to do the rest.

The metal tendrils extended from the central piece of the accessory as per usual, slithering around his joints and extending the embedded hypodermic needles. Joe started to breathe easier as he felt the prickling along his skin, only to tense up as alchemical fluid began beading along his skin. Tiny rivulets began dripping, and the Ritualist grumbled in low frustration as he realized the needles—while *prickling* him—had completely failed to penetrate. Shifting in discomfort was a mistake, as the sound of tortured metal rang out for a single moment, like a sharp scream from the accessory, and the tension around his limbs went slack.

"Don't tell me I just *broke* this." Joe wiggled back and forth, finding that the metal was now flexing like soft wire, buckling and bouncing with each movement. Slowly moving his arm away from his chest, he felt the brace around his elbow sag under its own weight and wobble uselessly. "Welp, looks like I just did the last thing I'll be able to do on Midgard for a while. At least it was good timing? Wouldn't want to finish the World Boss spawning quest at this moment anyway; I need to prep my Sect and build some superweapons to fight whatever pops up."

Taking a step away from the shrine and onto the meadow, Joe debated on whether he needed to leave the planet immediately or could function for a short while and take some time to practice moving without his inhibitor gear. His foot came down, and the ground complained, turning into packed dirt covered in a green syrup from where his boot had crushed the grass like a hydraulic press. Already halfway through his next step, Joe froze, his heart hammering as a system message flickered briefly into his vision before vanishing—a red window he was *positive* was the world warning him about his stats yet again.

"Take it easy, system," the Ritualist called in a calm, cajoling voice. "I wasn't ignoring your earlier warnings because they weren't important; I was just focused on jumping through the cascade."

He continued pacing around the shrine in slow motion, trying to get a handle on his strength so he didn't continue crushing absolutely everything in his path like a rampaging monster. By the tenth step, the grass underfoot wasn't reduced to goo, just a pulpy slurry.

Progress.

The system agreed with him, his tribulation effect coming into play immediately.

Skill offered: Pacifist's Pace (Beginner III). Few are those who seek to minimize the damage and destruction their basic movements can inflict on the world around them. Even fewer are those who follow through and maintain their peaceful ways permanently. Be it bugs or your good intentions, usually something is squashed. This skill helps you reduce all unintended damage you inflict and helps you maintain your peaceful ways by increasing the efficacy of stealth skills.

"Can't slap the ignore button fast enough." Joe chuckled a little too hard, causing a cloud of dust to form around his ankles as the ground vibrated with him. "Looks like I'm going to have to sit and wait for a while. Maybe I can take a couple extra risks on getting this under control if I let the levels of turbulent mana around me clear out some."

With utmost care, he lowered himself to the ground and shifted into a relaxed seated position. "No one around to accidentally hurt, no buildings to worry about breaking or monsters to mutate. Just me and a wide-open field I can practice in. Taking a break between rushing from one task to another never hurt anyone."

Skill offered: Gentle Touch (Novice I). A skill needed both for handling fragile artistry and your lady friends in-

"*Ig. Nore.* That's just rude. Novice *one*?" the Ritualist hissed as he closed his eyes and breathed deeply. "Just going to sit here for a little while and let the warped mana around me fade. Four levels means... what, four hours?"

It had been a while since he'd run into this issue, seeing as he hadn't been causing issues on Midgard for quite a while. After a short stint of pseudo meditation, he began to get antsy and decided to look through his combat logs from when he'd first been warned about generating turbulent mana around him.

"Ah, feces," the man grumbled as he looked at the warnings, "Twelve hours for the first... that's right, it doubles each time. Yeah, I'm not going to sit here for the next four days. Let's just leave."

The thought of getting back up and walking to the shrine over the next ten minutes so he didn't destroy anything accidentally caused Joe to *itch.* His eyes lit up as he remembered he had a different option, one that didn't require standing or any movement at all. "*Beam to Bifrost.*"

Immediately, his mana pool began sluicing away, and a deep grinding **thrum** filled the air as his location was practically broadcast to every last entity in the area. Joe's eyes cracked open as he swept his gaze around the area, hoping there wouldn't be anything foolish enough to throw itself at him while the mana field was rampaging around him with enough potency to blur him from sight. Ten seconds after the channeling of the spell began, power rushed to envelop him, only for the Ritualist to hold off and let it **click** into place, an instant-cast spell he could use later.

"Hmm. *Nothing* came over? Not even a normal creature?" Realizing this prairie was even emptier than he'd originally expected, Joe decided to do things the hard way. Pushing his fingers into the dirt, he slowly unfolded his legs and pushed himself into a plank position with his feet several inches off the ground. Once he was fully extended and parallel to the ground, he allowed his feet to come down and gently nudge the soil aside as he flowed upward inch by inch to a standing position. "I *knew* there was no good reason to practice yoga. Characteristics for the win."

Treating the planet as though it were a thin layer of ice over a frozen pond, Joe began walking back to the shrine with exaggerated care, distributing his weight with intentional control. With every twitch of a muscle or pull of a ligament, he started building a better understanding of how his body was affecting the area around him. "Quad Strength is absolutely the hardest to control. Technically, even walking is a movement technique, which means my body wants to *quadruple* the power I put into it. My Stoic Constitution plays into that, since my skin might as well be titanium for all the give it has. I'm just not getting the same tactile feedback I would be, were I weaker."

The only saving grace he had was the incredibly fine control his Dialectic Dexterity allowed him to exert, on top of his Karmic Perception allowing him to gauge the distance between the sole of his boot and the ground with immense precision. His Light Intelligence was zipping along, formulating equations for when he should stop moving with one leg and begin stepping forward, even if he didn't truly *feel* like he was on firm footing. Since every step on Midgard, even onto a boulder, felt as soft as sinking into mud, he was entirely reliant on planning out each movement.

"I can do this..." he egged himself on encouragingly. "My raw stats are the problem, but they're also the solution. Just need to figure out how to properly use my own strength."

Skill offered: Self-calibration (Journeyman II). You use your own Characteristics as reference points, devoting a portion of your thought process to continuously balancing your force and momentum in real time. Though self-calibration loses effectiveness if you are in an altered emotional state, such as being panicked, stunned, or-

"No." This time, the skill window froze for several seconds before fading away, as though it were surprised or offended that he'd turned it down. "Hey, don't be like that. I'm already doing exactly what that skill offers; why would I take up a slot for something only at the Journeyman rank that I can do *without* the skill? Just can't do it."

There was no response, which he greatly preferred, as his previous experiences had made him a bit gun shy toward the system getting into heated arguments over his viewpoints. That was how people got cursed, as he knew from personal experience.

Joe was inordinately pleased with himself when he finally returned to the shrine, reaching out and laying his hand on its surface without causing cracks to appear, whirlwinds to throw debris around, or, worst of all, earning the fifth layer of warp he was so worried about gaining. "There we go. From here, should I go back to the city of Towney McTownface? That's... no, that's a terrible idea. Someone will definitely force me to flinch and splatter them across the street accidentally. Accidentally for me, at least. On purpose for *them*, so they'd at least be getting what they wanted, but I'd still rather not cause an incident."

Going back to the capital city sounded like a terrible idea as well, as did visiting his duchy. There was no telling what the immense amount of turbulent mana he was dragging along with him might do to the crops, let alone the various animals they had gathered for milking. "Yeah... probably best to just head to Jotunheim and seek out Cleo. I don't mind gaining some more rewards after beating down a big boss like that whale. Abyss, now that I think of it, I went through all of that just for some crafting materials and an update to my quest."

Germinate the Cutting (Difficulty: Raid). You have captured three Places of Power in the Forest of Chlorophyll Chaos. Only one remains. Capturing any of them can give interesting benefits, and binding all four will germinate a force which has slumbered for centuries. One that may have been lost to time for a reason. Places of power captured: 3/4.

Reward: 1) Variable, depending on location. 2) Immediate access to The Cutting. (Major Raid). Recommended group level: 30+.

Reward gained: Control of the Ambiguous Cascade! You may designate a stable travel point in the Forest of Chlorophyll Chaos where the Ambiguous Cascade can always be found. The system's recommendation is to place it near territory you control, so it can be used as a natural resource and boost the productivity and profitability of your land.

"I mean, it's a good reward, and I'll definitely place that as close to my duchy as possible, but that's definitely a long-term-gains thing." Joe tipped his head back and forth as he thought over the situation again, pulling a face at the realization that, were he not already too strong for this world, the rewards likely would've been far better. "I guess I can't really complain that I didn't get a power-up after all that. Probably better to go figure this all out offworld and let the turbulence fade. Then I suppose I can come back, figure out how to get around without breaking the mana, and hunt down the last place of power."

Feeling good about what he'd accomplished, Joe interfaced with the shrine and chose to teleport to the base of the bifrost.

His view shifted in an instant, going from a peaceful pasture with trees in the distance to a wind-blasted almost crater with a stream of powerful energy rushing from the planet and into the depths of the universe. The Ritualist appreciated the intense damage marring the ground, as it gave him some comfort to know that he wasn't the only one who had trouble controlling his Characteristic output. Then, without further ado, he began taking careful, calculated steps closer to the rainbow bridge, knowing it would take nearly a quarter of an hour to walk the distance without having his inhibitor.

Eight minutes later, just as he passed the halfway point to the bifrost, the magical circles in the sky flared brightly, multiple rapidly descending forms hitting the inertial dampening magics and turning from streaks of light into forms recognizable as people. Joe sneered at the sight, "Great... now I'm going to have to pretend I'm moving this slowly because I *want* to. Ugh."

His fingers trailed up, brushing the silvery bell at the hollow of his throat and wondering if he should've activated his Karmic Shroud. It was practically the only method he had of going anywhere these days without causing a stir or attracting trouble, but he held off since the group descending from a higher world was already stepping out of the bifrost. Joe kept his eyes off of them and locked on his destination, while he put his hands behind his back as though he were simply admiring the view instead of trying not to crack a tectonic plate.

Unfortunately, the new arrivals weren't as willing to overlook his presence. After shaking off the vertigo of such rapid movement, the group noticed him and began heatedly arguing amongst themselves. Seeing as they were being so bold with their attention, Joe finally shifted his gaze to carefully observe them as well.

The group had formed a semicircle between him and the giant column of prismatic light, and his stomach sank as he realized each of them was wearing a tower insignia—this was clearly an expedition from Vanaheim. Joe closed his eyes and took a deep breath, muttering angrily at himself. "I don't care *how* comfortable these clothes are, if I'm going to be anywhere near a bifrost in the future, I need to put on something that stops people from recognizing my class and affiliation as soon as they see me."

Even as he said the words, he found himself not believing them: the robes were just *that* comfortable.

"You there!" It seemed the deliberations had come to an end, and though the majority of the group had resentment in their eyes as they stared at the man speaking, then to Joe, they did not interfere as he boldly approached the Ritualist. "I know you, don't I?"

"Not unless I purchased your assistance with goat cheese a few weeks back." The non-sequitur made the Vanaheimian pause momentarily, his face tinging red as he realized Joe was trying to brush him off.

"You've clearly been doing things on this world that you have no business doing, *Ritualist.*" The way the man stood with classic soldier's precision caused a familiar, unpleasant chill to travel along Joe's spine—already he could feel the impending violence. "The way the mana is practically *sick* due to your mere presence? You've been meddling. Is this how your Grandmaster became a Sage? You came to the weakest world and stole away with the Mythic Core? Perhaps you are here, even now, having taken pains to hide the methods you used to achieve it?"

"Nope." Joe literally and conversationally sidestepped the

person who was trying to pick a fight, deciding against giving a more verbose answer. There was no reason to share his life story with someone he'd just met, especially when they were trying to cause problems. "Just trying to figure out my Characteristics and keep myself under control. Wouldn't want to break the ambient mana, you know?"

"So you haven't been bouncing between secret locations? Capturing places of power in a blatant attempt at raising yet another Sage within your tower and thereby creating a supermajority on the Sage's Council, *Joe the Ritualist*?" The man hopped backward, once more getting in front of Joe, and this time clearly not about to allow him to ease past. "Spending a few days in your respawn room should give us enough time to undo whatever it is you've done. Prepare yourself for honorable combat!"

"Not super thrilled that you know who I am. But since you do... are you *sure* about this?" Joe straightened up with deliberate care, moving his hands away from his back and out to the sides, keeping them visible while his stance remained neutral. "I'm doing my best not to break things here. Do you really want to run that risk by attacking me?"

"Failing to control yourself means all of the punishment of the world falls on you anyway," came the confident response. The man stepped forward, his eyes bright and his hands rising into a chopping guard, fingers straight, palms angled to be all but hidden from Joe. "I see no risk to myself, as I can attack you here without inviting sanctions back home. You're a known accomplice of the Ascensionist faction; you snuck a Mythic Core through the blockade specifically designed to keep the world from devolving into civil war; there's a massive teleportation network being built in your name on Jotunheim, which no one from my faction can seem to earn access to, no matter how we bargain..."

"Then I come to find you doing sneaky things all the way down on Midgard. You have a very specific way of making things go wrong that we need to go *right*." The martial artist tensed, and Joe could feel that combat was imminent. "No longer. Not here. I've been sent to secure the Mythic Core of Midgard's World Boss, and I will not let your machinations cause me to fail. Now, for the glory of Sage Sergeant Sperlazza, *die* Ascensionist scum!"

The Master-ranked combatant swung his hand in a classic karate chop, and only by force of habit did Joe dodge to the side, even though there was no way the attack would be close enough to land. He grimaced as his reflexes shockwaved the air around him, but his face went slack with concern as a shimmer of light flashed through the space his neck had been a heartbeat earlier. A sound rang out behind him, like paper being slowly torn apart, and a lightning-quick glance back revealed a trench being carved through the blasted stone of the shallow crater they were in.

"Haa..." Joe practically deflated as he allowed the adrenaline to flow through him, realizing he may have no choice but to go all-out. "I think I can get *one* more level of warp before it becomes permanent... hey, what are you all about? Swords or something?"

"You...! The insolence!" Though his hand remained in the chopping position, it shot to his chest to indicate the imprinted emblem. "I am a practitioner of the grand marshal dao of *knife hands*! I have been trained by Sage Sperlazza himself-"

"*Skill* Sage Sperlazza, then?" Joe nodded as his interruption caused his attacker to blush a furious crimson. "Looks like it. You guys have a problem with sword cultivators, then? The comparison leave you feeling a little... inadequate? You know, long, girthy swords versus short, stubby knives-"

Skill offered: Perfect Taunt (Journeyman III). Hitting your enemy right where it hurts sounds great, right? What if the taunt only succeeded if you performed a critical hit with your Charisma check? That's Perfect Taunt, and-

The martial artist rushed forward, relentlessly swiping and throwing knife hands at the Ritualist. Invisible blades screamed past Joe's ribs, slit open slashes on his shoulders, and would've fully defaced his face had he not practically dropped to the ground in an instant dodge. Worry quickly filled Joe, as he'd been hoping his taunting would cause the other man to begin attacking without control, but... he was *far* more skilled than the Ritualist had bargained for.

In a blink, the distance between them was gone, and sizzling energy slashed into Joe. He cried out as he felt his left arm go limp, the tendons cut at the shoulder causing him to lose control of the limb. A gash opened on his abdomen, blood spilling out and seeping into the white fabric of his now-torn robe.

"You're going away for a few days." There was no anger in the martial artist's voice, only cold certainty. "And the next time I see you, the result will be the same."

Joe pushed off the cotton-durable ground as he jumped for the bifrost, only for his ankle to be caught in the offhand of his opponent and his momentum used to drive him into the dirt. He heard it before he felt it–a sizzling sound as a knife-intent coated hand plunged into his back, sliding between his ribs with a squelch and *staying there.* Moving slowly to draw out the agony, the martial artist began cutting up, aiming for the Ritualist's heart.

Then Joe realized he had one final option, which he should've taken before combat broke out. Willing it to happen was enough, the pre-channeled Beam to Bifrost enveloping him in a light that matched the rainbow bridge only a dozen feet away.

Between one instant and the next, the Ritualist had been launched into the depths of space, the angry cries of the Traditionalist following him for only a fraction of a second.

CHAPTER TWENTY-ONE

"That's the last time I'm walking somewhere, when I have the option to teleport." Joe coughed a mouthful of blood into the energy around him, for some reason finding the **crackle** of it hitting the boundary of the bifrost soothing. "Probably the pain. Anything distracting me is nice. Glad his hand didn't get cut off and stay stuck inside me; that'd be particularly nasty."

"Eh. Might have plugged the hole for a while, though. No... this is better. How would I go about asking someone to reach into my body and excise someone else's hand? Worse, what if I got some healing, and it trapped it inside me?" Pulling open his notifications, the Ritualist felt his jaw drop as he saw the enormous damage that had been done. "Abyss. If I had my inhibitor on, that would've killed me outright."

Damage Received: 2,519 Penetrative, Conceptual.

Debuff gained: Major Hemorrhaging. -55 health per second.

Current health: 4,239/7,966

"Well, looks like I'm not going to make it to the other side." His words tasted like iron and copper, and a quick swipe at his mouth coated his sleeve in fresh blood. "Still, I'm oddly proud of myself for not lashing out. Hope he at least got a level of warp for hitting me with that Master-rank attack."

There was one last message the system had sent him, and Joe carefully looked over it, worried that it was going to be a notification that his responses during battle had increased the turbulent mana to untenable levels. Instead, he found something that made him laugh through his pain.

Skill offered: Serene Cataclysm Body Art (Expert I). This is a passive internal discipline technique generally received only by Grand Berserkers. While lesser berserkers rage and sacrifice health for combat strength, this art allows the user to find ever-increasing control of themselves as their life burns away.

Effects:

1. *Gain perfect passive control over the first 200 + 10N points of each Characteristic's effects on your surroundings, with Expert 0 being considered 'N = 1' for purposes of this equation.*
2. *For every 10% of maximum health lost, the amount of perfectly controlled Characteristics increases by 8% of their base value.*
3. *This skill cannot be suppressed by disruptive effects.*

Accept? Yes / No.

"Figures I only get this *after* I'm leaving the planet." Joe decided that this was a potent enough ability that it would be worth collecting, and so made his decision, bringing him near the halfway threshold for his maximum skill gains. As the skill settled in his soul, he felt the entire foundation of his artificially enhanced frame shudder under the power of the system locking it in place, threatening to disrupt his ritual-inscribed mana channels. "Abyss, maybe I should've held off?"

Knowing he had only minutes to live and would have plenty of time for rumination later, the Ritualist simply accepted that he'd already made his choice and started thinking of how he could integrate this body art into his combat repertoire. "If this works the way I *hope* it does, so long as I survive severe damage, I'll be *that* much harder to hit. My Characteristics have been growing so rapidly, thanks to achieving Mastery tiers, that I know I don't have the best control of them. Certainly I haven't been using my *body* to its peak potential, at the very least."

He allowed himself to daydream about taking ninety percent of his health as damage and still functioning while getting the maximum boost to his Characteristic control. A chuckle escaped his lips, a bubble of blood lingering at the corner of his mouth. "I can just imagine it now. Someone manages to hit me easily a couple of times in a row, thinking I'm about to go down, only for me to suddenly be able to dodge with perfect proprioception. Out of nowhere, nothing they throw at me lands because I'm able to calculate everything with my Intelligence, see everything coming at me with my Perception, and move individual patches of *skin* out of the way of their attacks."

Going silent, he waited... and waited. At some point he had closed his eyes, not even realizing it, so when they popped open, he was shocked to find himself still on the bifrost. Confused as to what was happening, he opened his status.

Name: Joe 'Emperor of Mana' Class: Reductionist
Profession I: ***Codex-Keeper (1/20)***
Profession II: Ritualistic Alchemist (15/20)
Profession III: Grandmaster's Apprentice (15/25)
Profession IV: Ritualistic Metalworker (16/20)
Profession V: Ritualistic Numerologist (10/20)
Profession VI: Arcane Enchanting Theorist (5/5) This can now be used as a prerequisite for any enchanting-based profession!

Character Level: 30 Exp: 465,000 Exp to next level: 31,000 (Locked.)
Rituarchitect Level: 15 Exp: 105,700 Exp to next level: 14,300
Reductionist Level: 12 Exp: 90,472 Exp to next level: 528

Hit Points: 4,239/7,966

Mana: 24,975/26,640 (5,000 mana bequeathed to others. 6.25% reserved)
Mana regen: 281.89/sec
Stamina: 5,429/5,429
Stamina regen: 8.59/sec

Characteristic: Score
Quad Strength: 499
Dialectic Dexterity: 499
Stoic Constitution: 499
Light Intelligence: 494
Ritualistic Wisdom: 494
Dark Charisma: 494
Karmic Perception: 499
Red Luck: 497
Karmic Luck: 390

"Why isn't my health dropping?" Joe could still actively feel the giant hole in his back, how his lungs were flailing due to having access to the open air. He was fairly certain the martial artist had at least nicked the bottom of his heart, so by all rights, he should have bled out well in advance of this moment. "Don't tell me damage-over-time effects don't tick while traveling between worlds? That can't be right; I've definitely heard about people getting reduced to cinders while on the bridge... but maybe that was from the energy of the bifrost itself?"

Whatever the reason, the Ritualist suddenly found himself with a slight hope that he'd be able to survive the brutal attack. By his math, he'd have just over a minute, seventy-seven seconds to be exact, to find a healer that could fix him up before he exsanguinated fully and was sent to respawn. "Where would the nearest cleric be? This'll definitely require magical healing, and the likelihood that I get Jake the Alchemist to hand me a healing potion in time–scratch that, the likelihood of him even opening the *door* in under a minute is low. Dawnesha?

Yeah... maybe if I can get over to Tatum's temple in time, she'd have some heals ready to go."

After planning out his route from touching down on Jotunheim to sprinting to the temple and hoping for the best, Joe calmed himself and looked over the rest of his status. "Huh, my Reductionist *and* Rituarchitect experience went up? I wonder how much experience that whale was worth, if breaking it down paid off whatever debt I had for making that ritual in my soul. Capturing that place of power probably had something to do with it as well, now that I'm thinking about it. Those are always worth a ton of experience."

He thought back to the person who'd attacked him and scoffed at the idea of Mr. Stabby-knife-hands managing to swim through the cascade and capture the place of power at its center. "Yet another benefit for skipping any of the other requirements I was supposed to meet to capture the cascade. Gonna be really hard for anyone to retrace my steps and do it themselves."

The rest of his journey passed quickly, as he sank into light, meditative breathing to push his pain to the side. Though his health wasn't dropping, his nerves were still firing, letting him know he'd taken devastating damage. As Jotunheim grew large in his vision, he was shallowly panting for breath. "Feces on a stick, maybe I should've just gone to respawn instead of pushing through like this."

Even as he voiced the complaint, Joe physically recoiled from the thought, pushing it to the side as he broke through the top of the cloud layer surrounding the world of giants. He was no quitter, and even if success wasn't guaranteed when he landed, giving up certainly wasn't an option he would ever truly consider. Then he was exiting the base of the clouds, Novusheim looming large for a few moments.

"Seventy-seven seconds starts... *now*."

He hit the ground like a sack of meat hurled at a wall and immediately pushed out and away, Omnivault activating smoothly as he leaped into the city. He allowed his feet to touch down only for the skill to activate again, crossing nearly half a mile in mere moments. The harsh **crackle** of the sound barrier breaking caught up to him as gravity reasserted itself and dragged him to the ground once more. "Abyss, I forgot Jotunheim resists my movement better than Midgard does."

Damage taken: 110 bleeding.

Seeing his health sink like a rock thrown into a pond wasn't helping him, so Joe turned his attention to his surroundings, already knowing the exact route he'd need to take in order to get to the pantheon's temple on the far edge of the city. If it had been a straight shot, he would've already been there, but the buildings were tall enough that it was faster to zip through the twists and turns of the roads rather than get to the top of the buildings and waste time changing elevation.

The wide stone roads looked practically ornamental as he flashed across them, the worked rock easily taking the pressure of his boiling mana as it erupted from his legs with each push off its surface. His health dropped again, and a swift check over his shoulder revealed a trail of blood splattering along behind him. A good amount of it was still in the air, and very little was on the road itself–his momentum causing it to remain airborne until it splashed onto the walls of the buildings, startled people he was moving past, and the like.

Though he was actively dying and cringing from the gory fresco he was leaving in his wake, a small part of him simply exulted in the speed at which he could move.

Joe could already feel the effects of the Serene Cataclysm Body Art at work, interacting with his individual Characteristics and pulling them together into a unified whole. It wasn't perfect, but seeing as he was rapidly losing health, it was gaining power quickly. Even as his legs quadrupled his movement speed, the muscles themselves didn't overfire. His joints, which usually screamed as he pushed himself to his utmost, were instead smoothly shifting, tendons tightening barely more than they needed for optimal usage. As more of his blood flowed out of the gaping wound in his back, and his heart stuttered and missed a beat, his feet landed with ever-more-precise positioning.

Then he was outside of the temple, vision tunneling as he looked at a long line of petitioners stretching down the road to the doors of the temple itself. "Ugh... that's not good. I might pass out even before I fully lose all my health at this rate."

Unable to simply leap ahead, for fear of crashing into people, Joe pushed through as quickly as he could make himself move. After having crossed the distance between the bifrost and here in only six seconds, the next fourteen seconds of dodging and weaving through the majority of the group felt like a torturous tortoise speed. As the thirty-first second since landing on the planet ticked over, officially passing seventeen hundred total damage due to bleeding alone, the Ritualist was staring at the world through pinpricks as his tunneled vision collapsed further.

Even so, he slipped through the slowly moving crowd of people like a needle pushed through cloth by a master seamstress. His health continued to drop, yet his new body art pushed him to greater control with every ten percent of his health that he lost. As his blood trickled out of him–no longer a fountain, which was greatly worrying–and Joe's health dropped to thirty percent, he felt his control pass the sixth Characteristic threshold. Now he was moving as though he'd been carefully aligning his body and mind with each individual Characteristic he had gained to this point: three hundred and seventy-seven points of perfect control across all of his stats.

Angling his shoulders down a fraction, bending his spine just so, tucking one arm and flaring the other almost useless one just enough... the Ritualist carved through the empty space between people which should have stopped him cold or at least made him bump into person after person. He didn't push through, instead borrowing angular momentum as he slithered along, slingshotting himself around Dwarf and human alike. His smile went wide, yet somehow a deep part of himself understood that it looked beatific instead of manic or disturbing–his body art even granting him ever-increasing control of his Dark Charisma.

"I'm dying, but abyss if I don't look *good* while doing it!"

His words were a soft wheeze, barely reaching his own ears as he closed in on the temple doors. Unfortunately for those around him, while his movement was beautiful in a technical sense, like the marriage of a dancer and poet, the after effects were a study in macabre art. Each motion shook out yet another sanguine arc, leaving a mist of blood along the beards of the Dwarves at perfect face level with the hole in his back. Armor was splattered, fine robes had crimson droplets staining as his fluids smeared across them.

Usually half a second or so passed between Joe flashing by someone and a shout of outrage filling the air as they realized he was skipping the line. In many cases, hands reached out for him with fully justified frustration, only for the people being bypassed to freeze in realization–and sometimes disgust–as they actually looked at the bleeding Ritualist and realized the slick warmth on their outstretched limbs wasn't a drink being spilled on them. Their anger shifted into alarm, then uneasy silence as he moved deeper through the line.

"Not gonna... make it." Only the faintest spark of light was making its way to Joe's brain as his eyes stared at the still-distant doorway. "Brain... shutting down. Loss of consciousness imminent."

No longer concerned about the minor injuries he might inflict on people around him, Joe faced the temple entrance directly, then *leaped* forward, angling himself like a javelin... and promptly passed out.

His eyes fluttered open, and a soft groan escaped his lips as icy-cold water poured over his back and aggravated the inflamed edges of his wounds. The chill battled against the burning pain, quenching it ever so slowly. "*Mmumf.*"

"*Lay on Hands*!" came a familiar voice from behind him, giving Joe just enough of a warning to not flinch away as another dose of healing rushed into him, preceded by a small wave of water that collected on his back, gathered around the still-gaping laceration, and flooded *into* his abdominal cavity. "Couple seconds of cooldown, Joe. Tell me what happened to you if you can."

"Attacked." His reply was lost in a **glurble**, his lips submerged in the pool of blood he was lying in. The Ritualist wasn't about to try to arch his back to allow Dawnesha to hear him more clearly, at least not until his flesh had been properly stitched together.

"Yeah, I didn't get that. Should I send out the guard to find whoever did this?" Her rapid words were immediately followed with another casting of her healing spell. "Lay on Hands."

"Nnn."

"I'll take that as a 'no'." The high priestess's voice was tinged with annoyance, but it was greatly overridden by admiration. "Frankly, I cannot believe you managed to get here in time. The first three casts of my healing abilities only allowed you to have blood in your veins once more. You were a dried out husk by the time you sailed into the temple and slid along the ground. I legitimately thought we were under attack by a giant penguin at first. *Major Cure Wounds*!"

There was a disturbing sensation as his missing flesh was restored, the ragged wound bubbling and swelling like a balloon as his cells rapidly grew out and connected with each other. Dawnesha let out a sigh of relief as his blood finally stopped leaking away and undoing all of her hard work. "Celestials, finally. That one has *such* a long cooldown. Consider yourself stabilized, Joe. I'll hit you with a couple more healing spells, but will you be able to take over from there?"

Tilting his head to the side, the much-relieved Ritualist offered her a bloody smile. "I appreciate it. I'll be fine enough to get out of your way. There's a permanent healing ritual setup back on my Sect mountain; I'll just take it easy until I teleport home."

"But your healing spells?" Before Joe needed to answer with the awkward explanation, the air darkened slightly, and the

Dwarven High Priestess blinked rapidly. "Oh, I see. Tatum sends his apologies and deepest regrets. Please consider full restoration as a small token of his goodwill toward you and do not concern yourself with any form of repayment for my healing services."

"Hadn't even crossed my mind, if I'm being honest with you," Joe shamefacedly admitted. "I'll make sure to remember to have alloy ingots on hand for the next time I show up like this."

"Hopefully not anytime soon?"

"I wouldn't think so." After another splash of water sank into him, the Ritualist finally felt healthy enough to carefully turn over and pull himself into a seated position, still needing to heavily rely on the Dwarf's vise-like grip to get himself off the ground. "Got randomly attacked by a Master-rank combatant down on Midgard just as I hopped on the bifrost. Fun fact for you, it appears damage-over-time effects pause when you're traveling between worlds, then reactivate once you land. Don't know if this'll help anyone, but it doesn't hurt to know."

She offered a magnanimous nod to him. "Thank you for the information. Better to have an option of last resort when otherwise someone might give in to despair. Now, I do so hate to bring this up, but when you entered the temple, you damaged the doors..."

CHAPTER TWENTY-TWO

"Give me a few minutes, and I'll bring the structure back to tip-top shape." Joe tried hard not to roll his eyes, knowing that he could create a Ritual of Repair in under half a minute with one hand tied behind his back, all while blindfolded. "Thanks for letting me skip the line."

"If the Chosen Legend of Tatum can't get a little bit of preferential treatment at the center of his power on this world, what's the point of having the title in the first place?" Dawnesha winked at him as an orb of dark water formed over her palm, only to wash away more of Joe's wounds in the next moment.

"The temple isn't the only entity seeking damages," a nasally voice entered Joe's ears, making the Ritualist grimace and tense up as he slowly turned to face the Dwarven Master of Sarcasm, Stu. "Why is it every time we run into you, it's only after you've been an absolute menace to society? Look at this place!"

Before answering, knowing that would only give the Dwarf more ammunition to lob at him, the Ritualist actually followed the instructions. He swept his gaze across the area, noticing wood chips and cracked stone, crowds of people lined up at the various altars of the pantheon staring at him. Many people were annoyed, though there were scores of concerned faces. All of it, everywhere he looked, was literally decorated with arterial spray. "...Ah. In my defense, I was in a rather time-sensitive situation."

"Excuses are but wind. I've received over a hundred reports of people getting chunks of Joe in their chainmail. A new business appeared in the last five minutes, some entrepreneurial people immediately setting out signs offering discounted blood removal from walls and windows." The Dwarf slowly, sarcastically, began clapping at the seated human. "Everywhere you go, you create jobs for the common man. Sure, all of it is related to mitigation and disaster recovery-"

Raising a hand to forestall any additional dressing down, Joe simply gave the Dwarf a weary stare. "I'm guessing you're here to collect payment for cleanup, right? Do I have a tab I could put it on?"

Stu went silent, a rare accomplishment. He leaned back slightly, folding his hands behind himself, and the annoyance on his face shifted to somewhere between amusement and exhaustion. "I suppose this would be enough. If you'd like, I'll handle it for you."

"You." The word didn't come out as a question, but a flat denial of the reality of the Dwarf's words. "You'll just... fix the problem."

"As a matter of fact, yes. I find that I owe you a minimal favor, and this will set that right." Stu was surprisingly cheerful as he pulled out a small sack and revealed that it was filled with ingots of Jotunheim alloy. "So long as you accept my help, we can be done with each other. Until the next time you... Joe it up."

The Ritualist had to bite his tongue–almost hard enough to require healing–in order to stop himself from lashing out at the Dwarf using his name as though it were a curse. His eyes flicked to the side, and he was struck with the realization that, though he *could* repair the building, he had no method currently to handle the biological component of the cleanup. Before he could say anything, he looked to the Dwarf once more and narrowed his eyes.

A golden line appeared in the air between them, wavering back and forth like a silk thread in the wind. The karmic bond between them was minimal, just as the Dwarf had mentioned, but it unmistakably flowed from the bearded menace to himself. Sidestepping the agreement, Joe instead questioned the situation itself. "Why, Stu? Why is there a debt between us?"

"Funny thing, that." Stu stepped closer to the altar and dropped the entire pouch of alloy onto its surface. "If you'd remained as a Councilman of Novusheim, and we'd remained as peers, your help with my advancement would've merely been acknowledged as what council members should be doing to assist in the growth of our city. But since I convinced you to leave, only for that to be the final piece I needed in order to become the *Grandmaster* of Sarcasm-"

"Noo..." Joe's whine was quickly clipped off, and he coughed into his hand before trying again. "That is, congratulations on your advancement."

"Your appreciation is *noted*," Stu replied perfunctorily. "Now, can I take care of this issue for you, so I can be done with you forever? I guarantee that every last drop of... you... is collected, accounted for, and properly destroyed. Not a trace left behind that can be used to find, track, or attack you from a distance."

"When you put it like *that*... fine." Joe got to his feet just as another healing spell washed over him, and he nodded politely at Dawnesha as he started making his way toward the door, waving off her protests. "Goodbye forever, Grandmaster Stu."

"Thank goodness for that," the Dwarf replied in kind, tapping the altar. The sack of alloy vanished, leaving behind a black bubble of pure darkness that expanded rapidly, then popped... leaving a shimmer in the air that traveled out and away from the temple. "Done. I'll have my personal craftsman come and repair this door, High Priestess."

Stu quickly walked forward, intentionally barging in front of Joe and nudging him with his shoulder to get through the exit first. The Ritualist didn't even mind, as a narrow glare at the Dwarf showed the karmic bond between them fading in real time.

"You know what? I'd take the hit all over again if it meant not seeing that guy in the future." Glancing back at the altar, Joe looked at it with a newfound respect. "I didn't know these things had additional functions. Interesting."

"You'd be surprised what can be done with a large enough offering. Obviously." Dawnesha came up beside him, clearly wanting to discuss more than his health. "Before you leave, Tatum has a few things he'd like me to pass along."

"Oooh, where are they?" Joe went from annoyed to practically salivating in the space of a freshly-healed heartbeat. "Last time he had something for me, it was, uh-"

The Dwarf was shaking her head, and her hands were empty and at her sides instead of cupping gifts to lavishly ply him with. "Only words, this time around. Though... I suppose it has to do with the gifts you were given previously. While the message doesn't make much sense to me, I hope it'll be meaningful for you."

"Firstly, I'm told you have a weapon given to you that remains unbound. Tatum would like you to know that each day that goes by is another lost opportunity for *growth.* That was meant to be emphasized, and if it means what I think it does... congratulations, and perhaps bind that weapon before someone else finds a way to steal it without you noticing."

Her eyes were locked on him, and the Ritualist found himself utterly shocked as he noticed the naked greed in the *high priestess'* eyes. That was enough to make him realize that a deity-granted growth item was probably even more rare and valuable than he'd initially supposed. "I'll get right on that... as soon as I know how."

"Which leads me to the second part of the message." Dawnesha had to physically take a step back, inhaling deeply and slowly letting the breath out before she trusted herself to continue speaking. "Yeah. Go bind that as quickly as you can. Sorry, the message. Apparently, you should be able to get answers to a bunch of your questions so long as you–this is the part I don't really understand–so long as you seek out a *cat*?"

"Oh. Yeah, I need to hunt down a bunch of Verglas Leopards for a quest. That makes sense now," Joe lied with a straight face, not willing to break the secret of the Nyanderthal's society. "I can get right on that."

"That doesn't seem quite right, but I guess you know what's going on with yourself better than anyone else." The high priestess stared at him for a moment, the flat disproval in her gaze making Joe realize she likely had some ability to detect lies spoken in her presence. "Now, another piece of news I'm sure you'll be interested in hearing: Grandmaster Havoc has been apparently successful in his expedition into the depths of Jotunheim. He and his daughter Francine are both expected back in Novusheim within a month's time. Faster, if you managed to expand your teleportation network more quickly, now that you are here in person and can direct it out."

"Great!" Joe stepped back, trying to leave but not wanting to be rude to the person who had literally patched up his heart, lungs, and probably a chunk of spine while she was in there. "Thanks for the information; looks like I have a cat to find-"

"Here." Starting to get a bit frustrated, Joe looked back at the Dwarf, only to freeze in incomprehension as she passed over a thick packet. "This is also for you, but I'll take your word that you won't open it until *after* you manage to bind your weapon. It's sealed, and I'll know when you break the binding."

"What? Why do I need to wait?" Joe numbly accepted the package, glancing between it and Dawnesha in confusion. "Who knows when I'll manage to bind that thing? But I have the package here, now?"

"Please just do things in order. I know you are prone to jumping ahead and rushing off on new tasks when you have other things you should be doing." The sting of her words was mitigated by the soft smile she wore while speaking them. "Believe me when I say you will only be frustrated at knowing what this is before you are ready for it."

"I hate q-factor things like this," the Ritualist grumbled as he stored the document away. "You know what? I've got a gift for you, too. Why don't you take this, and let me know if you have any questions? I'm supposed to be your class trainer–actually, how do you feel about having some extra mana on hand?"

A quick explanation later, the high priestess was the proud owner of a new copy of the Standard Combat Ritual Manual, a thousand points of mana, and a few tips and tricks to help get her over the slump she'd found when trying to break into the Journeyman ranks with her Ritualist class skills.

Seeing as Joe was still technically her class trainer, though she was progressing much slower due to focusing on her responsibilities as high priestess, Joe felt this much was the minimum he should be doing for her–especially after he noticed her healing or changing the fates of other people in line after him without requesting payment, or at a rate he could tell was easily *far* under the true value of the services she provided. Instead of running off as he'd originally planned, he watched for a short while as the Dwarf worked her way through the line at a steady pace, her speed much increased thanks to the additional mana he had bequeathed.

"That was *definitely* a good idea," the Ritualist murmured to himself as he finally made his way out of the temple, planning on swinging over to the Aspect Tower and swapping out his lower-ranking aspect jars with the Natural Aspect Jar versions he had left in the city's trash and recycling center. "Helps her out, benefits everyone in the city, and it just so happens that she has a ton of skills rapidly progressing, thanks to the dual class she's acting as. The fact that I'll gain Mastery Merits from her like hitting the jackpot on a slot machine is just a coincidence."

As he walked over to the Aspect Tower, he felt a strange weight in his hand and looked down to see the sealed envelope being gripped tightly by his fingers. "Now how'd you get there?

Sneaky little package, I'm not supposed to open you. Then again, I *do* wonder if there's a way for me to look inside without breaking the seal...?"

There wasn't.

Incredibly intrigued as to what could possibly be in the document that he shouldn't have 'yet', the Ritualist quickly finished up in the city, greatly relieved to find a glut of Rare aspects waiting for him in the Natural Aspect Jars, and made his way to the teleportation pedestal which was still positioned outside of the city.

In an instant, Joe was spat out dozens of miles and thousands of feet in elevation away. The shock of the environmental shift made him want to gasp, but the shallow breath caught in his throat. Settling himself, he pulled in deeply through his nose, and the power-laden air rushed into his lungs—a heady feeling that made him feel oddly invincible and... just a tish bloodthirsty?

"Mm. That must be the boost we got from Aten killing off the titan. I can tell that's not directed at me, yet it still sends shivers down my spine. Okay... let's play 'how quickly can I get to my house and be left alone?'."

He had a goal and destination in mind, but now he didn't have the excuse of bleeding to death to allow him to skip his positional etiquette. Though he wanted to rush to his house, certain that he'd find Cleocatra there, as he'd been practically chanting her name in his head and aloud—the equivalent of spamming her with meeting requests—he was forced to slow his pace and walk across the top of his mountain acting like the 'First Elder of The Wanderer's Sect' that he was.

The training district he had personally designed spread out in front of him, the scaffolding for people learning to jump or training others if their own rank was high enough, towered above, reaching into the low-hanging clouds and *crawling* with people. He took a moment to look on as Novices trained with the simplest of tools, simply crouching and jumping to the top of a box like any workout enthusiast might do. As the rank of those learning the Jump skill increased, the physics of the motion became more and more bizarre, even Beginners actively defying gravity in their training area, hopping from pole to pole as a ritual underneath them adjusted their weight.

Coaches at higher levels barked corrections to them, their voice echoing with a metallic buzz as repeated impacts shook the metal framework of the skill training spire Joe had put together. As more people began noticing him, mistakes began quickly racking up. Novices hit their shins on the edge of their boxes, Beginners tumbled helplessly through the air, and Apprentices smacked headfirst into padded sections of the obstacles in their path.

Instead of focusing on any of those accidents, Joe simply caught the eyes of the coaches and inclined his head slightly, responding to their salutes and acknowledgment. Then he moved on, trying not to look as though he was hurrying, though internally the Ritualist was practically squirming back and forth with delight at not having been called over to help or demonstrate something.

His next obstacle was the large open field in the center of the space, his attempt at replicating the area around the Tower of Ritualist on Vanaheim. As he began crossing it, Joe found himself stuttering to a stop and looking around in surprise and mild disgust. “This place is *filthy*. What's going on here? Where’s Devoe?”

The field was churned to the point that it looked as though it had been freshly tilled and aerated. Large sections had been pounded flat inexpertly and were covered in half-completed ritual diagrams, chalk, bits of wire, and various components tossed around them as though they’d been carelessly discarded when they weren't needed for whatever design was being activated. Dozens of Ritualists had paused mid-conversation when they saw him, their eyes wide and uncertain, and Joe found that he didn't recognize *any* of them.

“Let's try that again.” Joe took a deep, measured breath, voice filling with subtle anger. “Why does the top of my mountain look like a trash pit, and where's the Ritualist I assigned to train you in my absence? *Where is Devoe*?"

"Abyss, I think he's the real deal. First Elder Joe."

The soft buzz of conversation made his ears twitch, and the Ritualist zeroed in on the young man speaking without seeming to have a care in the world. "You know who I am? Then you have me at a disadvantage, because *all* of you are new to me."

Seeing the group cringe away assured him that his displeasure had been clearly noted. The far-too-calm-for-the-situation Novice Ritualist waved at Joe with an easy grin on his face. "Heyo, First Elder! Pretty much everyone at the Expert rank and above was hired by the Sect to assist with repairs and some kinda secret project. Everyone else went along with them to get training in the field, help activate the rituals, stuff like that."

"When was this?" Joe quickly settled down, realizing that perhaps he'd reacted too strongly. "I was under the impression our mountain had been somewhat sequestered from the rest of the Sect-"

"*Nahh.*"

Joe's face went very still as the relaxed Ritualist cut him off with a shrug.

"That's all in the past. After this place stepped up during the attack by the titan, rescuing everyone, even leaving the safe area to go help out as things were going bad, we've got a whole new reputation in the Sect. Lots of new recruits, like yours truly, and everyone wants us to do work for them. Less permanent than an enchanter doing it but a whole lot less expensive at the same time, ya know?"

CHAPTER TWENTY-THREE

Folding his hands behind his back, Joe looked to the sky, staring at the shifting cloud layer for a few heartbeats as he pondered the information. "I suppose that does make sense. Hard for people to understand what it is we do until they see it in action... that still doesn't explain *this*."

He swept one hand forward to indicate the training field. "As you say, we have a reputation. One that certainly doesn't allow for us to stop taking care of the area and begin acting like slobs."

"Yeah, this place could really use some picking up."

"Yes, it could, *couldn't it*?" Joe stared at the young man who was now standing entirely alone, the others having taken subtle steps away during the conversation. "Tell you what. How about the people that made the mess go clean it up? Failing that, it's almost as if we have a large group of Novices who want to quickly advance this class and be a part of this 'new' reputation. Why don't you all figure out how to clean this place up and restore the surface of the field. I'll even make it a training opportunity and offer a reward."

Deciding against wasting parchment or other materials, Joe

merely lifted a hand, pulled out his inscription tool, and instantly created a Ritual of 'Little Sister's Cleaning Service' and left it hanging in midair. "This was one of the first rituals I ever created, which means I know any of *you* could do it as well. I'll give you a list of the components you need, and the first person to succeed and use it to get all this junk *off my grass* gets a reward."

"Grass?" The easy-going Novice blinked owlishly and looked around the churned, muddy field.

"There. *Should.* Be grass here." Joe's left eyebrow was twitching in time with his heartbeat. Moving his inscription tool once more, he created a simple Ritual of Glimmering with an overlay on it, choosing a simple orb with lines coming off it as the emblem to represent it going forward. "Here's the reward. Whoever makes the first ritual gets to learn how to interact with and alter rituals. You can learn how to do this and cancel rituals from your opponents, take down protective ancient rituals that have been guarding treasure for hundreds of years, or maybe even just directly take control and use it against your opponent, if they can't stop you."

To demonstrate, Joe allowed his Mana Dominion to expand, rushing against the Rituals of Elemental Burst two Novices were using to spar with each other. Both instantly stopped working, though the circles remained in place. Eyes still locked on the carefree Novice, Joe pulled on the diagrams, activating both at the same time and spraying him down from a distance.

"Hey! Who did that?" Another stream of water smacked the Novice, and he stumbled away, glaring at his contemporaries. "Trying to have a *conversation* here!"

Joe snapped his fingers, a bit of showmanship as he burst the rituals in the distance, causing them to pop with an outrush of mana that was slurped up by the clouds drifting just above the group.

"The next time I'm out here, I expect the area to be clean and tidy. Not only are you here representing the Ritualist class on this world, you're on the mountain of the First Elder. Your actions reflect on me. Please let them be *good* reflections."

With that, Joe stalked over to his house, eyes flicking to the Ritual of the Eternal Turtle in the distance, the main Sect mountain which was being repaired, the 'cloud six' peak that had been cut in half... Joe shut the door behind him, leaning against it and closing his eyes. "Ugh... so much to do, so much to get caught up on."

Standing straight, he brushed off his robes and turned to face the cat sitting on the table in the center of the room.

"Queen Cleocatra. Thank you for agreeing to meet with me."

"I'm only surprised it took this long." Joe watched as the cat all but smirked at him and was *sure* she would've been doing so if she'd taken on her humanoid form. "I know that if *I* had rewards coming to me from the monarch of an entire race, I certainly wouldn't be slow about collecting. Never know when a powerful person who owes you something might decide to sever their karmic bonds, hmm?"

"Ah." Joe lifted his hand and rubbed at his bald head softly grumbling. "Heard about that all the way down here, did you? Really not sure how I feel about Sage Pete at the moment. He's been good to me, but I kinda feel like he promised a whole lot of rewards with the knowledge that he wouldn't need to directly follow through on them."

"Meow does it make you feel, knowing the system compensated you directly out of what he would have otherwise gained? What did the world decide to give you as recompense?" Her tail lashed back and forth, and strangely enough, Joe hesitated about sharing the details.

"Feels... oddly intrusive to answer you?" Joe pushed past the awkward feeling, deciding to lay out his gains. "All of the sponsorship, training, and such turned into eighty-five Mastery Merits. Why was that so hard to say? Anyway, it's just rough to have to trade my growth for merits I would've earned eventually anyway."

The Nyanderthal shifted back and forth, crouching down as though preparing to pounce at his reflective head. "You need to change your perspective on this. Do you trust yourself to ascend through those skill ranks with or without his help?"

"Absolutely, it just would've been a whole lot faster with-"

"Now, how much do you trust everyone else training under you to have the same work ethic you've put in? How many Experts are you mentoring? How many Mastery Merits have you earned from training *them*?" Apparently the diminutive queen saw what she'd been looking for in his eyes. "Exactly. Generally you'll find that one Expert out of thirteen that you mentor will earn you a Mastery Merit on a skill you've been training them in. You might find someone who is fantastically proficient yet can never achieve *Inspiration* in a particular skill. Another might grow incredibly slowly, yet pass through that bottleneck as if it doesn't exist."

"Eight." Joe's voice was faint as he realized what she was getting at.

"What was that, now?"

"I've only earned eight Mastery Merits from other people. You were right; I was definitely thinking about this all wrong. I definitely trust myself to progress quickly and absolutely smash through bottlenecks by throwing myself at new challenges... but I'm starting to think I might be an outlier."

"Well, my fine young Ritualist," Cleo literally *purred* at him, "As they say, you have to be a little odd to be number one."

"I guess that makes sense? One is an odd number, and it's also very 'little'." He bobbed his head at her sage wisdom, though the disgruntlement in her eyes didn't seem to indicate she was pleased at his reasoning. "What?"

"*Nothing*." The word was spoken as a sigh, and she lifted a paw to get him to move closer. "Enough of that, shall we discuss your rewards?"

Joe's eyes darted to the side as he pulled up what he was owed from finishing the quest.

Quest complete: Dulling The Sword of Damocles. Your deeds have not only written your own legend but are closely tied to and therefore empower the hidden deity Occultatum. Though you have worked hand in hand, there is no doubt that he has benefited far more from your actions than you have. Every act you complete sharpens the blade, and if this tie were to be severed and the debt called in, you would be unable to survive the infusion of power.

Rewards pending:

1) External Karmic remapping of one of your skills.

2) Karmic wedge.

3) Karmic upgrade of an item.

"What would you like to start with, Joe?" the cat all but whispered, allowing him to bask in the excitement of the moment. "Depending on what we choose to upgrade or remap, just know that the bond tying us together may also be partially or even *fully* severed."

His eyes went wide, startled at the frank words. "I don't even know what these rewards really mean, but you're saying I could choose something you consider to be worth *two* life debts?"

"It's possible, especially when dealing with Karmic Debts directly." Her whiskers curled slightly, her slitted eyes narrowing mischievously. "The best part is, I am merely acting as the arbiter of karma in this instance and don't need to pay the cost directly. This means my services are being paid for out of the debt owed to you by others, which can be applied to the debt I owe you on behalf of my people. What fun!"

Joe hunched over the table slightly, his fingers drumming on its surface. "How long have Nyanderthals existed? I'm starting to get the sense that the ancient Egyptians back on Earth knew something the rest of us didn't."

"Ah, history gets distorted in all sorts of ways." The kitty-queen brushed off his perceptive comment. "We were far more willing to be all but worshiped than we were to rule, but that had several unfortunate consequences. One of them being we didn't get a say in the *policy* the pharaohs chose to enact. We were left to act only as the guardians of their fates, as we are uniquely qualified to do. Back to the matter at hand: as to what the rewards themselves do..."

She sat back on her haunches, wrapping her tail around and in front of her paws. "I'm sure you've guessed what the external remapping does, as it was specifically chosen as a reward to allow you to regain full control over one of your skills. We will essentially map out the pathways the skill needs to run along in order to function once more, and the excess will pump the broken skill full of everything it needs to repair itself."

Cleo paused as she saw the delight on Joe's face and delicately added a warning. "Seeing as this will be considered your own skill, yet not self-created, it will likely shift its name and function at least slightly. At *least* slightly. Possibly drastically. It all depends on your natural proclivities, as certain portions of the chosen skill may resonate with you, or other abilities, more than others."

"I already know which one I want to do." Joe pulled in a deep breath, unable to keep the brilliant, goofy smile off his face. "I'm literally falling apart not having Neutrality Aura. I don't look or smell good, I'm dehydrated all the time, my kidneys hurt, my blood doesn't clean itself up, showering takes *so* long, and don't even get me *started* on alchemy messes-"

"I *won't*." Cleo firmly interjected. "I'm glad to see you have your priorities in order. We can work on that now, or I could explain the other rewards?"

"Probably should hear what they are, right?" He nodded his head almost frantically. "I've waited this long; I can hold out for a little bit longer. Oh, and will I be able to learn anything about fixing my own skills by observing what you do?"

"*Purrrr*-haps," the queen replied with a non-answer. "Now, a karmic upgrade of an item is where things start getting *expensive*. Directly altering the tier of an item involves adjusting it at a deeper level than merely its molecular bonds. Did you have something truly significant that you would like to see empowered beyond its current form?"

"Not... really." The Ritualist could practically feel his robes sagging in disappointment even as he spoke. "Uh. My robes really want an upgrade, it seems. However, I will say I know that my codpiece is ready to reach the next tier?"

"Allow me to take a look." The cat looked at Joe with innocent eyes, and he stared at her with suspicious ones.

"Hmm. *Sure*." He swept over to his bathroom, closed the door, and only emerged after he was fully redressed, codpiece in hand. Even before he got close, the cat was shaking her head, sneezing furiously.

"Nope, never mind!" The Ritualist paused in confusion, only for it to be cleared up a moment later. "Perhaps we will explore this option again *after* you automatically clean the things around you once more. When's the last time you took that *off*, foul man?"

Deciding it was probably better not to disclose that information, Joe set the codpiece down a short distance from the table and once more waited, this time rather impatiently, for Cleo to continue speaking.

"Ah-*hem*." She turned and licked the fur of her shoulder for a moment to regain her composure. "Yes. The last option is an intriguing one. A Karmic Wedge. This is a gift to you, to allow for your ascension to Sage without causing your deity to have his power dispersed across the planet, destroying you alongside whatever continent you happen to be standing on at the moment, even as he's returned to mortal life."

A simple wedge, an item Joe could easily mistake for a shim used to level furniture, appeared on the table next to the Nyanderthal. The only oddity was a perfectly round hole in its widest end, which would make it useless in construction or actual usage. "Thank you?"

"The cost to use this is a single Mythic Core."

Joe choked on dry air, sputtering and coughing at Cleo's casual assertion. "*What*? Why?"

"I already told you why. Now let me tell you how. The Karmic Wedge will be used when you activate your own

Mythic Core, binding yourself to your selected skill." Her words were coming out with a calm impatience, as though waiting for him to realize the treasure he had in hand. "You may use the wedge to shunt off a single Karmic Debt as the others are paid in or out, depending on what you owe or are owed. Usually, this would be used in a situation like the one you found yourself in with Sage Pete, especially when you're the one owed something unique that the system can't outright grant you."

"Then, after I become a Sage, the Karmic Debt snaps back into place?" Joe let out a relieved laugh. "I was so worried that I wouldn't be able to become a Sage! Wait, why'd I need to go through the quest to get this? I mean, obviously so I could have it as a reward, but-"

"The name of the quest was *Dulling* the Sword of Damocles, not 'blunting' or 'you can ignore' the Sword of Damocles." Cleo tilted her head to the side. "It was never meant to be used to hold off the life debt of a *deity* to a *Novice*. There *will* be spillage. It just shouldn't be enough to cause you or your surroundings, ah, *permanent* damage."

Joe couldn't quite believe what he was hearing. "You're saying that, for me to become a Sage without popping planets, I'll need to have *two* Mythic Cores, and there will still be enough overflow power that I'm going to probably take serious damage from ascending?"

"But not *permanent* damage, yes." Cleo rolled her shoulders with satisfaction. "I will make sure to be in the vicinity during your ascension to assist. When you reach that stage and have all the required materials, you should already be strong enough to handle whatever gets thrown your way, but... there's no reason to take risks. Now, shall we remap your, what was it, Neutrality Aura?"

Even though he could tell she was simply putting him off, the Ritualist could also understand her reasoning. She was giving him a tool to use in the far distant future, making sure he was prepared no matter when it was that he became ready to take the next step. His situation was quite unique, and the fact that she could help *at all* was already something he should be incredibly grateful for. Pushing aside his concerns for the future, Joe allowed a smile to break through his stormy expression.

"I would absolutely *love* that." Only as he looked around for a chair did Joe realize that the rest of the room was entirely empty, every last bit of furniture besides the table having been taken away in his absence. "Huh? Wonder what that's all about. Should I sit on the floor, or, I don't know, in the shower?"

Cleo stared at him, allowing the silence to stretch before answering, "We aren't digging through your bones and scraping out impurities, Joe. We're tracing lines through your mana channels. Get comfortable however you want and do your best to focus inward. If you want to be able to replicate this process, or at least perform some facsimile, you'll need to pay very close attention indeed."

CHAPTER TWENTY-FOUR

Deciding against being fancy or allowing any distractions for himself, Joe opted to sit cross-legged on the bare floor in a lotus position. For a moment, his heart thudded wildly in his chest at the idea of being 'in a lotus', as the last time he'd been in one, it was a pod that stabbed him tens of thousands of times to inject him with magical materials. Even the minor association caused his breath to catch in his throat, and it took the Ritualist a long moment to comport himself.

"You okay there, Joe?" The Nyanderthal had impressive senses, and his sudden adrenaline rush hadn't gone unnoticed.

"Yep." He inhaled deeply through his nose, holding it for three seconds before letting it out over the same amount of time. "Just got a little reminder why I don't want to break the enchantment holding my mana channels together. There's only so many times I can be carved up with needles before I have some *other* permanent problems."

Queen Cleocatra observed him for another moment. "I'll let you keep your concerns to yourself unless you wish to share. If you'd rather not, are you ready to begin?"

"So ready." Remembering her advice to try and focus

inward, Joe went a step further and pushed into a deep trance using his Artisan Body to sink into his subconscious and view his Akashic Records. After only a few moments, he was within his mind, looking at the superstructure of his mind palace, delving deeper and quickly arriving next to the rubble of the structure his mind had formed to represent his Neutrality Aura.

"Stay entirely focused on the skill, and feel free to follow the tendrils of karmic energy passing through your body, if you can. Don't try to help. Don't speak while the process is happening; if you have something to say, say it after. Most importantly... *don't fight* the process. Don't worry if you can't see anything, you-" The Nyanderthal went silent as she shifted her perspective and found herself face to face with Joe, deep inside his mind. "**Mmrrraaow!**"

Joe tumbled backward, his eyes flying open as his head bounced off the ground. "Gah! What was *that* all about?"

The cat was staring at him from a few feet away, back arched and fur puffed out, turning her into a giant white cloud. "You were *in* your head!"

"Yeah, so were you. So what?" The Ritualist sat up once more, reassuming his position. "Were you not expecting me to be in there focusing on the skill? *You* told me to do it!"

"I had no idea you could directly access your Akashic Records." The queen stared at him with something akin to suspicion in her feline eyes. "You are no monk or... I suppose perhaps you count as a cleric?"

"That's not how I got the skill, but yes, once upon a time, I pretended to be a cleric for a good chunk of time. This is from a secondary effect of a body refinement skill." After his pulse slowed down nominally, Joe splayed his hands and dropped them to his knees. "Should we try this once more, or are you going to scream inside my brain again?"

"This changes things," Cleo muttered vaguely, looking away from Joe and toward the corner of his ceiling near the door. "Perhaps... you might actually have a good chance at figuring out how to do this yourself. I hadn't wanted to call out your arrogance, simply assuming it was ignorance, but now?"

"Arrogance? Because I want to learn how to fix myself, by myself?" Joe's eyes narrowed as his lips pressed firmly together. "Seems a little extreme."

Cleo's fur slowly relaxed, allowing her to return to her normal, regal appearance. "Time moves differently within your own mind. When you said you wanted to learn how to do this, I didn't explain what it will actually look like, unwilling to crush your ambitions. To an outside observer, remapping your skill will be *nearly* instantaneous. Karmic energy will flood into your mana channels, touch your skill, then race through each channel and node until the best, most effective, most energy-efficient route has been determined. The remaining energy will block the flow from moving along it then be recalled into the skill as fuel to rebuild."

"Oh, so, just Dijkstra's algorithm but for-?"

His question trailed off as it earned him a moment of scathing irritation from the Nyanderthal, "What did I say about questions? Save them for the end. Resume your focus; I'll see you in your mind."

"Wait, what'll the difference be, since I can... sorry, saving questions for the end." Closing his eyes again, shifting his breathing, and focusing inside, Joe quickly returned to the ruined structure, only to find the cat already there waiting for him.

"Ugh, you *can* do it at will. This is weird." Her grumblings had a strange, echoing quality to them as they bounced around inside his head. When she next spoke, it was firmer and with much more solemnity. "Joe. I, Queen Cleocatra, am here acting as an arbiter between you and a debt owed from another. As partial payment to you from the other entity, I will be pulling on the power owed to you according to the system. As my payment for services rendered, I will have a portion of their debt be weighed against the balance *I* have taken on. Should there not be enough debt, the remaining power will be pulled from other debts owed to you. Do you accept?"

"Yes." The Ritualist was under no illusions that there wouldn't be enough power, seeing as the bond between him and Tatum created a beacon large enough to track him across the cosmos. He wasn't here to ask questions–yet–so he simply replied as directly as possible, leaving nothing for interpretation.

No more words were exchanged as the eyes of the Nyanderthal turned to shimmering disks of purest gold. At the same moment, Joe felt a shift in his own perspective as his Karmic Perception overlaid his perception of his mind.

The calm, library-flavored air in the depths of his mind began to stir. The ambient lighting he'd never before put thought into shifted away from being perfect for reading during a rainy day into a brilliance that increased continuously, until he knew he would've been blinded were he staring at it with his physical eyes. Then came the sensation. There was no temperature shift, hot and cold being *far* outside of the purview of the swelling power. It was judgment, sharp and clean, an invisible line being drawn that perfectly delineated all that was admirable and what was detestable.

There was no room for shades of gray within the all-consuming light, and before anything else happened, Joe shivered as dust motes and fragments of destroyed skills–tiny remnants of Tatum's Divine Energy that had remained within his Akashic Records without binding to anything–were burned away. Not just within the focused skill, but swelling until the entire mind palace he'd created was shining from within and without, scrubbed and dusted to the smallest atom.

"A single act of recompense has been enacted, merely cleaning the mess Tatum created and failed to clean up. No longer will this damage remain and slowly build debt between you." Cleo turned her eyes to meet Joe's. "This is not a favor from me but simply the beginning of the remapping process. Attempting this without working in a sterile environment is practically asking for your soul to catch an infection."

"Soul infection. Oh look, a new fear unlocked." Though he didn't intentionally speak, they were within his mind, and his thoughts were laid bare, doubly so when they were this intensive.

The all-encompassing light began to narrow, turning from the heart of a sun to a flood light, then a spotlight focused on the remnants of his Neutrality Aura, a tractor beam holding the tippy building upright before condensing into a thick substance. Then the light pulsed, and his awareness traveled along with it as the leading edge washed into the shifting patterns at the edge of his mind where his skills connected to his class. There was a moment of resistance, then the beam fragmented into millions of tiny hooks that sought out the thinnest of gaps, swarming and searching like a school of fish looking to swim through a fractured dam.

The first filament that found purchase sank deeper into Joe's body, his mind alongside it in an instant. Hours passed, *years*, as he followed along every last bit of the geometric mandala that had been carved into his flesh and bones. Each cell had a connection point, being its own node that provided a route to every one of its dendrite-connected neighbors. Thousands of miles worth of area to cover, tens of thousands... then finally he was out of his brain and still had the remainder of his body to go.

A lifetime passed as Joe swam through the micro-currents of karmic energy in his very *self*, until finally his entire being was filled with light. Walking along his mana channels, Joe found that there were flavors he somewhat associated with a particular building. Smells that made him think of cleanliness and, oddly enough, the sharpness of cold water. He sought to understand how these sensations correlated and found himself stopping at individual nodes, sometimes choosing a different path as the distant memories became clearer.

At one point, he found himself pausing, realizing that, though the route he was on currently didn't have the exact same texture as he was looking for, somehow there was a coloration he deeply associated with the ruined edifice.

He walked those paths as well, touching corridors that led in the wrong directions. Unknown eons later, he found himself standing in front of rubble, staring at an edifice in confusion and wondering why it seemed so familiar.

Oddly enough, there was another creature there waiting for him, seeming to recognize him. Turning his ancient gaze to the project he had been working on forever, the entity watched as power pulled back, streaming in and reforming a foundation, walls, ceilings, beautiful artistic patterns, geometric representations he understood at an intrinsic level to hold the meaning he'd been searching for... endlessly.

"Done.," the other presence stated, the word reverberating and meaning *nothing* to the conception of what was once a man. "You need to get out of here. A full second has passed, and I think you're nearly drained."

It came closer to the center of the floating strands of consciousness, reaching out with a strangely fuzzy limb.

"Boop."

Joe's eyes flew open, and he gasped for air as mana erupted out of him. Power washed over his body, then filled the room. The lone table was blasted into smithereens, the fragments vanishing into particles of light before they could fall to the ground. The very air trembled as the structure of his house started to erode, threatening to collapse around him.

"Get a *hold* on yourself, Ritualist!"

Clarity of thought swarmed back, even as the thousands of years he'd just experienced turned into a dream. Then it was gone, leaving behind only an echo and a deep understanding that he *knew* himself. The power rolling off of him calmed as Joe recognized where he was, a glance at the notification awaiting him enough to explain the odd reaction.

Skill Changed: Neutrality Aura (Expert II) → Aura of Soothing Destruction (Expert II). A borrowed blessing remade, the Aura of Soothing

Destruction is now a scale judging not intent, but action. Within the bounds of this aura, neutrality is achieved by permanently ending problems.

Effects:

1. *Continuously dissolves unclaimed items, ambient filth, and residue within range. Any item the owner recognizes as 'not owned' or 'unwanted' is now automatically eroded.*
2. *Any items dissolved by this aura are automatically converted to aspects and stored in a compatible container if available, else they are dispersed into the ambient mana.*
3. *Negative debuffs on friendly or neutral targets decay at 200% normal rate. This decay is doubled against internally originating effects (poisons, infections, invasive unwanted mana).*
4. *Allied, non-hostile entities within range are healed at a rate of 1n health per second. Entities engaged in combat with the user are damaged at a rate of .25n health per second. All parts of any entities killed by this aura are instantly converted into aspects in their entirety, sans their core if applicable.*
5. *Moisture and blood gases are specifically targeted, destroying the barriers between the user and the environment to ensure the user is passively hydrated and properly oxygenated in all environments.*

Range: Anywhere the user's mana directly reaches. Cost: 10% reserved mana pool.

"That's interesting." Joe's voice was hoarse and scratchy, the result of not using it for so very, *very* long. He swallowed and was able to speak more forcefully. "The skill name changed, it was stripped of all divine influence, and the effects shifted. Looks like I incorporated Ascendant Matrix into its makeup, but... let me double check, yeah, it didn't get rid of that as a separate skill. Hmm. Doesn't reduce incoming magic damage anymore or work against positive effects my enemies have on them, but it does damage them directly now, and-"

His eyes bulged as he reread one of the lines. "It can

directly convert an enemy killed by this into aspects without me having to sit there and work on them piece by piece? Oh, this is absolutely becoming my final hit, even if I have to pull my punches to make *sure* it happens!"

"Whew, there you are." Cleo audibly gulped in relief. "For a minute there, I thought you were lost in the flow of karma. That would have been... not great."

"No, it was-" Joe stopped himself, realizing he actually had said what he meant. "It *was*. It was awesome. I learned so much about myself and about what karmic energy actually is. It has so many similarities to Divine Energy, but, correct me if I'm wrong: when I compare Karmic and Divine Energy, is it fair to say it's similar to ambient mana versus personal mana pool?"

"Not even–huh. Um. Kind of? But where ambient mana can be generated by anything at all, even rocks, karmic energy is formed by the choices people make. Only when people die without balancing their karma does it become free energy. Divine Energy is similar, but granted to the various pantheons through intentional acts of their followers." Cleo seemed incredibly hesitant to continue speaking on the subject, but Joe powered on nonetheless.

A hint of gold appeared in his eyes, causing the Nyanderthal's fur to slowly begin puffing up once again. "I finally understand what Karmic Luck is actually for, beyond the positives and negatives when trying to make something happen. Its combat potential alone is-"

"*No*!" Cleo hissed at him, claws extended, and to Joe's current perception, coated in a thin sheath of the very power he was casually discussing. "You... even having been able to see how the skill remapping functions, this insight is beyond the pale. You didn't just see or feel it, you resonated with it. That's the second time you've shown an affinity with karmic energy *no one* beyond my people is meant to have. Even *deities* only begin to have access to this much connection upon their ascension. How, Joe? Are you one of my people masquerading as a human, somehow able to fool even *me*?"

"Humm? No, it's probably because of one of my traits." Joe's answer caused the cat to sputter, and by the way she hadn't put away her natural weapons, the queen was waiting on a more informative one. "Some things happened, and I had a lesser trait that kind of ballooned up. It was so long ago, thousands of... no...? During the settlement of Jotunheim? No, Alfheim, just after the shattering of the Dwarven race. I gained a trait called Karmic King, and all it does is let me understand Karmic Luck a little easier."

"Abyss..." Cleo sagged to her haunches. "'All it does', he says. Do you know who the last person to hold that trait was? I'll give you a hint... I have a similar trait, called Karmic *Queen*."

"Uhh... we weren't married in a past life or something... were we?" His haphazard guess earned him a scathing glare, but he didn't pull the question back until she shook her head, at which point he let out a greatly relieved sigh. "Thank goodness. I mean, you're great and all, but that makes me think there'd be some kind of prophecy forcing us back together or something."

"Yes, I understand you have *very* specific allergies when it comes to commitments outside of your field of study." Cleo huffed impatiently as Joe glanced at her without understanding her meaning. "Now, it appears the remapping was a success, so two of the three rewards I owe you have been granted. Shall we finish with the third, and see where-"

"I'm not gonna let this go." Joe's hesitant words caused the Nyanderthal to freeze, and she let out a knowing grunt as he voiced his thoughts. "If you don't explain this to me, I'm going to end up trying to figure it out for myself, Cleocatra. Karmic Luck is a weapon. If I'm correct, it's the *best* weapon."

Her reply was far more patient than Joe had expected after her initial threatening posture. "What do you *think* you know?"

"As far as I can tell, adding Karmic Luck to my attacks..." The Ritualist's eyes shone brightly as he clenched his hands into fists, mind already on the crystalline whale that had been nearly impossible to kill. "...will let me inflict *True Damage*."

CHAPTER TWENTY-FIVE

"Oh." Cleo blinked in surprise, calming down in an instant. "Well, yes."

Joe waited a moment, but the little queen didn't take it upon herself to elaborate. "That's it? A moment ago, you were ready to cut my head off for even suggesting I could use it for something, and now you're just *fine* with me figuring out True Damage?"

"I highly doubt you have enough Karmic Luck available to you that you'd be able to permanently damage someone *beyond* merely using it as a method to ignore their armor class," the Nyanderthal dismissively explained. "You're also unable to harness the debt owed you, which means... never mind. Yes, theoretically you could spend your Karmic Luck, so long as it is positive, to deal a portion of your damage as True Damage. Realistically, you would merely use a single point as the tip of a spear, allowing the rest of your natural damage to flow through that singularity and into your target."

"What were you thinking I was thinking?"

"Joe," Cleo replied with a flat stare. "I was about to start cutting you down simply for saying something out loud; why do you think I would let you know what it was, if you *hadn't* already figured it out?"

The Ritualist hummed lightly as he regarded the cat, deciding it was probably best to put this topic to the side for the moment, but he found himself unable to stop from pushing just a *bit* more. "Understood. If I have a breakthrough on this, are we going to have a problem?"

"Unlikely, as you aren't the sort of person to abuse the power it would grant you," Cleo explained with a hint of sadness in her voice, "When someone learns how to do so, they are usually put down permanently or go on the run from us forever. If they intentionally use it once, they *will* use it again. The power is far too seductive. Better that you don't know."

"'Us' meaning the Nyanderthals?" Once again, the only answer to his question was a slow swishing of the cat's fluffy tail. "*Fi~ine*. Shall we work on the third reward, then?"

"I'll take a look at that codpiece after you figure out how to reactivate your remapped skill without causing everything around you to crumble." Cleo's words caused Joe's eyes to light up, as he *intentionally* activated his Aura of Soothing Destruction for the first time.

Mana flowed out of him, wrapping around his body like a thick cocoon yet held tight to his skin. Immediately he felt better, his health ticking upward to finish the job Dawnesha had started back in Novusheim. His clothes felt cleaner, the white fabric gaining luster as though it had been freshly bleached, the studs on his gloves shining as though polished, and his Decury Duelist patch shimmering as though challenging the world around him to a fight. "That's–oh, right! Its range is 'wherever my mana reaches' now. I'm holding it close so my Emperor of Mana title doesn't mess with stuff, but..."

Carefully extending his Mana Dominion, Joe could see the effects on the world around him in real time. The cocoon he'd formed split open like a rose unfurling its petals, and the air began sparking with static electricity as the lazy spiral of dust filling the room touched against his aura and simply ceased existing. "That flash must've been grime turning into Trash aspects, right?"

Knowing he was simply talking to himself, Cleo didn't bother to respond, seemingly content to enjoy the show as Joe struggled to conceptualize the fact that he needed to intentionally view the items in his room as 'not trash' long enough for his aura to recognize them and simply clean the miniscule amount of filth away instead of destroying–for instance–the floor. In no time flat, his baseboards were clean, the stone foundation was gleaming with a mirrored polish, and the air swiftly began... drying?

Smacking his lips, Joe frowned slightly as the moisture in the air continued to plummet, even as the tight, papery feeling behind his eyes he'd long since grown accustomed to faded away. Rubbing his fingers together, he heard a scratchy rasp then felt a shift deep inside him–as though his kidneys were jumping for joy. "Ahh... automatic hydration. Was I really *that* bad?"

"Please open the door or something to let some humidity back in here." The Ritualist glanced at Cleo and had to force himself to keep a straight face as he saw her fur lifting into the air, the fluffy cat now a giant ball of static electricity waiting to be unleashed. "Perhaps you have a jug of water you could dump onto the ground? Go turn your shower on?"

"That one." Walking over to his bathroom, Joe pulled on the spigot handle and put the shower on full blast, only to flinch away as the entirety of the output was diverted away from the drain and onto his skin, where it sank through the surface and directly joined his bloodstream, quickly rehydrating every last cell in his body. After two full seconds, the water began pounding against the floor, and the Ritualist took a deep breath with lungs that expanded fully and *didn't* have a leathery **crackle** to them any longer. "Alright, I get it now. Maybe that cleric that gave me an IV a while ago was more serious than I realized."

Flexing his hands, Joe inspected himself with a slow and

unguarded grin spreading across his face. "No grime under my fingernails. No sticky sweat or blood clinging to my skin. Oh, Aura of Soothing Destruction, I've missed you and your predecessor for *far* too long."

"Leave the shower on to steam the air, and let's get this over with! I have other places to be." Cleo's voice had a hint of annoyance in it, and Joe knew better than to test his luck with this powerful, yet oddly lazy monarch.

When he emerged from the bathroom, he was holding a perfectly clean Legendary storage codpiece in his hands, which was reverently placed on the floor where the table had once stood. "I've had this for years now, and if there's anything I own that deserves an upgrade to the Mythic rank, it's this."

Cleo extended one paw, slowly reaching out and brushing the little toes on her footpad against the item. "Mm... yes. This has everything it needs, except... its mind is still too young to form a proper Mythic baseline. Or, should I say, too far too singularly focused. A direct upgrade would merely increase its storage capabilities, sorting, and total amount of space."

"You won't upgrade it for me, then?" Joe was rather crestfallen, having been certain he'd finally be able to repay his gear for all of its hard work and efforts.

"I didn't say that. Yet, I feel we would be doing this codpiece a great disservice if we did so. Who knows what it could eventually become, were it to ascend naturally?" Joe perked up at Cleo's words, as she slowly explained, "This is a truly ancient item, and I believe it has been naturally growing its entire existence. There are signs that it was created as a *Rare* item, and the energy emanating from it is entirely its own. As far as I can see, it's never once been pushed to ascend, which means it will likely be able to make its way to the next rank on its own."

"I mean, Mythic is as high as it goes, so would it be so bad to help it on its way?" Joe's words were met with silence, and his eyes went wide as he made a realization. "Mythic *isn't* as high as it goes? Divine? If we let it grow on its own, does that mean we could maybe push it to the next rank after-"

"Sorry, Joe. That's information I either don't have or can't give to you." Cleo's voice was overly loud as she interrupted him, making it clear she wasn't speaking for his benefit alone. The Ritualist understood that some unseen watcher, likely the system, must be eavesdropping on their conversation. "This is your reward we are talking about, and if you want to use it on this item, I'm not going to stop you."

Rubbing at his chin, Joe hesitated, but only because he was sorting through all of the various items he owned, trying to figure out the best usage of this one-time offer. "No... but I'd love to know how to help it grow naturally, if you can share that information?"

"I suppose it depends on how your reward is chosen to be used," Cleo replied, clearly picking her words very carefully. "Still, I would love to tender my reward now. The offer is made, and if you don't use it, I can only say that I tried to give it to you. When I leave, you'll have to seek me out in order to get it. I won't come and find you to offer my services."

Clasping his hands in front of him, Joe slowly blew a hot breath onto his fingers. After a moment, his eyebrows shot up. "Oh! I have an idea; what if you helped me with this?"

Grabbing his codpiece, Joe looped it over his shoulder and cupped his hands in front of him, then drew out the ritual orb Tatum had given him after a year of non-interaction. Even with his Characteristics much higher than when he'd first gained the weapon, he still strained to hold it aloft and slowly sank in place until he was forced to set it on the ground. It wasn't a physical weight, more of an assault on his mind that made holding onto the item incredibly difficult.

Glancing at Cleocatra, the Ritualist felt gratified to see her mouth hanging open as she read over the orb's information. He joined her in admiring it for a long moment.

Deific Ritual Orb (Bound) (Growth). This exotic weapon is one piece of a set of weapons usable by Ritualists only. While it can be bound to anyone at any level, it is a Sage-rank weapon and therefore the immense strain it produces makes it unusable for anyone without enough mental power to control it. Requirements for use:

1 Sage-rank Ritualist Class skill OR

5 Grandmaster-rank Ritualist Core Skills OR

3 Grandmaster-rank Ritualist Core skills, 1 Master-rank Exotic Weapon skill specific to Ritual Orbs, and 1 Master-rank skill which passively supports the Exotic Weapon skill.

Binding this weapon to yourself early will allow it to grow over time based on your experiences, even if you are unable to actively use it in combat.

"I'm not going to try to get you to upgrade this, as something tells me that's probably not going to happen." Joe awkwardly chuckled as he stood straight and rubbed the back of his head, his eyes curved into crescents as he smiled at the cat. "However, it'd be really cool if you could help me bind the orb. I know I can't use it for a long time, but I'd like to bind it to my Karmic Luck, and I just have... ya know, *no* idea how I'd even go about doing that."

"A... a good choice," Cleo finally managed to sputter out as she tore her gaze away from the glowing weapon. "This is a Peak Mythical weapon, and once it's bound and has the opportunity to grow further, it will definitely become... I have no idea what it will become."

Once again, her words turned stilted and robotic, though her eyes widened at Joe knowingly. With an exaggerated nod, she asked in a casual tone, "This is certainly something within my *purr*-view, and I would be willing to assist in the binding of your weapon to your Karmic Luck. Now, it's not what I promised you, but I am also the only person who could properly assist with this. Are you willing to trade a direct upgrade for assistance of this kind?"

"Is this something I could do without you?" Though it was obvious she was trying to get him to jump at the chance immediately, and Joe knew it was probably the best option, he didn't know when he'd have another opportunity for an instant powerup again.

Cleocatra opened her mouth, only to close it with a troubled expression, wrestling with her thoughts longer than Joe expected. "Before today, I would've likely told you this wasn't possible without my help. But now? After learning of your Karmic King trait and seeing your affinity for karma in action? Yes, I think this *is* something you could do on your own, *eventually*. Most likely, after binding a ritual orb to each of your Characteristics, you will gain the insights into the process you would need in order to bind your Karmic Luck. Perhaps, after a few decades of careful introspection, studying *The Ties That Bind People-*"

"Eh... hold on," Joe held up his hands. "Studying interactions between people? How words can have a positive meaning and still get a negative reaction? Really diving deep into the territory of Charisma, most likely? Can we skip all of that and maybe just let me accept this as a reward?"

"It would be great for you; I hope you understand." Cleo spoke with all sincerity. "Eventually you'll need to follow that path, if you hope to get the most out of this trait."

"If I'm being as honest with you as possible, it's a little too..." Joe fluttered his fingers as if emulating confetti falling from the air. "Ya know? How do I quantify a Karmic Debt? How do I control it, have a repeated cycle, apply scientific thinking in a way that lets me use 'em? Nah. I'll stick to magic, thank you very much. If I learn cool things along the way, that's great. But going out there and making a deep study on what I can only call, as generously as possible, *soft* magic? I'll leave that to 'soft' people like yourself. By that I mean fuzzy, not weak."

"I understood." Cleo seemed to greatly relax, visibly relieved at hearing his decision. "I could teach you, you know? Take your understanding to a new level, over the next half decade of dedicated study and learning in both a classroom and practical environment?"

"Nah. Rituals are my jam." Joe gestured at the orb on the floor. "If it's all the same to you, I'd like this to be my reward?"

"Prepare what you need to prepare," Cleo ordered after a heartbeat of distracted decision-making, letting out a soft sigh of acceptance. "I will begin spinning our debt into a usable thread and allow you to imbue it with... you do have a positive value in your Karmic Luck currently, yes? Good. Then we should have no problems."

It had been a while since Joe had gone through the process of binding his Characteristics to a ritual orb, mainly due to the fact that he was working with Expert-ranked versions currently, and they had the unfortunate habit of breaking during extended combat sessions. A glance at the nearly solid-black, silver-speckled orb on the floor put those concerns to rest. "I'll get right on that. Just need a bit of alchemy work, a ritual, and I'm *pretty sure* that was glowing gold when I first got it. Did I break it?"

"Probably just an effect Tatum placed around the weapon to make sure you didn't misplace it when he first created it." Cleo brushed off his concerns easily. "Would've been quite the incident if someone else had managed to come along and scoop that up without you noticing it existed in the first place."

Joe shivered at even the suggestion, twice as glad to be permanently binding the weapon to himself as he'd been only moments before. Pulling out his alchemy equipment, he ignored the amused stare the queen shot his way as he deadlifted his Abyssal Bloom cauldron and began packing aspects into it.

With each orb he bound to himself, the requirements both for the alchemical reagent as well as the ritual circle he used increased by a rank. Seeing as he was a Master in both of those Core Class skills and currently only had three of his Characteristics bound, it was barely the work of an hour to produce everything he needed. Even then, it was only because he was including the time Cleo needed to do... whatever it was she was doing.

Joe was directed to sit in a meditative position around the orb, his legs slightly extended so as to grant the Nyanderthal access to the weapon. She circled him once, then twice, her padding steps silent against the stone floor. As she went around him again, the Ritualist found himself blinking, trying to rid himself of the odd after-image of her passing–as though an echo of the queen was following half a step behind the original.

"You've bound Characteristics before." Her soft voice came directly from behind his left ear, though the Ritualist could see her walking directly in front of him. "Having someone else do it for you means granting them access to not only your Characteristics, but your own mindset. How you view what those Characteristics *are*. How they affect you, how they form your being from the inside out. I tell you this, not to scare you but to warn you. This will not be painful. Yet it will feel... wrong. Misaligned. The sensation *will* pass."

Fidgeting slightly, Joe decided to fish for information while she was being chatty. "Are there a lot of people out there who bind their Characteristics to weapons? Stuff, maybe?"

"To all manner of things." Her voice spoke each word in an alternating pattern into his left, then right ear, then back again. Immediately, he felt a hint of nausea and went to close his eyes, only to find them open again without his intervention. "They might bind themselves to weapons, and yes, that is the most common variation. But someone like your mother? Her robes would not protect her nearly so well were she not willing to give up the part of her that is willing to harm others, no?"

"How do you know my-"

Joe's words were cut off as Cleo spoke onward, "Mages often bind to various foci which will allow them to cast spells beyond their abilities. There are even those focused on Charisma who will choose to bind to a musical instrument, thereby granting themselves the slightest edge over their competition. Rulers or monarchs who are bound to a location, such as a singular city? That isn't mere hyperbole; often their thrones and their very selves are literally tied to each other in service of their kingdom. So yes, not only is this more common than you might believe, but I have assisted with the process many times before."

There was a lingering silence, and the Nyanderthal seemed reluctant as she murmured, "I will say... not many are willing to go this far. Karmic Luck is the most ephemeral of the stats, even beyond Luck itself. While the other Characteristics come from yourself, allowing you to have a hand in how they grow, this one is how the world sees *you.* Your choices and your actions, yes, but not your *intentions.* Because of this, it's usually impossible for someone to bind this on their own. You could've been one of those few, but I understand your... hesitation."

Joe blinked, finding that Cleo had stopped opposite him and raised a paw. There was no light gathering, no flare in the ambient mana. Yet the space between her outstretched limb and the orb seemed to shift, as though he were looking at the Nyanderthal through a concave lens. For a moment, it seemed as though her paw were ten times its original size, hundreds, as distant as the horizon, yet still expanding to fill his view.

In one motion, she scooped him and the orb up, though he remained exactly where he was. She wasn't tugging at his skin or his mana channels. Instead, it was a sideways pull, and he felt *seen* in a deeply uncomfortable way—as though the eyes of a large crowd were quickly turning toward him, one after another. A stadium's worth, a kingdom's worth, then one enormous, burning gaze from deep within the void of space.

Energy trickled out of him, golden in his suddenly shifted sight. Immediately, patterns bloomed across the surface of his ritual orb, lines curving and intersecting as images began to form, only to slide away as new ones replaced them.

He looked closer without realizing, seeing a battlefield where he had dropped to his knees, on the verge of giving up as others paid for his stubbornness and choices with their blood. A silver silhouette of a quiet room with an empty fireplace, where he had looked at various books in the room without reaching out for any of them, turning away and making a choice which had greatly benefited him. A hand being offered in friendship, another hand only pretending to do so. Promises he had kept where it would've been easier to ignore them, joined with promises kept only to the letter of the agreement instead of the spirit.

Nothing lingered, shifting and fading endlessly, and Joe intrinsically understood that he could stand there for his entire lifetime and watch his past unfold in front of him from the moment he gained sapience until now. As he pulled away, the depth of what he could see faded, until they were merely reflections on disturbed water, then were hidden by the endlessly deep darkness of the surface of the orb.

"It is done." Cleo wobbled on her feet, her eyes crossing and uncrossing as she struggled to focus on Joe. "That's... that was more than I wanted it to be and less than I still owe. I need rest. *Purrrrrrrrrr*-haps a week of sleep or so. Yet, it's not quite enough. Ask me your question, and consider the quest completed."

Joe's mouth fell open, for an instant unsure what she meant, though his mind caught up quickly. "Yes! First, thank you for this, it's perfect. I'll read the notifications after you go get some sleep, but... the question. What do I need to do to get my codpiece to the Mythic rank naturally?"

"That's easy." Cleo sleepily smirked at him. "Just let it hold on to some Mythic materials or a Mythic item for a while to get a baseline for what it's trying to achieve on its own. Then, feed a Mythic Core-"

"Oh, come *on*."

Joe's protestation cut off before it could truly begin as she finished, "-into its storage for a while, and it will absorb the runoff energy and ascend naturally without having to consume it. Not a terrible plan, since you're going to need two of them to become a Sage in the first place. Just remember, don't die while you're holding onto a Mythic Core, because it will *always* drop from your corpse."

As though the word 'drop' had been a command, the cat

fell to the floor and curled into a snoring furball the next instant. Joe scooped her up with one hand and the orb with the other, freezing in place as he realized how easy it was to move the weapon now.

Not sure what else to do, the Ritualist pulled a comfy chair and a large pillow out of storage, gently placing the exhausted queen on its surface before leaving his house and quietly closing the door behind him.

CHAPTER TWENTY-SIX

The silence on his mountain was somewhat startling, especially with the sun high in the sky. Joe looked around, seeing only casual sentries posted up near the outskirts of the peak. After a moment, he snapped his fingers. "Right! Two weeks of sunlight per day. Of course people have to sleep and such, even when daylight's burnin'."

With that micro-mystery out of the way, Joe's world briefly reduced to the singular object resting in his open palm. The ritual orb didn't glow, hum, vibrate, pulse, or even reflect the sunshine sloshing across the Sect territory. It simply remained in his cupped palm, as black as spilled ink with only the silver flecks in its depths revealing that it was anything other than solidified shadows.

"Now how is it..." Joe nudged at the ritual orb with his mind, knowing it was unlikely to lift into the air, yet was still minorly disappointed when it didn't even wiggle. Pulling back slightly, he reordered his thoughts. "How is it that a peak-Mythic item can still be a *growth* weapon? I know it has some kind of intelligence already, otherwise it wouldn't have reacted when I made a joke about cracking it apart and using it to make templates for other versions. Maybe that has something to do with it?"

The fact was, the Ritualist had only one other Mythic item, the Karmic Shroud around his neck, which he could activate to hide his karmic bonds from the world and therefore avoid having horrible situations chucked at him in order to 'give him rewards he was already due'. But he'd been wearing it for a while, and it hadn't shown any indication of shifting or changing, which meant he would have to learn as he went. "Hmm... both of these are *karmic* items now. I'd say that was some kind of pattern, but it only became that way after I bound it, so that *can't* be the only thing that's necessary for items to reach that level."

Poking and prodding at the orb as he walked around the area, Joe tried tightening his focus, wrapping it with mana, and even just tossing it into the air. Pressure built up in his head, a usual occurrence when using the psychically directed ritual orbs for long periods of time, yet there was still no reaction—the weapon may as well be a gorgeous paperweight. Picking the weapon up off the ground, his eyes crinkled in slight interest as to the fist-sized crater it had formed. "Okay, as a last resort, I can just *drop* it on someone. It's bound, so I'm not about to lose it. Good to know."

With a sharp inhale, Joe tried a different, far more *aggressive* approach.

The world around him **hummed** and sparked as his Mana Dominion extended to its full expanse, and he *grabbed* the orb with a thick ball of coalescent fusion-formed threads. Power flooded out of him as he worked to hoist it into the air, inviting the item to absorb his mana if it wanted. Yet even with the air thickened and shivering as if in fear, the orb simply fell to the ground as if it were a standard rock.

A short, sharp laugh erupted from Joe's chest. "There's a mind in there, all right. Looks like you just don't care to play *ball* right now, huh? Get it? 'Cause you're an orb? Nothing? I see, you mustn't be able to understand my language. Otherwise you'd at least be spinning in place with laughter."

Seeing as he couldn't use the weapon, Joe plucked it off the ground and went to put it into his codpiece, knowing that it would gain all of the benefits of being bound, no matter where it was. On that note, his codpiece would also see growth, according to Cleocatra, as it accommodated something above its own rarity. "There you go, help each other out. See you after I get a few more skills to the Master rank... what's this, now?"

Deific Ritual Orb of Karmic Luck (Bound) (Growth). This exotic weapon is one piece of a set of weapons usable by Ritualists only. While it can be bound to anyone at any level, it is a Sage-rank weapon, and therefore the immense strain it produces makes it unusable for anyone without enough mental power to control it.

Effects:

1. *Uses the wielder's insights into Karmic Luck to deal a different damage type on hit with each attack. The damage dealt against any target struck will depend on your knowledge of their bonds and debts.*
2. *Unknown.*
3. *3-9 Unknown.*

Requires a minimum of 1 point of Karmic Luck per attack.

"Now isn't *that* interesting," the Ritualist murmured as he stored away the Mythic weapon, hoping that, when he was able to wield it, the orb would have grown enough to have multiple effects already. "Seems like it'll have at least nine different possible effects on it. Hopefully when I can actually use it, it'll give me a bit more information. How much damage does it do, seeing as it's three tiers above my other weapons? Lastly... I lose Karmic Luck just by *using* the orb?"

Unfortunately, he'd need to wait to find out for a good long time. A system notification popped into place, alongside a feeling of being absolutely bloated... then compressed.

Skill increase: Celestial-Arcane Interaction Lore (Master 0 → Master

I)! All Characteristics +5, except Karmic Luck! Excess Characteristics deferred!

With that increase, he had officially dragged each of his Characteristics to a total of four hundred and ninety-nine points each, the main component necessary for breaking through into the next threshold. In fact, there was a glut of points stored up that should be enough to put him well into the five hundreds for most of his Characteristics... and yet... there wasn't a single hint of the system doing any of its usual intense displays to show he was about to break through.

Faced with multiple situations which didn't have any answers readily available, the Ritualist could only straighten his shoulders and look around the cloudy peak. Not for the first time, Joe was faced with an overly familiar question that always seemed to loom large when he came to liminal spaces between active goals:

"Now what?"

The mountain air was still, yet charged with potent mana. Distant rituals caused the ambient power to pulse in time, the Ritual of the Eternal Turtle still endlessly draining energy from the clouds and converting it into a semi-permanent defensive layer.

Even as he watched, Joe could practically see the sister peaks of the Sect growing, while his remained the same height—an effect of the Ritual of Stoneheart Compression at play. His mountain was actually growing at the same rate as the others around it, yet it was never going to be the same height. Even so, that was a point of pride. He leaned down and patted the ground fondly. "*Our* mountain is going to have an absolutely unshakable foundation."

After a few minutes of admiring the hard work his Sect members had been putting in, Joe turned toward the teleportation pad in the distance and began moving toward it. "If I don't know what to do, it's never a bad option to check on infrastructure. Let's go see how the growth of the teleportation network is going."

**Wahmp.*

When Joe was nearly halfway to the teleportation pad, a messenger in a brightly colored uniform appeared on top of it, looking around with slight disorientation as he regained his bearings. As the man took a hesitant step off the pad, his eyes landed on the Ritualist and lit up.

Joe felt his heart sink as the runner darted toward him, only to skid to a stop with his boots tearing up some newly planted grass. The messenger had a bright grin on his face as he pulled out a letter and waved it around. "First Elder Joe! Message for you, express postage from Midgard. I appreciate you making it so easy to find you; this is the easiest major payday I've had in a good long time."

The Ritualist reluctantly accepted the letter, moving to open it but pausing as he saw the runner remain awkwardly in place, staring at him in expectation. "Thank you for the letter?"

"No problem, no problem!" The messenger shifted slightly, his grin fading from full-power to customer-service. "Don't suppose you'd like to add on a tip for prompt delivery? We recommend thirty percent-"

"Here." Joe picked up a rock and dropped it in the grinning man's hand, and the messenger froze in place as he stared at the Ritualist in confusion. "I just brought this to you, a special order from Vanaheim. I know you have no idea what it is, you didn't ask for it, and you might not even want it. Anyway, how about you give me a bunch of money because I gave it to you?"

The messenger's face went sour, and Joe rolled his eyes in exasperation. "Buddy, you just told me this was the easiest delivery you ever had. Probably because you were able to use the teleportation network *I set up* to travel across the surface of Jotunheim to the top of a mountain with just a thought."

Grumbling about out-of-control tipping culture, Joe stepped onto the teleportation pad and set his coordinates to all zeros. With a soft crackle of blue power, he found himself in the 'Joe-to-Go' headquarters, feeling somewhat aggrieved at the ugly glare the messenger had been giving him as he vanished. Sweeping his eyes over the room to make sure everything was in order, his gaze landed on a curtain hastily set up and dividing the large open building in two, hiding whatever was on the other side from his view. "What's that all about?"

"That's a surprise!" the Ritualist on duty called over in a weary tone. Even so, the individual had lit up upon seeing Joe arrive, so he likely didn't have malicious intentions. "Aw man, you're here *way* too early. Could you ignore that for a little bit? My shift is ending, and I know Nixie was one of the people they gave all the information to. She should be here anytime now."

"I can give it a little bit, but I... kinda feel uncomfortable having surprises waiting for me in my own buildings? Should go without saying that this place is pretty important to the ongoing success of the Sect..." Seeing the other man frantically nod and begin working on a message spell, Joe grumbled softly and turned away, looking at the sealed letter he'd just been given.

Pulling at the wax, the parchment unfolded into an extensive missive from someone with near-perfect handwriting, and a quick glance at the signature at the bottom let Joe know that it had come from Boris.

Joe,

I hope this letter finds you in good health and preferably not in the middle of something that would explode if you've set it down to read this. There is nothing in here that is dire or terribly time sensitive, so please focus on your current project before feeling the need to delve further into this letter.

Joe looked away, letting his head fall back as he stared at the gorgeously intricate ceiling of the Legendary building he was in. "Come on, Boris. That can't be how you really think of me, right?"

Feeling put-upon, he turned his eyes back to the letter and read on.

If you are receiving this letter, you must be on Jotunheim. As I am uncertain where else to find you, I had this delivered to your Sect. If you received it right away, fantastic. If not, please look for a secondary letter that might be coming to you with a few details listed below. As you know, news travels in fragments between worlds, with large lag times depending on the frequency of messengers being available to make the trip.

As we had discussed, I have taken the liberty of beginning the process of regaining tenure with the Scholar Society from my end. I have no illusions that my research in the Pathfinder's Hall, novel though it may be, will be enough to re-secure my standing. Therefore, included with my request, and the synopsis of my current research, I added in a third point of information I felt would be extremely relevant to my reinstatement, namely the fact that the originator of the Scholar profession is still active on Vanaheim.

With great care and choosing of words, I informed them that I could have overturned their decision without any preamble, yet am hoping to return through the standard process. Seeing as I was removed from the Scholar's Society due to my association with an Occultist, yet it has come to light that the originator of the Occultist profession is also the founder of the Scholars… I have great hopes that they will reconsider my case and reverse their decision forthwith.

I am certain that my formal reinstatement will require your involvement, but as you know, I'm not content to sit and wait to be rescued. If an opportunity presents itself, I intend to be prepared. Should the society respond and grant my request for an audience, I only ask that you make yourself available as soon as it is practical. Please be on the lookout for another letter in the near future.

With great respect, and fingers crossed,

Boris.

A deep humming stole his attention as he tucked away the letter, and Joe felt some of the tension leave his shoulders as a school of fish appeared in the center of the room, starting to fly on streamers of iridescent clouds, only for the enormous teleportation pad beneath them to activate and send them away. The room lit up once more as the mana accumulator refilled the storage, laminar streams of light pumping fresh power into the ritual to recharge it. A veritable rainbow of aspects joined the beam of mana, injecting the materials required to summon yet another swarm.

"Looks like everything is working the way it's supposed to..." The Ritualist shot one last, uneasy glance at the curtain before walking over to the aspect jar storage plinth and pulling it out of the ground. Unsurprisingly, the higher-tier aspect jars were near full to bursting, while the lower-ranking ones were only *partially* filled, at best. "Looking good, let's see... still have plenty of Common and Uncommon, but Rare and Unique are pretty much out. Oh? There's a couple Artifact aspects gumming up the works here; how'd those get in here?"

After pulling the aspects into his new jar, Joe took the opportunity to recover all of the Natural Aspect Jars and replace them with standard versions, which didn't regenerate on their own. Still, each of them were full to the brim, while the natural versions were all but empty. "Okie-dokie, at this point, everyone knows how to use the network, and it should be self-sustaining by now. If not, it'll be on *them* to make sure it stays well-fed."

A quick stop over at the hidden panel later, Joe was the pleased owner of dozens of Common and Uncommon cores, with a couple Unique and a handful of Rares in the mix. "Less than I was expecting, but I suppose not many people are throwing entire corpses down the trash chute these days. I bet these come from people out hunting who leave a monster on the pad to pay for their travel, not people in the Sect properly butchering their kills."

Popping over to the Ritualist on duty, Joe took a look at the tablet detailing the extent of the current network, letting out a low whistle at the thousands upon thousands of miles the network now covered. "Have we been able to see any curvature with all of these, yet? Once we can get a baseline, we should be able to extrapolate out how big the planet is as a whole."

"Yeah, about that." The man manning the tablet zoomed out slightly. "As you can see, while there are currently thousands of destinations, they are generally clustered in a grid pattern in a large sphere of influence. There have been requests to shift the distribution into a straight line, making a belt around Jotunheim instead of a slowly expanding circle. Thoughts?"

Joe shook his head after a moment of consideration. "No, the point of this system isn't only to get around the planet. It's also to seek out powerful opponents and the like."

"Oh good, because we send a daily report, and the Sect has been making kill quests for anything at the Artifact, or, ya know, Master rank. Good experience for our people, lots of materials flowing in. Even if it's only been one or two of them, they take *days* to process."

Joe's eyes flicked to the once-again-hidden plinth, a hint of glee filling him as he realized the Artifact aspects likely hadn't been a fluke. "Good show. I'll have to swing by more often and keep an eye on things. I appreciate your hard work, and now... I'm going to have to take a look behind the curtain."

"Aww, don't do that!" Joe edged away from the whining man, uncomfortable with his too-familiar attitude. "Just hang on-"

"I'm here!" Nixie's bright voice echoed through the room as she appeared with a crackle of blue light, breathless and looking around wildly until she saw Joe's bald head shining in the mystical light given off by the energies sweeping through the room. "Tell me you didn't look yet! No, of course you haven't; you wouldn't be looking at me like that. Yay!"

"Not a fan of surprises in my own-" Joe began to growl, but the enthusiastic female Ritualist rushed over and grabbed his hand, pulling him toward the curtain—even if he was somewhat reluctant to follow.

Without further ado, she gripped the curtain and ripped it away with one pull. As the expansive bolt of fabric fluttered to the ground, Joe's objections died quietly.

A full half of the enormous, square building was filled from floor to ceiling with machinery. There were intricate, interconnected pipe systems, pressure chambers, drums, and an enormous alchemical setup which used only basic equipment; yet it existed on a scale he'd only witnessed in the Pyramid of

Panacea itself. Vats the size of small buildings lined the eastern wall, while refrigeration units created from enormous containers with various rituals carved into them caused the air to shiver with frost. Directly opposed to that were kettles and pressurized tanks letting off enough heat that the air was distorted like a mirage.

"It's... beautiful, but what is it?" Joe blinked rapidly as the ubiquitous chrome of the machinery shifted colorations along with the magical lights emanating from the mana and aspects which were actively generating rituals and fish to expand the teleportation network.

"It's the Sect's way of saying 'thank you'," Nixie informed him with a guileless grin. "For stepping up and saving the Sect here and on Midgard. For jumping in when the titan was choking out the main Sect mountain, and evacuating everyone who needed to go. Letting them know they always have a place they could escape to when things are at their most dangerous. That, and setting up the teleportation system. Everyone loves that."

Joe took a slow step forward, inspecting the logo carved into every major surface: a stylized coffee cup with lightning bolts crackling off of it instead of steam lines. "It's a *gift*? But... what is it?"

"It's a *coffee machine*," Nixie explained with a grand flourish. "Large enough to supply coffee to everyone in the Sect and Novusheim, as it stands now. There are more modules coming, and once it's fully done, you should be able to run coffee to anyone across the entire planet without running out."

"They made me a coffee machine?" He shook his head. "Let me try that again... they made me a coffee-production *factory*?"

"A *planetary scale* coffee machine."

Joe swallowed hard, placing a hand on his chest. "It's all I've ever wanted. How'd they know?"

"One minor detail, but pretty important to operating this thing." Nixie chuckled dryly at his over-acting. "You're going to have to figure out how to secure coffee beans for this. It's a one-time gift, not an endless supply, you know? Anyway, we've had hundreds of people working on this, and this thing is absolutely *stuffed* with rituals. It should be able to make pretty much anything anyone wants. See those injectors over there? That's just flavored syrups. The refrigerators have all sorts of different milks, from cow, to goat, almond, coconut, penguin-"

"What was that last one?" Joe's question was ignored as Nixie continued extolling the virtues of the system they had created, and soon his doubts were forgotten. The Ritualist felt... odd, in a way he couldn't quite pinpoint until it came to him in a rush. "Oh."

"Something the matter?" Only then did Joe realize that Nixie was holding a large crystal, obviously recording his reaction to show other people after they were done here.

"No, quite the opposite." Joe gestured helplessly at the miles of tubing, vast array of distilling chambers, alembics, and drip stations. "I'm just not sure how to react. They didn't need to do this; there was no quest for it or anything. I guess I'm just surprised. I believe this is the first gift I've gotten in... in a long time. Something that wasn't tied to obligation, you know?"

Nixie's beaming smile softened and she stepped close, pulling him into a half-hug and holding the crystal up to take a selfie. "Yeah, we all figured it was well past time. You deserve nice things, too, ya know? You've done a lot for us, and we all know it. If you want to pay us back... just keep pushing the boundaries of what's possible, and maybe put together a few super weapons we can use to fight off the worst monsters around here?"

"No." Joe blinked a few times, unsure why the room had gone blurry, or why he couldn't control the smile on his face. "You don't pay for gifts. The superweapons I design are entirely for fun. There's no reason to complicate matters beyond that."

Nixie only laughed, fully aware that he was doing his best to banter but was all but short-circuiting from the unexpected generosity of the Sect. "Well, once you secure a way to start filling this machine up, I know you're going to have plenty of customers waiting for a fresh cup of joe."

"Yeah... I wonder if I can repurpose part of my duchy to start growing coffee bean trees or bushes? They're going real hard at standard farming though, so I don't know if-"

Joe paused as something thumped against his hip, and he glanced down to see his Ebonsteel coffee mug violently squirming back and forth. Unclipping the carabiner, he lifted it as Mate spilled up over the rim, staring around the room with his own analogue to wide-eyed amazement. Ever so slowly, the Elemental turned to look at Joe, its normally chipper voice a hushed whisper.

Wait.

To both of the Ritualists' great concern, the summon dived back into its cup and vanished.

CHAPTER TWENTY-SEVEN

The minutes slowly ticked by as Joe and Nixie waited for the Elemental to resurface from the mug, and soon both of them were getting antsy. As much as he wanted to move to the next project, the Ritualist knew better than to ignore a friend when they spoke in such a deliberate, almost pleading manner.

"It wasn't just me, but Mate sounded *concerned*, right?" Rubbing his bald head, the bright-eyed Ritualist looked at Nixie, who'd already given up on standing around and had started doing her job after relieving the previous teleportation grid minder. Once on the clock and sure the elemental wasn't coming back right away, she'd moved directly into fiddling with the tablet and mapping out more teleportation points.

Nixie half-shrugged, not looking away from the grid she was forming. "I can't really understand that thing like you can. It's all just liquidy sounds to me. Kind of like if someone has a three-year-old and they can figure out what they're asking for, but no one else has a clue?"

"I... guess?" Drumming his fingers on the mug, Joe shifted back and forth, his eyes beginning to wander around the room. Hesitating only a moment, he clipped the mug back onto his belt then walked through the elaborate machinery, still quite touched at the gesture from his Sect. Even so, there were only so many pipes he could admire, vats to knock on to see how sturdy or hollow they were, and active rituals to look at with a hint of superiority in his gaze, knowing he could've integrated them better if he did the work himself. At some point, he had to simply step away, appreciate the gift, and twiddle his thumbs as he waited for the Elemental to return.

Half an hour passed, and there was no caffeine-infused liquid gathering out of his mug. Just fish appearing, becoming very excited they could fly, then getting teleported away. Releasing a long-suffering sigh, Joe leaned against a wall, staring at the ceiling and admiring the lights while pulling out his ritual orbs and practicing intricate maneuvers in a five-foot space.

"Are you really just going to stand over there and play with your balls like that?" Nixie's words made Joe's jaw drop, and only the smirk on her face kept him from sputtering in surprise. "You have to have something to do other than toss those around, right? They're weapons, after all. You shouldn't practice indoors when there are other people around."

"First off, they're *orbs*, thank you very much." Joe caused the weapons to swirl in a tight double helix, increasing their speed to the maximum he could still control and causing the air to hum. "Secondly, this is about as safe of an area as I can work with them. There are monsters outside, and this is a Legendary-rank building. The orbs are only Expert rank, so I'm not going to hurt anything in here."

"Right, no *thing*. But *I'm* in here," she reminded him while keeping a wary eye on the glowing, icicle-shaped Ritual Orb of Intelligence. "Could you find a different thing to do with those other than whip them around at high speed only a few dozen feet away from my head?"

"I could-" The weapons came to a standstill, frozen midair as though they were ornaments with an invisible wire holding them in place. "Abyss, hold on."

Reaching inside his spatial storage, he pulled out a thick,

sealed packet he'd almost entirely forgotten about. "Can't believe I get to use this so soon; somehow I got the feeling this was supposed to be opened maybe even *years* from now."

"Hey, man. Whatever gets you to put those things away so I can focus." Nixie shot him a firm-lipped grin, her raised eyebrows clearly displaying how she was beginning to become annoyed with his antics. "I mean, sure you could be messing with the huge factory present we assembled in the room, maybe writing thank-you notes or something...?"

But by the time she looked up from her tasks to see if mumbling in a lightly-peeved tone had caught his attention, Joe was practically in his own little world.

He reached for the seal on the packet, pulling it open and frowning slightly as it resisted. With a grunt of effort, he ripped the seal off the paper, rolling his eyes as a shockwave of mana collected around the document, forming into an alert that raced off into the distance. "Seriously? Dawnesha must've *really* not trusted that I was going to follow her instructions. I'd bet fifty pounds of alloy that she's going to come at me like a tornado in a trailer park the next time she lays eyes on me."

Luckily, that was the only unpleasant surprise he had to worry about, though Joe carefully scrutinized the documents within, looking for additional traps or the like before pulling out the various parchments. His eyebrows climbed as he looked over the absolutely *ancient* ritual diagram in his hands. Fingers trailing across the text at the top of the vellum, he murmured the name he could just parse, as language had shifted over time.

"Rite o' Awaecnung Gehygedes. That's... *old.* How would that translate? Probably 'Ritual of Awakening... something'. Gehygd. Hmm. 'Hygd' *could* be 'mind', but as a singular word, maybe it's something closer to 'the thinking of the mind'. Maybe thought or understanding? So altogether it'd be the Ritual of Awakening of the Mind-"

The words on the document flared, not quite gold, and shifted ever so slightly into a more recognizable format. Joe tried a few different combinations, with the words shifting until they flared with golden brilliance and became completely recognizable as he muttered, "Ritual of Ascending Sentience?"

Getting more excited with each passing moment, he read over the details of the ritual, his eyes drinking in the concentric layers inked with painstaking precision. It was beautiful and intricate, beyond almost any other design he'd seen before. This was–without a doubt–a Grandmaster-ranked ritual. Gently caressing the edge of the parchment, Joe shook his head as his growing smile threatened to cut his face in half. "But you don't *have* to be that difficult, do you?"

While the ritual in his hands clearly represented the culmination of a lifetime of effort, it suffered from the same issue he'd seen on similarly aged designs. In short, it was *deeply* inefficient. The equations connecting the rings were sound but so incredibly dense and filled with bloat that it was nearly laughable. From the Novice circle to the Journeyman, Joe was able to pick out at least three dozen chains of justifications which existed purely because the original creator of this ritual hadn't had access to higher-order mathematics.

In essence, while the ritual would still remain immensely complex when Joe managed to modernize its design, it would no longer need to explain itself to reality with every single step it took. As it was, redundancies were nested inside redundancies, regulators were created as entire sub-arrays instead of singular conditional gates. The design was incredibly verbose, because it *needed* to be, at least when it was first created.

Joe let one of his fingers hover over the document, humming softly as his Magical Matrices leaned on his Calculus and Number Theory, the two skills pointing and laughing at the archaic algebra and barely keeping each other from dropping to the ground and rolling around from sheer mirth as he traced along a spiral. "This entire section exists because calculus hadn't been invented yet. The sheer brute force this represents is more equations than it took to land on the moon the first time around."

Letting out a soft, happy sigh, the Ritualist carefully packed the document away. "I can't even imagine how many levels that's going to earn me in my skill when I fully adjust it. Taking a Grandmaster ritual like that, even if it only brings it down to a lower level within that tier, is going to be... just *so* much skill experience. Maybe I could get it to mid-Master? Lower?"

The best part was how the majority of it wouldn't be that terribly much of a challenge, though the reintegration of the modernized equations would absolutely mean careful examination and planning. While he couldn't work on the project at the moment, Joe was certain he'd be making time for it in the near future, especially now that he understood its actual function. When Joe looked at the ritual again, the system prompt had updated itself, confirming his assumptions.

Ritual of Ascending Sentience (Grandmaster). By measure and reckoning, the unthinking is granted the means to know itself. The growth of a millennia is hastened to mere decades, the silence of sleepy sapients shattered.

Effect: Accelerates the development of sentience in a magical item. Growth rate of intelligence scales with the target's initial level of sentience with a multiplier applied based on the efficacy and rank differential between the item and ritual.

Limitation: The target must be a magical item capable of achieving sentience. The user of this ritual must have personally created or had significant direct involvement in the construction of said magical item.

"Good, hopefully that'll keep clarifying as I get a better handle on all of the nuances." Joe dropped the packet back into storage, his mind whirling with the possibilities of the ritual. "I'll need to calculate out exactly what sort of multipliers that'll create and figure out the best way to maximize the return. Maybe I can spend some time with Master Darling and get her to explain what sort of things help with growing the minds of enchanted items. Do they need schooling like a child's mind? Or examples of already powerful items they can emulate?"

He rubbed his head, the goofy grin not falling away as he stared into the distance, planning and plotting the best way to use a design such as this. Only then did he have an 'aha moment'. "No wonder she told me not to open this until after I bound my orb. Abyss, I want to chuck everything else to the side and focus on this for a few months right now... actually! There's nothing else I need to-"

Burble.

The distinctive voice of his coffee Elemental pulled a reluctant Joe away from his thoughts, but the wet *plopping* of things landing in his hands captured his full attention immediately. Resisting the instinctive urge to drop whatever had been dropped there and shake his hand clean, he instead managed to hold still and look down at the various items. His gaze shifted over to Mate, who was looking at him with a hopeful expression, then back at the pile of coffee grounds and... other stuff.

Somehow Mate had managed to create multiple distinct piles, one of glossy grounds that smelled rich and earthy, another with a lighter roast with a sheen of oil coating it releasing floral notes. 'Different grounds' was the trend for the majority, but the final pile was a single bean coated in a thick, glossy white sauce. Slowly and deliberately, Joe moved his hand further from his body, hoping he didn't accidentally let whatever *that* was drip onto his robes.

"What... ahh... have we got here, buddy?"

Nixie picked up on his resurgence of conversation and looked over, frowning as she squinted at his rigid palm, then her eyes going wide. "Is that-"

"It's fine, let's just let Mate explain himself."

"I mean, I knew you *liked* coffee, but this is-"

Ahh-faaa-gato! Mate's words were drawn out and extremely high-pitched, and between his concern bordering on disgust and the hard-to-understand speech, it took the Ritualist a few moments to understand what was being said to him.

"Avocado? No, wait, *affogato*? Is *that* what you're saying?" Relief flooded through Joe, and he closed his eyes momentarily before explaining to the other Ritualist in the room, "Affogato is a dessert coffee. Well, technically, it's hot espresso poured over gelato or ice cream. If I remember correctly, it literally means 'drowned in coffee', which, by the way, is the best way to get sent to respawn I can imagine."

"I have other thoughts on that." Nixie relaxed minutely, turning her eyes back to the tablet now that the situation had somewhat resolved itself, though Joe could tell she was listening in as Mate started trying to explain himself.

The tiny Elemental launched into a long-winded explanation filled with burbles and bubbles, alongside a few intelligible words. The literal stream of information splashed in one ear and out the other, and finally the Ritualist had to hold up his empty hand and gesture for the summon to pause. Ever so reluctantly, the coffee quieted down, though it was practically vibrating in place as it looked between the distinct piles on Joe's palm and the man himself with a determined expression.

"You need to go slower." The Elemental puffed up slightly, but Joe quickly stepped in once more. "Let me see if I'm following along, okay? I know caffeine loves speed, but we have a bit of a language barrier. This obviously is important to you; I'm going to make sure we get it right."

Some of the tension went out of the liquid, and it let out a tiny sigh before starting again. This time, the coffee began pouring out of the cup, and Mate's tiny head remained exactly as it was while an enormous, nearly humanoid muscular upper torso appeared above the cup, flexing back and forth. Joe ignored Nixie's low whistle of appreciation, working to figure out the charade correctly. "When you aren't here, you're doing something you can *only* do because you're stronger? Stronger than other Elementals like you, or just because you are an evolved version?"

Yuppers! Strong coffee. Bubbles break Bucha. Burble. The concerningly defined musculature flowed back into the cup, leaving only Mate's usual representation on this plane. **Bluubsie too weak.**

"Is that why you've been speaking less when you're around? You're exhausted?" Joe couldn't imagine what could possibly be so draining that a creature made entirely out of 'wake up juice' would be tired. "I'm sorry it took me so long to start asking questions, little buddy."

The conversation slowly sped up, with Mate trilling and replacing far too many words with sounds that Joe realized must be its actual language, not just what he interpreted as the sound of a carafe of coffee being carefully poured into a mug.

Blurble.

"That bad, huh?" Joe stared into the dark surface of Mate's head, not sure if he was understanding every detail exactly correctly, but getting the gist that it had been a trying time for his Elemental. "But you still went back? You went alone? You shouldn't have done that."

"*Buurrrble.** The mug trembled as Mate's liquid surged in a vortex, then stilled suddenly, hard little bean eyes boring into Joe's.

The man winced away. "There's *always* a choice, Mate. But at least it worked out, so I can't say that you did the wrong thing. Which one of these is that friend?"

A pseudopod made of coffee branched out and pointed at the oily, weakly scented grounds. The Ritualist grimaced, shaking his head slowly. "I don't know, Mate. Don't take this the wrong way, but if I saw that in passing, I'd assume it was... decaf."

Gasp.

"Don't look so betrayed; that's the *reason* you brought it here, right?" Joe's demanding words caused Mate to hesitate, then slowly and sadly nod. "I'm just not getting a clear picture on all of this. Why are so many of your friends... injured isn't the right word, correct? Weakened?"

...burble.

"Ah, *diluted*." Joe nodded in understanding, then flinched back as Nixie practically exploded out of her seat, throwing her hands in the air.

"Are you putting on this little show for me? Why? There's no *way* you're actually understanding what your Elemental is saying." Nixie all but stomped her foot with indignation as Mate and Joe both looked her way with wide-eyed surprise. "It's been 'bubbling' and 'brewing' and *splattering* for like, twenty minutes! You're just making junk up at this point, and it's nodding along because it's made out of coffee! Coffee doesn't have problems you need to solve for it. What's really going on?"

"That's *incredibly* rude." Joe turned away from his fellow Ritualist, returning his full attention to Mate. "Don't worry, little buddy. I know no one understands you like I do. Keep going."

However, Mate was still staring at Nixie, quivering in place and losing his ever-present good cheer. Suddenly he went from a medium roast to a *dark* roast, grin falling away and shifting into a blatant frown as the contents of the Ebonsteel mug heated up, the scent emanating becoming more acrid and potent. "Mate? Careful, you're going full Espresso-"

B-Burble! The indignant sound burst from the Elemental, just before it sloshed up into the air once more, four arms as large as Joe's forming, as though the summoned entity had become half a spider. The limbs sharpened into long, pointed tips, then shot toward the bald man holding the cup up. Having seen something like this before, Joe managed not to fight against the caffeine injection, simply allowing both arms and legs to be punctured, though it took a few moments for his skin to part enough for the liquid to begin absorbing.

As Nixie watched on in horror, starting to race over to help Joe, her full-blown sprint slowed to a run, then a jog, then practically a crawl. The Ritualist blinked, realizing she was midair, and her right foot was only slowly moving toward the ground. His eyes shifted slightly, his head not moving fast enough to keep up with the motion.

Mate loomed large in his vision, and Joe felt his jaw drop ever so slowly as the Elemental's words shifted from unintelligible cute noises... to something else entirely.

CHAPTER TWENTY-EIGHT

*-Burble brubble beans aren't just beans, they are the targeting components for your Planar Shift spell and ritual. Each of these is one of my comrades who has been helping to fend off the invasion, but essence has been diluted to the point where they are, as you correctly surmised, are nearly... *decaf*... on their way to being little more than *tea*. Time is short, so here is the pertinent information-*

The rich voice and intensely articulate words hit him like a hammer. Joe looked on with his vision tunneling from the massive caffeine rush, his heart fluttering like a hummingbird's wings as his veins slowly blackened from the sheer amount of coffee pumping into him, which was absolutely necessary for keeping him in this connected state.

Ritualistic Wisdom has visualized a new ritual design!

Ritual of Quad-Ra-Mate (Journeyman). This ritual is designed to impact currently summoned Elementals, altering their binding to distill them into a more potent form, while allowing them to inject others with their unique capabilities.

Effect: When used with coffee Elementals, the intended target of this ritual, the target will be able to increase the perception of time and connectivity with another entity, potentially allowing for the sharing of information.

Caution: Even with the intended target, there is the potential for a severe debuff during or after the infusion of Elemental power. Effects will vary, but will generally appear in the form of the inverse of the applied power or potential.

Joe slowly turned to look at the hand on his shoulder, where a very concerned Nixie was gently shaking him back and forth. "-okay, Joe? Come on, talk to me! I didn't mean to insult your summon; I thought you had good enough control over it that you wouldn't get attacked-"

"*Shh...*" The Ritualist managed to hiss out as a pounding headache set in. "Water. Please."

She rapidly yanked out a large water bottle, jaw dropping as she pulled the cover open and the full container turned into vapor in an instant. Conversely, Joe let out a soft exhale of relief as his Aura of Soothing Destruction grabbed the liquid and directly converted it, undoing a good amount of the damage the overdose of caffeine had inflicted on him. He could feel the gases in his body rebalancing, the extreme overabundance of coffee being destroyed and directly converted into aspects, stored safely away in his codpiece.

After a dozen seconds, he was able to open his eyes carefully, wincing but not completely overwhelmed by the shifting lights in the room. "Well, that was new."

"Can you tell me what just *happened*?" Nixie frantically half-shouted, glancing at his coffee cup with a hint of fear in her eyes. "That was *insane*!"

"Just, not so loud, please?" The Ritualist lifted his empty hand to rub at his forehead, squeezing his eyes shut. "Short version is still pretty long, but what's going on is that Mate has been essentially in the middle of fighting a war for the last few years."

"That's not what I'm talking about. You were just injected

with..." Nixie blinked as the insanity of his words washed over her. "Don't go telling me you could get actual conversation out of that splashing, or I'm going to call a healer to check out your head."

"If you don't want to hear the truth, that's fine," the Ritualist calmly groaned, but when he cracked an eye open, Nixie was standing with her hands curled into fists at her sides. After a moment, she reluctantly nodded at him. "Good. Short version. Mate was percolated up the ranks of Elementals by being connected to me and having access to so much free mana. His evolution made him one of the stronger entities on his plane, though obviously there are higher forms of coffee, if they can promote him like that."

"Oh, yes, *obviously*," Nixie sarcastically grunted, rolling her eyes at his lacking explanation. "War in the plane of Elemental coffee. Makes total sense."

"Just? *Okay*?" Joe flapped his hand at her, continuing on before she could protest further. "Apparently there's a new Elemental domain that's expanding, and it's at war with coffee and tea at the same time. Coffee's holding its own, because the Elder Elementals are extremely potent. But the weaker ones are getting diluted to the point where they might get converted, and Mate's trying to save some of his friends."

He lifted his hand, indicating the grounds still contained on his palm. "Apparently these *de*volved, all except affogato, as it's simply not well-known enough to be commonplace and absorbing power from multiple locations. Plus, as a dessert coffee, it'll likely always be weaker than the more concentrated versions."

Nixie's head was shaking softly from side to side in agitation, but at least she wasn't interrupting.

"Mate brought me these different samples so I could potentially summon the corresponding Elementals and have them function here in conjunction with Joe-to-Go. They'll be safe, and over time they'll get stronger, faster than they ever could on their own, thanks to both the clean mana that'll run through them as well as the consistent feedback loop from empowering people across the planet. That combination gets more power for themselves in turn." He regarded the samples sadly. "I can't go there and fight their war for them, but I can give these survivors somewhere safe to grow."

"You *know* how ridiculous this sounds, right?" His counterpart burst out with an exasperated growl. "There's a *war* in the Elemental plane of coffee? They're teamed up with tea to fight against the invader. What sort of enemy is it? You said it's a new Elemental plane?"

"*Kombucha*," Joe stated in a steely voice, righteous anger filling him on behalf of his liquid friend.

"I'm done." Nixie began to turn away, then paused for a moment. "Should I tell the Sect you've figured out your coffee supply chain issue?"

Joe pressed his lips firmly together, slightly put off by how little care she was giving the subject. "I suppose technically, yes?"

She didn't respond, instead giving him a single nod and moving on. For his part, as his skills reversed the damage Mate had unintentionally done to him, Joe glanced down at the various coffee items on his palm and felt something **click** in his mind.

He carried the items over to the machinery with utmost care, separating them out and putting a lid over the grounds to ensure they didn't blow away from someone's careless actions. As for the cream-covered bean... Joe carefully scraped that off, holding his skills in check to ensure no part of it was accidentally destroyed. Then, looking down at the tiny particles that represented Mate's friends, Joe tilted his head from side to side and released a satisfying **crack*.

"I might not be able to win a war for you, but I'm happy to say that this doesn't seem like a problem that needs an epic hero to charge into battle. You guys need infrastructure, and that just so happens to be my specialty."

Tapping a tune on a nearby shelf, he closed his eyes and

considered what he needed first. "How can I make this a permanent solution? Reusable summoning rituals means stable and damage resistant diagrams. Gonna have to forge 'em, in that case. Nixie!"

"Wh-"

Even before she could finish speaking, Joe was on the move to the teleporter, "Don't let anyone mess with those coffee grounds! I'll be back soon; I just need to get a few people moving."

The next few hours quickly blurred together, as he personally saw to many of the tasks he needed completed but didn't hesitate to delegate to anyone he felt could help. But when it came to forging the diagrams, exquisite quality was non-negotiable. Even if creating the ritual required for his Planar Shift spell was simplistic, Joe wasn't about to hand it off to someone else. He was doing this for his friend, Mate, who had saved him many times and had been there for him when even *water* wasn't.

He used Jotunheim alloy alongside a hint of arcane aspects to form the ritual circles he required. Journeymen-rank diagrams were *laughably* easy to create at this point, seeing as both of his relevant skills were Master rank. Even so, several times the gyroscopes he made had tiny imperfections which would lower their lifespan only a little bit, yet he tossed them aside without hesitation to be melted down. Only when they twisted and turned in a perfectly smooth, balanced rotation did he allow himself to move on to the next step.

Enchanted Tokens were necessary to ensure he could take the summoning foci Mate had given him and turn them into a permanent method of calling the specific Elementals to Jotunheim. His minigame style of Enchanting soon had him sitting in the center of a ring of glowing cast-offs; nearly a dozen of the coin-sized enchantments discarded when the process showed more than a five percent deviation from his desired outcome. Only when the enchantment had been created as perfectly as he could realistically expect with his surgical precision and laser focus did the Ritualist allow himself to clean up.

His body didn't need much rest–not on Jotunheim, where he could let loose his massively enhanced Characteristics–so he only allowed himself a brief breather to send a message to Nixie, letting her know that, in the next couple days, the Joe-to-Go headquarters would begin producing coffee for the masses. They would need as many employees as she could manage to secure to run coffee on his behalf, so he hoped she could come through with a large number of recommendations.

Then, even without waiting for the messenger to get all the way out the door, he dove into working with his Abyssal Bloom cauldron.

Joe knew that he needed to be able to summon each of these Elementals regularly, as one way or another, they would be dispelled eventually. This meant that purification, flavor isolation, and contamination suppression were of the utmost importance during the alchemical process. It wasn't *only* that he was a coffee snob; the Ritualist was simply doing his best to make sure that these particular blends stayed as true to their origin as he could possibly make them.

Finally, he had five solvents, which were as perfect for the situation as he could possibly make them, going by his limited knowledge and lack of experience with a situation like this. Lifting one in the air, he swirled the cerulean Tonic around, forming a tiny whirlpool before carefully storing each way for later use. "When I add the grounds or the creamy bean to the mix, I should get an injectable I can use for the tokens. My Magical Matrices is telling me all of this should line up, with only a five to eight percent chance of failure. All that's left is... doing it."

A half-dozen people were in the headquarters by the time Joe returned, an uncomfortable number in such a delicate environment. If he hadn't recognized everyone, it was highly probable the Ritualist would've gone on the attack, thinking someone was about to attempt sabotage on the location. Instead, he controlled himself with an iron will, trying to be polite as he greeted each person then went to pick up the grounds.

They stared at the back of his head with excited expressions as he got to work, and the Ritualist did his utmost not to get *itchy* under their attention. Still, a ritual cluster was never far from hand, and more than once, he reached for one after someone made too sudden of a motion in his periphery. Only when they realized he was going to be working for a while did they give him some space, allowing Joe to calm down and give the task the focus it demanded.

He started with the strongest of the materials, a standard medium roast coffee he was under the impression would become the baseline drip coffee people could add cream or sugar to as they wished; though his recommendation would always be for them to drink it black. Sprinkling *all* of the remnants into the first Tonic had him gritting his teeth with concern. The cerulean fluid churned and pulsed, only to shiver into a singular tan liquid with a bluish tint. Letting out an explosive exhale, Joe allowed a faint smile to touch his lips. "One down..."

The next four went without issue, much to his great relief. Alchemy was still his least favorite of the five core skills, simply due to needing to repetitively create the same products over and over to supplement his main rituals. Rarely did he deviate from those formulae, which tended to lead to a hint of anxiety when doing so eventually became necessary.

The next step was practically routine, as he took the solution and slurped some of it up with a syringe, literally injecting it into a minuscule cavity carved into the Enchanted token. Once each of the various imbued tokens had been placed within their associated gyroscopes, Joe decided to summon each Elemental in turn *before* assigning them a vat to live in—no reason not to let them have a say in where and how they lived.

The first to appear was an Elemental slightly darker than Mate's usual appearance, and the Ritualist nodded politely at the confused creature as it swirled into being out of nothing.

"Hello, there! I wasn't given a name for you, but going by your composition and the honest, straightforward, resilient nature I needed to carve into the enchantment focus, I believe you are drip coffee? Is there something you'd like to be called?"

**Dr~rip.* The Elemental's voice was surprisingly deep and had a... southern twang to it?

"Drip it is." Joe waved at the various storage containers, "I assume Automate told you I'd be trying to summon you, so I shouldn't have much to explain. Feel free to select one of these to live in and plan on hundreds, perhaps *thousands* of people asking for you every single day."

The Elemental's tiny jaw dropped, and it wiggled back and forth in pure excitement, flowing up the side of a thousand-gallon tank and dribbling inside of it.

Joe raised an eyebrow at its massive new home. "*Bold* choice. But I guess that tracks."

Skill offered: Coffee Discernment Lore (Master V). With a single inhale, you are able to draw the properties of coffee into your lungs, allowing it to roll through your senses with immense acuity. The fragrance reveals the beans' lineage, while the roast speaks to you in a lower register. A single sip can satiate you for days.

Effect:

1. *Understand the lineage and harvesting of the coffee or coffee blend you are smelling so long as you have access to its fragrance. This will allow you to understand its needs when growing it, whether it should be on a rapidly draining mountainside, rain-soaked field, or allow for rapid growth in a lowland. +25n% growth rate when selecting ideal conditions.*
2. *Having a masterful understanding of the roast will allow you to improve the effects of coffee you make or in any way create. Plus 25% to strength buffs and all positive effects of caffeine.*
3. *You are able to remove up to 25n% of the arrogance modifier from an overly smoky roast or the impatience flowing through someone drinking a scorched blend.*

"I... I want it so bad." Joe's fingers hovered over the 'yes' button, pupils dilating as he reread the information twice. For the first time, he felt the true agony of needing to give up a skill he truly wanted in order to survive his Paradoxical Heart Demon Tribulation. "It's... I can't do it. *Ahh!*"

With trembling hands, he refused the skill and returned to the summoning circles—feeling as though he had taken a punch straight to his stomach. The next to arrive was Americano, which was summoned with its own tiny cowboy hat made out of old coffee grounds woven together. It nodded at Joe and selected a tank much smaller than Drip's, though with a larger water supply connected to it.

Cortado flashed into existence with a tiny roar, looking around wildly and latching on to Joe with fervent attention before ever so slowly calming down. "You okay, little guy?"

Nope!

Getting closer, the Ritualist could see that its panting form was heavily diluted and spent a short while helping it through various distillation pipes and even a brief round in a centrifuge before it flashed him a relieved smile and stood tall, though it was less than a quarter of the size of Americano. It relaxed into a superheated small tank with an audible sigh of relief, and a grim-faced Joe hurried to summon the next—fully uncertain what condition it would be in.

Latte appeared smoothly, fully content to let Joe pick a spot for it, and cheerfully accepted the three-sectioned tank which would allow for chilled milk, water, and its own heated relaxation area. Finally, Joe moved to the final ritual diagram, and the air turned frosty as the summon was slowly reconstituted on this world.

Affogato was shaped like a snowman, with a hardened outer shell of chilled gelato and a liquid core that could be seen when meeting its eyes. Joe ushered the nonverbal Elemental over to a chilled tank, where it quietly settled without complaint or excitement. It was clearly exhausted, and much like

Cortado, had likely been embroiled in battle before the Ritualist had pulled it away.

"All done?" Devoe's gravelly voice pulled on Joe, and he turned around to regard the half-dozen Ritualists watching him excitedly. "That went faster than we expected; you got everything set up and in place in only a couple of days. I really appreciate that; you've no idea how many ingots I earn in the betting pools. You'd think people would catch on by now that they shouldn't be underestimating you."

"Hey." Joe mock glared at the Dwarf. "If that's a real thing, I need to know how to get access."

"Can't bet on yourself. Conflict of interest," another of the Ritualists immediately chimed in, though his words were regretful instead of concerned. "Otherwise we'd cut you in for sure."

"I've got thirty-seven people wanting to run coffee for you and nearly a hundred that are showing interest but want to see what the business looks like before they commit to anything," Nixie chimed in, hoping to shut down the sidebar conversation. "Any thoughts on that? How're you going to be doing distribution? Taking orders? What's the payment structure for people who want coffee and for the employees you have working for you?"

"If they're all Sect members, I'll pay them in contribution points." Joe nonchalantly waved that point away, and she hesitantly nodded in acceptance–for now. "As to payments and taking orders, I want none of that for the first week."

His words were met with silence, but finally Devoe managed to sputter out, "N-no *payment*? Are you out of your-"

"No, we are definitely going to pay the people doing the work. I mean that I want to give out free coffee. For everyone. Planet-wide." Joe firmly spoke over the Master Ritualist. "We're going to flood the market, putting up no friction or barriers to them getting access. Just good coffee everywhere."

"...He's lost his mind." The Dwarf pulled on his beard in

consternation, but before he could try and talk Joe out of it, the Ritualist explained his plan more fully.

"The more people who drink the coffee, the stronger these Elementals will become. By next week, we'll have kiosks, standardized menus, and a sales license from Novusheim. When the free coffee goes away, people will be *fighting* for their place in line, and everyone will know where to go to order their drinks."

Each member of the group looked around at each other with conflicted expressions, but eventually the Dwarf managed to fight against his centuries of grasping for every possible advantage and returned a sharp nod. "If that's what you want, that's what's gonna happen."

The six of them got to work and were soon carrying out enormous trays of coffee cups filled to the brim with the various options. Of them, Nixie wore the brightest smile, as her tray was loaded down with half-cups with steaming ice cream filling the containers. Once each of them had vanished through the teleporter, Joe allowed his calm facade to fade away and allowed his excitement to bleed through as he stared at the enormous machinery.

Pulling out a notebook, he wrote his thoughts out carefully, rereading the words twice before slowly closing its cover.

Five blends for the free folk of Jotunheim, the world of giants.
Latte for comfort,
Americano for strength.
Drip for the many.
Cortado for balance,
And Affogato, sweet and potent,
To drown their resistance in sugar.
One habit to bind them all.
A coffee empire to shake them.
And with the dawn's inevitable call,
One ritual to wake them.

"But none of them were deceived, because this was the plan all along." Joe chuckled to himself as he set aside his melodramatic note and checked on the comfort of the Elementals one last time. Then it was time to head off to Novusheim; if he wanted a business to thrive in the Dwarven city, he needed to make sure to play by their rules.

"Shouldn't take long to get a license from the council... they *love* me over there!"

CHAPTER TWENTY-NINE

Joe stepped out of the Dwarven Council chambers of Novusheim with a stamped, rune-etched business license tucked securely into his codpiece and a knot in his chest that refused to loosen. He was breathing hard, hands clenching and releasing as he did his best not to stomp along the roadside like a petulant child.

On paper, the meeting had gone well.

The negotiations had been smooth, even better than when he was still a member of the governing body. Each councilor had listened, perhaps asked a few quick questions, figured out his logistics and distribution plans, then cheerfully approved the license with barely a concern raised between them. Sure, there'd been some haggling over taxation and a truly insulting fee for 'adding nothing with longevity to the city with this business' since his products were all consumables, but Joe had agreed to it all without complaint.

He could afford it. In fact, he had an account with the city he hadn't even known about, where stacks of ingots as tall as he was were secured in his name. At first he'd been excited, but the part that stuck with him was how Grandmaster Stu had leaned back in his chair, fingers steepled, beard twitching as he failed to keep his smirking to himself.

"Industrious," Stu had *complimented* him in a voice thick with satisfaction. "Efficient. Structured. You've got a good head for business on your shoulders. Reminds me of the old ways. Establishing demand before profit extraction. You're not just selling coffee, are you? This is something humans *crave.* You're building dependency."

The Dwarf had added his seal to the business license with a **slam**, staring at Joe with mocking eyes. "I suppose every empire starts somewhere. Should I look forward to your induction as a proper Jotunheim Oligarch in the next few months? It's just so strange; I really thought you'd be seeking power through knowledge, and here you are, just looking to build your wealth like the rest of us. Maybe I was wrong about you. Or maybe... just maybe... I was *right.*"

Joe sucked in a sharp breath as he rounded a corner, slowing his pace and being pulled back to the present as he found himself on a main thoroughfare, the flow of the city moving around him. Dwarves passed by in pairs and trios, and groups of laughing humans excitedly chattered as they hurried to wherever it was they were going—many of them clutching steaming cups of coffee stamped with a Joe-to-Go insignia.

"Brooding again?" A gravelly voice came from near his elbow as Grandmaster Snow approached, her heavy boots silent despite their size. She stroked her mustache thoughtfully as she inspected him, a genuinely happy smile on her lips. "You look better. It's good to see you've regained access to your mana."

Though he was *indeed* brooding, Joe tried to resurface enough to have a pleasant conversation. "Couldn't have done it without you. Thanks for all the time and effort you put into helping me establish a baseline."

"I didn't do much, but we all do the best we can. Don't we?" She reached over and patted his arm, her smile gentle now and her eyes filled with knowing as she met his gaze. "Still. I'm immensely proud of you for finding your own path back."

Joe felt his heart clench and bobbed his head in thanks for her words. They walked together for a block or so, speaking of small things: training, the oddities of Jotunheim, and the titan the Sect had managed to hunt. Then their time together came to an end—as she had a schedule full to the brim with the daily operations of Novusheim—but though their time together was short, the Ritualist was incredibly touched that she'd made some for him.

Once more walking on his own, he moved along until he found the source of the steaming cups in people's hands, watching as his new hires handed out cups of coffee to anyone who'd take them.

"They're moving as fast as I wanted." Joe tried to push down the bitter aftertaste that came with that realization, which only existed thanks to Stu's particular method of getting in his head. As he looked around, realizing that nearly every street corner had a runner stationed with an insulated crate, the Ritualist calmed down and allowed himself to remember that there was a *purpose* for his coffee business that went far beyond simply adding to the pile of alloy he apparently had sitting in a vault somewhere. "This will provide jobs, empower the coffee Elementals, and *so* much more. Maybe Stu's just mad because he didn't think of it first?"

Not sure what else to do with himself, Joe simply stood on the sidewalk and watched for a while, surprised to see how wary the Dwarves were about anything being handed out for free. The vast majority of the passersby declined the offered coffees with curt nods, but a large number of the passing humans excitedly took the free sample at face value.

It took time, but soon enough, people were drinking the coffee without ill effects—or being asked to pay after drinking it down—that there was a rippling shift in who accepted the offerings. Then there was a steady stream of people lining up to take a cup, and finally the tide turned entirely.

A high-ranking Dwarf, going by the sheer amount of metal in his beard, accepted a cup of drip coffee and sniffed it suspiciously. Eventually, he took a cautious sip... and froze. The crowd around him sucked in a breath, only to let it out slowly as he took another long pull from the cup.

"Huh," the Dwarf muttered with an approving nod. "It's a bit weak but has a surprisingly robust flavor. Can't say I've had another drink like it."

One word of acknowledgment from this Dwarf was enough to send all the others in earshot scrambling for a position in line, wanting to see what was different about this drink compared to the drink they already knew.

The coffee quickly ran out after that, only for a fresh runner to race into the area, an oversized crate in their arms as they swapped theirs for the empty one and took off running with it.

Joe exhaled slowly, full of relief to see his venture gaining ground. Simply going by how much of the luxury beverage was being taken in by the minute, he was certain the Elementals providing the coffee would see a return to their previous power and beyond in no time flat.

A ripple of movement as the crowd parted drew his attention down the street, where a battered wagon rolled along at a lazy pace, its driver hunched forward, reins slack in one hand. In the back of the wagon lay a figure wrapped in layered blankets, motionless save for the slow rise and fall of their chest. A runner jogged alongside the wagon, holding up a cup.

"Care for an Americano?"

The driver shrugged, fully focused on not allowing the muzzled leopards pulling the wagon to get too close to anyone. "If you want. I don't have any money for ya. We're just passing through. Don't want no trouble-"

"-ricano?" A sleepy voice echoed from the interior of the wagon, a hand extending out of the blanket and grasping around sleepily. "Yummo."

The runner hesitated then carefully pressed the cup into the outstretched hand. Joe looked back to the place his new hire had set up, trying to calculate how many cups of coffee would be necessary to satisfy the crowd that had formed, only to feel the wind get knocked out of him as the world *lurched.*

A sudden, massive draw on ambient mana pressed down on the crowd, causing the air to shimmer and warp. The faintest aura rolled outward from the wagon, compressing reality for a heartbeat before snapping back into place, every last iota of power put back where it had come from.

The figure in the wagon had sat up.

Joe, along with everyone else in line of sight, stared at them as they finished off the hot drink, nodded once, then promptly fell back asleep. Pale as a ghost, the runner staggered away from the wagon, even as the driver swore under his breath and snapped the reins—the leopards happily speeding up and forcing their way through the crowd, smacking the sturdy Dwarves out of the way with leather-blunted-claws where necessary.

Joe moved without thinking, long strides eating the distance until he matched the wagon's pace. "Mind if I walk with you?"

The driver flinched away, eyes still facing frontward. "Just passing through. Don't want no trouble."

"I was headed toward the teleportation pad anyway; not going to try to cause issues." Joe remained quiet for a few moments, staring at the lightly snoring person in the back of the wagon. "Not that it's any of my business, but... what was that all about?"

"You're right. It's not." When his gruff demeanor wasn't enough to scare Joe away, the driver sighed, "Figures. Do what you want. Just don't make him get up."

Joe remained staring at the unknown person, and perhaps it was due to loneliness or simple aggravation, but the driver of the wagon finally broke down and answered the question. "I'm bringing Staybre, the Sleepy Warlock, on a world tour."

"Sleepy Warlock? Is that a title, or..."

"He's a Class Sage." Now that the man was talking, he blurted out information as though he hadn't spoken to anyone else in weeks. "Chose it in his sleep, matter of fact. Didn't even know until three weeks later. Severe narcolepsy. Sleeps through specializations, skill gains, the works. Wakes up to fight, and now, *apparently*, to try *coffee,* of all things. Should've known better than to travel through a city like that. We've been traveling Jotunheim for decades, and... well, we rolled into the area last month. I couldn't pass up the chance to see a *real* settlement. Winter's gone, there's stuff to look at out there, and *still* the thing I miss the most is having a traveling companion who does more than sleeptalk at me."

Joe went quiet again as he thought of all of the times he'd found himself alone after long periods of intense excitement and how it had pulled at him. Doing his best not to have any ulterior motives at all, he tried to sympathize with the guy. "Listen, I understand you're on your way out of here. I'm the First Elder of The Wanderer's Sect, and I truly think that no one should be on their own for too long. Why don't I show you how to use the teleportation network, and you can pop back to a populated area whenever you need to see a friendly face?"

"Here we go again." The driver snorted darkly. "He's not going to fight for you."

"*He's* not the one I'm worried about," Joe replied calmly, earning himself a searching glance as the man looked at him for the first time since the conversation had started. After a long beat, the driver nodded slowly and pulled to a stop as they came level with the teleportation pad. The Ritualist showed him how to use it, and moments later, the man and his wagon were gone.

"What a strange day," Joe rumbled as he stepped onto the pad. "Wonder if Master Dreamstrider knows about that guy. Maybe they could hang out."

Before he teleported away, Joe took one last look at the city and felt the lingering effects of Stu's words finally fade fully. Yet, in its place, a slow realization grew. "On Midgard, I'm a Duke in charge of a massive farming operation on the frontier of the kingdom. On Vanaheim, I'm making my way toward

Class Sagehood. Across the worlds, I'm one of the elite in the most powerful human Sect in existence. Here, on Jotunheim?"

His lips twitched in annoyance as he realized *why* Stu had been getting into his head; the dwarf was likely using him to grow a skill or two. "I'm definitely on my way to becoming an Oligarch, or at least that's what they'll call me as my business expands and I need to regularly deal with the council."

He shook his head, shocked at the dawning realization that, on each world, he'd been following their standard methods of moving up the social strata. "How odd. I don't even really need to do that; it's... maybe it's just kind of a side quest for me? Actually, not like I *asked* for it. Perhaps it's just that, when people see you accomplishing things, and they know you can do more, they want to pull you into their faction and have you be competent alongside them? Yeah. Know what? I can get behind that."

A blue static washed over his vision, and his surroundings were replaced by the now-familiar peak of the First Elder's mountain. Joe took his first step toward the training field, hands behind his back as he prepared to settle into a casual stroll. "Swing home, check on any messages, see if anyone needs personal training, then maybe a few weeks tinkering with rituals... this Ritual of Ascending Sentience is just *begging* to be reworked-"

The sound of many feet marching in unison sent a shiver down his spine, and the First Elder slowly turned to assess the formation of incredibly well-equipped combatants moving toward him. Happily, their eyes were on the teleportation pad, allowing him to let go of some of the instant tension he had accumulated. "The Ascender's expedition? What're they up to?"

To his increasing concern, the expedition from Vanaheim looked *happy*. That was the first clue that something was about to go terribly wrong. The second was the intense gear they were wearing.

Joe had seen plenty of weapons and armors as he traveled

through the worlds, but there was a qualitative difference between what someone was going to be wearing on a daily grind session and... *this*. Warriors especially tended to save their most expensive, useful, and hardest-to-repair equipment for when it really mattered, and every last one of them was decked out in their top-of-the-line gear.

He had a moment of cognitive dissonance as he looked at the shining armor etched with hundreds of moving sigils which were clearly *not* bound to the metal itself. There were blades layered with shifting geometries and even enormous rucksacks that had clearly been turned into spatial storage containers with enormous capacities. Every face among them was familiar, thanks to his Perception and Intelligence allowing him to cross-reference his memory with the current situation, but not one of them was wearing something he'd seen before.

At least, not until he saw Grandmaster Fari.

She was wearing a Talisman Master robe, which looked like a tattered bed sheet covered in shapes and squiggles, but was actually an enormous number of talismans woven together and draped across her form. This was particularly impressive, seeing as the Wolfman stood head and shoulders above Joe, giving her even more space to fill with the potent magical weaponry. As her gaze met his, her chin rose in the air, exposing her throat as a gesture of respect. "First Elder!"

"Grandmaster." Joe slowly lifted his chin as well, mirroring her actions instead of the usual nod he would give another person. "You seem bedecked for war... have you found the Traditionalists' encampment? Hopefully it's far away from any population center-"

"Hah! No." As she barked out a laugh, her troops let out a whoop of excitement alongside her, the sound rolling across the peak. "You have impeccable timing! Not only did we just deliver your cut of the World Boss materials to your house and complete our preparations for the next assault on the Jötunn, but one of your people just arrived with the coordinates of its respawn site!"

Skill Offered: Impeccable Arrival (Novice V). Having been constantly bathed in the flow of karmic energy, you are-

"Refuse."

Skill Offered: Impeccable Arrival (Journeyman V). Having been constantly bathed in the flow of karmic energy, you are subconsciously tuned-

"No."

Skill Offered: Impeccable Arrival (Expert III). Having been constantly bathed in the flow of karmic energy, you are subconsciously tuned to the ebbs and flows-

"What-"

Skill Offered: Impeccable Arrival (Master I). Alright, you got me. Look, this is already impacting you, ya might as well just make it official. Having been constantly bathed in the flow of karmic energy, you are subconsciously tuned to the ebbs and flows of the world and will arrive precisely at the most appropriate moment where your presence will have the most impact, for good or ill.

"If it's already affecting me, then I don't need it as an official skill, *do I*?" The notification stayed in place even as he refused it, forcing him to shove it into the corner of his vision so it would at least get out of his way. Joe's small success turned into a stiff smile as a hint of concern began growing in his chest as Fari bounced from foot to foot, clearly wanting to be on her way. "Ah. You've won the lottery, is what you're saying."

"Indeed! Just as you predicted, when the monster returned to life, it damaged your network in such an obvious way that a single scout was able to confirm its reappearance. As we have kept our promises to you, now you have kept yours to us. Even now, we are on our way to secure the Mythic Core."

Fari's voice dropped to a lower tenor as she stepped close, "I don't suppose you could close the teleportation network behind us once we leave? Just to make sure there are no unexpected visitors from Vanaheim once word gets out that we are on the hunt?"

"What about you? Won't you want to make your way back

as quickly as possible?" Joe's hopes rose slightly at the thought that he might have more time than he expected.

The Wolfman splayed her hands, forming a gesture he didn't quite understand. "The battle will be different this time. The Jötunn is unlikely to be wreathed in flame, so I am expecting injuries of a new sort after the battle. Getting to the core will also require us harvesting at least a portion of the World Boss, and I can guarantee that none of us will want to leave before the work is fully completed–though the core is our goal, the materials we harvest are ours to do with as we please. A bonus, if you will."

"Spoils of war. Makes sense." Joe didn't flinch as the Grandmaster's hand shot into the folds of her robe, pulling out a stack of what looked like nothing so much as papers.

She tossed them into the air, allowing them to flutter like confetti for a moment before gripping them with her will and activating them one after another–tearing the talismans in twain and releasing their stored magics. Her expedition grouped closer together, waiting with professional calm as ribbons of light wrapped around the damaged papers then unspooled to sink into each of the members of the raid group.

Joe's skin prickled as buffs and boons exploded into being, empowering the people in extremely obvious ways. Muscles swelled up to thirty percent larger, the vasculature in their limbs and forehead going from thin straws to quarter-inch garden hoses. Heat began building around each of them, slowly ramping up and reflecting from one unit to the next. Mist began pouring off of the troops, sweat instantly steaming away as their breathing deepened, and their eyes dilated.

Grandmaster Fari turned away from Joe, having said her piece to him, and addressed her troops. "We cannot afford dalliance nor variance. Do not rely on luck, as the world will bend to injure you this day. We bring *certainty* to the field of battle, and by nightfall tomorrow, the Jötunn will be slain! Within a week, our packs will be full, our injuries healed, and we will return triumphant to Vanaheim!"

The expedition team shouted, their voices easily an octave lower than before the buffs had been cast on them. A thick feeling of pre-battle euphoria struck Joe, tinged with bloodlust and avarice as they thought about turning the Mythic monster into usable magical materials. The Ritualist had to hop to the side as they marched to the teleportation pad, vanishing fifty at a time to some distant location in the world of giants.

As the last of them winked away, accompanied by a thin sheen of blue static, Joe hurried to follow up on his end of the bargain. "Need to shut down the teleportation network, let's say within five hundred miles of wherever they landed. But first..."

Sprinting to his house didn't exactly leave the impression on his Sect members that he usually hoped for, but Joe had other things on his mind than public image at this moment.

"When they secure the Mythic Core and return to Vanaheim..." Joe burst through the door of his house, expecting the room to be utterly packed with material, only to find himself slightly taken aback when there was a single oversized rucksack in the center of the room. A glance inside the seemingly ordinary hiking bag showed castoff Mythic materials the Wolfman leader had deemed unnecessary for their goals: toenails, entrails, the aqueous humor of the Jötunn's eyes frozen solid and cut into iceberg-sized cubes. Seeing as their agreements weren't punishing the Grandmaster, he could only assume she had followed through and given him a fair portion.

Strapping the rucksack on, he rushed for the teleportation pad, finally allowing himself to finish his train of thought. "When they get back to Vanaheim, they're going to kick off a planet-wide war. I've got somewhere between one to two weeks to get the Tower of Ritualists ready for that. Hopefully, we're the only people who'll know what's coming."

Visions of doom and gloom flowed through his mind as he grimly remembered how people acted in times of war. "Even if the tower tries to stay neutral, people with a bone to pick with us are going to use the chaos as an opportunity to attack."

The instant he shut down the teleportation network around

the expedition, leaving firm orders to the workers in the headquarters not to reopen it for at least two weeks, Joe activated his pre-channeled Beam to Bifrost and raced across the surface of the planet.

As he joined with the bridge between worlds and launched into the depths of space, the Ritualist could only grit his teeth in frustration that he could only move between planets *twice* as fast as anyone else.

CHAPTER THIRTY

Joe emerged from the bifrost fully focused on getting back to the Tower of Ritualists, only to immediately need to come to a halt as dozens of strangers blocked his path and began interrogating him from all sides. The Ritualist stared at them coldly, trying to decide whether or not he wanted to cause a problem—frankly, if one of them attacked and managed to send him to respawn, he'd just get back to his tower faster.

The blockade had shifted somewhat since the last time he'd come through here, the two factions having clearly and cleanly separated the space around the bifrost into their preferred setups. One side had metal walls bristling with weapons, while the other had a nearly purely magical barricade blocking anyone from leaving. Joe felt the sensation of active searching magics and intrusive skills washing over him and allowed his hands to drift into a good casting position, on the cusp of summoning a stack of ritual clusters-

"Ah, abyss, it's someone from the Tower of Ritualists." The outcry around him shifted immediately as someone finally noticed the insignia on his robes. Instead of the harsh demands for answers, the two sides merely checked the output of their scans, then offered him strained politeness while allowing him to pass–neither group being willing to offer offense to his Tower. The newly ascended Sage could tip the balance of political power with a single word and cause everything they'd been working toward to be for naught... but only if they overstepped and caused him to break his neutral stance.

While the Ritualist hurried to make his escape, he caught the eye of an immensely armored man who was fractionally shaking his head in immense aggravation. "No idea how you keep getting off the planet. I've repeatedly warned you to stop. I look forward to the day..."

"When *what*?" Joe turned and directly confronted the Grandmaster, who had trailed off, leaving his threat vague and implied rather than explicit. "What *exactly* would you be doing if you didn't have other people around you keeping you in check?"

The rigid man didn't back down, though his grip on his weapons tightened noticeably as he leaned forward. "I look forward to the day when I can *properly* explain why it's a good idea to listen to those with more experience than yourself. Or maybe you can just start listening to your elders and *stay on Vanaheim*."

"You know what?" A faint smile touched Joe's lips, though his eyes remained steely. "I think I'll stick around until all of this... *posturing*... is resolved. I appreciate your repeated advice."

More than one weapon remained trained on Joe as he turned on his heel and stormed off, unwilling to waste his time arguing with people. He could feel dozens of angry eyes following him until he rounded the corner. Heart drumming with adrenaline, he gently thumped on his chest as he raced along the roads, frustrated at how easily he became angry when he was nervous and distracted. "I could've just ignored him. Why do I *always* feel the need to challenge people who're just trying to look important by talking down to me? Shouldn't I be *better* than that by now?"

Omnivault allowed him to rocket along the planet's surface,

and in what felt like the blink of an eye, the Tower of Ritualists loomed ahead. Much of his anxiety fled as he crossed into the large, open field around the tower, knowing that the protections his fellow Ritualists had been building into the location had been ramping up in recent weeks. Any aggressor would likely quickly find themselves buried under damage-over-time effects, curses, and enough debuffs to bind them in place without the need for so much as a single strand of twine.

He didn't linger and chat with anyone as he passed through the gates of the tower, instead making his way toward the stairs to the penthouse immediately. Even so, his arrival had somehow been noted.

Jenny emerged from a side corridor at a dead sprint, notebook tucked under one arm, and her expression set with a determined cast. "Tri-Master Joe! Welcome back, I have so many things that require your attention-"

"Not *now*, Jenny!" Joe was up the first flight of stairs in an instant. "I need to see Sage Pete immediately."

Her half-shout stopped him dead. "Wait! He's in closed consultation, probably not even in the tower right now."

The Ritualist grit his teeth and bounced in place before turning back with a grunt and descending the stairs. "Okay, when will he be done with that? I'm not joking when I say I come bearing urgent news."

"As your assistant, please allow me to assure you that I'll make an appointment on your behalf as soon as he becomes available." Her words tumbled out with a practiced smoothness, even as she flopped her notebook open and stepped in close. Then, having turned to an apparently random page, she spoke to him in a much softer tone. "What I really need to talk to you about is your Inscription Momentum skill. I did some calculations, asked some casual questions, and probably annoyed half of the Enchanters in the tower-"

"Look, I said I'd consider teaching the skill. You'll be one of the first in line if I do, but right now I-" Joe stopped speaking as his heart **thumped**, then went still for a single second too long, causing his chest to painfully constrict. He bent over and *wheezed*, magical energy zinging across his skin and shocking him across the entirety of his body.

"Master Joe!" Jenny stepped close, offering him a shoulder to lean on as he staggered in place. "Were you attacked? Should I get-"

The bald Master waved her off, already fully aware of what had happened. A notification from the system was blinking in the corner of his vision, and while he took a few deep breaths to regain his balance, he read over the information with a glare.

Congratulations! Planar Shift has reached the Expert rank!

Skill increase: Planar Shift (Journeyman → Expert). You are a summoner who splits his time between entities which can attack and those who show great utility. Almost never do you place your summons in harm's way, making them far more apt to wish to continue the relationship you are building with them.

Effect:

1. *Allows the summoning of a planar being of your choosing from the tome.*
2. *Comparatively easy control over any creature of Expert rank or below, doubled if they have been summoned by you previously.*
3. *Summoned creatures now receive a passive minor Regeneration effect. This healing is permanent while they remain summoned, repairing injuries over time and enhancing longevity during sustained combat.*
4. *Increases the amount of time a summoned entity can remain per summoning by (Skill level *favorability). Favorability can be increased by allowing summons to act in alignment with their desires and minimizing the damage they take during your contracted summoning.*
5. *Entities summoned specifically to provide defensive capabilities are 50-(skill level/2)% more difficult to summon and control.*

Standardized skill progression: To increase the level of this skill, maintain summon control for one hour per current skill level.

Probing at his body, Joe found that the enchantment holding his mana channels together had settled once more. He patted Jenny on the shoulder, trying to alleviate some of her concern, even as he allowed his Aura of Soothing Destruction to eradicate the dribble of blood leaking from the corner of his mouth. "Not sure why that... sucked so bad."

Immediately the Ritualist's priority shifted, and he pulled away from a still-concerned Jenny, eyes returning to the stairwell. With each step he took, he felt stronger and more in control of himself and soon was climbing with a sense of purpose.

His assistant kept pace beside him. "You've got to let me make my case for why you should stop everything else and focus on teaching Inscription Momentum for the near future."

"No, I need to find Master Darling and figure out why my enchantment feels like it's going to kill me." Joe glanced at his climbing companion from the corner of his eye, almost amused by how frustrated she appeared. "But I don't have anything else I'm doing on the way up... so if you keep pace, no one's going to stop you from talking."

"You clearly don't understand what this'll mean to the tower if you manage to begin teaching the skill. I don't mean someday or eventually, I mean *now*." Words poured out of the young Ritualist as a constant stream of consciousness, as she attempted every method she could think of to convince him. "The hardest bottleneck after actual cost of materials is the time requirements for higher-level rituals. Making an Expert-rank ritual, on average, takes the better part of a day. A Master rank?"

She shook her head, frustrated tears welling in her eyes as she let more words fly. "The only reason we aren't considered completely incompetent in combat is that we can set up our spells in advance, and they constantly refresh themselves. I'm sure you've seen a mage, or a warrior, or some more specific class toss out a Master-rank attack in the blink of an eye. Anything we can do to bridge that gap—even *slightly*—will put us in a better position."

Heaving for air both from the emotional appeal, as well as trying to keep up with the breakneck speed climbing of the stairs, Jenny grabbed his wrist and pulled Joe to slow him. "We *need* this edge. Faster inscription means more defenses, rapid response countermeasures... you'd probably bring about the first Ritualist dueling corps specializing in emergency inscription! Not to mention the *bubble*. Do you have any idea how rare skills with time dilation effects are? Studying this skill as an outside observer could open an entirely new branch of ritual magic!"

Joe was taken aback by how much thought she'd put into this request and felt his gut clench as he realized that, just *perhaps*, he'd brushed her off a little too casually during their last conversation. "The requirements for the skill have to be pretty harsh, but certainly there has to be *someone* who's figured this out already? It's not a unique skill or anything like that."

"If there's anyone who knows it, most likely that would only be a high-level Enchanter who's done inscriptions for decades or even *centuries*. It would be the edge that allowed them to become a Sage. *Guaranteed*. Which means they'd never share that secret, not even with the members of their own tower." Seeing that she was making headway, Jenny switched tactics slightly. "Beyond the practical side, think of how much respect this would garner you and all of us. By the time someone reaches the Grandmaster rank with the skill, they could be tossing Master-rank rituals around like candy in a parade!"

Joe knocked on the door of Master Darling's office, rubbing his knuckles as they buzzed from the enchantment it was inscribed with. Seeing her opportunity about to vanish, Jenny pointed at the office and met his gaze directly. "The first person who would benefit, at least get the most benefit, is in *that room*! What do you think she'd say if we asked-"

"I'll make some time for it." The Ritualist hastily lifted a hand to shush his assistant, not quite ready to deal with the endless requests for training that would inevitably arise once he'd made knowledge of this skill known to even a small group of people in the tower. If the head of the Enchanted Ritual Circles branch learned about it right now, he was certain to be pestered until he gave in. "Make a list of... pick ten other people who you think would benefit the most from this *and* be able to teach others. We'll get them in a room, do a demonstration, and see what they have to say. Now will you *shush*—he~ey, Master Darling!"

The door of Hilda's office swung open just a crack, and she stared between the two intruders, clearly able to see that something was amiss. "What's happening?"

Jenny leaned forward, cheeks swelling as if she were about to explode from keeping Joe's skill a secret, but the man himself stepped forward and put a hand over his heart. "I was hoping you could take a look at the enchantment? I passed a skill threshold, and it felt like I was about to fall apart."

The door opened wider, clear interest and a hint of concern looming large on Hilda's face. Joe turned his head to stare at Jenny meaningfully. "I believe you have a list to put together? A meeting request to... request?"

"On it." Far from disappointed, Jenny turned with a heavily determined expression and rushed off, descending the stairs twice as quickly as she had climbed them. Joe shook his head in slight aggravation then stepped into Hilda's workspace.

"This is exactly what I had mentioned we needed to speak about the last time we interacted. I didn't expect it to be necessary so soon... tell me more about the pain you went through." Hilda didn't exactly ask, instead speaking in an entirely professional manner as she shut the door behind them and made her way to her desk, quickly pulling out several tools Joe had never seen before. "Did it feel like your limbs were being twisted out of their joints, your skin was being shredded, or was it more akin to getting hit with a low-powered lightning bolt?"

"Uhh, the last one? Are the other ones... coming?" Joe inquired with trepidation. "Seems like you were expecting something like this?"

Master Darling didn't answer immediately, instead slowly circling him as she touched her tools along the mandela of geometric lines on his head, neck, and wrists–the only places he already had exposed skin. "Already this advanced? Why are you more than halfway through all possible tier transitions or skill gains? You must understand that seven is the *maximum* number the enchantment can sustain, right? I'm certain I was fully clear about this."

"There's only been four so far!" Joe defensively countered. "Do you have any idea how many skills I've turned down over the last weeks?"

Master Darling adjusted her glasses as she leveled a flat *look* at him. "Weeks, Joe. *Weeks.* Is the path to the next Characteristic threshold so easy to race along? Some of my colleagues have struggled for decades now and are only approaching the barrier now. Personally, I've needed to entirely change my life plans and accept a new class in order to have the *possibility* of pushing to the Grandmaster rank."

"Well, I don't want to say it's exactly easy, but... I *am* almost done? Just not sure what else needs to happen." Seeing her disbelieving, somewhat disappointed countenance, Joe decided that trying to convince her with spoken words was destined to fail. Instead, he pulled open his status sheet and shared his Characteristics directly.

Name: Joe 'Emperor of Mana' Class: Reductionist
Profession I: Codex-Keeper (1/20)
Profession II: Ritualistic Alchemist (15/20)
Profession III: Grandmaster's Apprentice (15/25)
Profession IV: Ritualistic Metalworker (16/20)
Profession V: Ritualistic Numerologist (10/20)
Profession VI: Arcane Enchanting Theorist (5/5).

Character Level: 30 Exp: 465,000 Exp to next level: 31,000 (Locked.)
Rituarchitect Level: 15 Exp: 105,700 Exp to next level: 14,250
Reductionist Level: 12 Exp: 90,972 Exp to next level: 28

Hit Points: 7,966/7,966
Mana: 24,256/25,940 (6,000 mana bequeathed to others. 6.25% reserved)
Mana regen: 284.74/sec
Stamina: 5,429/5,429
Stamina regen: 8.59/sec

Characteristic: Score
Quad Strength: 499
Dialectic Dexterity: 499
Stoic Constitution: 499
Light Intelligence: 499
Ritualistic Wisdom: 499
Dark Charisma: 499
Karmic Perception: 499
Red Luck: 499
Karmic Luck: 390 → 314

Master Darling glanced at his status once, did a double take, then goggled at the numbers she was seeing with unrestrained shock. "What in the *world*?"

"I know, right?" Joe was looking at two sections he had somewhat glossed over over the last few days in all the excitement. "It took seventy-six points of Karmic Luck just to bind my weapon? Hold on... I only need *twenty-eight* experience points to get to my next class level? Excuse me, I might have to go take care of something real quick-"

Instead of leaving the room as he'd planned to do, Joe went very still as the Enchanter's hands clamped down on his wrists. "You have a capacity of nearly twenty-six thousand mana? But... you had more before? That's still an insane amount, but how did it go *down*? Wait, I do want to know, but first I need to know how you managed to get all of your Characteristics so high in such a short amount of time! You haven't been experimenting on yourself even more since you left here, have you? What am I saying, of course you have. Maybe I should do a more intensive examination?"

He slowly broke her grip, gently patting her hands as they slid bonelessly off of him. "Combination of different skills increasing through the Master ranks. Mostly Lore, but a few other things have been going on in the background."

She studied his face, pupils darting back and forth as she examined every inch of skin. Her voice was faint when she spoke again. "You seem healthier. Even beyond just what happens as you gather Characteristics. I hope it's not weird to say, but you also seem... shall we say more *refreshed*?"

"Yep, I don't stink *nearly* so bad anymore," he quipped, enjoying her reflexive wince. "Managed to get a few of my skills working again. Here-"

Joe extended his Mana Dominion carefully, observing the space around him and intentionally designating all of the items in the room as 'not trash'. There was a light **crackle** as the faintest of smudges vanished from one of Hilda's cheeks, specks of dust along the floorboards vanished, and a strangely empty scent permeated the room as all lingering dust and molecules were eradicated by his Aura of Soothing Destruction.

After a moment, the Enchanter blinked rapidly, her skin plumping and tightening softly as her internal hydration was maximized, and every *hint* of soreness was healed in an instant.

"Oh!" She cracked a smile for the first time since opening her door. "That's quite pleasant; I can see why you like it. Odd, I hadn't thought my office had a smell, you know? But now that it's gone...?"

"Seems to stand out in retrospect, right?" Joe chuckled at her reaction, as it was everything he'd been hoping for. "Sorry to have to get back to the main topic, but you seemed to know I'd be experiencing getting shocked?"

"Yes." She immediately returned to her standard professional demeanor. "I had been meaning to warn you. It's a safety measure I built into the enchantment to make sure you realized when you were approaching the maximum capacity of the enchantments. I wanted you to have every alert available before you went overboard and accidentally broke it."

The Ritualist stared at her blankly, trying to reconcile her words with her actions. "So... if I have this straight, you built in a pain sequence, which nearly killed me even at *four* of the seven slots being used... all to make sure I didn't progress too fast?"

"Exactly."

"I guess... thanks?" Joe couldn't quite make that logic work in his head, so he shifted the direction of the conversation slightly. "Right. Well, hopefully it won't be a problem for too much longer. I just need to break into the next Characteristic threshold."

"Which you understand requires *anchoring*." Hilda nodded along with his words, her head slowing slightly at Joe's apparent confusion. "Come now, you must've had this conversation with someone already. If you want Grandmaster-rank Characteristics, you need a Grandmaster skill your body can use as a template. That's the third requirement, alongside surviving or completing your Tribulation and gathering your Mastery Merits."

"Oh, yeah. That. I just hadn't heard it called 'anchoring' before." The Ritualist relaxed, dispelling the panic that had been welling up in him. "Working on it."

"I suppose if you've already reached the Characteristics threshold, which is usually the very *last* thing anyone achieves," she grumbled softly at the unfairness of his rapid ascent, "you should stay in a safe location and focus on accruing Mastery Merits to the exclusion of all else. Luckily, you have an entire tower packed to the brim with Journeymen and Experts champing at the bit to learn from you. Just be aware, the closer you are to success, the more your Tribulation will try to break you."

Thinking about the massively reduced requirements for earning amazing skills and how it constantly tantalized him with options both fantastic and horrible, Joe could only grin in excitement. "My Tribulation is going to throw even *more* at me? You don't say...!"

CHAPTER THIRTY-ONE

"What brought you back to the tower? I was under the impression that you would be running around the world of giants for a few months having fun jumping back and forth, leaving craters from the rituals you set off in your wake." Now that they'd moved past the serious topics—or so she assumed—Master Darling's voice took on a lightly teasing quality, only for her face to fall as Joe stiffened up and regarded her with a grave expression.

"Right. About that-"

Congratulations! Two of the Experts you have been training in the way of 'Jumping' have received Inspiration and broken through the Expert bottleneck!

Current Merits earned from skill source: Omnivault. (3/100)

Total unused Mastery Merits: 95.

"What?" Hilda reached out and poked Joe when he remained silent.

"Huh? Oh, sorry about that. Heh, just as I'm trying to let you know about a serious issue, a couple people back on Jotunheim figured out how to jump real good." Dismissing the notification, even as he squeezed one fist tightly with excitement at how close he was getting to achieving Grandmaster rank, the Ritualist took a deep breath and tried again. Without allowing himself to get distracted, he explained the situation with the expedition and how it was incredibly likely that they would be returning with a Mythic Core in less than two weeks.

When he stopped speaking, he expected follow-up questions, but instead found Hilda already halfway to her desk, rolling up her sleeves as she began pulling books off shelves and vanishing them into some storage device. "What're you doing?"

"Leaving," she replied without missing a beat. "Why are you asking? You just told me a war is inevitable. I need to mobilize the members of the Enchanted Ritual Circles cohort and get them working on a full defensive position. We have just over a week or so to set up large-scale deterrents. I'm thinking curses layered with debuffs that will follow any aggressor for *days* at the minimum. Might not be enough to stop all of them, but they should make it painfully clear that trying for an attack of opportunity on the tower would be a terrible decision that would weaken them for the entirety of the war."

"Entirety? You don't expect it to last long, then." That was a surprising factoid, as in his experience, even at the quickest wars tended to drag on for weeks or months at a time.

"Mmm." Hilda snapped open a briefcase and began dumping components out of the drawers of her desk. "As soon as one side raises a Sage, there's an automatic calling of a meeting of the Sage's Council, where they'll demand a vote. Not attending is the same as abstaining, which means every last combatant of note will be forced to leave the conflict behind. The losing faction will do everything they can to delay the Mythic Core's arrival, or steal it, or *perhaps* hold out long enough to have one of their own delivered. But once it reaches the intended Grandmaster's hands, the war will end all but immediately."

"Ah." Joe's mind drifted back to when Pete had ascended and how practically everyone across the planet immediately knew of the occasion, due to the door being left open. Someone ascending publicly would certainly have an even greater effect. "Well... in happy news, I'm going to do a skill demonstration for you in the near future, and try to teach it if you're interested."

"Thank you, but I highly doubt anything of use will come of me learning a skill and having only a few days to work on it," Hilda replied with perfunctory politeness. "If you don't mind, I need to get going, and I'd prefer to lock the door to my office behind me..."

With that she swept out, not *quite* pushing Joe in front of her, only to leave the bemused man standing alone. His sudden solitude lasted all of thirty seconds as Jenny's voice preceded her running down a hallway, a thin strip of paper clutched in her hand as she waved it back and forth to catch his attention. "Tri-Master Joe! Meeting scheduled with the Sage! It's, well, it's twelve hours from now, but it's the very first appointment he was willing to take. I wrote that the meeting involved the safety of the tower as a whole, so I hope I didn't accidentally make you a liar."

She slid to a stop in front of him, and he plucked the paper out of her hand, glancing at it to absorb the details before stuffing it in his pocket. "Nice work! Hey, Master Darling left to get some people working on... some stuff..."

Jenny's eyebrows shot up at his evasiveness, but she managed to keep her mouth shut as Joe pushed himself to say more.

"I think that teaching session you were interested in should be scheduled for tomorrow, sometime after I talk to the Sage. If you can make sure Hilda attends, that'd be probably for the best. She might be... resistant to showing."

"She's at the top of my list." Jenny paused with a smug smirk on her lips. "Didn't realize she was at the tippy top of *your* list as well."

"Alright, get out of here." Joe waved a fist in her general direction then immediately reversed course. "Actually, hold on.

Before you do that, I need a favor. I'm going to write out five notes, one for each of whoever is the top person in each Core Class skill that–I can't stress this enough–that *you* think should have access to Inscription Momentum. I'd rather have the most appropriate people have this skill than the strongest."

Rubbing the back of his bald head, Joe glanced down, wondering if there was anything else he should say. Snapping his fingers, he looked up and locked eyes with Jenny to show her how very serious he was as he said, "Make sure you tell them the same thing I'm about to tell you. Keep this quiet. We need to prepare defensive measures for the tower, as if we're going to come under siege. I want no announcements, nothing getting out to the public until the Sage decides to make it happen."

Jenny's excitement and levity faded away, realization dawning in her eyes. "Something big is happening, isn't it?"

"Not just yet, but soon," Joe candidly admitted. "I'm only telling you this because you need to know enough to get past anyone blocking your access to what I'm assuming is going to be a large number of Masters. There's... let's call it a ninety-five percent chance that one of the factions is going to be returning with a Mythic Core in under two weeks. We need to ride out the storm that's going to be crashing over the entire planet, and that's only going to happen if we're ready for it without anyone being able to undermine us."

"Okay... okay." Much to her credit, Jenny absorbed the information after only a few deep breaths to conquer the surge of fear his words elicited. "I'll take care of it, but what are *you* going to do?"

Joe reached into his pocket, gently caressing the Codex Key that had been calling his name for the last long while. "I'm going to find a good book to read. If I need to sit and wait anyway, I might as well enjoy the time."

They parted ways, Jenny racing off, while the Ritualist meandered through the halls until he found a nice, secluded dead end. He pulled his key out and slid it into empty air, giving it a twist and causing a portal into the sub-dimension to pop open. He stepped inside and allowed the door to close behind him, drinking in the stillness of the space.

Sparing a moment to light the fire, Joe perused the books whispering through his Magical Synesthesia about the knowledge they contained, until he came to a slim tome that had caught his eye the last time he'd been in here. "Multiplicity of the Myriad Mind. I think I can finish you in twelve hours."

He was gratified to find that this book wasn't chained in place like many of the others, though it was heavier than it looked, the cover a strangely cool metal that felt pleasant beneath his fingers. After settling into the comfortable chair, he opened the cover... only to find a deeply theoretical roadmap instead of a magical explanation. The first chapters were explorations of group identity, divergence from preconceived notions, and the limits of single-path progression. The author argued that specialization was a trap, and not because it limited growth-

"But because it limits perspective." Joe read the final line of the chapter out loud, pausing for a moment to decide if he agreed or not. "Eh. I guess anyone trying to figure out a problem for long enough has run into something like this. You're hammering away at it for what seems like forever, then someone with a fresh set of eyes comes in and solves it in no time flat. I can get behind this."

Only in the final twenty percent of the slim book did theory give way to application. Joe's pulse increased in tempo as he unfolded an archaic ritual diagram. "Master rank, huh? Ha! For *now*, you non-math-knowing precursors!"

The diagram was extremely clear as to the ritual's purpose: it created clones of the user, bound to an item that could be easily transported. Each clone had only a single skill they were created with, and although they were temporary creations, they were *not* illusions but instead independent entities.

"They'll use whatever skill they're given to the extreme. I feel like I've pushed the boundaries, but it'll definitely be interesting to see what the ritual considers 'seeing them in ways I'd never think of'." The applications for this ritual quickly grew more exciting as he thought about testing his assumptions on skills and especially identifying his blind spots when it came to magic he'd already had for long periods of time. "Refine my own capabilities, maybe even fight? Ooh, even better... compete with myself! Why is this locked away, I wonder?"

"Hmmm, here. 'Warning, never give one of the clones the ability to use this ritual, as it is the only skill they have, they will assign it to every clone they create, which will in turn do the same'. I guess that makes sense. If someone found that out, it means it's because they *did it...*" He found himself lost in thought while staring into the crackling fire and slowly allowed his eyes to close.

The next thing Joe knew, there was a sharp chiming coming from his pocket, alongside a concerning vibration that had him smacking at his robes before he was fully awake. "Get it off of me!"

The thin paper Jenny had given him fell out of his pocket, fluttering to the ground and bouncing around as it vibrated and strobed with light. The Ritualist let out a sigh of relief when he saw what had been 'attacking' him then pushed himself up out of the chair. At that moment, the fire in the hearth **popped**, sending a small spray of sparks upward as if reminding him to put it out before leaving.

Letting his mana fill the space around him, Joe activated his Aura of Soothing Destruction. The effect on the space was immediate, as the lingering grogginess he felt vanished, a faint dryness in his throat and eyes fixing itself even as the patches of the flaming logs in the hearth were deemed 'trash'. They flared brightly for an instant before being converted directly into aspects. Pure plasma remained above the no-longer-burning wood for a single tick of a clock before puffing out of existence.

Skill offered: Fire Destruction (Expert IX). Firefighters look at you with awe and admiration, being able to-

"Skip. Clearly I don't need a dedicated skill for that." As he stepped out of the sub-dimension, Joe glanced at his status to see if there'd been any changes, but his Codex-Keeper profession remained stubbornly stuck at level one. "I suppose, while that book was useful, it didn't exactly open my mind to new subjects. I'm betting some of those chained tomes will *literally* make me wrestle with unfamiliar ideas... no reason to rush this profession, I suppose."

He took the stairs rather than Omnivaulting up through open air, though the temptation was real. Sage Pete had kept him waiting half the day, and while Joe wasn't trying to be petty, he was certain his meeting alarm had gone off early to ensure he'd arrive by the time the Sage was *actually* free.

The door to the penthouse swung open just as Joe strolled up to it at a leisurely pace, further reinforcing that he'd made the right decision. When he stepped inside, the ritualist found Sage Pete standing near the enormous bay windows, looking out over the tower-covered planet. Though he appeared young once more, Pete still had the mannerisms of a centuries-old man.

His hands were clasped behind his back, stance wide and commanding, until he turned to regard his visitor. "Ah! Joe, m'boy! Welcome, welcome. Tea? Oh, right, apologies. Coffee? Before we get started, I'd love to let you know the findings of my investigation into this 'controller' situation."

"That would be very nice, actually. Both the update and the drink." Joe lifted his mug from his belt, the motion enough to summon Mate, who looked around the room with only a quick glance before topping off two mugs and vanishing back to fight its war on another plane.

"Mm. Good stuff," Pete happily muttered as he sipped the drink, manifesting a biscotti and dipping it into the coffee. "Ah-*herm*. Now, the investigation. I'm sorry to say that, though we have checked in on the obvious candidates, no one we have looked into has the kind of reach or power that would allow them to control groups of Masters on Vanaheim, let alone across entire planets. Whoever you've been running up against hasn't been using any obvious brute-force-domination techniques. Unless you are terribly mistaken, which I don't think is the case, someone is working against you in a subtle, layered, and patient manner."

Setting a bag on the table, he began pulling out one block of cheese after another. "That said, my digging into your situation hasn't been wasted effort, exactly. I've uncovered three separate coercion plots, a mid-ranking scribe rewriting vows after negotiations had concluded—terrible for their tower's reputation if it comes out publicly—and a surprisingly large smuggling ring run exclusively by Experts in various classes. Since you paid for the work to be done, the bounties I've earned on handling those situations come back to you. A significant amount of cheese and a few thousand points of Honor."

"I guess it was too much to hope this would be something cleared up quickly." Joe took in all of the information then shook off his disappointment and tried to refocus. "I appreciate all this, and I'm glad at least something good is coming out of it. I totally understand this isn't an easy thing I'm asking of you. But, look, here's the thing... or, do you already know why I'm here?"

Pete shook his head, his smile appearing more like a grimace. "Only some hearsay, which I have to assume has a kernel of truth, seeing as the Masters of Enchanted Ritual Circles have begun unspooling miles of silver wires across the entirety of the training field out there. War approaches, does it not?"

"Yeah." Joe's voice was heavy, but before he pressed on, the Sage lifted a hand.

"Some *good* news for you first, then. Mirascible has returned to Vanaheim, having finished whatever he was hunting on Jotunheim. He requests your presence... he said you'd know where." Pete took a sip of his coffee, staring at Joe over the rim of the mug. "It was very cloak and dagger. Quite... odd to see from such a *direct* personality."

Joe leaned back in his chair, lifting his Ebonsteel mug in the air for a toast. "*Fantastic* timing. Knowing we have an ally of his caliber on the planet certainly helps me put my mind at ease. As to my news... let me tell you a little story about an expedition, a deal, and a Mythic Core arriving in only a few days."

As he laid out the details of what had been going on, the Ritualist was gratified that Pete didn't interrupt once, though his face was deeply lined by the time Joe stopped speaking. "-Which is why I think we need to get our tower positioned for a siege at the minimum. I don't really understand the politics of this world quite yet, but you don't have to have been born here to know what happens when two groups want a resource there's only one of. Especially when the people who want it have the power to crack continents with a casual strike."

The Sage set his mug down on the table with a soft **clink*. "Ah... war. It's been hundreds of years since Vanaheim has tasted actual war, instead of the posturing and Honor duels to which we've grown accustomed."

Silence stretched between them as Pete's fingers tapped once against the armrest before he reopened conversation with a question. "It seems you've thrown in your hat with the Ascensionists. No, I understand you haven't made any formal agreements, but that's the way it *seems*. It is likely better that we open negotiations with their faction now, before they know they're about to have a Mythic Core in their hands. If they are about to win this political bid, it's best that we join the winning side ahead of time. Lightly and with as much political neutrality as possible."

"How can you align with them and still remain neutral?" Joe was genuinely curious, as his connection to Occultatum meant this sort of thing *should* come naturally to him; but human nature was endlessly varied and difficult to understand.

Pete seemed pleased to be able to explain, a subtle reminder that he expected that Joe would eventually outrank him, even in this tower. "I'll reach out to the faction leader and offer them a safe haven for their noncombatants should total war break out. I'll begin the process of allying with them from there, while refusing to set foot among the Sages' Council. I won't risk forcing anyone's hand by being the tie-breaker with their voting."

Joe started getting up from his seat. "I can start putting together some-"

Once again, the Sage interrupted him with a gentle gesture. "While I appreciate your courage, and the Decury Duelist patch on your shoulder announces your combat role to the world, there is a qualitative difference in what we can offer. You are powerful, but a Master fighting in a battle of Sages is like comparing a candle to the sun. If I may be blunt, you can spend the next week creating a masterpiece in an attempt to fight if needed. But at the end of the day, someone like myself, someone with overwhelming power, will simply ignore it. Or..."

The Sage leaned forward, his gaze intense. "Or you can spend the short amount of time we have teaching us that amazing skill you've stumbled upon and find ways to collect Mastery Merits by the *fistful,* so that the next time a situation like this arises, you will be able to choose whether to be on the front lines or not. But unfortunately, Joe, this time around, that choice is not yours to make. Your strength isn't enough for this fight, and, to drive home my point, let me give an example. I'm certain some of the people who will be taking the field against us would be able to directly undo the efforts you've put into restoring your mana channels."

That stopped Joe cold; his shifty side that had already been trying to make plans to counter a Sage freezing like a deer in the headlights. "Undo my efforts? You mean to tell me someone could come along and... and rip the alchemical ritual straight out of my skin?"

"In essence... yes." Pete tilted his head to the side, confusion writ large on his face. "You hadn't considered what it might look like to throw yourself against a Sage? A Sage of a general skill is incredibly powerful, oftentimes *multiple* times as strong as a specialized variant. This is simply due to the vastness of their experience and deep foundation of supporting skills; but it doesn't make it any less true. Were you to go up against a Sage of Alchemy or Enchanting, it's highly probable *either* of them could directly siphon your imbuement directly out of your body."

"I'm certain it would be an unpleasant experience, to say the least." Seeing that his words had hit their mark, Pete de-escalated slightly and moved to change the topic. "Why don't we make a plan together to maximize your time here over the next few days? Once we have that, and with my backing behind you, it shouldn't be difficult to start moving pieces into position."

CHAPTER THIRTY-TWO

The Sage settled deeply into his chair, fingers steepling under his chin as his eyes focused on a hazy point in the distance. "Let's put together what your next few days should look like. Not as a 'maybe this should happen' wishlist, but a proper schedule I'll task someone to keep you on track with."

"*Ugh.*" Joe grumbled softly enough that he didn't interrupt Pete's spiel.

"We have a fixed window of time, even if we don't know its exact length. Let's assume... ten days before things go from their current level to openly hostile. This means that every hour we have needs to be put to work. Every minute accounted for."

"Ugh."

"*Yes*, yes. No one likes to be told they need to work extremely hard, even if it's only for a short period of time." Pete rolled his eyes as Joe flushed slightly at being caught whining. "In my mind, you have one goal, earning enough Mastery Merits to become a Grandmaster, which comes together as three distinct tasks. First and foremost, teaching Inscription Momentum to a select group of people who will be able to pass it to others quickly. In my mind, these should be Masters of each of our Core Class skills, people who have deep insight and understandings into how their disciplines function at the highest level. None of them should need any hand holding, so long as you're willing to teach them."

Joe half-raised a hand. "I also promised my assistant she could be part of the first batch."

"Jenesequa?" The Sage's nose crinkled as he tried not to pull faces at the Decury Duelist sitting across from him. "Why in the world would you try to teach a skill like this to someone under the Expert rank? Skills with a time dilation component are among the most difficult to comprehend abilities that *exist*. No, wait... this might actually work in your favor. It should give you a good handle on the reasons Masters tend to instruct Experts and leave the training of even Journeymen to those at the Expert tier. If nothing else, it should benefit your Teaching skill immensely, and you'll be able to determine the variance in time requirement necessary to pass Inscription Momentum along. Who else?"

"You?" Joe's half-asked answer earned him a droll look from the Sage, but then the Ritualist considered the question more seriously and lit up. "Speaking of my Teaching skill, the way it works right now, the *type* of student I instruct matters a whole lot. Beyond those with high-level Core Class skills, bring in whoever has the highest Teaching skill. Since they can pass along what they learn from me at half efficiency, as if I were teaching it directly, they should gain a bunch of benefits and levels quickly. Rapid propagation is the goal, after all."

"Wise choice." Pete wrote down a few names then turned to the next point of conversation. "Even if... there's a stipulation I have for this plan. You've seen the effects of Karmic Debt and how accruing too much can close off the future ascension of those who are laden down with it. To that end, I'm going to require that anyone who learns this previously unknown, *immensely* beneficial skill acknowledges *you* as their teacher. Until you hit a full one hundred Mastery Merits earned from this skill, anyone who learns it *must* give you full credit."

Even as Joe slumped in his seat, running a hand across his face, he could see Pete's advice was sound. "I don't like bottlenecking the spread of knowledge, Sage. Plus, it kinda feels like I'm forcing people to have an obligation to me-"

"They will have an obligation, whether you like it or not," the Sage cut him off bluntly. "In this way, you are only enforcing *attribution* instead of attempting to put them under your control. There's quite the difference. After you have all the Mastery Merits you require, you could choose to make the skill itself a tower secret or further spread it to other inscription-focused classes such as Enchanters for benefits of your own. But that choice must be yours; and this is the only way to make sure it happens that way."

Silence stretched between them for a moment as Joe struggled with his personal preferences, but eventually he acquiesced. "I understand why you're making that rule, even if it's not my favorite."

"Then we have our first priority locked in. Well done." Pete moved on immediately. "I'm going to assign you a mid-sized lecture hall for the next few weeks, a working space reinforced to withstand failed attempts at rituals."

"I'm just going to be teaching, aren't I?" Even as the words left his mouth, the Ritualist winced and lifted his hand before the Sage needed to explain Joe's own skill to himself. "Right, nevermind. How are they going to learn Inscription Momentum if I'm not demonstrating it? So I'll be working on a ritual at the same time, then?"

"Right you are. That brings us to your second, hmm, let's call it short-to-medium-term goal." Pete couldn't hide the grin on his face, the wry laughter in his eyes making Joe squirm in his seat with embarrassment. "I'll assign you a large group of Experts and below to assist you in the creation of any ritual of your choosing while you demonstrate. I will seal their senses partially so that they won't be able to learn what you are teaching the Masters–this is standard practice, don't look at me like that."

"Couldn't we just get the same oath from them and let them learn if they can?" the Ritualist inquired, trying to hide his disgust at the idea of forcing people to participate in something without letting them even know what they were doing.

The Sage appeared surprised at the idea and rubbed his chin pensively as he considered the words. "That depends. Will your Teaching skill support them or hinder your instruction of those you're intending to teach?"

"It'll..." Joe double-checked the skill just to be certain, but answered confidently, "Bystanders are able to learn any skill I'm teaching at a reduced rate. About fifty percent less, but it'll still give them a chance."

"Interesting. Most people, when they reach evolutions in Teaching, tend to narrow their focus. Generally they intend to teach small groups of people. Notably, it's usually professors or other general education teachers who advance their skill the way you are going. Generally *not...*" he waved at Joe's entire body, "exceptionally talented people who seem to pluck unique or incredibly rare versions out of thin air. I'll triple the number of Experts I was going to assign, in that case."

"Neat." Thinking of having so many helpers had Joe quickly going through the catalog of rituals he had available, and he grinned at the thought of not just double but *triple* dipping. "I think I have the perfect design to use. I recently acquired a ritual that allows me to give people a chance at directly learning any skill being used in a set area. Learning might actually be a strong word for it... maybe directly transferring the skill to them would be a better description? No training sessions or prerequisites, just directly bypassing the learning requirements."

"Mmm." Pete's eyebrows lifted with barely restrained interest, and he bobbed his head thoughtfully as he wrote in his notebook with a suddenly shaky hand. "Don't suppose you'd be willing to sell a copy of that one to the tower? What's the rank?"

"Master."

"I figured it'd be around there." Pete remained in place, quill quivering above the paper as he waited for an answer. "It could benefit hundreds of people and allow us to quickly bring people focusing on one Core Class skill up to snuff in the others. *If* you are willing, that is."

"You know, I'd *give* it to you if you'd take it." Joe pulled out the diagram and held it out to the Sage, who stared at the vellum as though Joe were thrusting a hissing snake in his general direction. "But then you'd think there's a debt between us."

"No *thinking*. There just *would* be." Pete didn't take his eyes off the document, "Please don't tempt me. I'd take it and do great things with it. Even with the material cost, having this as an open-source reference would bring the power of our tower to heights we've never seen before. But I can't bear that burden alone... which is why the tower must *collectively* purchase it from you."

When Joe stored the ritual away, Pete closed his eyes for a moment and allowed himself a quiet sigh of relief. When he opened them, he was all business once more. "Well, there's your first and most important two goals. Since you'll have an adequate supply of mana from everyone helping, and I assume you can bring your own stabilizers for safety purposes...?"

"I have a Master-rank stabilizer, but I'm missing a key alchemical component to fully realize its potential." Joe pulled out his notes, quickly leafing through until he tapped on a starred section. "I need an 'Ichor of Overflow' that'll allow me to combine the stabilizer and upgrade it into an-"

"Eclipsing Aurora Chalice." Pete grinned fondly at some distant memory. "I've made a few of those Ichors in my day. I'd offer to make you one in return for the skill you're going to teach me, but an Artifact-rank alchemy item isn't enough of a payment for me to learn the skill. However, that would be a perfectly valid request from Master Gabrielle Syme. I'll send her a work order to have it ready by the time she arrives for class. Nothing quite like paying off your debt before you accrue it, you know? I'm sure she'll appreciate the opportunity."

"I could just make it myself-"

"In your immense amount of free time?" The Sage held Joe's gaze. "Not only would it take you longer than you should be spending on it, doing so would rob her of an easy repayment of this favor. I can't *stop* you, but then she would need to figure something else out. Something of equal value."

Joe merely grunted, acknowledging the point and nodding to show that he understood.

To his credit, the Sage knew better than to belabor the point. "Obviously, you will need to take a short break at some point in the next few days and meet up with your combat mentor, or Mirascible will come back and drag you out of here, but in every other spare moment, I do have an idea for what you can do to maximize your opportunities for earning Mastery Merits."

The Sage had a mix of emotions flash across his face, a hint of pleasure, excitement, but surprisingly... mostly envy. "This isn't an option I've ever been able to point at as a possibility, but you can essentially gain individual merits directly if you are willing to create Master-ranked Lore books for the scholarly among our ranks. There are dozens of people, even among the highest echelons of the various disciplines, who've been unable to gain Inspiration in their associated Lore skills. I'm certain they'd be more than willing to purchase an Artifact that would allow them to sidestep that barrier and directly attain Mastery. Far from an equal exchange, frankly, you could hold an *auction* for who gets to go first."

"Please no." Joe shuddered at the thought of only passing on incredibly useful information to the highest bidder. "Whatever won't cause them to load me down with their Karmic Debt, that'll be plenty of payment. Whoever asks first gets it, unless they're someone I wouldn't want to empower above their peers."

"Well said." Pete chewed on his lower lip for a moment. "I

may have a bias, but again, I'd like to request Master Gabrielle gaining this opportunity first. She's worked under me for decades and is an incredibly dedicated and passionate Alchemist, yet the final step of theory has held her back for a very long time. I firmly believe advancing her Lore would likely allow her to gain the Enlightenment she needs to become our tower's next *Grandmaster*."

"Good enough for me, man."

"Man?" The Sage's countenance shifted slightly, and when he spoke again, he clearly felt awkward. "While the statement is true, and I understand we're alone, please do remember to act more formally around me when we are in public. Your etiquette will do you harm in higher social strata, unless you have the power to force people to accept your nonchalance."

"Like Mir."

"Very much so." Pete shrugged apologetically. "Please take my advice in the spirit it is offered. There are all sorts of Sages who've been alive for centuries who can and *will* take offense, whether you mean to offend them or not. Sometimes a single negative interaction will cause them to work against you until they feel their honor is satisfied. With a Sage-level conflict looming..."

"Got it, I'll be on my best behavior." Joe crossed his heart with one hand then offered a winning smile as he showed a double thumbs-up to the Sage. "Teaching a class directly and a group of people indirectly. Working on a ritual to bypass having to teach in the first place and plugging all the gaps with generating at least one Lore book. Add in a touch of politeness and remember people's titles. Anything else?"

"I think that'll about do it." Pete's frosty stiffness faded as he finished writing in his notebook then tore out a few pages, sending them elsewhere in the tower with a flash of green light, then handing the final one to Joe. "These are who I recommend for your course, the first five being the top Masters in the tower in their respective disciplines, and the next are teachers with attitudes I expect you will greatly approve of."

Then the Sage got to his feet, dusting off his hands as he looked out the great window. "I'm off to begin playing politics and securing alliances with the faction I expect will be winning. I do hope you are correct that the Ascensionists will be the first to return with a Mythic Core, as I am going to be throwing our lot in with them rather deeply."

"I mean, all I know is..." Joe's mouth went dry as he realized he had no idea if the Ascensionists had succeeded, or, more specifically, would succeed *before* the other faction.

Pete gave him a nod of quiet support. "I understand. You've given me information to the best of your ability, and I'm not overly concerned with the alternate outcome. It's not like Mythic Cores are something you can just pick up along the side of the road, so knowing they have a high probability of success is enough for me. I will let your assistant know your schedule for the coming days and send her my shortlist of learners as well. Seeing as you have a few hours before you're slated to show up for your first lecture, I'd recommend taking this time to visit with Class Sage Mir."

Without further ado, the Sage sharply gestured at his door, and Joe reflexively jerked his head to follow the motion. There was a flash of green light, and by the time he looked back, Pete was gone.

The Ritualist couldn't even be too annoyed, seeing as he'd also discovered the joys of using his abilities to vanish while among people. "I just hate that he can *still* manage to sneak past me."

Even so, as he exited the office and let the door swing shut behind him, Joe's stomach fluttered with excitement and nervous energy. "This week begins the big push for *Grandmaster...*"

The word echoed in his head, circling around to put itself at the forefront of his thoughts over and over. As he made his way down the enormous winding staircase that circled the entirety of the hollow tower, the Ritualist needed to remind himself to watch his step more than once. Excitement had stolen the spotlight even from the concern over the upcoming conflict, and he needed to continuously bring his thoughts back to the present so he didn't trip over himself and tumble the rest of the way down.

Watching other people and seeing what they were up to helped Joe ground himself. He soon found his attention pulled toward how each of the different core discipline groups worked as they interacted with people in their own circles, as well as the way they meshed or clashed with other Ritualists outside of their area of focus.

He quickly found that the upper floors belonged to Enchanters and those pursuing the heights of ritual circles. To his great surprise, directly below that were the rooms and offices of mathematicians studying Magical Matrices, followed by advanced Alchemy–not on the same floor as the kitchens–and finally Ritualistic Forging just above the general study areas and housing.

The layout surprised him, as he'd assumed that the more 'prestigious' classes would be up on the higher levels. He had only seen the math club in action, not the actual class... classes. Then Joe saw a young man, likely only a Beginner in Ritualistic Forging, dragging a crate of materials on a dolly. Even with the wheeled contraption, the youngster was red-faced and heaving for breath as he pulled on the handles to get the wheels over a step, only for it to lurch up as it passed the halfway point.

Suddenly the classes with lots of heavy materials and components being situated lower in the tower made much more sense, logistically speaking.

After taking a moment to help the forger by grabbing the crate with one hand and quickly hauling it up a few flights, Joe resumed his journey. Soon he was crossing the training field and was swallowed by the ecumenopolis of Vanaheim.

As he walked through the mostly empty streets, Joe examined the towers he passed with a critical eye. Each of them had the same base material yet had been worked in some way by the people living there to give their home a distinct look and feel. In the distance, the Ritualist saw Mak's cheese wagon go rumbling by, the usual tagalong cart kiosks squeaking along after the enormous carriage.

He almost altered his course to go and chat, but the thought of making conversation right now ate at him. "I'm supposed to be spending every minute I have carefully. No need to go make promises to bring fancy cheeses to the world or tease the coffee-cat. Gotta get to work."

As he hustled to the ouroboros statue–which he was technically not supposed to use to get entry to the Inverted Tower, now that Mir had shown him a better option for entering–Joe felt a yearning sadness fill him for the current state of this world.

Vanaheim was, for lack of a better word... *easy*.

There were wide streets, parks, a distinct lack of monsters, and endless opportunities for advancing your class. Every tower was essentially a combination of community and university. Entire family trees had grown up in them, and magic was everywhere. Even fighting was regulated and polite, at least when compared to the death matches such fighting would end in on a different world.

As he jumped on top of the enormous sphere surrounded by a snake, pressing the hidden recessed button and making the entrance appear at its base, Joe had a deeply uncomfortable question fill him.

"How different is this place going to look in just a few weeks?"

CHAPTER THIRTY-THREE

"Thought I told you not to come in through that path!" Mir barked at Joe as the Ritualist finished winding his way through the ancient corridors and entered a large modernized common area. "It's degraded, and we let it get that way for a reason."

"Sure, but why would I go back where people know I can be found and attacked?" Joe reminded the Elementalist. "Remember that? We popped out, you showed me how to open the door, a group of people saw me and went berserk, and you thought it was good training for me?"

"Was I wrong?" Mir countered in his usual direct manner. "Do I need to draw you a map to every possible door? Aren't you supposed to be able to figure this out on your own, as it's kind of the whole *point* of the profession?"

"A map would be handy, thanks." Joe easily ignored the attempted slight, moving on quickly so he could hopefully point back to this conversation and actually snag one on his way out. "Good to see you. Pete said you were looking for me? Err... Sage Pete."

Mir raised an eyebrow at Joe correcting himself. "Looks like someone got in trouble with their class leader. *I* recommend challenging anyone who calls you out for not using their title to a duel and sending them to respawn until they give you 'permission' to call 'em whatever the *abyss* you want to call 'em."

"It's a plan." Joe's agreement seemed to take the Class Sage by surprise, and the ancient powerhouse's lips twitched–his version of a beaming smile. "Now, what can I do for you?"

Mir eyed him up and down, arms crossed with a slightly sour expression on his face. "I don't need you for *anything*. You've gotten a bit stronger, but you still look like a stiff breeze will scatter your sense of self into three distinct pieces. There's some interesting times coming, I hear, so I'll just keep an eye on how you handle yourself in battle. Nah, Nathaniel wanted to see *both* of us."

The Sage seemed to have reached his daily word limit and ignored Joe's subsequent questions until the Ritualist finally fell silent. They descended for long minutes, and Joe could feel the pressure building in his ears until he let out a huge *yawn,* and his eardrums finally **popped**. When the stairs finally opened into a broad landing, he picked up the pace, more excited about the impending conversation than he was to be at his actual destination.

As they approached it, the door to the basement penthouse swung open without a sound. The squeak of their footsteps on the floor caught Nathaniel's attention, and the Gnome twisted from his position–standing on a stool behind the desk and rummaging through a stack of papers nearly twice his height–to offer them a cheery wave.

"Ah, my Codex-Keepers!" He hopped to his chair, taking a seat and motioning for them to do the same. Joe sat down... Mir remained standing. "Joe, I noticed you had entered your subdimension yesterday, so I wanted to call you here and make sure everything is functioning in a straightforward manner. It's all meant to be user friendly, at least entering and exiting the library, but how did you find the books themselves?"

"Well..." Joe let the moment stretch before answering. "I found them by looking at the shelves."

The Gnome's face went blank for a moment then seemed to collapse in on itself. For a moment, the Ritualist was sure he'd messed up, then Nathaniel burst into laughter, slamming his tiny hand onto the desk and setting the clearly sturdy furnishing to bouncing. "He looked at the shelves! Mir! Did you-"

"I heard him." The Elementalist shot an annoyed glance at Joe.

"Oh! It's been so long since someone's told me a proper joke." The Gnome wiped at his eye, where a mirthful tear had appeared. "Thanks for that. Ahh... now, any problems accessing the information? Did you find something in your wheelhouse?"

Joe inclined his head, feeling somewhat sheepish as he answered, "I did manage to make it through one of the books, but in the end, I fell asleep. It's a *very* comfortable library. I was wondering, though I made it through the first book, I saw no shift in my profession. What does progress look like, in terms of getting to the higher tiers?"

Nathaniel's face shifted with pleasure, his craggy face wrinkling from his cheeks to his eyes as he considered the question. "Excellent, excellent. Don't worry about sleeping in there; this profession is meant to be welcoming and... extensive, in terms of the requirements for advancement. This isn't something you can race through, as your profession will only gain levels once you've not only read but *understood* more than half of the material presented to you in each sub-dimension. Plan to be level one for *quite* some time."

Pursing his lips, Joe reluctantly accepted the information, having assumed something like this was likely.

"Oh, come now, don't be disheartened! This profession is a stewardship and gives you access to power beyond any of your similarly ranked peers, should you learn how to use it." The Gnome leaned forward on his desk, fingers steepled as he gazed fondly at the new Codex-Keeper. "How about I offer you some advice, which will give you something to look forward to?

I only ask because, well, I'm told that sometimes the dangling of rewards you will potentially gain in the distant future, after years of study, may seem more cruel than encouraging."

Perking up immediately, the Ritualist eagerly agreed to hear what was possible. "Are we talking about what my profession could eventually become or extra benefits I might gain? Maybe you could let me know some of the libraries I'll be able to get a key for?"

"The last one." Nathaniel chuckled, even as Mir shifted around uncomfortably. "Don't *worry*, Mirascible, we'll get to why I called you here in just a few moments. Now, Joe, you know that each profession rank grants you another key, but you already have access to the lost and hidden Ritualist documents. It follows that, when you enter another library, it will be the information for a *different* class. It could be focused on crafting, combat, support, or utility, and you won't know for sure until you begin to read! Seeing as whatever you find will be outside the bounds of what you're focused on, you'll need to learn them on your own, and at a disadvantage. Now... given the option, what would you *want* to learn?"

Joe considered the options for a moment, deciding to ask questions before giving a firm answer. "You're saying I could view things lost to, say, Alchemists and the like? It makes me wonder, what sort of designs would be in a codex for something like Forging? What could possibly be made that they would have taken away from them or intentionally repressed?"

"That *is* the question, isn't it?" The Gnome's eyes twinkled mischievously. "I can tell you this: be careful what you decide on when you do rank up, as your words may be misinterpreted by the system... intentionally or not. When you say 'forging', I assume you mean various works done in a smithy, such as all of your ritual needles, stabilizers, metals that hold intent long after you've released them from your service? There are at least two Codex Keys which fit the name you have given, and the other would be 'forging'. That is, falsification of documents and... so on."

The Ritualist leaned away, rolling his eyes in annoyance. “Watch out for the monkey paw wishes, and choose the key *very* specifically when it appears. Got it.”

“Very good, glad you’re such a quick study! I can't tell you how many times Keepers have locked themselves out of their originally planned library over the years.” Nathaniel's grin turned impish as Mir let loose a soft growl. “Still, there's nothing wrong with learning about things you didn't think would be helpful. Now, back to the original question...?”

Joe struck upon an idea and shot a sly smile at the Gnome. “Which Codex Key would I need to pick to have the fewest books to read and understand?”

“Healing.” The response was so swift that Joe's excitement faded petulantly–obviously the Grand Archivist had answered this question many times before. “*Heh,* no need to look so dour! Everyone thinks they will be able to rocket through the profession using that method, but... if I told you the truth, which is that there are only *two* books in that library, why would you think that I don't recommend *anyone* choosing those keys? At least, not while they still need to read and understand the information in each library they choose to advance their profession?”

“Either the information is so incredibly difficult to understand...” Joe paused when Nathaniel nodded along but continued after a long moment of remaining uninterrupted. “Or it’s so dangerous that even having access to it... affects them? I suppose I’m not sure.”

“Mir, what’s in those books?” The Gnome finally pulled the Class Sage into the conversation properly. “Feel free to tell him; you won't be punished. This is an object lesson.”

“First book is how to make the Fountain of Youth, a method on rejuvenating someone’s body and mind so they can achieve limited immortality outside the bounds of the system.” Mir huffed softly as he spoke, his eyes filled with derision, for some unknown reason. “The second book is how to use healing to conquer the world.”

Joe's jaw didn't quite drop, but it was a near thing. Nathaniel swept back into the conversation, tutting at the Elementalist. "You have such a *unique* way of spoiling dramatic reveals."

"How many times have we done this?" Mir crossed his arms and rolled his eyes at the pouting Gnome. "Besides, they're both useless."

"Oh, I don't *know*. At least five." Nathaniel sighed heavily as he turned back to Joe. "The requirements for generating the Fountain of Youth rely heavily on a deep understanding of the physiology, morphology, endocrinology, and *psychology* of the intended target. Even if someone were to fully master the contents of that book, the spell within it can only be cast on the same person once per year. It will de-age them by, wait for it... *one year*. Leveling up the spell is so horrendously difficult and time consuming that the creator of the spell has only achieved the *Apprentice* rank in the multiple thousands of years they've been alive."

"Is it you?" Joe's simple inquiry completely derailed the Gnome—who sputtered furiously before sending a harsh look at Mir. "No, he didn't tell me, it's just... that would make sense? You're the only Gnome I've ever seen, and there has to be some reason you're still around when the others aren't."

"Yes, well." Nathaniel sat back with a groan. "Now there are *two* spoilsports in my tower. Moving on, I *guess*. The second book is less dramatic than Mir made it out to be, mainly because there's an unfortunate cost to Healing which causes the best of them to be forever trapped as a Grandmaster. This may come as a surprise to you, but if a Sage of Healing dies, it's usually the *worst* among them who takes their place. I don't mean they're bad at healing, I mean... they are not generally good people."

As the silence stretched, Joe realized the Gnome was waiting on him to be an active participant. "That seems counter-intuitive, doesn't it? Shouldn't the best person who's also the best Healer also have the first opportunity for ascension?"

"Which brings us to the unfortunate fact of Healers." Nathaniel glanced out his enormous bay window, where a plume of vapor was floating by, obscuring their view of the core of the planet. "When you are healing other people's injuries, fixing their issues, cleansing them of their maladies, and often saving lives... what do you think happens?"

His recent experience and exposure to the requirements of advancing to Sage rank allowed Joe to grasp Nathaniel's meaning immediately. "Ah. They have so many life debts owed to them that becoming a Sage is all but impossible. Which would mean... the Healers out there who refuse to heal without payment and ignoring anyone asking for free help *don't* have that same debt leveraged against them. When it comes time to ascend, they can, and others can't."

"Which is why the Sage of Healing is considered one of the worst people on the planet, as was their predecessor, going back *millennia* at this point." For some reason, this was more shocking to Joe than the idea of the Fountain of Youth being real. It shook his worldview, as Healers were paragons of prestige and helpfulness in his mind. "The book Mir was referencing was a way to counter the debt... but in a horrifying way. Essentially, it allows the Healer to use the Karmic Debt they've accumulated, taking what is owed them from the people they've healed the most, and forcibly turning them into warriors on their behalf."

"Spend enough time pretending to be a false saint, building up lots and lots of goodwill over the years, maybe even open a free healing center and become a major attraction-" Mir's example was cut off as Nathaniel joined in with his own.

"Or perhaps join a group of people you're constantly going to be healing, choosing to run with *only* the most powerful people who get hurt the most, knowing they have a Healer they can rely on no matter what. Then, when the time is right... subvert them to be under your command."

Joe pondered that horrifying thought for a moment, doubly glad that he had his own healing skills and didn't need to rely on someone else. "Is this one difficult to understand or just hidden away because of its immense potential for being used in terrible ways?"

"Hidden away," Mir answered immediately, though Nathaniel hesitated for a beat before agreeing.

"Yes. There are other requirements it has, which make it nearly impossible to use before the peak of the Grandmaster rank, unless someone has a specialized skill set. Harvesting Life Debts is no easy task. Although, when someone understands how to do it, and they try it for the first time, there's simply no going back." The master of the Inverted Tower stroked his long beard. "I can't imagine the damage that could be done should the current Sage of Healing gain access to this particular spell."

Joe had a different thought and found himself idly wondering if he *should* actually go after that library with his next key. Between his Karmic King trait and his easier understanding of karmic energy, the idea of being able to harvest debt owed to him seemed like a potential off-ramp for his current situation with Tatum. "When you say it harvests debt, can you explain that a little better? Does it only allow them to seize control of another person? How long does that last?"

Nathaniel shook his head, expression going grim. "I see your beacon, Joe. That's part of *why* we're having this conversation in the first place. Please accept my apologies for leading you to this line of questioning, but I felt it was necessary long before you ever had the opportunity to gain access. There's no good that can come of taking a Life Debt and turning it toward other ends. As to how long it lasts, that depends on the strength of the debt."

After letting his words sink in, the Gnome finished in a quiet voice, "The worst part is, once the debt bond has been fulfilled, only the most powerful of people will be able to realize that they were acting outside of their own interests. Most simply think they chose the path they walked upon."

"Book is called 'Empire of the False Saint'," Mir helpfully supplied. "Something Nathaniel failed to mention was how anyone who's *ever* used this particular spell died within a few weeks of assuming control. Not from the backlash of the spell itself, as far as we can tell. Out of nowhere, they were found sliced into five pieces. Every last one of 'em."

Joe's brow furrowed for a moment, then his face went pale as he remembered the pearlescent light glimmering around Cleocatra's claws as she asked him what Insight he had gained into using karma as a weapon. Knowing that the secrets of her hidden race weren't for him to share, he kept his mouth shut, even as the Gnome looked at him with sudden interest. "Thank you for the warning. I'll... keep this in mind when selecting my next key."

"Good. Good. That's all I can ask." Nathaniel allowed Joe to keep his thoughts to himself, though he pushed back from his desk and watched him closely. "We are stewards of forbidden knowledge, but just because others have used it for terrible ends doesn't mean it should be forgotten or ignored. Once it's been fully lost, it has the most *abyssal* way of being rediscovered in a new form somewhere on the worlds. Beyond that, we only have one other duty..."

Trailing off, the Gnome looked at the Ritualist encouragingly, while Mir looked on with a bored expression, clearly having been the subject of this gentle nudging for many years. Joe looked on blankly for a split second, not certain what he was supposed to say in this situation. Then he remembered the oath he'd taken in order to become a Codex-Keeper in the first place. "Right! Above all, we keep the serpent asleep."

"Such a quick study!" Nathaniel clapped encouragingly, not a hint of sarcasm in his manner. "If this world is destroyed, all of the knowledge locked away in the subspaces connected to the Inverted Tower will be hurled out for anyone to claim. It's happened half a dozen times over the last two millennia, and each time, I've needed to recollect and store away what was lost."

The master of the Inverted Tower shook his head, annoyance filtering across his face. "I tell you what, many of these books are actively resistant to being found once they escape... and whoever finds them tends to fight with everything they have in them to keep what they've found. The spells try to propagate out as much as they can, to give me false leads I have to track down. Then, when *everyone* has access to forbidden knowledge..."

"It's less effective? When everyone has it, it's not really special anymore?" Joe tried to guess, wondering if this was another test.

"What? No!" Nathaniel shook his head vigorously while Mir snorted out a laugh. "They *all* use it and destroy each other at the same time! It's like they forget the basic tenets of mutually assured destruction."

"Ah. Got it. Then, how do you keep them from just continuing to use the spell after you get the book back?" This question had been niggling at the back of Joe's mind ever since he first realized that the spells and information had to come from somewhere. "It's lost now, but certainly someone would've taught an apprentice or something? Do you just hunt down everyone who knows the spell and obliterate them?"

"Nothing so dramatic, unless they try to attack *me*." The Gnome's eyes glinted with a savage light rather unbecoming on his grandfatherly features. "As you may imagine, going after someone who has access to *every* forbidden spell from *every* class—and the means to use them—tends to not end well for the attacker. No, as the Grand Archivist, I have the capability of using *my* key, the master key, to forcibly lock away the spell, if I can get my hands on the first edition of it."

"I've got things to do. War stuff," Mir interrupted, finally unwilling to contain himself any further. "Do you have something to say to me, or can I leave?"

"Yes, yes." Nathaniel looked at the door meaningfully. "Never feel bad about coming to me for questions or explanations, Joe! As there are only five Codex-Keepers, scattered as they may be, I have *more* than enough time to help you with anything you need to know. Anytime you need help, I'm here.

Except right now, as I need the room to have a conversation with Mirascible."

"You got it. See ya around, Nate." The Ritualist took the words with good humor, stepping outside the office and patiently waiting as the duo had their conversation. When the Elementalist stepped out nearly fifteen minutes later, a grave expression on his face, Joe had the good grace not to press him for information. If he was *supposed* to know what was happening, he would've been included in the first place. "So about that map you were going to give me..."

"Brat! Fine, if you're not gonna figure out the entrances on your own," Mir grumbled and pulled out a large folded parchment. "Here, come on. I'll at least walk you out."

Belatedly, the Class Sage shook his head and mumbled, "I can't believe he let you get away with calling him *Nate*. The last known Gnome, millenia old, with enough power to make lesser deities run with their tails tucked between their legs if they offend him... and you give him a nickname on your second meeting."

"Tha~ank *you*." Joe plucked the document and stored it away, carefully ignoring the admonishment as he moved alongside the Class Sage. They climbed the stairs in silence until finally approaching a familiar hallway. Each time they passed one of the creatures working, hidden away by their brown robes, the Ritualist looked longingly at them, wanting nothing more than to pet the petite penguin he knew was hiding beneath the garment. "How do you just ignore them, Mir? They're just so adorable!"

"Practice," the irascible man grumbled as he tapped a sequence of bricks insultingly slowly so Joe could follow along. "There you go. Practically spoon-fed to you. Next time I see you, there'd better be some combat going on, or I'm going to start getting *antsy*."

Thinking about the impending conflict that would likely embroil this entire world in the next few weeks, Joe grimaced and shook his head. "I'll see what I can do, but something tells me it won't be a problem."

The door swung shut behind him, and the Ritualist noticed that the tower wall he was standing next to had a brick-like design. "Ah... same pattern to get in as out, I'm guessing."

Pulling open his map, Joe looked at it for a long, searching moment before heaving a sigh and putting it away. "O~of course."

The map only had one access point marked: the one he'd just come out of. Even as he had looked over the parchment, the entrance had appeared and turned green. "At least it'll update as I figure more of them out... probably."

Seeing as he didn't have the time to hunt down the Class Sage and ineffectually attempt to strangle him, Joe merely grunted in annoyance and made his way back to the Tower of Ritualists. Halfway there, he paused, and a slow grin slid across his face. "Hold on a second... can I still...?"

Pulling the enchanted map out of his storage, Joe attempted something he hadn't tried since he was on Midgard. Focusing hard, the Ritualist barked out a laugh as the map vanished, binding to himself and creating a tiny minimap in the upper portion of his vision. "Yes! Ha. Been a long time since I had something this useful. Thanks, Mir."

Glancing at the minimap, he expanded it out slightly, finding a dot he hadn't noticed at first glance. It showed the entrance he'd used to enter the Inverted Tower, under the ouroboros statue. "Deprecated entrance, center of *th' underplump*. Huh. Finally, I have a way to see what the districts are named."

With a spring in his step, and whistling a soft tune, Joe hurried back to the tower with far more enthusiasm—now able to glance at the permanent map in his vision and pick out the best route to use.

He had a class to teach and very little time to prepare.

CHAPTER THIRTY-FOUR

"Who has the highest mana pool?" Joe pointed both of the Expert Ritualists who raised their hands instantly, each glaring at the other, to the innermost area. "I'll have you both in the Novice ring; I need as much stable flow as possible."

"As an Expert of Enchanted Ritual Circles, I will make sure that you have the smoothest experience you could possibly-"

"Mmmn-*ye~es*," the other Expert interjected in a smooth tone, "because Enchanters are known for the stability and shelf life of their creations *in progress*. As an Expert of Alchemical Ritual Circles, long used to keeping each distinct ingredient contained perfectly-"

"Sounds great! Why don't you both compete to see who can do the best job here and *now*." Joe left the peacocking individuals to glare at each other in the smallest ring, turning to sweep his gaze over the fifty-five other Ritualists here to assist with the Master-rank ritual he was going to be preparing. "Standard prime number layout; please arrange yourself according to your own mana pool and control. Other than the first circle, if you think your control is better than someone else's, move forward a ring. Else, move outward."

As the large variety of Experts and Journeymen shuffled into position, some of them with far more enthusiasm than others, Joe began working on his own setup task. Directly between the two Experts in the Novice circle, he placed his Master-rank stabilizer, the low table or altar that would hopefully achieve its new form today. Once it was in place, there was barely enough room for him to squeeze in as well, just enough for him to not be out of position so long as he was economical in his movements.

By the time he was satisfied with the positioning of not only his tools, but his humanoid resources, the first of his actual students for the day was entering the large lecture hall. Jenny waved from what felt like a football field's length away, and Joe halfheartedly returned the gesture, even as he looked around the space and examined the reinforced stage he and his assistants were on. "Abyss, if this is only a *mid*-sized lecture hall, I'd hate to be teaching on whatever they think of as the largest. There has to be some space shifting trickery going on, otherwise there's no way this would fit in the tower."

The entire room was shaped as an amphitheater, with the stage being directly in the center so it could be viewed from all sides. The closest sets of seats were positioned so that most people would just barely have their heads above Joe's, giving them a perfect, clear view at whatever he was creating or teaching about onstage. Just below the raised platform was a permanent ritual, an enormous shield generator rated to the peak of Master rank. Anyone caught within the bubble when rings went haywire would be rushing back from respawn only a few minutes later, but anyone in the crowd was all but guaranteed to be protected from backlash or malfunctions.

"Tri-Master Joe," Jenny formally called out as she approached the stage, obviously doing her best to put on a good show for the assistant Ritualists near him. "I'm greatly looking forward to today! Would you mind if I did a roll call as people arrived, to ensure the only people gaining access to the room are the ones who are supposed to be here?"

"Does that really matter *so* much, Jenny?" Joe was quite tired of the barriers people kept creating between each other to make sure information remained siloed when it just wasn't all that important. "They're all going to take an oath, aren't they?"

"Oaths can be broken, if you don't mind taking on a Warlock title," she smoothly replied, pulling out a small ledger. "Oaths in *conjunction* with an Alchemical ritual the Sage is bringing that'll boil their guts into goop for a few years should they break it? Still not perfect but *less* likely to be abused."

"Fine." Joe shortly waved with great agitation, his mind focused on the sheer amount of work he wanted to get done over the next few days. "Start with the assistants, would you?"

His declaration rang across the room, the acoustics of the place making sure every person already present could hear. Not one of them failed to perk up excitedly, and it was only after Jenny was halfway to the first of them that someone spoke aloud the question on all of their minds.

"Wait... *we* get to learn a skill that the heads of the disciplines are all going to be in attendance to get for themselves?"

"Also the *Sage*, yes," Jenny answered in Joe's stead. Raising her voice, she spoke to the crowd, who thankfully *didn't* leave their earmarked positions to hurry the process along. "To be clear, all of you are only going to be getting the opportunity to learn the skill. You will not be the focus of Tri-Master Decury Duelist Joe's Teaching skills, although he does have a bonus to teaching others outside of that core focus, so-"

"What rank is the skill?"

"Will you be quiet? Obviously, if the Sage is coming to try and learn it, it's got to be awesome!"

"I don't care if it's a *walking* skill, something's giving tri-Master Joe an edge, and I want in."

The sudden buzz of conversation died instantly as the door at the top of the lecture hall was thrown open with enough force that it bounced off the wall and closed halfway. A Dwarf swept in, the multiple coils of metal in his beard clanging together loudly enough that it was clear that he'd set them up to act as veritable wind chimes as he moved.

Jenny returned to Joe's side in an instant, speaking softly enough that he could just barely hear her–meaning no one else would be able to do the same. "Glanak Onyxmaul, peak Master of Ritual Circles. He's the one I warned you about a while back if you remember. Very demanding of his students and requires an oath for Mastery Merits at the *minimum,* no matter what skill he's teaching."

"Why's he here?" Joe kept his voice a low susurration, his expression neutral. "I told you to extend invitations only to the people *you* thought should have access to this skill."

"He got a direct invitation from Sage Pete." Jenny's voice took on a sour note, "Trust me, if *I* had gone and offered him the chance to come learn something from another *Master*, he would've never shown his face here. Since he's the head of the Ritual Circles discipline, the Sage must've thought it would be inappropriate not to involve him."

"Suppose I can see that." As the glaring Dwarf came too close for their conversation to continue, Joe inclined his head fractionally and offered a warm smile. "Master Onyxmaul, it's a pleasure to meet you. I don't think we've been formally introduced yet?"

"Correct. Some of us have hundreds of students to teach and can't simply go galavanting around the universe on a whim." The Dwarf raised an eyebrow as he looked at Joe critically, what the Ritualist understood was a scathing assessment of his lack of facial hair alongside being bald.

In Dwarven culture, everything from age, to experience, to marital status could be read from the plaiting of their facial hair, so Joe's total lack certainly wasn't helping first impressions. "I am duo-Master Onyxmaul. It is my great pleasure to be introduced to you, tri-Master. I'm told your focus is Ritual Circles? I'd love to compare insights over a drink sometime. My treat."

Wanting to get back to work, Joe brushed his hand to the side. "Ah, there's no need for formalities-"

"Yes. There are," the Dwarf replied bluntly, turning and walking to the second row of seats and dropping into one of them, arms crossed as he very obviously critiqued the way Joe had set up his assistants.

"Oh. I suppose, in that case, I should go and update my robes," Joe stated breezily. "Didn't know it was so important for etiquette. Is it quad-Master, or is there a different title I should be going by now that I have *four* of the Class Skills Mastered?"

"Of *course* you got another one Mastered," Jenny heaved with a combination of excitement and envy, breaking the sudden tension emanating from the Dwarf, who had gone *very* still. "Duo-Master Onyxmaul, present and accounted for."

After checking his name off her ledger with a flourish of her quill, even as she turned her back on the Dwarf, Jenny gave Joe an 'I told you so' look. Then she hurried to go between each of the helpers, even as more people began arriving for the actual demonstration and explanation.

The next to arrive was Master Cosmo, the Wolfman bounding down the aisle enthusiastically and thrusting his fist forward to bump against Joe's with just a *hint* of force. "Your delightful assistant gave me a short description of what we could be looking forward to today; I cannot wait to learn from you! Also, we should set up some combat rituals together, I've triangulated the best positions to place them for maximum carnage! Oh, uh, my seat. What do you think the best spot would be?"

Joe directed him to the front row, seeing as his easily eight-foot-tall frame would allow him to have a great view practically no matter where he sat. Still, he picked a comfortable chair with a direct-line view to where he'd be standing next to the stabilizer, and Cosmo enthusiastically thanked him for the advice before claiming the chair with all the intensity of a king laying claim to a contested territory.

The next to arrive was Levi Redips, the Master of Ritualistic Forging Joe had only run into when he first joined the tower. The seeming human–though his canine features told perhaps a slightly different story–merely nodded at Joe politely before taking a seat opposite his Dwarven counterpart. Master Darling arrived next, appearing flustered and surprisingly unhappy to be there.

"Joe, please tell me this is more than just a briefing about what you informed me of yesterday," the Master of Enchanted Ritual Circles questioned in a tired voice. "We've been adjusting a wide-scale curse all night, and I had to hand it off to a dozen of my subordinates who won't be able to get a single thing accomplished without a full vote among themselves."

"I'm hoping it'll be worthwhile," Joe replied evasively, unwilling to go into any more detail. This earned a grunt from the Master, which was echoed by Glanak in the same instant.

Five more people entered just then, a small cluster Joe had never met. They seemed perfectly comfortable in the lecture hall, even with the other Masters looking at them critically. Each of them spoke softly only to each other as they sat together in the second row.

As Jenny came around, her list almost completed, the Ritualist thrust his chin out to indicate the newcomers. "Who are they?"

"Those are..." she hesitated for a moment, brow furrowing as she studied their faces, before obviously recognizing one of them and relaxing. "Ah! Those are the *Distinguished Professors* of the Core Class skills. Think of them as the dean of students for each of the different schools or disciplines of the Ritualist class."

"Shouldn't that be the top Master or eventually Grandmaster?" Joe subtly indicated the other people seated in the chairs around him.

"When would *they* have time to teach everyone?" She resumed her efforts as if her words were enough explanation, though she paused with her quill held aloft. "Oh, I guess you could say more... general studies. Think of them like the professors who instruct in large lecture halls like this one we're in, filled with people who're being taught about the class skills.

The top Masters and above *might* do small group sessions or take on an apprentice, but there's a couple thousand people in the tower trying to learn at any given time."

"Right. Got it, thank you." His attention was caught by the newest person sweeping through the room, an Elf he'd met at the same time as Levi. "Master Gabrielle Syme! What a pleasure to see you again."

"Tri-Master Joe." Her tone was surprisingly cool as she approached him, lips pressed firmly together as though holding back unkind thoughts. She reached into a satchel, pulling out a five-gallon *bucket* shining with orange light as it churned in its container. "I was told to bring you an Ichor. Here it is. Please use it immediately; then we will discuss payment afterward."

"Payment...?" Joe quizzically blinked at the Elf, even as he accepted the oversized bucket carefully. She tensed at his words, jumping onto the stage and falling into step alongside him as he approached his Master-rank stabilizer in the center. Very carefully, he tipped the container over, allowing the Ichor to flow into the incredibly delicate-appearing chalice atop the low table. "Didn't Sage Pete tell you what we were going to be trading for?"

"Must have slipped his mind." The Elf's salty comment was somewhat muted, seeing as she knew better than to divert his attention when a dangerous substance like the Ichor was out in the open. "If you'd be so kind as to inform me why I had to use my *personal* stock of Artifact-rank herbs for this, I would be greatly appreciative."

"The skill I'm going to be trying to teach all of you today is unknown to the Tower of Ritualists," Joe explained as he waited for the incredibly viscous material to **slurp** its way out of the bucket. "Sage Pete himself is coming to learn it today and asked that I allow you to prepare this as an equal trade, so that there'd be no debt between us. Something about prepayment being the best way to do things?"

She relaxed fractionally, obviously put at ease by the Sage

himself–her former instructor–being the one to suggest the trade. "Must be quite the skill."

"He certainly seems to think so." Joe's eyes went wide with panic as the rest of the Ichor slopped out of the bucket in a rush, splashing onto the top of the chalice and immediately beginning to overflow. "*Abyss*! What do I do?"

"Be patient?" Gabrielle chuckled softly at the sudden display. "Obviously, there's too much to fit into the chalice; how else would it continuously stream to the stabilizers and act as both empowerment and cooling system? If you want something to be *truly* concerned about, the next time we're trading favors, I'd love to teach you how to create a Ritual of Lethality. Master rank, single target. Generates a poison that will continuously stack on the target with each successful hit, creating a quadratically scaling damage-over-time effect."

The Ritualist sucked in a breath, greatly surprised by the sudden shift in direction the conversation had taken. "That would be cool... I haven't been able to find too many applications for my alchemical ritual circles, if I'm being honest. Actually, know anything about tattoos? I got a neat adjustment to my Class Skill when it reached the Master rank with Alchemical Rituals."

"You *what* now?" The Elf looked at him with mild surprise, scanning his outfit and not seeing the ornamentation of a Master of Alchemical Rituals. "Should probably get your robes updated. Some people get feisty about not being called by the correct title, but if you're not even showing your rank, you don't have any room to complain."

"Wouldn't whine about it anyway," Joe muttered, his eyes locked entirely on the Ichor slowly oozing over the entirety of his stabilizer, trying to figure out what it was doing–and how.

The low table had all sorts of channels etched into its surface that had appeared to be more ornamental than functional, though less so after each of the stabilizers from Expert all the way down to Novice rank had been correctly slotted into place. Now the lines were being filled as the Ichor swept along the channels, as if through a process of rapid osmosis. It sloshed over the bounds of the lines at each connective point, pooling in deep grooves and wrapping around joints as it slithered up the extended stabilizer bars in defiance of gravity.

Every part of the shining chrome surface now had a decidedly burnt orange tint, with thick orange 'veins' along the previously ornamental etching. Thick knots of amber had solidified at each of the joints, though a gentle tug let Joe know that the metal could still articulate as needed. Overall, the stabilizer had greatly shifted in appearance, gaining a decidedly organic appearance. The majority of the Ichor remained in the chalice itself, and even as he watched, it collected in on itself, growing denser and crystallizing, until the cup still appearing to runneth over was filled with a brilliantly orange gem perfectly fitted within.

You have created a new item! Well, new to you. Congratulations! Your Master-Rank stabilizer and Ichor of Overflow have combined to create a single item: the Eclipsing Aurora Chalice.

Item: Eclipsing Aurora Chalice (Artifact). The culmination of two Masters fusing their work into a singular item of ritualistic engineering, the Eclipsing Aurora Chalice is the single best known stabilizer of rituals below the Legendary rank.

Effects:

1. *Continuously detects and corrects minor instabilities where structured and ambient mana interact, reducing the risk of cascading failure by 70% by absorbing and storing it into the gemstone lattice.*
2. *Autonomously articulates each housed stabilizer, repositioning emerging stress points along the entirety of the ritual being undertaken. Stress points will be highlighted with orange light, allowing for easier soothing of mana flow and issue resolution.*
3. *Decreases the total mana and material cost of Master-rank rituals by 5%, increasing by an additional 5% per tier when working with lesser rituals.*

Caution: The chalice containing the overflow gemstone lattice is not and cannot be attached to the surface of the stabilizer. If the chalice is knocked over, the Ichor will destabilize within 5 seconds, releasing all stored mana as a single burst.

"This thing is *so* cool," Joe whispered reverently as he ran the tips of his fingers along the organic-looking surface, pleased to find that it felt of metal and gemstones instead of fleshy, as its appearance would suggest. "It's like walking around with a massive piece of jewelry."

"Don't forget to properly discharge the mana at the end of your creation." Gabrielle spoke after giving him a moment to admire his work. She showed him how to do so, pointing out a sigil he could connect to with his mana to vent the power. "You can store it for a while if you need to, but don't wait too long, or the lattice will begin to destabilize. Eventually it *will* explode."

Joe immediately began thinking of where he could let the energy go, and his first thought was to vent it within the Grand Ritual Hall on Midgard, directly empowering the mana reservoir of the building. After deciding to test that in the near future, he realized the Elf was walking away and quickly called out, "Oh! I'll need ten thousand experience points worth of cores from you."

She stopped cold, turning around with a harsh glare. "Look, *Quad*-Master Joe. I don't even have the skill yet. Can you at least let me make sure I can learn it before shredding my cheddar?"

"Wha–oh, I'm not trying to nickel and dime you." Joe quickly waved his hands in front of him, showing empty palms to make sure she subtly picked up on his 'I'm a friend' cue. "But I just figured a bunch of standard cores is a better option than a single Artifact-rank core. That's... you don't have any idea what I'm talking about. Got it. Let me explain. Sage Pete asked me to create an Alchemical Lore book for you at the Artifact rank, which I'd be paid for with the Mastery Merit I earn from you using it to hit the Master rank with the Lore skill. Even so, I still need you to offset the experience loss I'll take."

"You... you can do that?" Her demeanor shifted in an instant, going from near-Glanak-grumpy to Cosmo-friendly as if he'd flipped a switch. "How soon? Are you sure you don't need any other payment? Is there any way I could get you to skip this demonstration today and focus on-"

Sage Pete arrived at that moment, and the Elf bit her lip as she bounced on her toes, wanting nothing more than to continue her request, but knowing it was no longer possible: the Sage's time was far too valuable to waste.

Striding down to the first row, Pete nodded at each of the other Masters present, inclining his head with great respect at the various teachers. Only after a moment did Joe realize everyone had gotten to their feet as soon as the man entered the room and only sat back down after he did so. He clicked his tongue. "Another piece of etiquette I need to learn for Vanaheim. Why am I *still* not getting offered a skill for that? Am I just so bad at it that I *still* can't meet the requirements when they are reduced by ninety-five percent?"

"Ahem." The Sage's voice rolled through the lecture hall. "I'm sure our newest addition to the tower hasn't yet mentioned this, but against his wishes, I have a requirement for everyone participating in the attempted skill instruction today. If you want to be a part of this, you will need to swear a binding oath to accept Master Joe as your teacher in this particular skill and not to share it with others within the tower unless they agree to the same oath."

As if that weren't bad enough, Pete added additional stipulations without allowing the instant outcry to overwhelm his words. "There will be no sharing of this outside of our tower, except by the originator of the skill himself. To reinforce the oath, I've spent the last few hours creating a rather intensive alchemical ritual which will melt the innards of any violators the moment they attempt to pass on this information incorrectly."

All of the assistant Ritualists on the stage took his words in stride, but each of the people in the audience were on their feet, some having a shout startled out of them, some clearly needing to hold themselves back from leaving.

Glanak was by far the most vocal. "I don't care how many Class Skills he's Mastered, I *refuse* to accept an oath to *anyone* under the Grandmaster rank!"

CHAPTER THIRTY-FIVE

"Then you may leave..." Sage Pete informed him mildly, letting the implied threat hang in the air before expounding slightly, "...and find yourself surpassed by your peers within the year."

The room went still, each person casting inquisitive glances at Joe, who was fully relying on his Aura of Soothing Destruction to keep his nervous sweat from soaking through his robes.

"You can't *truly* think it's that good of a skill?" The Dwarf's gravelly voice cracked despite, or perhaps because of, his defiant, ramrod-straight stance. He waited for an answer as his hands balled into fists, yet Sage Pete merely settled into his chair, steepling his fingers as he maintained his deadlock stare with the Dwarf.

"Perhaps we should have Quad-Master Joe explain the skill for all of our benefit? After he does so, you are welcome to make the oath, or you may join the *end* of the line for learning it when you realize your mistake in the future."

There was a sharp inhalation from nearly everyone in the room as the Sage *publicly* admonished the reticent Master. All of a sudden, *everyone* was focused on Joe, very carefully not looking over at Glanak's rage-flushed face. Grounding himself with a deep breath, the Ritualist pushed his shoulders back and tried to leverage every bit of his Charisma even while doing his best to keep the 'Dark' aspect out of it.

"Thank you all for coming today. What I'm planning to teach is a skill currently unknown to the tower, according to Sage Pete. Inscription Momentum. It's a passive increase which applies to *any* form of inscription, making it effective for all Ritualists, yet doubly so for the Enchanters among us."

He nodded in acknowledgment toward Master Darling without breaking his flow. "As a basic description, when writing out magical diagrams, the speed with which you can do so without inducing errors or feeling like you're rushing yourself increases to a maximum of the skill level as a percent. At the Expert rank-"

Already there was murmuring, especially among the professors who were sitting close to each other. "-once you've achieved at least twenty-five percent of your maximum increased speed potential, you form a limited bubble of time dilation around yourself *and* your project. This will allow you to work at full speed while also minimizing the disruptions to the ambient mana outside of the area of effect."

"-*time* dilation?" Even the people on stage were whispering excitedly among themselves, knowing exactly how rare it was to have such an effect added to any skill or spell. Joe gave them a moment to remember themselves–and who they were on exhibit in front of–before pushing on with his impromptu lecture.

"The goal of today is getting you access to this skill, after which you'll have the opportunity to study the time dilation effect in detail." Joe gestured at the Ritualists arranged behind him. "As you can see, I'll be working on a Master-rank ritual. When it's ready to be activated, whoever I feel was the most helpful among the people on stage will get the opportunity to have the effect of the ritual used on them... hopefully giving them access to the skill directly, transferring over my skill levels, or at least a portion of them."

Once more, the helpers were unable to hold back from speaking amongst themselves, though each of them now had a fire in their eyes as they straightened up, ready to do anything they could to stand out among their peers. Joe shot them a grin, knowing they hadn't come here today with the expectation of *any* reward, other than being allowed to participate in creating a Master-rank Ritual. "Since it's a seven-circle design, this would normally take us a solid sixteen hours of continuous effort-"

"*Sixteen*?" Cosmo was the first to notice the discrepancy, his ears perking up at the unfamiliar number, and Joe winced as he remembered that the time requirements had been halved, thanks to having the Ritualist class as his *base* class.

"Unrelated, but yes, that's approximately how long it should take me without this skill." Half a dozen hands went up, but he merely shook his head. "As I said, that's unrelated. I'm also unable to... actually, I'm not sure if I can pass on the means I use to cut down the basic time requirements. I'll have to discuss that matter with the Sage before anything else."

Many disappointed hands dropped, with him pretending not to notice. "The best part is, if I manage to get Inscription momentum up to full speed as quickly as possible, there is the potential to finish in *eight* hours. Theoretically, that is, since my current rank is Expert zero in the skill. Imagine that... only a standard work day to create a Master-rank ritual! We begin by-"

"I'll have to ask you to pause there, Joe." Sage Pete smoothly cut him off, turning to view the others in the room and allowing his eyes to linger on Master Onyxmaul. "I believe we all have a decision to make. Jenny, if you would prepare the tea?"

Joe hadn't even seen his assistant leave the room, let alone return with the rolling tray laden with saucers, mugs, and kettles. She went from person to person, starting in the center of the stage and rotating out until she was dropping the drinks off with each of the Masters, hesitating only a moment before dropping one before the now-pale Dwarf.

He didn't say a word as she left the dish and moved on, her

rounds culminating by very carefully placing a cup in front of the Sage and pouring for him. Then she took her own position and a deep breath.

"If everyone would repeat after me..." she spoke the words of the ceremony, and as the oath completed, Joe swept his gaze around the room, taking note of the sixty-seven thin bonds now connecting him to each other person in the room. A heartbeat after the others, one more sprang into existence, the Master of Ritual Circles not meeting Joe's eyes while sipping his tea.

"With that, we have all agreed, and the diluted ritual *Injection* I slipped into the kettle will help us all remain true to our words where we otherwise might fail," the Sage carefully stated, seeming not at all concerned with the horrified reactions his words elicited. "After all, what is a tea ceremony, other than a small ritual performed to create trust between teachers and students?"

"He dosed 'em with compliance juice." Joe shivered as he muttered the words under his breath, thinking about how much Grandmaster Havoc would likely enjoy the Sage's company. Handing his own cup over to Jenny, he waited until she was eventually back in her seat before beginning to lecture once more. "Unfortunately, as I was saying previously, were I able to maintain the skill for the entire time, we could cut our time input by nearly half. Unfortunately, between my Teaching skill, Inscription Momentum, as well as the actual requirements of the ritual I'm going to be creating, my stamina won't allow for consistent usage throughout the process-"

"*Really*?" The words slipped out of Master Levi's lips, and he had the good grace to look embarrassed when people turned his way. "Sorry. That's just... teaching's not exactly a physically intensive process, is it? You're not exactly pounding on metal for twelve hours, ya know?"

"Never picked up a Stamina regeneration skill." Joe shrugged nonchalantly, trying not to show how uncomfortable he was with so many people being surprised at his lacking Stamina. He couldn't even force himself to look in Master

Darling's direction, not wanting to see how she would internalize that information. "As I was *saying*, in the moments when I do have it all activated, please make sure to pay as close attention as possible-"

"No. That won't do at all." Sage Pete waved Joe over with a single hand, just like an impatient father might use to pull their unruly child to their side. Deeply disgruntled, Joe hopped off the stage and approached the powerhouse, only for the Sage to pull out what looks like nothing more than a stamp someone might use to apply a mailing address. "Left glove off, please. We can't have you be drip feeding us opportunities; let's get eight straight hours of you teaching."

With that, he stamped the back of Joe's hand, and the bald Ritualist hissed in pain as the item was pulled away, leaving behind a bright green Expert-rank ritual design on his skin. The Sage reached over and activated the ritual with a quick tap of his index finger, then motioned for Joe to return to the stage. "Fear not, that's a temporary tattoo. The ritual will activate when your resource pool hits zero, siphoning off a portion of any mana you're channeling at the time and converting it directly into Stamina. Perfect for long rituals such as this."

Caught somewhere between annoyance, shame, and delight at the opportunity to grind his skills for an extremely extended period, the Ritualist decided to go all-in on delight and cast the other useless emotions aside. "Fantastic! Let's see how far we can push the envelope. Is everyone ready?"

Without waiting for an answer, Joe lifted his inscription tool and plunged it into the prepared surface of the stage he was standing on. The Novice-rank circle was inscribed in a flash, and Joe began detailing the process aloud as he went, explaining how the skill was currently active and letting him go even faster than normal. Glanak scoffed at Joe's showmanship, which the bald man figured was fair—any Master of Ritual Circles could create a Novice version this quickly, under ideal conditions.

The Beginner circle followed just as quickly, but it was only when the Apprentice-rank circle formed in just the blink of an eye that the Dwarf went ashen-faced and became truly attentive.

Lines formed faster than some of the Experts helping out could comfortably track. Each stroke of Joe's inscription tool was perfect, each curve smooth, even without the use of any other artistic tools. As he started the Student-rank circle of the ritual, he was already feeling the strain of Stamina depletion. The Ritualist tried to breathe through his nose, slow and deep, but could feel the energies pouring out of him as he worked.

The twenty-five-points-a-second upkeep cost of his Teaching skill was being paid by his Stamina, as his mana was far too precious to use on anything but the ritual itself. With Inscription Momentum drawing from the same pool, Joe was losing thirty-five points each second. Even if it was offset slightly by his regeneration of eight point five, Joe's Stamina pool hit zero only a few minutes into the extremely long work day ahead of him.

Green light flared out from under the edge of his gloves, and the Ritualist felt a cool, minty sensation wash over him, even as the dozens of Ritualists assisting him with his work grunted from the unexpected drain. Joe had never needed to call on the mana of people helping him out this early in the process, but as his speed ramped up ever higher, he couldn't help but enthusiastically accept their very minor sacrifice.

Joe stopped explaining what he was doing at the eight-minute mark, when he glanced over and realized that the people in the stands around him appeared to have been frozen in place. Even the Sage himself had been slowed ever so slightly, as though moving through water when he repositioned himself.

Those he was meaning to teach directly had their eyes locked on him. Even looking through a curved bubble of dilated time, Joe was impressed to see their hands flickering as they wrote out notes and thoughts on what they were seeing in their notebooks without breaking eye contact. He returned his full attention to the ritual, making steady progress until he hit the Expert-rank circle, where progress slowed down dramatically.

Still humming a merry tune, Joe crawled around on his hands and knees as his fingers flickered back and forth, aspects and mana flowing out faster than water could pour through a sieve. Every once in a while, he'd spare a moment to check on his helpers, but with the burden shared amongst the group, none of them showed any signs of strain as of yet.

"I forgot to mention this to the group at large." Joe's words pulled a few drifting eyes to himself, though he didn't decrease his pace one iota. "To those of us in the time dilation bubble, it'll still feel like we're spending the full amount of time working on the ritual as it requires. We'll just be able to fit two full days of work into one! Isn't that *exciting*?"

Oddly enough, few of them shared his enthusiasm.

Only an eighth of the way through the circle, sweat rolled off of him and into his robes, soaking in and vanishing from the fabric, though his skin remained hot and sticky. With such a powerful diagram in the works, he needed every bit of mana he could get access to and so had been forced to deactivate his Aura of Soothing Destruction before starting.

Even so, as his work continued apace, with both his passive Teaching and Inscription Momentum skills toggled on, his Stamina dropped like a guillotine. A green flare of light from under his glove bloomed once more, followed by a sharp gasp from each person connected to the ritual.

Stamina: 0/5,429.

Stamina: 250/5,429… 500/5,429…

Joe wasn't exactly certain what the conversion ratio was, but he frankly didn't care. The very instant his pool hit zero, his stamina increased by two hundred and fifty points with each **tick** of the tattooed ritual until it was full once more. The best part? The process repeated itself endlessly. Seeing as his resource didn't try to drop below zero, his Inscription Momentum chugged along at maximum speed.

As he finished the Expert portion of the diagram and

moved on to the Master, now drawing *deeply* from the mana pool of each person involved, Joe realized he was having a *blast*.

For the first time during the ritual creation process, the Eclipsing Aurora Chalice **hummed** to life. The gemstone lattice in the chalice gained a soft luminescence that slowly brightened over time as Joe went deeper into the diagram. Molten, amber orange colorations ever so slowly approached the original neon hue of the Ichor when it had been in its bucket. Stabilizer arms moved, swaying like the boughs of a tree in the wind, thin threads of bright orange pulsing along the veins of the low table and sparking through open air between the articulating limbs of the stabilizer.

Wherever the potent semi-liquid moved, Joe could feel a sudden stillness in the space around it as ambient and structured mana were separated out like iron filings and sand when a magnet passed over them. Tiny failure points stabilized without Joe having to do a thing, a chunk of mana infecting the design siphoned back into the gemstone lattice. Knowing he had the Artifact backing him up, the Reductionist allowed himself to get deeper into the zone, shutting out all other sensations as he bent the entirety of his will to the task at hand.

Hours passed in a blur, Artifact-rank aspects moving into place without complaint, seeing as they were no longer strong enough to fight against Joe's extremely tempered willpower nor the iron grip his Mana Dominion used to control the typically unruly materials.

When Joe connected the final lines of the Master-rank ritual, he was nearly surprised–sixteen hours of experienced time had passed in a haze. Glancing down at his hands, Joe noted that the ritual placed by Sage Pete was nearly entirely gone, a minuscule outline all that remained of the rich colors and details it had originally been infused with.

"If I had that activate every, let's say five minutes or so, for simplicity's sake..." Joe did some quick math, chuckling heartily as the numbers rapidly reached ridiculous heights. "Twelve activations an hour, sixteen total hours. Maybe a hundred and ninety activations? All told, a little over a million Stamina used to make all this come together. That's *wild*."

As his inscription tool vanished back into his spatial storage, the time dilation effect–surrounding him, the ritual circles, Eclipsing Aurora Chalice, and his helpers–vanished like a mirage in the desert. Relieved groans and thankful sighs filled the air as people got to their feet, having long since sat in a meditative position while focusing on whatever mana recovery skills they had.

A series of notifications swept over Joe, demanding his attention even before he could interact with the audience members who hadn't moved except to breathe and take notes the entire time.

Skill increases:

Inscription Momentum (Expert 0 → Expert VIII).

Teaching (Master I → Master III).

Serene Cataclysm Body Art (Expert I → Expert III).

Ritual Circles (Master VII → Master VIII)

Congratulations! You have earned 15 Characteristic points in each Characteristic, except Karmic Luck, for increasing your Mastery skills thrice! (Deferred). It is a rare opportunity to teach an old Sage new tricks.

Congratulations! Your Specialization, Reductionist, has reached level ***13****! As a reward, you have gained a minor permanent boon attached to this class, 'Treasure Sense'.*

Treasure Sense: When you are near a large amount of materials at the Unique rank or above that you are entitled to, you will have an innate sense as to what the most valuable treasure is in the area. Only you can decide whether you will use this to reduce the best materials for yourself or harvest them to gather the material for sale.

Skill offered: Jade Breath-Plundering Doctrine (Expert III). Having been exposed to the constant loop of emptying your Stamina, only to draw from the wells of power of those around you and convert their collective energies into your own, your mana channels have grasped the essence of this process without need for additional outside input.

Effect: When channeling mana, you may instead choose to siphon up to n% of the current amount of power flowing through you and convert it directly into Stamina. You may use this skill with your own mana at 50% reduced efficiency.

Great for canceling spells you didn't mean to cast!

"Well, abyss. Can't exactly say no to that, can I?" Knowing the next few moments were going to suck, Joe accepted the skill and dropped to the ground, writhing in pain as the enchantment imbued within him 'warned' him that he was approaching the limits of its maximum usage. "Celestial feces, it's the 'feels like my limbs are being twisted off' one!"

Through the haze of pain, Joe glared at Master Darling, her face a study in serenity as she stepped in to let everyone know that he wasn't in any danger at the moment.

CHAPTER THIRTY-SIX

By the time he could fully function once more—merely a few seconds, though with his enhanced Characteristics it felt like hours—Joe had already received a message he was dreading.

Skill increase: Mental Manipulation Resistance (Journeyman IV → VI). Throw off the shackles pain inflicts on your mind! Get rid of every *unwanted sensation. Do it!*

"Abyss..." Joe grumbled as he pushed to his feet, going from prone to upright in a flash. Coughing slightly into his hand, the Ritualist glanced around the room and met the curious eyes of the onlookers. "Did everyone get the skill?"

Each person in the stands around the stage inclined their head to acknowledge that they had, indeed, acquired Inscription Momentum. Letting out a soft sigh of relief, Joe pumped a fist in the air. "First try! Yeah! Any questions?"

"What skill did you get at the end, there?" Master Darling was the one to raise the question, but she certainly wasn't the only person interested in the answer.

"Let me try that again." Joe merely smiled in reply, as he was unwilling to share the details of his long-winded skill. "Any questions pertinent to *today's lecture*?"

There weren't any, though there were plenty of people who had intrigued expressions on their faces, as though they'd gained far more from the last eight and three-quarters of an hour of carefully studying him than they had expected. After giving everyone the option to speak, Joe simply shrugged and maintained his pleasant expression. "Then there are only two more quick housekeeping things to discuss before we disperse. The first is the secondary benefit you'll get going forward."

Double checking his Teaching skill to make sure he gave them correct information, the Ritualist did some quick math and finished his thought. "If you paid attention the entire time I was teaching, you should get a bit over six and a half hours of time where my Teaching skill, at Master rank three now, will boost your capabilities of instructing others in the skill. They'll essentially get the same benefit as if I were teaching them directly."

The handful of professors in the room perked up, giving him nods of respect when they realized he had refined his ability to pass on knowledge to such a high degree. The other Masters didn't seem *quite* as enthusiastic, though obviously they were wise enough not to pass over free bonuses. "The second item on the agenda is... the reward to the person I thought was the most helpful today! That'd be you–Wolfman on the third circle, Expert rank. Did you manage to learn Inscription Momentum already?"

The Expert he'd called out crouched slightly, his enormous frame shrinking slightly as all eyes turned to him, a show of deference built directly into him by his heritage. "Quad-Master, I'm sorry to say I failed to grasp the essentials of the skill. I-"

"Exactly." Joe tapped on his nose then pointed his index finger at the Wolfman. "You were a constant source of mana, and throughout the entire process, stayed in a deep, meditative state to make sure we had all the energy we needed. How you managed to maintain a stable channeled flow at the same time is beyond me, but you picked up the slack when the others around you found themselves completely tapped out. This gave them more opportunity to observe, but you remained focused the whole time. Come here, move to the central position and activate the ritual."

Seeing as the ritual was fully created and empowered, the Expert needed only to do the equivalent of throwing a switch to make it fully operational. As he stepped from the third ring to the center, his stance shifted, and he stood taller–proud of the fact that his efforts had been recognized. As he came alongside the Eclipsing Aurora Chalice, he paused and looked at the activation sequence in confusion. "Where's the... what am I looking at here?"

Joe followed his gaze, realizing with a chuckle that his Magical Syntax Lore effect had come into play, his Master's Mark creating an overlay which hid the details of the circles from onlookers unless they managed to force their way past his defenses. As far as this Expert could tell, he was looking at an emblem of a brain with an arrow pointing at another brain–a cartoonish caricature which frankly had no place on such a powerful piece of magical working. "Right, sorry about that! Force of habit. Touch the base of the brain stem on the left-hand side and send a thread of mana through there."

The Expert did as he was instructed, and the ritual sprang into motion. A thin orange light surrounded his anthropomorphic features, and a circle wide enough for five people to stand side by side appeared on the edge of the ritual itself. Joe quickly stepped into the targeting circle, not wanting to waste even a *moment* of this ritual's potency. Pulling out a simple enchanted parchment, Joe began inscribing an Apprentice-rank ritual diagram, flying through the different circles for several minutes.

Long before he actually finished the inscription, there was a flare of light as the circle around Joe collapsed into a single point then shot in a straight line at the Wolfman a short distance away. As it hit the haze surrounding his head, the single point split into two streams, which beamed directly into the wide, startled eyes of the Expert.

"I! I got it-" His excited bark cut off as his eyes rolled up in his head, and his nearby peers lunged forward to catch him just before his bulk collapsed onto the overcharged chalice.

"Close one."

"Nice catch."

The rival Experts looked at each other with something akin to grudging respect as they hauled the Wolfman away from the center point of the still-active ritual.

A few minutes passed before the unconscious Expert stirred once more, freezing as he found sixty pairs of eyes staring at him. To help him get out of the slightly awkward situation, Sage Pete gently called, "Everything work out for you, youngster? Any issues assimilating the skill?"

"Sage!" The Wolfman shoved himself to his feet, where he stood unsteadily for a moment as he caught his breath. "Reporting. I did gain the Inscription Momentum skill, at... at *Expert rank two*!"

"I'd like a copy of this ritual diagram." Master Darling conversationally tossed the comment toward Joe, but it may as well have been a hand grenade for how the room exploded.

"I'll pay *double* whatever she would offer you!" Glanak was on his feet, hands gripping the chair in front of him as he leaned toward the stage, clearly having to physically hold himself back from jumping over the barrier and attempting to directly inspect the working himself.

"It's interesting, but–nah." Master Hollows was shaking his head even as the professors vied for Joe's attention, making a dozen arguments a second about how this would revolutionize their teaching capabilities.

Once more, the Sage had to speak up, and his insights caused the room to go quiet once more. "I do believe he has more to say..."

All eyes turned to the Wolfman on stage, who was fidgeting slightly. Lifting his chin out of respect for the assembled powerhouses, he spoke once more, louder this time. "I also gained the skill *Ritual Lore*... at the Journeyman rank."

"Abyss." Joe spat quietly under his breath, the calculus behind how he'd be using and disseminating this ritual shifting in an instant. He'd only intended to pass along Inscription Momentum, but if the ritual took all of his currently in-use skills into consideration as something to just *hand out* willy-nilly, he couldn't risk some of his more potent abilities going out without strong stipulations in place. Forcing himself out of his ruminations, the Ritualist inquired, "Is that why you passed out?"

"I think so." The Wolfman winced as he rubbed his clearly aching head. "There was such a massive influx of information... I didn't have the skill at all before. Yet, I feel like, if I could have handled it better, if I had managed to stay awake, I would have achieved a higher level. My apologies for wasting the opportunity."

"Your nose is bleeding." Master Hollows, as a Wolfman himself, noticed the physiological shift before anyone else. "Please take a seat and rest. Make sure you have a few trusted individuals keeping an eye on you for the next few hours as you recover. Joe-"

"Quad-Master." Glanak spoke under his breath, obviously uncomfortable with the familiarity being shown in front of such a large assemblage. Cosmo didn't even notice, his attention fully on the bald man on stage.

"-this changes my mind on wanting the ritual." His tongue flicked along his muzzle, yellowish eyes burning with excitement. "It still has more uses, clearly shown by its stability. If we could funnel the math club through here, I would be more than willing to attempt to impress upon them the intricacies of Calculus and Number Theory. In fact, just allow me to use the remainder of the charges on this ritual, and we can cancel our previous agreement for lesser versions of the Lore books you were going to make us."

"Done," Joe agreed instantly, trying not to squirm as he realized he'd all but forgotten about that deal. He felt an immediate sense of relief, as a weight he hadn't noticed slowly increasing on his shoulders vanished. "As to the actual schematic itself, I need to discuss the proper requirements for dissemination with the Sage. Obviously, there are potential side effects we hadn't considered. Still, this might be an amazing tool for bringing trusted apprentices through the ranks quickly."

"The amount of Honor it'll cost them to directly gather skills from Masters is something we'll need to work out." The Sage was shaking his head, obviously beginning to consider the same ramifications Joe had been. "We don't need people jumping ranks only to find themselves bound to their instructor for the rest of their lives. Now, since we're on the subject of debt..."

Sage Pete stood from his chair with deliberate motions, his presence reasserting itself as the dominant force in the area. "A skill of this caliber, taught directly and for such a long period of time, with multiple additional benefits, constitutes a mid-Master-rank service requirement in return. Before anyone leaves, we will make plans to settle accounts. Each Master will provide quad-Master Joe with payment appropriate to their mutual ranks."

His gaze swept over to the professors in the stands then to the people onstage. "Expert-ranked instructors owe a commensurate payment, with the tier difference between you demanding a peak Expert-ranked remittance. Those of you who assisted with the ritual have already contributed enough, as you had previously agreed to work for nothing and earned benefits only indirectly."

People on the stage brightened, while a few of those in the stands grimaced. More than one gaze went distant as each individual calculated what they would be offering. The Sage's eyes shifted to Jenny, but before he could say a word, she cheerily waved at Joe. "My continued assistance as your assistant remains a cheeseless position, as direct instruction has always been what I was after in the first place!"

"That'll do." The Sage returned his attention to Joe. "My payment will be somewhere in the middle, a Grandmaster-rank favor, whether it be a particular item, ritual, help learning a particular concept, or something of the like."

"Ooh, an open favor," Master Levi mumbled enviously. "That's *good*. 'Specially from a Sage."

Jenny went from person to person in the stands, her easy-going attitude and bright smile easing the sting of having to agree to take on a debt. Only one person stood out from the crowd, practically gleeful as she smugly looked around. When Master Gabrielle caught Joe's eye, she smiled broadly at him, making her way to an aisle and strolling toward him.

"*Absolutely* worthwhile to have paid out beforehand. I apologize for my initial bitterness when I didn't know what was coming. Thank you for accepting a low-Artifact Ichor as payment. If I would've waited until *after* I gained what I did, that wouldn't have been enough." She fractionally bowed toward him, but when the Master of Alchemical Rituals stood straight once more, her stare had turned *hungry*. "Now, before all of this excitement, you had mentioned... a Lore book?"

"It'll take a couple days, but I can get to work on that... right now, actually." Joe lifted his hands, palms up, and focused on his Alchemical Lore skill. As bright orange aspects began pooling in his cupped hands, then floating up alongside a wash of mana, they took on the form of various formulas, imagery of shimmering herbs, and metals that glowed with a radioactive light. He winced at the notification that his Base Class experience had dropped below full, ten thousand points portioned away and locked to his current project.

Eyes going wide, the Elven woman leaned forward, pulling back just before the tip of her nose would have brushed the energetic materials. "Oh! Perhaps you should do this in a safe location? That seems rather unstable."

"It's fine as long as no one *touches* it," Joe stated with more nonchalance than he felt, and his raised eyebrow made her chuckle in acknowledgment of his concern at her closeness. She leaned away, and he immediately breathed easier. "If you wouldn't mind preparing ten thousand points worth of experience in cores, I'd be happy to hand this over as soon as it's completed."

She nodded vigorously, only reluctantly stepping away. Before she made her exit, Gabrielle turned and looked at the slowly forming book with a different question in her eyes. "I don't suppose the creation of Lore books in this way is a skill you'd be willing to pass on?"

"There are some nuances to the skill that make it unlikely that I can do so," Joe carefully hedged. "Though it has evolved from its original form, this was once a Deity-granted skill."

"Ah. Many thanks." He was pleased when the Elf merely nodded in understanding and turned away, hurrying out of the room–no doubt to secure payment and impatiently pace back and forth until she had her hands on her key to another Master-ranked skill.

"It's *all* favors," Jenny stated sullenly from next to his elbow, nearly making Joe flinch and reflexively chuck the unformed aspects in her face. "It's so strange to me. Not one of them came to the lecture with the idea that they would actually need to have something ready to go? I mean, sure, Master Gabrielle did, but the Sage set that up behind the scenes."

"No problems, though?" Joe cast around for the best place to set up then shrugged and slowly walked into the spectator section around the stage, settling in on the first row. "Master Glanak seemed as though he was someone who would like to be out of debt as quickly as possible. I'm surprised he'd walk away with only a binding promise of a favor. You know, I think you might've judged him a little harshly?"

"You *what*?"

"No, really!" Joe doubled down in the face of her disbelief. "I've got a lot of experience with Dwarves, and I think he's just a hardcore orthodox member of their race. Dwarves don't like owing other people, and they have an extremely strict hierarchical society. In my mind, he's just bad at recognizing how the other races in the tower interact. He's probably uncomfortable *all* the time with how things are being done; you can really see it in how, even though he wasn't exactly my biggest fan today, he spoke out in defense of my position when he felt I was being disrespected."

"Eh... he just seems like a sullen old fuddy-duddy," Jenny disagreed gently, though she swept the room before speaking to make sure Master Onyxmaul had already left. "What can I do for you? Need some food? Water? Pillows, if you're going to be here for a while?"

"Food, yes. I'm good on water... *forever.*" His smile widened at being able to say that out loud once more. "I figured I'd stick around in here and watch the math club file through and nerd out."

"If you're just going to be sitting here, want to take some meetings while you're at it?" she gently prodded, pulling out her enormous notebook and flipping to a section clearly labeled 'meeting requests', with a subheading of 'don't you dare try to put your name in above someone else'. "Err, as you can see, I usually let people write their own names in here."

"Got it." He would've done the same, so didn't quite understand why she wasn't able to meet his eyes as she spoke. "Seems efficient? Some of those names have to be pretty unique. Bring 'em on; that'd be a good way to pass the time as we work on this."

The next forty hours passed in a surprisingly pleasant blur.

Jenny managed to keep a steady stream of visitors arriving, ushering them in one at a time so that Joe could answer questions, discuss theory, and offer insights he'd gained–both through throwing himself at problems and the smooth progression of his knowledge offered by his Loremaster skill. Some of them, seeing what he was doing, requested an easy solution in the form of a Lore book to push them over the edge they'd been teetering on sometimes for years.

Each of them got a simple shake of the head, a quiet explanation that he was only able to create a limited number of books per year, and a deeper conversation than they might've been expecting. Even if he couldn't hand every last one of them

Inspiration, which they *literally* needed in order to achieve Mastery, Joe could ask them questions about the issues they were facing then reframe the problems. By pointing out blind spots and offering perspectives they may not have otherwise considered, he hoped that they'd be able to ignite the spark they'd been missing.

Everyone left having had a slightly different experience. Many of them were thoughtful, some frustrated, but a few left with hope bubbling up in them. Though he never asked for it, each person who arrived hoping to advance their Lore swore that, if they broke through, they would name him as their Master in that discipline. It got to the point that Joe looked at Jenny with great suspicion, but she had a simple explanation for him.

"There's no one in the tower who directly teaches Lore. Among the Masters, the going consensus is that Lore is someone's personal understanding and relationship with their craft." Jenny's words tickled a memory in Joe's mind–specifically how getting a skill high enough tended to generate a Lore skill, and the combination might create something unique, like his Mantra of Metal or Tokenization Mindset.

"No wonder there isn't someone going out of their way to push the study of Lore," Joe murmured to himself as he made the connection. "They don't want to take away the potential benefits of someone advancing on their own."

Still, the fact that no one actively tried to help uplift someone across the chasm from Expert to Master seemed shortsighted. He could only shrug and gratefully accept the fact that *he'd* be the one to collect the Mastery Merits on the way out.

Between sessions, he watched the math club funnel through onto stage, where they would activate the ritual for a long moment while Master Cosmo sat in the orange circle that would appear, thinking deep thoughts about calculus. It became a mark of pride for someone to last as long as possible, though almost inevitably everyone went unconscious as the flood of knowledge overwhelmed them.

Only one person—eyes, ears, and nose pouring blood—managed to withstand the entirety of the transfer. When the orange light faded on its own, and he remained standing, though swaying in place, the entire club burst into applause.

"Direct increase to the Master rank!" the surprised recipient shouted as he lifted his trembling arms in triumph, getting swept up by his peers and carried out of the room on their shoulders to celebrate.

Only a few hours later, the ritual finally faltered, fully expended. No one was unhappy with how long it had lasted, as there'd been massive gains made by a couple dozen people. Cosmo cheerily waved at Joe as he and the remainder of his club made their way out, and soon Joe was left alone to contemplate the nearly complete Artifact.

"Good thing that ritual only counted down when it was actually active, or it wouldn't have gotten nearly as many people through." Even as Joe finished his thought, someone slid into the seat next to him. Expecting the next person signed up for a meeting, the Ritualist tried to get his mind in the right space for another deep conversation. A smile on his face, he turned... only to find Master Gabrielle staring at the book in his hand with unrepentant greed and open excitement.

"Perhaps it is my overeagerness, but I thought it had been forty hours already. What're you thinking? Five more minutes?" Her voice came out in a near-whisper. "Give or take?"

Realizing he didn't need to hold a conversation, Joe gratefully remained silent and watched as the remnant aspects pulsed out of his hands and into the book. As the last mote of power slid into place, and a slight shockwave vibrated the air to announce the creation of a new Artifact, he directly handed the Lore book over.

The Elf accepted it with both hands. Much to Joe's surprise, she directly absorbed it instead of cracking the cover and beginning to read. Within five seconds of its creation, it had vanished in a burst of light and seeped into her skin.

"That's *it*?" she gasped, and at first Joe thought she was

upset with what she'd been given, only to realize she was all but slapping herself in the forehead. "That's *all* I've been missing? This whole time, it was just... are you *kidding* me? Now it all makes sense. It... it *all* makes sense!"

Her eyes went wide as a wave of golden energy exploded away from her, sweeping around her in a small sphere before collapsing in on itself. The Elf staggered as the weight of her *Enlightenment* nearly suffocated her, drowning out the Inspiration she had gleaned from the absorption of the Lore book. Seeming to move almost mechanically, Gabrielle's fingers twitched slightly as she interacted with whatever system messages were appearing.

Then a different weight settled across the area, the unmistakable feel of a *Grandmaster* making its presence known.

You have been brushed by Enlightenment! Skill comprehension is increased by 20% for the next 12 hours!

"Oh, abyss." Joe could practically feel dozens of skills trying to edge into his mind, but he held them off as he watched the tears of joy trickle down Gabrielle's face. She dashed them away quickly, turning to him with a beatific smile.

"Hey! Want to go get new robes together? Looks like we both need an upgrade."

CHAPTER THIRTY-SEVEN

Skill increase: Enchanted Ritual Circles (Expert VIII → IX).

Joe stared at the skill increase notification with immense trepidation, holding perfectly still, as though that'd be enough to keep the suddenly increased skill from tipping over into the Master ranks. "Note to self... it's a lot easier to gain skill levels when you're flush with enlightenment energy."

He'd been putting the finishing touches on creating a token for his Carnage Pulse cluster. After seeing the effects of even the *temporary* tattoo Sage Pete had stamped his hand with, the Ritualist had been reminded of the potential power he was missing out on by ignoring the new effect that had been added to his alchemical rituals skill. At first, he had planned to work out some kind of boost for himself, but Joe realized early on in his research that nothing was going to push him over the boundary he was already currently stuck on—he was hard-capped at four hundred and ninety-nine Characteristic points across the board.

Instead of looking for ways to boost himself, the Ritualist decided to go the other direction entirely, trying to find a way to make his current clusters even more deadly than they already were. The results sat in his hand: five small, shining tokens, each of them keyed to a combination of the Ritual of the Red Cascade and a Brew of Reverse Homeostasis. All three of the items were at the Expert rank, and they, in combination with the repayment of the favor he had immediately requested from Master Onyxmaul, would serve him well in combat.

"Just need to figure out how to tie all of this in with my normal approach. Usually a mid-range fighter, stamping someone with a tattoo puts me a little closer to the action than I prefer." Joe replayed the ambush by the controlled Masters who had been sent after him, how he had ducked and weaved, doing his best to maintain distance while his ritual orbs and ritual diagrams did the heavy lifting of isolating and whittling down his opponents. His heavily enhanced mind let him pick out a few places he might have been able to land a strike with something held in his hands, but there was one major problem.

"Am I going to need to put a hundred percent of my focus on pushing through the defenses of whoever I'm fighting against to get the tattoo in place? That's basically *planning* to take a hit, at the bare minimum."

Storing away the tokens, Joe next reached for his Abyssal Bloom cauldron, which had been cooling down in the fireplace of the small library for the last half hour. "Cool enough to store without causing issues. Good."

After he had packed up and cleaned away all of his mess, Joe fell into the comfortable chair and reached for the book on the nightstand next to him. He took a quick glance around the sub-dimension library once more before sticking his nose into its pages and allowing the information within to consume him.

The last few days had passed with deceptive calmness, giving him all the time he needed to work through his various projects. The subtle shifting of his fabric drew his attention to the fact that he was still wearing his same old robes, having been turned away by Minya the moment she saw him walking alongside the newly ascended Grandmaster. To be fair, she had solid reasoning, and Joe couldn't help but chuckle at the memory of her words.

"If you can tell me with a straight face that you aren't about to be a Penta-Master in the Core Class skills, I'll whip you up a new set while you wait. Otherwise, get out."

Gabrielle had offered him an apologetic smile but then vanished into the depths of the room to get fitted for her new gear.

Truly, Joe didn't mind. After wandering around until he found a hidden alcove, he had pulled out a Codex Key and settled in to get some work done, culminating in his relaxing reading session. Soon, the book was slipping from his hand as his eyes pressed closed, allowing himself the luxury of a short nap to recover from the endurance work he'd completed in the ritual and Lore book creation. Still, a full hour was plenty for him to recover and *then* some.

The biggest problem was that, when he woke up, he'd been offered a slew of sleep and dream related skills, stacked precariously enough that when he'd brushed his hand to dismiss them, he had *almost* accidentally accepted a few of them. Joe had decided on the spot that there would be no more napping, at the *very* least until his Tribulation didn't have the super fertilizer of Enlightenment energy to feed on.

Yet, his Tribulation had found another way to impact him, as his *comprehension* of skills was artificially boosted alongside the requirements being dropped to attain them. Slowly turning a page, Joe split his attention between the words he was reading and his thoughts on the matter. "I mean, it's not like I don't *want* to become a Master in Enchanted Ritual Circles, but the *timing* of it is important, too."

He allowed his eyes to flick to the side, where a system screen holding a running tally had been slowly creeping up over the last few hours.

Current Mastery Merits: 98.

There was also a handy-dandy breakdown of the origin of the merits, leaving Joe shocked at how a simple conversation with a few people had led to near-immediate breakthroughs for them. He resolved to make that one of his main focuses while on Vanaheim–clearly there was a desperate need for someone to offer their insights on Lore. Pushing that thought to the side, though keeping the plan in mind, he blinked several times and focused on the new chapter.

"Dispute over the Ritual of Corruption." He raised his eyebrows in absent-minded acknowledgment of having seemingly found the reason this book was deemed 'forbidden' and locked away. "With a name like that, it can't be anything safe. Let's see..."

There are many ways to end a civilization. Fire, plague, a Sage-level Ritual of Flattening to reshape the terrain into a completely flat surface from the point of origin and out to the horizon. Yet the Ritual of Corruption nearly brought Vanaheim to its knees in a far more subtle manner.

Joe looked away to indulge in a moment of power fantasy, already envisioning himself lifting a hand and crushing a mountain, cities, forests and raising rivers with a single magical effect. "Ritual of Flattening... going to have to keep an eye out for that one someday."

It does not rot flesh, twist minds, or inflict any other grotesque status, as the name suggests. Instead, this ritual allows the practitioner to sacrifice a measured amount of their own health to alter the apparent age of a non-living target in such a way that it will fool all attempts, magical or otherwise, to discern its true age.

Yes, dear reader, the Ritual of Corruption nearly took down Vanaheim by a simple manipulation of its currency: cheese. A Ritualist, at a height of power that suggests he should have known better, devised the plan to counterfeit the age of his currency, and, working in conjunction with a healer of similarly low moral standards, produced products that looked, smelled, and tested as decades-aged wheels, mass-altering entire warehouses full of cheeses.

While the currency of Vanaheim is endlessly stable, due to the endless consumption of whatever can be produced, the Codex-Keeper reading this disquisition will have an understanding that, when the cheese had been portioned out in a manner designed to keep the Jörmungandr asleep, only to have practically day-old cheeses being fed to it instead of a magically dense lattice of power that would last days on end, the world itself was nearly destroyed as the creature began to awaken.

This very ritual led to the great purge of Ritualists throughout the planes, as they were deemed too dangerous to all civilization. It was only after this ritual was locked away and long forgotten that they were slowly allowed to return to society as a whole.

With this warning, remember that corruption will always remain the most effective way to topple a society… ritual or no.

"What." Joe flipped to the back of the book, taking a look at the ritual it contained and wincing away in pain as he tried to take in the Grandmaster-rank concepts it touched on. "No *kidding,* he should've known better. What kind of Grandmaster Ritualist is hurting for money? Preposterous. But seriously? *This* is the reason the members of my class were exterminated throughout the universe? Falsifying *cheese*?"

He closed the book with a sigh, unwilling to read more of it at this moment. Looking across the shelves, Joe found himself lost in a moment of wonder. "I guess almost setting the World Snake free is a good reason for punishment, but extermination across all of the worlds? *Wow.* How much history has been locked away like this? Obviously, Nathaniel did it to save my class, but... how many others has he done the same for over the years?"

Newfound respect for the millennia-old Gnome who was nearly singlehandedly blocking the systematic destruction of various paths to power flowed through him at that moment. Getting to his feet, Joe twisted back and forth, simply taking a moment to enjoy the freedom of movement he felt. "Maybe I should go for a walk, just take it easy, and don't accept anything the system tries to give me. Don't look into anything too hard... or maybe I should just stay here."

Waffling over his desire not to push his enchantment too far, and the sheer antsyness of being stuck in a tiny room for so long, Joe finally decided to step out of the sub-dimension. The portal snapped shut behind him as the Ritualist stepped into the first basement level of the tower, moving directly to the stairs and ascending to ground level. He took a deep breath, letting it out slowly as the far fresher air of the huge open space washed over him.

"Ahh, there we go–what *now*, Jenny? Wait, how? It's been five *seconds* since I-" Joe grumbled as his relaxation was immediately interrupted, his assistant rushing toward him in all but a sprint. Her face was set in a way Joe had come to recognize as 'serious business', but there was no tension in her shoulders or around her eyes to indicate something was wrong, per se.

"Master Joe!" Jenny came to a stop a respectful distance away, offering a shallow curtsy to appease the many eyes on them at the moment. The Ritualist braced himself, but her following words left him far more intrigued than anything else. "I've been looking for you for hours now. You have a visitor, and I promised them I'd fetch you as soon as possible. Where have you *been*?"

"Busy." He nonchalantly gestured with an ambiguous motion. "A guest, you say? Someone from outside the tower, then, but... who would come here looking for me? No, don't tell me. Uh... unless they're here seeking a duel? No? Perfect. I like fun surprises. Lead the way."

They didn't have far to go, as the room she led him to wasn't one of the distant lecture halls, workshops on a separate floor, or anything of the like. Instead, there was a simple antechamber directly off the main entrance, clearly designed to keep people not a part of the tower from getting a chance to snoop around and gain access to things they weren't supposed to see.

"A messenger? No? An emissary from another tower, here to try and bribe me? Feel free to let me know if I get it correct. That's not it, huh?" Joe scratched at his neck as they approached the door. "Heartpiercer? Socar and his cat? None of those, *really*? It's not going to be Master Surge, 'cause you said it wasn't someone trying to fight me."

His excited smile froze with confusion as the door opened and the visitor was revealed.

"Boris? What're you doing here?" Joe froze up for a moment then changed his question, "Wait, *how* are you here? Shouldn't walking around on this planet literally crush you?"

"Characteristics do not determine everything about a person. I am a *Professional.* I have my own means of staving off..." The elderly Scholar stopped speaking, his breath turning ragged as he cut himself off, squeezing his eyes closed. Boris was hunched on the edge of his chair, hands clenched together so tightly that his knuckles had gone as white as his hair, and the spectacles on his face slid down his sweaty nose as he whipped around. "No... that doesn't matter right now. Joe. *Joe*, I messed up."

Crossing the room, the Ritualist reached out a hand to support the elderly man, guiding him back into his seat before his swaying form could collapse into it. "Take it easy. Breathe. *Breathe*, man. Did you break the Grand Pathfinder's Hall or something? I'm sure whatever is going on, it's fixable. We're having a bit of a situation here on Vanaheim, or I'd get back on the bifrost with you right now-"

"No. It's here. Vanaheim itself is in danger, due to my *abyssal* impatience." The man's chest hitched, and Joe realized with a jolt that he was fighting back tears with everything he had. Perception and Charisma intermingled, allowing the Ritualist to notice grief, guilt, and a thick layer of exhaustion swirling through the aged researcher. "My message? To the society? They got it, alright."

"Which is why you sent it in the first place," Joe reminded him gently, not quite sure where this line of conversation was leading. "Meaning it all went according to plan?"

"Yes, well." Boris swallowed hard, and words tumbled out now that he'd begun. "I've managed to reconnect with one of my oldest friends in the society, Sir Liz R., who had promised to keep me abreast of the situation as it unfolded. He's apparently been trying to reach out to *you* on the sly, which is the only reason I caught him. Joe... I was just supposed to be getting acknowledgment that my letter was received, that they were even considering my reapplication! Instead..."

He cupped his hands behind his head and leaned back, trying not to hyperventilate. "Instead, they officially declared the founder an *apostate*. An existential threat to the purity of the Scholar profession, due to being corrupted by the ways of an Occultist! They've dispatched an entire Alumni Association to find him and destroy everything he has touched... and anyone associated with him."

"I guess we found what we're going to use this token on, haven't we?" Joe smirked as he pulled the small disk of metal out of his storage, fully prepared to consume it to overturn the ruling. Before he could open his mouth and try, Boris reached out and grabbed his hand.

"The Alumni Association has cut all contact with the Scholar's Society until the deed is done. They cannot get messages. In fact, they were ensorcelled to not see, hear, or even *smell* another person who has had dealings with the Scholars' Society until their task is done–specifically to counter the founder's ability to overturn the rulings of the provost." His hand slowly dropped, seeing that Joe understood what a waste it would be to use the precious item. "They've decided to find Nathaniel on their own and fix their 'problem' at the source. I don't know what to do, but we have to warn him."

Joe tried to shake off the tinge of fear Boris had infected him with, offering a smile to ease the other man's spirit. "I don't think you need to worry so much. This isn't, you know, *great*, but it's not exactly like Nathaniel is defenseless. He has enough power on hand to probably take on a half-dozen Class Sages at a time, all on his own. I know for a fact that the other *single most powerful* combatant on the planet is his ally and friend as well.

Not to mention, he lives in a hidden location and is incredibly well protected."

"Well, there's a problem with all of that," Boris cut in, his voice cracking as his eyes begged Joe to take this seriously. "They're *not* alone anymore. I saw things on my way here, slipped into the meetings that were happening, by dint of my scholarly appearance and pretending like I belonged. In fact, in this instance the geas they are under acted in my favor as, though I am excommunicated, I am as of yet a *Scholar* originally of the society. They couldn't even notice me standing next to them, even as I blatantly read their documents, attended their meetings, and learned of their plans."

Joe began to get a very bad feeling, which only grew as Boris pressed on. "When they arrived, they were welcomed by hundreds of people in heavy armor and escorted into a tower. As I said, I followed along. The alumni brought news from Jotunheim, warning that an expedition had been successful, and a Mythic Core is on its way... to be delivered to the Ascensionists? A faction of some kind, I'm certain."

"Don't worry about that; what are they *planning*?" The Ritualist pressed, even as he pushed aside the musing of the elderly man.

"Yes." Boris ordered his thoughts. "A small contingent of the alumni was escorted around the planet and found signs they believe will grant them access to this hidden tower you mentioned to me. There was great interest at that finding, as the... Traditionalists, as they called themselves as a whole? Yes? The Traditionalists assume that entrance to that tower is the key to finding a World Boss on *this* planet. Are they correct in their assumption that leading an assault on that entity is their only chance for getting a Mythic Core before the expedition from Jotunheim returns?"

"Probably?" Joe felt his stomach roil as he realized the end result of their actions. "They're going to hunt the World Boss? That'll destroy the planet, even if they *succeed*!"

"It will," Boris agreed gravely, the light flickering off his half-moon spectacles as he held Joe's gaze. "They all came to that same conclusion and agreed that it was preferable to allowing a path for the deities in Asgard to descend. There was much talk about what would happen should they be allowed to walk among mortals once more and the warping effect they would have across the myriad worlds. I have to tell you... the proof they have is concerning. It's a convincing argument, if you listen to it."

"I'm sure it is." The Ritualist shook his head in disbelief. "I need to bring this to the Sage immediately. You stay here. Rest. I'll make sure someone brings you some food and water, and perhaps finds you a more comfortable space where you can freshen up."

His Aura of Soothing Destruction unfurled through the room, removing the grime of travel that had accumulated on the Scholar's skin and clothes. The elderly man let out a soft huff of appreciation then settled back into his seat. "I suppose I have nothing more to do. I must leave this matter to you. I've... I've already done far too much damage."

The Ritualist didn't take any measures to look good to the onlookers or spare his mana or Stamina as he rushed out of the room. Omnivault sent him ping-ponging up the tower, his Quad Strength turning what would've been a hundred feet of vertical distance traveled into four hundred feet *per jump*. Even before his resources bottomed out, Joe was outside of the Sage's penthouse, fist pounding on the door.

There was a flicker, and he found himself slamming into a chair, the entire piece of furniture falling backward halfway before stabilizing and slamming back to the ground. Only then did he register the sound of the door violently shutting behind him, and see the infuriated face of the Sage only a few feet from his own.

Pete was clearly trying to control himself, but his voice still emerged as a gravelly growl, "I'm certain you have a *very* good reason for interrupting me in such a decidedly *improper* and aggressive way."

"Celestials, Pete... Sage Pete," Joe quickly amended as the glare intensified. "Yes... I come with dire news."

As quickly and respectfully as he could manage to the out-of-sorts Sage, Joe explained the situation, his own concern growing as Pete appeared to be *understanding* something he already knew rather than being unsettled by the information. Once all of his words had run out, Joe waited for an answer, but the Sage merely pulled on his beard in consternation.

"Well, that explains *that*." Pete glanced at Joe sharply. "Conflict has broken out in the open across multiple regions, escalating far faster than we anticipated. Yet, there isn't a single sign of Mythic Core energy having been detected... so no one knew why the Traditionalists have chosen this moment to disturb the peace. We are moving to contain them, and the alliances I've made are already being called upon. The Sages we've aligned with are in fact are on their way at this very moment. Now... now at least *I* know it's all a smoke screen for the true target."

"Looks like the rest of them are going to find out pretty quick." Joe inclined his head toward the enormous windows, and the Sage followed his gaze, watching the various streaks of vibrant light in the air as humanoid missiles approach their tower at calamitous speed.

"Before they get here, you should know that a large group of the Sages in the Traditionalist faction have vanished. No one knows where they are at the present moment, which leads me to believe they're likely already staging an assault on the Inverted Tower. Even so, you are not ready to engage in the upcoming conversation. Remain silent, or I *must* send you away for your own safety."

Pete took a few sharp breaths, letting his hands bounce up and down as he tried to bleed off some nervous energy. "Frankly, I'm not sure *I'm* ready for this meeting."

The room flashed with multiple instances of bright green light, and Joe found himself standing in a corner of the penthouse as a dozen people were teleported into the center of the room.

One voice rang out before any others could dominate the discussion, the Sage of the Tower of Ritualists stepping forward with his hands wide to draw attention to himself. "New information has come to light. We've found the reason the Traditionalists are attacking and need to position ourselves to counter them *immediately*."

CHAPTER THIRTY-EIGHT

Pete began walking through the situation Joe had outlined for him, all while the bald man himself remained standing in the corner, constantly buffeted by the waves of pure conceptual energy emanating from the room full of Sages. As each of them began to realize the gravity of the situation, their anger ratcheted up, and the strain the mere Master was under reached ever greater heights.

"At least we know why they are moving and what they want. The fact that the Traditionalists are using the surface conflict as a smoke screen aligns perfectly with our concerns over the Sages that have gone off the grid-"

He came to a sudden stop, moving in a blur from the center of the room where he was addressing the gathered people to the bay window of the penthouse. A foul curse erupted from his lips, and Pete vanished in a flash of green light only to reappear on the other side of the window, just as an enormous burst of light appeared on the horizon in all directions, an aurora of scintillating energy streaking across the sky and approaching with deadly inevitability.

Skill offered: Danger Sense (Expert VIII → Master I → Master V). Duck and cover!

Joe clapped his hands over his ears, almost forgetting to refuse the skill as the windows began rattling, vibrating faster as death approached without leaving an avenue for escape. Pete's strained scream barely reached the ears of those in the room, but it was impossible to miss the apocalyptic volume of mana surging out of him.

The Tower of Ritualists responded.

A heavy layer of what looked like paint peeled itself off the tower, reverting into a dense liquid after countless years of being held solidly in place. The entirety of the training field around the tower lit with millions of arcane symbols, nigh-instantaneously fading as the long-dormant power was pulled into the alchemical substance that had been coating the tower. As the two met, the paint turned into a river of iridescence then reformed into an enormous cloud bank centered above the tower.

For all of his insight into the class he wielded, Joe could still only just barely make out the fact that the thunderhead above them was actually a singular ritual, even then *only* because storms didn't arrange themselves into clean lines.

Just before the aurora collapsed in on them, the ritual activated, and an opaque fog surrounded the tower in its entirety. Joe waited, but only the sudden silence and cessation of the glass trembling was ringing in his ears. Glancing down to double check that he hadn't been sent to respawn, the Ritualist held his position, not sure if he had permission to leave the corner of the room. "Pretty sure any sudden motions will get one of those guys to pop me like a *bubble*."

Pete reappeared this side of the window, staggering over to his desk and maintaining his upright position only by bracing himself against the sturdy wood. "Safe. Filled with *scalding* rage, certainly, but safe."

As the Sage spoke, the dense fog lifted, not vanishing but becoming translucent enough to see through. Joe staggered toward a window, entirely unconcerned with propriety as he went to the glass and stared through it in utter shock.

"Master Darling is going to be *furious* that all her work over the last few days is gone." The training field, the massive circle surrounding the tower, was now a single pit full of molten rock, churning like soup. It was obscenely hot, shown by bubbles the size of carriages rising and bursting, sending splatters of lava airborne before plopping down to rejoin the liquefied surface.

Even more horrifying was how the towers around the perimeter had been affected.

One–no! *Two* of the towers had been cleaved directly in half and were already settling into their strewn-about positions, haphazardly leaning on their neighbors or blocking entire roads. Others were missing chunks of themselves, crumbling sections still sliding off and falling as weakened areas gave way beneath the blistering heat and force.

"Our deepest apologies, Sage Pete," one of the new arrivals stated uneasily. "They must've been tracking us, waiting for a large enough group to get together."

Pete brushed off the conciliatory words. "None of that. I chose this alliance willingly and am happy to be able to prove my worth to the cause... even if it was far sooner than I had expected to need to do so. I'm gratified to be able to tell you that my offer of a safe haven to all of your noncombatants is officially invoked. I am effectively removed from the board, as I'm now unable to step out of the tower, as the ritual is being maintained only due to my presence."

"Abyss, I had hoped we could get you to the Sages' Council and force a vote," another of them grumbled, though he looked properly relieved not to have taken the attack head-on. "I'm certain a secondary strike would hit as soon as your ritual goes down, so we cannot exactly blame you for this choice."

"That's the signature attack of *Class Sage* James Archemental!" Another stepped forward, clenching their fist in front of them, even as the air began to ripple around him, as though he were being viewed from underwater. Tiny sea creatures flashed by, almost too quickly to notice, and only the splash of blood from where they met convinced Joe that he wasn't just imagining them. "Total war it is. I'll... I'll need to handle him. This was an alpha strike against an assumptively unprepared neutral party. This isn't what happens when people are trying to win a fight; it's what they do when they are trying to remove the option to *defend* yourselves."

"Class Sage Scuddy..."

"You can't mean to try and face him directly! One of you is *certain* to be slain."

Sage Scuddy cut off the conversation with a sharp motion. "I am the only one among us who can plumb the depths and find, let alone *contain* him. It must be me, and truly, this has been a long time coming. He has been my friend, my rival, and now... it seems, my enemy. Farewell, and I hope to see each of you upon the morrow. I can only hope my ambitions match with my expectations when this is over."

He vanished, leaving the tower under his own power and moving too quickly into the distance for Joe to track. A heartbeat of silence followed his exit as a misty spray of seawater washed over them all.

"I can't *imagine* what would have happened if the Tower of Ritualists had been directly destroyed." Pete's soft words echoed across the room. "All of my people slain in an instant, with nowhere to respawn? Please, contact your own towers and make sure they're taking measures to defend themselves."

The oppressive energy in the room shifted considerably, as each of the Sages immediately followed the advice and looked into the distance as their skills, spells, talismans, or other items established a connection to their homes. Joe finally peeled himself from the window, edging closer to his shaking-with-adrenaline Sage.

"How'd you manage that?" His words were low, but he was under no misconception that he'd be able to keep his conversation private. "That was a Sage-rank alchemical ritual;

you would've needed a Mythic Core just to design it. How? *When?*"

Pete bit back a sharp reprimand, taking in Joe's equally shaken visage, and decided to explain while they had a moment to themselves. "Not made by me, and a *long* time ago, Joe. We've never had a Sage before myself, but we've had plenty of Grandmasters who worked to create our final defensive option. Without you and your assistance with my ascension, it would have remained inert... even as we were obliterated. Unfortunately, it's a single-use activation. Once it powers down, it's gone. I can maintain it for the next couple of days, and happily, this means we are currently standing in the single safest place on the entire planet right now."

He raised his voice to ensure everyone could hear him, allowing them to stop pretending politely that they couldn't. "*All* our allies are welcome, unconditionally. I'll make sure to prepare our largest lecture halls, filling them with entertainment and excitement for any families, tucked away in the deepest bunkers to make sure the littles do not catch a whiff of the ongoing atrocities."

Thankful nods came from all present, and Joe marveled at the masterful move the Sage had just pulled. It was a facet he would've never considered–having been nearly *exclusively* in combat scenarios, around powerful people, or focused on his own craft since he had first entered Eternium. He'd all but forgotten that Vanaheim was home to more than just the elites of each respective class. Likely, the vast majority of them had children, grandchildren–multiple generations of family living in their atmosphere-piercing towers.

As the conversation quickly shifted to logistics, Joe's attention drifted back to the sudden devastation viewable only when the miasma of the alchemical ritual was thin enough to pierce. "By the abyss, what kind of attack even *was* that? To have that much range and area of effect? It feels like a meteor, but there's no rubble remaining. Some kind of energy blast, but... the pattern of it? It's like all of the lightning in a thunderstorm was discharged in a single moment, but was riding along the ionosphere before dropping."

"S'called shootin' skip," a nearby man offered plainly. "They didn't ride the ionosphere; they bounced the attack off of it, allowing it to originate from a single point on the other side of the planet and rebound down from all sides. *All* of us should've been caught in that, and the Ascensionists would've immediately lost ten percent of their effective combat power until we came back."

"It's not an instant respawn for you?" Joe did *not* enjoy having that bit of knowledge.

The Sage shook his head. "Not exactly instant, but still fast. No, the real concern is how that would've likely destroyed all of our defensive gear, weapons, spatial storage devices... if it can penetrate the walls of the towers, then that was an attack designed to destroy *things*. Our death would have merely been a fortunate side effect for our enemies."

"Let's discuss options!" someone else called from the other side of the room, and each of the Sages drifted toward the conversation. "We need to immediately get in position to counter the fools going after the World Boss. I can handle tight-quarters combat. If anyone needs wide-open spaces, this may not be the mission for you, but please nominate a substitute."

"Illyria, Skill Sage Supermassive." As she spoke her name, Joe was yanked off his feet, pulled toward her as though she'd suddenly become a gravity well. Happily, the effect lasted only a fraction of an instant, causing him to sail across the room instead of directly into her. He managed to land on the wall comfortably, sliding to the floor as she finished, "I'll be fine in close quarters. I can be our vanguard, turning whatever they throw at us into our own power."

"Aranu. Sage of the Gravitational Sword." Joe dodged behind the couch just before it was sliced to ribbons, the pieces caught and all but bolted to the floor.

"I don't mean to be rude, but can we *please* halt the demonstrations?" Sage Pete spoke out, looking around at his destroyed furniture with a hint of sadness. "I'd hate for my protective ritual to keep the tower intact while the interior is destroyed from the inside. By my allies, no less."

"Oh look, it *wasn't* my blood you had to worry about. *I* didn't ruin the upholstery." Joe thought he had spoken under his breath, only to earn himself a dirty look from Pete. "Err... sorry about your favorite couch."

"Sage Nosaj." Only then did Joe notice there was a person standing in that space. At first, the Ritualist assumed the man would be an assassin, but the person resolved behind a curtain of shifting light, his features hard to make out. "As a Class Sage, my involvement in direct combat would be... less than ideal. However, I will send one of my Skill Sages with you. If your gear is destroyed, you will only become more powerful."

"Ha!" Another spoke out, grinning knowingly at Nosaj. "Been a while since I've seen you send a 'flash mob' into combat."

"We *always* used to run onto the field of battle completely nude." Nosaj sighed with fond nostalgia as Joe inched away from him. "There is no quicker way to demoralize your enemy than to make them realize their weapons are useless if they can't land a blow in the first place."

"You realize that's why people keep assuming your first name is 'Poor', right?" No one else laughed along with the duo, so the speaker lifted a hand nonchalantly, "You all know me. Yeren Almas, Class Sage. Same deal: I'll send a subordinate along. Look for Big Red on the field of battle. Although my favored druid's focus is crafting, he is more than capable of handling a few *defenders.* Especially if you'll be underground."

Joe was having trouble focusing on this person as well, though for a far different reason than the first. He was... blurry, as though constantly in active camouflage that caused him to blend in whenever he held still for the smallest amount of time.

"Calarose," came a gentle voice. "I will be focused on bringing everyone to safety, as I'm certainly specialized enough in herding cats to ensure they remain safe throughout the journey. My apologies, I will not be able to join you in the depths."

"Reynard Kogitsune." This Sage had features similar to Master Levi, a hint of canine that was just noticeable enough to indicate they were clearly inhuman. "Trust me when I say the Traditionalists' safety is but an *illusion*."

Before the next person could speak, Sage Pete clapped his hands harshly. "I know we love nothing more than to have the opportunity to showcase our power as we rarely get the opportunity to step outside of our towers, but can we *please* move forward with the operation! The literal fate of this world is riding on your shoulders. If you can't go, don't! But please, don't grandstand without first making a choice."

That refocused the group, and they quickly began readying themselves to go... only for one of them to bring up a rather substantial concern.

"Where are we actually... going?"

Joe face-palmed, immediately knowing where this conversation was headed.

"Huh, yeah. The Inverted Tower is an open secret, but its physical location is... an *actual* secret."

All eyes turned to Sage Pete, only to follow his gaze and land on Joe. For his part, the bald Ritualist merely squared his shoulders and stepped forward. "More than happy to get you there, if you'll have me. I'll be in your care. Ya know... cause I'm *definitely* going to die out there."

There were a few chuckles at his good-natured acceptance of his fate, especially since they all knew it wouldn't be a permanent state for him. As Pete raised a hand to teleport them away, the door suddenly burst open.

"Wait! I'm coming with you!" Jenny shouted, face bright red and immediately shivering as the keyed-up Sages focused their attention on her. Her next words came out far weaker, though still firm. "I need some practical experience if I'm ever going to grow."

"Taking the field among Sages is *not* the way to get practical experience," one of the visiting powerhouses gently admonished her, though neither Sage Pete nor Joe said a word.

The Ritualist looked at his assistant, a question in his eyes. When she met his gaze firmly, he shrugged and motioned for her to stand beside him. "Hope you know what you're doing."

Green light obscured his vision, and as he blinked it away, Joe found himself and the entire group suspended half a mile in the air outside of the tower. A wave of dry heat rolled over him, practically sucking the air from his lungs as he adjusted to the atmospheric conditions above the still-molten field.

Now outside of the barrier around his own tower, he could hear the screams of pain and cries for help coming from the destroyed towers in the vicinity and had to hold back his visceral reaction to sprint toward them and offer to help and heal–yet it was being suspended in the air and *not* able to move under his own power was the true deciding factor.

Thunderous explosions echoed through the streets, and signs of distant combat and guerrilla-style strikes on wandering squads were easy to pick out from this vantage point. Joe's mind went blank, a sharp rushing sound filling his ears as the needs of hundreds of people pulled on his heartstrings.

"Where are we *going*, Master Joe?" An impatient voice reminded the Ritualist of the situation they found themselves in.

The Ritualist firmed his shoulders, shaking his head and reminding himself that *none* of these people would be better served by him allowing the world to be destroyed. Checking his minimap, he thrust a finger into the distance. "The closest entrance is in the center of th' underplump!"

His head rocked back and forth almost hard enough to snap his neck, giving him a severe case of whiplash that his Aura of Soothing Destruction needed to step in to mend. He shot a glare at the Sage holding onto him, only to go still as he looked down at the position marked on his map and found a smoking crater where the entrance to the Inverted Tower should've been.

"Well, *that's* not gonna work." The group of Sages turned steely eyes on Joe, "Where's door number two?"

CHAPTER THIRTY-NINE

"I think one of those towers collapsed on the other one I know about." Joe snapped out his thoughts rapid-fire. "But there's a deprecated entrance under the statue of the Ouroboros circling the world-"

Joe's words were forced back down his throat as they rocketed across the sky, and he needed to pound on his chest to force his lungs to release the overinflation of air as they came to a stop. "Will you *stop* doing that?"

"In case you forgot, we don't exactly have the luxury of endless time. Also... plan C?"

The Ritualist stared down at the smoldering statue, mind going blank as he saw the only other entrance he knew of twisted and smoking. "Abyss, they must be going through the tunnels and closing off entrances from the inside. We need to hurry... but... I don't know where."

"Please quickly prove your worth to our mission." The Ritualist dropped a few feet as the Sage holding him aloft contemplated tossing him aside, only to seemingly reconsider at the last moment, "or I'll need to figure out a different way to get what we need."

"Celestial feces, *give* me a second!" Joe zoomed in on his minimap, trying to reconcile the underground labyrinth of entry points to their surface world locations. "Okay, we need to go a quarter mile north, then an eighth west!"

He braced himself for rapid transit, only to realize the impatient group was looking at him uncomprehendingly. Reynard leaned in, "You can trust me when I say that north, west, and so on, are only an illusion on this world. Just point."

Joe did so and quickly found himself above what should be an entryway into the tunnels leading to the Inverted Tower. Thankfully, this one had either been overlooked, or more likely, simply hadn't been visited and imploded like the others just yet. "Just need to figure out how to open the door-!"

After being set on the ground none too gently, he began scanning the area and taking a rapid series of notes under the disbelieving gazes of a double handful of Sages. Jenny sidled up to him, not bothering to lower her voice, fully aware it wouldn't stop anyone from hearing her. "What are you doing? Just open the door!"

"This is a profession-based tower," he explained as calmly as he could manage while under so much pressure. "There are contextual clues in the area that a Scholar or an Occultist can pick out. I need a few minutes."

"Can I help? I have a ritual that might be perfect for this." Jenny only got a distracted nod in reply, as Joe was fully invested in figuring out this mystery. He did glance over curiously at her as she pulled out a multi-use ritual, which had clear signs of frequent activation and degradation. To his surprise, she blushed furiously when she caught him looking over. "So, yeah. Have you ever wondered how I managed to find you so quickly after you got back from vanishing in the tower? I wasn't trying to track you, exactly... just find you, I promise!"

The ritual activated, and two tiny spectral rabbits faded into existence, already looking around with great interest. Jenny leaned closer to the solid black rabbit, which had an odd hat and half cloak draped over it. "Sherlock, find clues to open a hidden entrance in the area. Watson, guide Joe to them."

"You named them Sherlock and Watson?"

Now she had Joe's full attention and sheepishly admitted, "This was one of the first rituals I ever purchased. I swear, they're not just cute, they are really good at finding lost things, people, hidden paths. Stuff like that. This is the Ritual of The Hare-ald's Revelation... in case you were wondering..."

The Ritualist shook his head vigorously as Jenny's words trailed off, not sure how much he should react in front of such a prominent group. "We'll talk about you using summoned creatures to stalk me at another time."

"Oh, don't say it like that," Jenny mumbled with obvious discomfort. "Makes it sound weird. I was just trying to be a good assistant."

**Squee*!* The black rabbit impatiently cried out as the white bunny with brown spots bit at Joe's robes and tried to drag him away. To their credit, the first rabbit gripped a section of flooring which looked natural, only to yank away a thin sheet of material and reveal a partial word below.

"Got it." Joe immediately got his head back in the game, able to use the angle of the word to quickly find another secret section, snowballing into triangulating another portion, and from there rapidly uncovering the method to open the hidden pathway. As his hand depressed the panel they had revealed, he had barely a moment to register the fact that the rabbit had manifested a smoking pipe and was giving him a nod of acknowledgement before it vanished like a pleasant daydream. "Neat ritual, Jenny. You're right, I'll have to snag a copy of that."

The ground smoothly slid apart, revealing a concealed stairway everyone present immediately began moving toward. Cold air filled with a dense minerality rolled out of the opening, and the Ritualist couldn't help but notice the difference in quality between this entrance into the labyrinthian tunnels leading to the Inverted Tower and the deprecated version he'd been using previously. Just as he was about to begin his descent, Joe was pulled from his thoughts by a gentle hand on his shoulder.

"I've left a beacon for Class Sage Barkmane and disabled the mechanism allowing the door to close. He's already linking up with every last allied Sage on the planet and coordinating our logistics from afar and should be able to get our reinforcements following us swiftly. Your task is done." Sage Supermassive stepped in front of him, her grip on him firm without being forceful, yet unutterably irresistible. "I'll take point. You should make your way back to the Tower of Ritualists-"

"I appreciate your concern," Joe cut her off as respectfully as possible, "but these tunnels wrap around the entirety of the planet. If you don't have a map or know where you're going, you could end up lost in there for a pretty long time, even moving as quickly as you all do."

Firming his stance, he followed the Sage down the stairs, "I came here knowing that I'd be sent to respawn at some point. While I'm not looking forward to it, I'm not going to shy away from some pain when the literal fate of this world is hanging in the balance."

"Well said." Another immense aura pressed down on Joe, and his Mana Dominion immediately began working to rebuff the weight settling over him–finding only limited success. A well of despair flooded through him, though only a tiny fraction of her concept escaped to impact him. As the Ritualist let out a hiss of effort, the overwhelming sensation swiftly pulled away. "Abyss! Apologies. I'm so focused on the upcoming fight, I didn't mean for that to bleed over onto you. Ah, right, we haven't been introduced, I am Sage Nokomis."

"Joe," he replied respectfully to the chatty lady, thankful that no one seemed to be worried about moving in silence. Delving underground for an unknown length of time was bad enough, and doing so when everyone was incredibly stressed to the point of being nonverbal would have been far worse. "Which tower are you here to represent?"

"Ahh... now there's a long story." The Sage immediately began recounting some of her great successes and failures, leaving the Ritualist blinking in surprise at how open and talkative she truly was, especially after having remained quiet until this point. She spoke about how she had achieved her power as a 'Corrupted Vitalist', basically the direct opposite of a Healer, and had spent decades on the edge of life and death, only to return to her tower and find that all of her efforts had led to... becoming only a Skill Sage, the Class Sage having ascended in her tower only a few months before her return.

Joe listened with as much attention as he could spare, thoroughly entranced by the story and taking many lessons from it—not the least of which was: when he had the option to ascend, he should make sure he took it at the first opportunity, no matter *how* unlikely it seemed that someone could manage to slip through to the finish line before him. But, as much as he wanted to lean into the tale and begin taking notes, he needed to keep a close eye on his minimap the entire time, redirecting them in ways that seemed inane or counterintuitive in the extreme.

The tunnels beneath the surface of Vanaheim were vast in a way that had to be a deliberate readjustment, magically stretched, expanded, and angled so that it was impossible for someone even attempting to strip mine the crust of the planet to find them. If they hadn't come in a proper entrance, the tunnels may as well have not existed in the first place. As they hurried along the massive warren of corridors, the walls curved in ways that made distance hard to judge, generated endless loops someone might unknowingly follow for weeks before succumbing to exhaustion, and subtly distorted space to ensure those who were lost remained as such.

"We need to turn left here." Joe immediately shifted, trusting in the cold logic of his map over the seemingly correct path laid out in front of him.

There were a few protestations, especially since the direction he'd indicated led to a stairway angled upward, back toward the surface of the planet, but after only three paces, the sounds of people behind him entirely vanished. Joe glanced over his shoulder, seeing an endless, empty corridor behind him, only for the group to appear moments later, phasing into existence as they were shunted into a new location entirely. The Ritualist inclined his head and turned to face forward, only for his eyebrows to raise in surprise when he saw the sharp downward slope now in front of him.

Skill offered: Map Reading (Master III). You can read maps so good, you're like the best at reading maps.

"Ignore." Joe chuckled at the most recent attempt from his Paradoxical Heart Demon Tribulation to trip him up, but happily inane skills such as this wouldn't be enough to make him gamble on his future advancement, even if they *did* start at the Master rank.

"I take back my previous statement; it wasn't foolish of you to stay with us," Sage Reynard called from the back of the group, earning himself a questioning glance. "Oh, right, forgot. I made sure you couldn't hear that part of our conversation. Disregard!"

That only made Joe wonder what *else* was going on around him that he wasn't aware of, but he had no choice but to shove his doubts aside and press onward. Progress was slow by necessity, especially as they came to a thick knot of tunnels twisting tightly and branching constantly. The blatant teleportation they'd been subjected to reminded all of them that, if they lost the path or fell behind the group, they may never meet up again–at least not in time for it to matter.

When the hallway they were moving along suddenly spat them into a wide chamber, the Ritualist looked around suspiciously, wondering what fresh abyss they were about to experience. They weren't alone in the room, but although the strike force around him went tense, Joe relaxed as he took in the cluster of small figures huddled together on the other side of the space. Barely waist-high, round-backed, and brown robe covered, the helpers of the Inverted Tower were pressing against each other for support as they communicated in soft warbles and distressed **clicks*.

"Don't worry about those, they're just-" Joe waved his hand without concern as he hurried to get through the archway on the opposite side of the room, only for the creatures to turn toward the group as one and surge at them with horrific speed. Their hoods fell back, revealing split beaks stretched wide and hungry. That wasn't particularly strange, as penguins *always* looked horrifying when they had their mouths open, but as their robes flapped open, their bodies were revealed.

Instead of the normal, adorable fluffiness Joe had witnessed on previous occasions, now they were coated in a viscous black substance which glistened under the ambient light. Their feathers were matted and clumped, eyes glassy and unfocused as they shook and flapped with exaggerated and violent motion. Flinging themselves around with reckless abandon, the penguins splashed and splattered the oily liquid everywhere around them... and where it landed, it crawled up the walls and expanded over the floor, releasing a sweetly rotting scent that had Joe scrambling back to dive behind the Sages before his rational mind had caught up to the situation.

Flippers windmilling wildly, the lead penguin hurled itself forward, only for Sage Supermassive to casually step forward and lift her arm, forming a buckler made out of what looked like nothing other than a black hole. Each of the penguins was drawn to her, tumbling through open air and angrily squawking.

Then they were gone, compressed to cubes no wider than a finger, and only Joe and Jenny were surprised in the slightest.

"What just happened?" The wide-eyed young Ritualist turned to Joe. "There were little cloaked things over there, then they started screaming and vanished... and now the whole place is covered in *mold*?"

Joe didn't admit that he hadn't noticed what the liquid turned into, having been far too focused on the near-instant start and end of combat. A quick scan of the surfaces revealed that Jenny had been correct: the oddly organic stone they were moving through now had massive patches of greenish-black fuzzy mold coating it, giving off such a lively sensation that he knew it would happily cover the entirety of his body in an instant if he allowed himself to physically interact with it. "I don't understand, I've seen those things all over the place down here, and they've always been..."

"Let's keep moving." The order came from the depths of the group, and the Ritualist could only comply, even if he were lost in thought and shocked by the shift.

"I'm surprised you've been able to bypass those things, even if they were friendly previously." Sage Supermassive sent a measuring look at Joe. "Artifact-ranked beasts like that typically would never allow such an easy food source to escape."

"*Artifact*?" Joe's realization that those no-longer-adorable penguins could individually stand toe to toe against him made goosebumps roll across his flesh. "Those are... Nathaniel had mentioned they were the ecosystem maintainers of the World Boss, but I thought that meant they'd remain passive unless it woke up? No, it couldn't be that-"

A Sage with an incredibly lithe body caught Joe's eye and shook his head fractionally, the powerfully enchanted bow in his hand so bright that the Ritualist was forced to look away after his first cursory glance. "The planet remains intact. Therefore, the World Snake remains asleep."

"Ah." Joe could only gulp and take a few deep breaths as he realized how quickly the situation on this world could devolve. "Thanks for letting me know, Sage..."

"Umbra." The taciturn archer remained focused forward, his eyes flicking to the sparks generated by Joe's Aura of Soothing Destruction frying the mold and cleaning the stone as they moved to the other end of the chamber. "Sage of the Arrow Rain."

"Umbra? Not a Shadowmancer, but an Archer?" Though he waited for more information, the bowman remained silent, and Joe realized he may have become a bit spoiled for conversation after the fascinating discussion Sage Nokomis had been offering. Instead of trying to force familiarity, the Ritualist examined the green and black mold outlining the edges of their path as his aura cleaned it away as glittering sparks. "Is that... *why* is it so familiar?"

"Machismo." Uncertain how to react to Sage Supermassive's words, Joe shifted to face her, only to find that she was staring at the dense mold with something akin to reluctance. "Ah... if only I could bring some of that back to my tower; within the year, we would look at our current wealth as a pittance."

"Strong or aggressive masculine pride would make you wealthy?" Before Joe could delve deeper into the subject, Jenny nudged him with her elbow and shot him a look.

"No. Ma-*cheese*-mo." She rubbed at her forehead when he merely stared at her uncomprehendingly. "Right, you didn't grow up with this stuff. The Jörmungandr is known for having immensely powerful, um, poison isn't the right word. Let's call it alchemy-like abilities? When it begins to circle a planet, it releases a constant drizzle of black rain that coats the world in mold, converting all living things into a cheese-like substance over time. Machismo is the name of that substance, and if it could be cultivated in a tower, they would be able to supply a near-endless amount of cheeses perfectly suited for the monthly tributes to keep the World Boss asleep."

"Tributes?"

"It's taxes, but it has the same effect," Jenny explained with a careless wave, as if there *wasn't* a massive difference between the two terms.

Joe considered this new information, still uncertain whether she was messing with him. Unfortunately, all his additional questions needed to wait. Though combat had been brief, the shrieks of the birds had been loud enough to draw attention to their counter-attack. As they stepped into the next chamber, someone was there waiting for them.

"Sage of the Bound Page?" Reynard stepped forward, his slightly canine features matching up quite well with the person standing in opposition to them. "Why? Why would you be here? You're a known crafter. *Respected.* Known widely as neutral with only the *slightest* leanings toward Traditionalism. Why would you be part of the strike force to unleash death on this world?"

"I'll... *I'll be here.*" The Sage's voice echoed unnaturally as he leaned forward, both hands gripping a large staff. He cocked his head to the side, eyes gleaming with an unnatural sheen. His pupils were dilated far too wide for the brightly lit environment, his movements a fraction too stiff to seem natural. "You're... you're gonna go. I've been sealing entrances. This section is slated for collapse; turn back now, or I'll drop the ceiling on all of us and entomb you here."

Only then did Joe's eyes become opened, his Magical Synesthesia suddenly whispering to him. The voice of magic came from all directions; above, below, *all* around him. Now that the traps had been shown, the Sage's hand revealed, the Ritualist could see thousands of papers scattered across the area, even back down the hallway they'd just emerged from. Even worse was what the magic was telling him.

"Ruinance. Calcination. Spallation. Ablation. Catabasis. Subsidence."

It had been his experience that the more layered the meaning of any word the skill whispered to him, the more immensely potent the effect would be were it unleashed. It had been a long time since Joe had direct access to a thesaurus, but he was fairly certain the papers around him would annihilate this section of the tunnels, burning, melting, shattering, and sinking them from an outburst of immense stress and heat. Before he consciously made the choice, he was already backing up-

Bumping into a Sage who drifted past him, silent as a shadow, before turning to look at the group. Catching their gaze, he nodded meaningfully and gestured grandly for them to go forward. Reynard, face drooping with despairing reluctance, heaved a breath and halfheartedly tried to stop his fellow from moving forward.

"Sage Skazzy... we can find another way." Reynard's words were met with another subtle shake of the silent Sage's head and a more demanding gesture. There wasn't a second attempt made, and Joe found himself suddenly horizontal as he was lifted and hauled along with the group as they hustled past the furiously gesturing Sage of the Bound Page, waves of mana reaching for the traps he had set... only to be rebuffed.

As the archway they ran through vanished into the distance behind them, Joe kept waiting for a detonation or at least some sign of combat or acknowledgment that two immensely deadly forces were colliding. "What just happened?"

"We just lost the only chance we had to leave this place without spilling blood." Sage Nokomis grunted with immense discomfort coloring her voice. "But no one else could've prevented the destruction of this path in time. Abyss. Without the Sage of Violent Silence here to neutralize all lethal effects, we're going to have to put down the next impediment to our progress the *instant* we lay eyes on them..."

"...or all is lost."

CHAPTER FORTY

The group moved at a dead sprint, Joe snapping out shifts as they rushed through the tunnels, Sages flashing forward and slaughtering penguins. Only the sound of their hurried steps echoed back at them until finally the resounding clamor simply ended in silence—the corridor expanding out into absence.

It took Joe a moment to reconfigure, realizing that the absence wasn't an end point, but the confined area opening into the ground floor of the Inverted Tower proper. "We made it!"

Barely had the words escaped his lips before the Ritualist was grabbed and bodily tossed backward, tumbling through the air and bouncing off the ground painfully as he scraped along until coming to an ignoble halt by hitting a wall. His Aura of Soothing Destruction was already moving to fix the minor damage he had accumulated, and a stiff rage flooded him though he knew it was his *allies* who had tossed him away. "Was that *necessary*?"

His shouted query received an answer immediately, as a chunk of the hall in front of him literally evaporated, increasing the total space of the open area by nearly eight percent. Seeing as the first floor was hundreds of feet wide originally, that was quite the substantial increase. Joe's gut shriveled as he pressed himself against the wall, realizing only then that Jenny was crumpled next to him, battered and bleeding from receiving the same treatment. He quickly extended his mana, wrapping her in his aura and undoing the suffering she was experiencing.

Without hesitation, the Ritualist Tossed out a full dozen barriers, half of them directional, meant to block anything coming directly at them. The second were omnidirectional, bubble-shaped shields meant to catch any incidental damage. As the Parchments and vellums left his storage, moving into position, Joe's mind went very still. His eyes went wide, trying to take in every detail of his first experience with full-blown Sage-level combat.

A kaleidoscope of motion and cascading energy resolved into individual fights as he did everything possible to push his Perception to its utmost.

Skill offered: Peripheral Survival Instincts. The mouse escapes the lion only because it isn't hungry enough to waste its time with such a tiny morsel-

Joe began automatically denying anything the system put in front of his face, with the skill offerings coming thick and fast as he observed the battle and was bathed in the runoff of various conceptual energies. Shattered stones slit open his skin, only for the fragments embedding themselves bone deep to be converted into aspects and the wounds–from deep lacerations to micro-fractures in his jaw from his teeth being rattled so hard –to quickly fade beneath the power of his aura.

The first of his rituals activated, a thin layer of energy popping into place and catching random stone fragments.

Sage Supermassive faced off with an Elven woman dressed like a paladin, all-consuming buckler locked with its opposing twin, a radiant shield spinning with divine geometry. "Aleyona! It doesn't have to be like this!"

"Hello... Cuzzzt-" The paladin's words were slightly slurred, shifting upward as her lips pulled into a rictus grin. Her arms snapped back and forth, sword and shield flashing around to block everything thrown her way, parrying spells, projectiles, and weapons with equal ease.

Sage Supermassive tensed as the Elf began glowing with a sudden upsurge of power, just managing to duck behind the gravity well strapped to her arm and catching a serpentine stream of radiance in its entirety. She was thrown back but managed to keep her footing long enough to reset her stance.

Joe pulled Jenny behind him as one of the bubble-shields finally surged into existence too slowly to stop the *gentle* portion of the light filled with the power of retribution carved into them. He cried out in agony as the entirety of the front of his body blistered as though his robes weren't even there.

He could only thank his lucky stars that his codpiece was made of sterner stuff.

Simultaneously curling up like a shrimp from pain *and* doing everything he could not to move as his skin was destroyed and remade within a second, Joe forced his stinging eyes back open and looked through layers of shielding—only to see that the entire field of battle had already changed.

Skill offered: Pain compartmentalization. High synergy detected with skill 'Mental Manipulation Resistance'! This-

"Not just no, but *Abyss* no," he spat out as his eyes landed on a gracefully dancing man holding a sword seemingly made from raw shadow-stuff. Joe's roiling emotions calmed slightly as confusion overlaid the pain and doubt. "What? He's not... attacking? Just trying to show off or something?"

The longer he stared at the man dancing with his blade, the more the Ritualist's heartbeat pounded with hope. Maybe they *didn't* need to fight to the death? If someone could just posture hard enough, maybe everyone would be more willing to have conversation instead of-

Skill increase: Mental Manipulation Resistance (Journeyman IV → V… VI… VII).

The sudden upsurge of his most concerning skill snapped Joe out of the trance the hypnotic motions of the sword had inflicted on him, though all he wanted to do was return to watching the impossible rhythms of the shimmering sword as it lengthened and thinned, widened and-

Skill increase: Mental Manipulation Resistance (Journeyman VII → VIII).

Congratulations! One of the Experts you made time for has followed through on their promise to attribute you as their master as they broke through the Expert bottleneck!

Current Merits earned from skill source: Smithing Lore. (1/100)

Total unused Mastery Merits: 99.

Skill offered: Captive Audience (Master I). Have trouble keeping your students focused as a teacher? Need your enemies to stay in place long enough for your attacks to land? Instead of hoping for the best, why not make *it happen? You-*

"Gerkis!" Sage Reynard let out a chilling laugh as multiple versions of himself appeared, his illusions reaching out and drowning the swordsman beneath a tidal wave of bodies, only to spit out a lesser version of the dancing Sage. "Finally... I get to test myself against you *properly*."

"*Ahh*!" Joe bellowed as he clutched at his face with both hands, digging his fingers into his temple and earlobe and physically turned his head away from the dancing Gerkis and swarms of Reynards being sliced to ribbons, not forgetting to refuse the skill offerings out of sheer principle.

A roar split the air as though in response to Joe's own scream, as a gorgeous woman sprinted across the room and leaped into the air, her flesh ripping and altering mid-motion. Her shriek of almost-pain turned into a bestial rumble as scales rippled across her shoulders, and draconian wings tore out of her back. She descended like a meteor, claws and flame joining together to turn the Sage of the Gravitational Sword, Aranu, into a splash of radioactive charcoal.

A swinging blade met her halfway, arresting her momentum and sending the human-dragon hybrid upward as gravity reversed. Wings flapping, the Draconian Sage fought against the shifting gravity and hurled herself at the swordsman, claws and elemental fury somehow missing time after time.

Joe's mouth dropped as he realized she should've already won the fight, but... he focused harder, watching as she somehow missed yet again. Her wing faltered here, talon hesitating there for just a heartbeat, allowing the swordsmen to slip away. As if to remove all doubts, a blast of supercondensed flame hit... angled half a degree off course, thereby charring Aranu's skin but failing to immolate the man.

"She's fighting for control?" Suddenly Joe could see it clearly. Where the other Traditionalists' eyes were gleaming with certainty, hers were only sparkling. Perhaps it was that her hybrid form was more resistant, but the Ritualist was absolutely certain that this Sage wasn't as deeply entrenched in whatever was influencing them as the others *must* be.

His vision shifted suddenly, and the room exploded with scintillating golden threads, thousands upon thousands of tiny streamers digging into each of the Sages fighting against the group focused on saving the world. They were karmic bonds one and all, but tipped with tiny hooks, as though the bond had been staked into place instead of accepted as a natural consequence of true *debt.* Suddenly the draconic resistance made perfect sense, as there was no way beasts—highly magical or not—could be expected to have the same demands made of them as sentient, sapient entities.

"What's happening?" Jenny whispered hoarsely as she peeked around him, staring into the room with incomprehension writ large on her face. "Is it over?"

Only then did Joe realize the intense machinations of the conflict in the room were actively invisible to his assistant—the Sages were moving so quickly, unleashing abilities so far beyond the scope of her understanding. To Jenny, the room may as well have been empty, but for various strobing lights and deadly blasts of what must've seemed like fire.

Unable to answer without losing track of what was happening, Joe merely extended his arms to the side and did his best to shield her from the onrush of effervescence forming welts across his body and bursting in tiny explosions that sent blood splashing into the air as power rippled through his shields. One by one, the defenses evaporated, only to reappear in the next moment as the ritual reinstated the magic.

"Joe!" Jenny gasped in horror, but when he didn't even cry out in pain–his aura kicking in to reverse the damage–she merely accepted the thin protection he offered and hunkered down.

Skill offered: Presence of the Singularity. Never again will you-

Skill offered: Aegis of-

Skill offered-

"I *refuse*!" Joe's words were accompanied with a deep surge of blood and fluid as a portion of his throat dissolved and reformed.

"Life is a present that is but *borrowed*, Sage Harmony Elizabeth!" Nokomis bellowed as tendrils filled with immense vitality shot toward a rapidly moving opponent, controlling her deadly threads as though she were unspooling a massive ball of yarn. Though she missed her target constantly, the sheer confidence on her face gave Joe the impression that she only needed to land *one* for the fight to be over. "It's time to pass the gift you were given to another!"

Joe finally managed to match the movement of his eyes to the endless momentum of her opponent, the streak of light resolving into a white-haired woman with long ears like those of a rabbit extending from her head. The Sage remained silent, even as she vaulted around, flipping and twirling as she provided support to her allies. With every jump, she positioned herself to perfectly intercept projectiles, interrupt devastating spell bursts, or force someone out of place long enough to put them in a disadvantageous situation.

Staring at the bunny woman, the Ritualist felt his heart *thump* with excitement as Omnivault began resonating with her movements. Energy collected around him as Enlightenment crept along the edges of his vision, subtly changing and reinforcing the immense Insight he'd already gained into the skill. At that moment, he knew he was watching the Sage of Jumping in action, as she unreservedly used her power without trying to hide her motions or the reasoning behind them.

Then their fight took them out of his view, and Joe felt a deep sense of loss as he absorbed the last remaining flow of Enlightenment, which he wouldn't even have noticed had the system not informed him that it had left a souvenir behind.

You have been brushed by Enlightenment! Skill comprehension is increased by 20% for the next 12 hours!

A sudden detonation took Joe off his feet, slamming him into Jenny and crushing her against the wall with a startled yelp even as they crashed through three layers of shielding. She cushioned his impact, and his aura immediately got to work setting their bones and knitting their bruised flesh back together—but Joe was too woozy to fully appreciate that fact until the instant concussion debuff faded, allowing clarity to return to his thoughts.

"Sperlazza, you go too far!" a charming voice rang out, concern pitching the sweetly feminine voice higher as one of the few Sages in his team Joe hadn't yet interacted with tossed up barriers, one after another.

Another person *not* dressed in robes stepped forward methodically, thrusting his hands out and sending shimmering distortions at the faltering barrier Sage. The first of his projectiles to strike the barrier was reflected, but the sturdy man—who wouldn't look out of place in an old school military movie—easily sidestepped his reflected attacks and sent another which pierced through and detonated with a snap of his fingers.

Joe hadn't seen many Sages who looked older, as they seemed to have the ability to adjust their features on demand. He wasn't precisely certain how long someone must have lived to decide that physically appearing to be in the late fifties was what they went with; but it was clear this was a man who'd been a warrior for a *very* long time. From the simple dark green shirt he wore, to the craggy, weathered lines in his face and sharp, high-top haircut he sported, this man *exuded* competence.

As Sperlazza closed in, an arrow cloaked in darkness suddenly pierced his extended wrist, pushing his follow-up attack off course and giving the Sage on the back foot a chance to create some distance between them. Sage Umbra stepped out of a shadow, arrows flying from his bow so quickly that they began blotting out the ambient light around the no-nonsense Sage. "Juniper Jade, prepare your best. Make it... a sphere turned inward."

"Umbra! *Don't!*" The Sage who'd been tossing barriers up froze for the tiniest fraction of a second, nearly catching a flying flask to the head for her inattention.

An herbaceous scent filled Joe's nostrils as the flask struck the wall. Wherever its contents splattered, the incredibly difficult-to-damage material was simply wiped away, revealing the dirt and stone of the ground beyond its boundary. A glance into the farthest boundary of the room showed that a section of the area had been warped and replaced with a large garden, with a man calmly yet continuously reaching for petals and flowers, plunging them into potion bottles and flasks before whipping them with unerring accuracy across the room.

When his allies were hit, wounds vanished, their speed increased, and their attacks hit harder. It was quite the opposite for the man's enemies, who howled in pain and lopped off chunks of their own flesh to remove the deleterious rot rampaging through their systems.

"Big Red! Turn his plants against him!" The demand caused the redheaded, seemingly half-*tree* Druid to split off from where he had joined in working to take down the dancing swordsman.

Handling the bottle-hurling Sage was a fully necessary action, seeing as how, without anyone focusing on the–Joe had to stop himself from thinking of the word 'Alchemist', as his own Lore skill rebelled against the incorrect terminology. The concept of 'Apothecary' flashed through his mind, and the Ritualist could only accept the designation for the moment–without anyone focusing on the 'Apothecary Sage', he was able to move with impunity.

In a flash, Big Red had entered the fray, his powers pulling on the plants the Apothecary was using to generate reagents. He puppeteered the herbs, trying to keep them pry them apart where they were being compounded. Others still in their pots and places in the manifested garden were instructed to shift around, or do their best to wrap the Sage in roots and branches. Those that were too far from the man instead knit themselves to their neighbors, intertwining with each other to make an unmanageable mess not easily turned into consumables.

"*Now*!" Sage Umbra screamed out his demand from a place of agony, and Juniper Jade hurled both arms forward to release a massive portion of her power in a single burst. Just as Sperlazza slammed his flat palm forward, the tips of his fingers penetrating Umbra's heart, an arrow sprouted out of the ground below them, sinking through the bottom of his throat and emerging from the top of his head. The old soldier still somehow managed to blink, the light in his eyes shifting into something approaching rationality, and his gaze becoming confused.

Then both Sages died simultaneously, erupting with enough power to mimic the force of a nuclear detonation. Joe was instantly blinded, his optic nerves fried to a crisp, powerful Characteristics notwithstanding. A scream tore out of his throat, perfectly matching Jenny's as radiation turned his body transparent, burning her even through the shadow of his near-corpse. The Ritualist nearly wept with thankfulness as she moved a moment later, his aura pushed to its limits trying to keep them alive.

After Joe survived the initial wash of energies, his vision was restored just in time to look on in wonder at how the violence of the Sages' deaths had been caught and contained in a massive bubble–power striking all angles and rebounding on itself, disrupting and destroying the miniature fusion reaction that had sprung into existence due to the compression. The tiny star quickly died as the source of its energy vanished, fading into the ambient background energy of Vanaheim in only a few seconds.

From his new position on the floor, holding himself in a loose fetal position as his muscles reconstituted, Joe watched in wonder as the Ascensionists regrouped, pulling together into a loose formation and preparing to throw themselves back into the fight.

**Sqwaa!*

"If it wasn't bad enough already, now the penguins are coming to join the fight?" Joe spoke around chunks of burned skin floating around in his mouth, spitting out the remnants as he glanced into the tunnels they had come out of. Then he heard something else, from deeper in the tower, that caused his muscles to lock in place as though he had stuck a fork into a power outlet.

Tsk.

The sound rolled over everyone present like a gunshot, causing them to flinch. It wasn't enough of a warning.

A sharp clattering filled the air, a human skull rolling across the chamber at impossible speed, bone unfolding and thickening as it *grew*. It hit the formation of Sages dead center, bowling them over and shattering dozens of barriers and protective items, talismans, and incantations before finally coming to a halt.

"A seven-ten split. Not my best work." The soft sound of feet slapping against stone echoed through the room, and Joe found his eyes drawn with a deep sense of inevitability to the figure stalking toward them. "I guess it doesn't really matter, so long as you all promise not to tell anyone it wasn't a strike. If we can come to an accord, perhaps I will *spare* you."

CHAPTER FORTY-ONE

An intense smile was on the face of a man dressed in a set of clothing that all but *screamed* 'evil overlord'. A complex series of snaps, buttons, and fasteners of every shape and size adorned his seemingly simple vestments, though the skulls sitting on his shoulders, jaws clenched to hold the trailing cape in place, belied the man's seeming simplicity.

Seeing that no one was answering, though all combat had screeched to a halt, the newcomer pulled out a fresh skull with a flourish, manifesting a silk handkerchief in the other as he began polishing the gleaming bone.

"Gerkis Hansmellon, you aren't trying to upstage me with your Shadow Daddy Sword Dance, are you?" Although the fastidious Sage was speaking lightly, huge smile stretching across his face mimicking the skull in his hands perfectly, the soft threat in his voice was no joke. "Why don't you put those sharpened shadows away for now? Oh, Ariadne *Ever-changing...*"

His words were almost a sing-song tone as he flashed across the room, catching the draconic hybrid under her wing and pulling her to the ground just before she could launch herself at

Sage Supermassive. "Easy there. It's all better now. Back to human form with you. Harold. *Harold.* Sage Theapoth!"

The third time he called at the potion-flinging apothecary still engaged in combat with Big Red, the newcomer's caricature of cheerfulness had fled, finally causing the oddly catatonic man on the other side of the room to stop plucking flowers, disengage with the druid, and slowly look over.

"I will *thank* you to pause at *least* until after I have finished picking up what I've come to collect."

Juniper Jade, the Sage who'd managed to contain the immense death energies of the Sages who had fallen, pushed herself into a kneeling position and managed to force out a question. To Joe's immense confusion, the tone she struck was... *respectful.* "Class Sage Dur'Ax... *why*?"

"Why what, youngster?" Dur'Ax settled slightly, his cheery rictus grin reappearing as he fiercely rubbed at a stubborn spot of filth on the skull in his hands. "Why have I come out of seclusion after a century? Thrown my weight behind the Traditionalists? Invaded the Inverted Tower? Or perhaps you're wondering why I haven't torn your spine directly out of your body and added your skull to my collection? I'm sorry to say, you're going to have to be a bit more *specific.*"

"I appreciate keeping my spine where it is. Thank you for your benevolence." Juniper's voice came out as a harsh whisper, waiting until Dur'Ax nodded graciously before she tried again. "Why would you initiate a fight? Simply making an appearance in the Sages' Council would be enough for any among us to stop our infighting. If you didn't want the bifrost open to Asgard... all you needed to do was *ask.*"

"Ah. I see the confusion." Dur'Ax spoke gently, as someone would to a child. "I don't care about that at all."

"Then..."

"Shh, wait a moment." The grinning Class Sage turned toward Joe, looking past him and down the hallway. "I want to see what happens. You've all had your fun, and Sage Mir was so *certain* his protégé here would be arriving alongside you... no matter how out of his depth he is. He was right, and I want to see what gave him such *surety*. Go, little Ritualist. Show me why Mirascible has such faith in you."

Two penguins burst out of the tunnels at that moment, cloaks tattered and torn, leaving a trail of machismo behind them as they flapped wildly. Initially, they sprinted into the large open space, yet after only a moment, they were back at the start of the tunnel, exiting it once again, to their apparent confusion. The third time they rushed out of the tunnel, they were slightly angled–pointed directly at the bald Ritualist and his now-healed assistant.

"Jenny, I need you to stay as far away from this as you possibly can. Stay in the layered shields as long as possible." Joe spoke as calmly as he was able, even as he sent his ritual orbs forward and caused them to unspool into an Expert-rank ritual. "Both of those are Artifact rank; you don't stand a chance-"

"Just like you didn't stand a chance against the Sages down here. That didn't stop *you* from trying to help!" Even as a fistful of vellum appeared in Joe's hand, a stack of parchments nearly as thick made its way into Jenny's. "The only thing I have on me that might have any effect on monsters this strong is some illusions, but I'll add whatever I can think of!"

Mana flooded out of Joe, activating the Ritual of Abrasive Momentum just in time for the penguins to sprint into its field of effect. The oily substance coating the birds burst into flame, sparking away as a cloud of spores lit up and detonated with a continuous **pop-pop-pop** like firecrackers being tossed into a metal trash can as the Ritual of Extended Ember Forced the initial Sparks into a full-blown conflagration. Even on fire, coated in flames thirteen percent hotter than they should be, the monsters didn't slow down or even seem to notice the damage.

Then the creatures were practically on top of him, and Joe threw himself sideways with a twist of his ankles, staying low to the ground in order to redirect himself as needed. His choice was proven to be the correct one as the flightless birds swished around, reorienting on him in perfect synchronicity as the oily gunk continuously pouring off their feathers allowed them to treat the ground as though it were a frictionless surface. With only a slight curve added to their vector, they honed in on him without losing any momentum. Driving his heels into the ground, Joe tossed himself upward, reaching the ceiling in less time than it took to take a breath.

To his consternation, the Artifact-rank threats stayed on him, their powerful bodies *more* than up to the task of following him only a few dozen feet into the air. As he pushed off the ceiling at an oblique angle, a beak snapped closed next to his ribs, close enough that his robes fluttered. Joe twisted harshly, eyes narrowing on the flurry of sparks erupting between him and the birds, where the machismo they were gratuitously splattering about reached the boundaries of his Aura of Soothing Destruction and were converted into aspects. Gritting his teeth, the Ritualist realized the process wasn't instant–the mold-inducing grease was too powerful of a material to be directly broken down.

"Keep it off." Joe sucked in a sharp breath as the ground approached. He exploded his Mana Dominion out to its maximum range, and the machismo pooling across the floor was rapidly degraded. "Abyss, that stuff is everywhere!"

Whipping his ritual orbs up and behind himself in a tight curve, he felt gratified to hear meaty thumps as the weapons struck the penguins, their Expert-rank design barely enough to inflict damage. Happily, it seemed that the main concern with these creatures was the toxin pouring off of them, leaving their defenses lacking. Joe bounced back and forth, hitting the floor, wall, and ceiling in a triangular pattern, seeing as there was no fourth wall for him to interact with. He wasn't in any hurry to try and enter into the main room, where the various Sages were watching with expressions ranging from interest to despair.

If he were treated like the creatures had been, and was put back in the same spot he had started if he crossed some arbitrary boundary, Joe knew the momentary distraction of having to reorient himself would allow the penguins to gain the upper hand at the bare minimum. As it was, he was reliant on his mobility to keep the squawking and screeching birds moving through the Ritual of Abrasive Momentum. "If I can keep lighting them on fire, beating on them with my orbs, and letting my aura destroy a hundred and thirty-eight health a second... I should be able to whittle them down."

Each time his weapons retracted, spinning around him and slingshotting away once more, they flared with sparks as the oily substance coating their surface was converted into aspects. Then, gleaming with reflected light, each of his weapons whizzed away once again to strike at the endlessly aggressive beasts. Unfortunately, at this rank, his opponents had intelligence of their own and quickly split apart to catch him in a pincer attack. Fearing for his assistant, Joe risked a glance in her direction, only to see an impassable wall where she should have been.

"Illusions! Perfect, stay safe over there." Now feeling more confident in Jenny's continued existence, Joe was able to firmly place all of his attention on the creatures closing in on him from either side. One bird was trailing along behind him, snapping and flailing at whatever part of the Ritualist was closest. The other had streaked along the ground, sliding across the surface of the floor as though coasting down an iceberg in preparation to plunge into an ocean.

It whipped around, its momentum vanishing as a flood of machismo erupted out of its flapping wings, allowing the bird to come to a halt, horrifying beak fully extended in preparation of clamping down on the Ritualist rocketing toward it. For half an instant, Joe's muscles locked in place as he saw his death approaching at speed. Then he narrowed his eyes, recognizing this as an opportunity to flip the script.

With one hand, he reached out to grasp the Ritual Orb of Strength, hauling himself to the side even while in midair. With the other, he yanked an enchanted token out of his spatial storage ring, entirely relying on his Dialectic Dexterity as he flicked the coin-shaped object straight down its gullet. Joe immediately paid for his falling 'T-pose' position as iridescent machismo spattered across his right forearm before he could pull the extended limb out of the path of the trailing bird.

Letting out an involuntary shout of pain as his skin was immediately covered in spots of mold that began to rapidly expand out–eating away at his flesh with the sensation of ten thousand fire ants chomping with their greedy little mandibles–Joe hit the ground and bounced, failing his Dexterity check for the first time in a long time. Mana wrapped around the wounds, threads of power slicing through his skin and excising the foaming impact sites. "Never been so happy to see *blood* pouring out of me."

Skill offered: Flesh is Weakness (Expert III). You've found a way to directly strip the flesh from your very bones. With this skill, you can begin replacing the torn away meat with a dense weave of mana. Once this has gained enough power, there will be no more need for food, water, or other things which entice the base mammal you once were. Upon reaching the Grandmaster rank, you will be able to directly change your race into that of one of a handful of energy-based-

"Nope, same problem as I had with the shade race change offered way back when. I still like being able to enjoy things." Looking at where his torn-out wounds had landed, the Ritualist had to force down his bile as he saw easily a dozen disks of cheese rolling away. "My turn!"

An enormous stamp appeared, and Joe grasped the oversized handle with his left hand, seeing as his other arm was currently regrowing its meaty bits. Pulling out a beast vellum, he inserted the ritual the stamp would use as a template and reared his arm back. Already, the internal reservoir of the chunky item had been filled with the Brew he had put together, allowing Joe to brandish the taglock-tipped forged stamp and use it as the weapon it truly was. "Thanks, Glanak... let's see if getting you to make this for me was worth a peak-Master favor!"

Lunging forward, he jammed the base of the stamp into the

penguin's chest, seeing as it had tilted its head back and was working its throat, trying to huck up the energetic disk it had inadvertently ingested. The force of his strike caused the entirety of the Brew to be injected into the bird in a single motion, the myriad taglocks acting as hypodermic needles and directly forming an alchemical ritual tattoo. "Time for the hard part!"

Having never tried out this method before, Joe wasn't sure how exposed he was going to be, but even so, the Ritualist didn't hold back as he connected with the material he had just embedded into the bird. Mana flooded through the stamp, into the ritual...

All sensations faded away: the burn in his legs, rasping for air, and even the agony of his clenched fist and left arm being covered in the machismo that had splashed off the penguin as he slammed the item onto its body. In that instant, Joe's mana connected with the creature's health pool, and the two resources struck each other with what felt like the force of two celestial bodies colliding in space.

As an Artifact-ranked creature, the penguin was by no means weak. Its Constitution was high, allowing it to rage against the invasive attack. If this were some form of poison, disease, or even regular damage... the monster would have thrown off the attempt nearly contemptuously. But the Characteristic was attempting to go head to head against the Emperor of Mana–and didn't have a chance to understand the difference between them before energy surged through its veins, connecting it to the enchanted token *already behind* its multiple layers of redundant protections.

The multi-pronged invasion allowed the ritual to set firmly in place, mana threading through the creature's veins and bolting the diagram in place as the token anchored it from the other side.

As the ritual flared to life, Joe grunted with effort as he twisted additional mana into the threads he was leaving behind –causing them to swell with thousands upon thousands of spikes. Instead of thin cables threading through veins and arteries, as the Ritualist pulled away, they resembled nothing more than the vines of an overgrown rose bush. With every minute motion the monster made, more midvein micropuncture mangling manifested.

The Ritual of the Red Cascade fully activated, using the internal bleeding as a template for how it should treat the creature it had been used upon. Having already punched through the resistances of the penguin, thanks to Joe's actions, the embedded ritual responded violently. The barbed tendrils the Ritualist had sunk into the monster erupted, turning the pinpricks into huge lacerations all contained within the bird's body. Outwardly, the only sign of the *cascading* wounds was how the bird spasmed. Each twitch increased the damage it took, until its interior no longer resembled anatomy, but instead a catastrophic snarl of crimson ruin.

Howling with fury as it entered a mindless state, no doubt pushed past the brink thanks to the Ritual of Berserking coming into effect, the dying monster hurled itself at Joe. He dropped to the ground, allowing the lunging creature to take the full force of the impact of its fellow, who had swooped in to take advantage of Joe's moment of distraction. The impact caused a wave of machismo to sluice off the duo, forcing the Ritualist to frantically spin, rolling across the ground as liquid fell like rain fractions of an inch from his face.

His breathing became easier as the Ritual of Fresh Air wiped away the ancient, musty scent that had been ever-present in the inverted tower. Surging to his feet, Joe crouched and pushed back, eyes on the pair of monsters. The undamaged one was currently slapping its flipper against the other's back, as though trying to dislodge something caught in its throat. Its fellow was hunched over, hacking and coughing up enormous gouts of blood—which flowed across the floor for only an instant before the mold coming off the birds fully engulfed it, leaving odd three-dimensional designs hanging in the air.

"Planar Shift." Joe took the moment of respite to link with

his Ritual Orb of Constitution, summoning Morsum around the weapon. The pseudo-Lich had only a fraction of a moment to get its bearings before it was slammed mouth-first into the heavily damaged penguin. Machismo coated the skull fully, but the summon took the oily substance in stride—draining health from the creature it had bitten into to stave off its own imminent demise.

"That's enough! I've seen everything I need." Joe nearly fell over in shock as the Class Sage appeared right next to the similarly startled birds, staring at the pseudo-Lich skull Joe had summoned with vague interest. "Been a while since I've seen one of these things. Interesting use... they are meant to be little more than alarms for the various Necromancer classes. I absolutely adore the fact that you've shown me something new to do with a skull. That *never* happens!"

The eyes of the penguin rolled up, and it toppled backward; vanishing in a huge burst of bright orange flames that swirled through the air and directly funneled into the spatial storage of Joe's codpiece. Before he could dodge away, the Ritualist remembered with great relief that any enemy killed by his Aura of Soothing Destruction would be fully and instantly converted into aspects. Morsum dropped to the floor, collapsing into a pile of dust, his summon instantly dispelled, now that he wasn't offsetting the damage being taken.

An Artifact-rank core hit the ground, bouncing a few times before being casually scooped up by Dur'Ax and tucked away in one of his pockets. He shot a wink at Joe, who was glaring at the Class Sage as if he had just mugged him. "Waste not, want not, and all that! I'll take care of this. As a little bonus for being so entertaining, I'll let you go *collect* your partner."

The undamaged penguin splattered against the far wall as the Class Sage casually backhanded it, but Joe had already fully turned his attention to the set of shielding still in place behind the illusion of a wall. Something about how Dur'Ax had said 'collect' put him on edge, and he hurried to check on Jenny.

"Come on, you've got to be okay in there. I saw probably thirty different times you were putting active effects in the field."

Shoving through the false wall, Joe felt his heart sink as he saw a thick layer of machismo covering the ground and fully encapsulating his assistant. Letting out a shout, he dashed forward, dismissing the rituals as he ran—fully intent on getting rid of the substance as quickly as his Aura of Soothing Destruction could manage. He wrapped her in his mana, even before he arrived next to her still-standing form, and the mold boiled away in moments under the intense focus of his skills.

The black fuzz vanished, and he locked eyes with Jenny as she stared back at him. Or, more accurately, as her perfectly detailed eyes, frozen in the last position she had been in, stared unblinkingly into his face.

Pale, dense, and subtly marbled, his assistant was now a perfect sculpture, as though someone had carved her out of a massive wheel of aged cheese with enough detail to get every last *eyelash* correct.

"I think that display was worth your little assistant's weight in cheese, don't you? Luckily, looks like you've already been paid!" Even as he swallowed his fury at Dur'Ax's words, the Ritualist didn't fail to carefully store away the sculpture. After taking a moment to regain control of himself, he rounded on the grinning maniac still waiting for him.

"Is she gone for good? Or will that send her back to respawn?"

"Oh, it's good she's gone." The Class Sage waited a moment after his non-answer, as if waiting for Joe to laugh. When he didn't get the reaction he had been hoping for, Dur'Ax sobered up and looked between each of the others, including his own ostensible allies in his next question. "Moving on, since his question failed to meet the standard of an inquiry to which I would give an answer. Do you know what's *in* this tower? Do *any* of you?"

"The... World Boss," a hesitant voice offered.

Joe spoke up, compelled to do so by some force the Sage

was emanating. “Forbidden knowledge. You want whatever it is that’s been hidden from your class.”

“Ah, he speaks. Good, good. Thought I broke you there.” Dur'Ax turned his smile to the Ritualist. “So, *so* close. But no, I don't care about something so *boring* as knowledge.”

The air above the man was suddenly filled with hundreds of skulls, all shapes and sizes, varieties and ages. All of them were polished and gleaming, their eyes filled with light as they stared down menacingly at the assemblage. A sheen of energy swept out of them, forming a flat plane that yet another skull projected images onto, a live performance from the penthouse of the Inverted Tower.

“First, I was *asked* to be here. I accepted only because it just so happens that my goals align with hers, at least enough for us to work together for now.” The Class Sage’s tongue flipped across his lips, teeth chattering slightly as he shook with excitement. “No, there’s something truly unique here that I’ve been after for a *very* long time. In order to complete my collection, I need the rarest skull of them all...”

“...and there’s only one Gnome I can possibly take it from.”

CHAPTER FORTY-TWO

"*Mmm.* I truly appreciate your haircut." Dur'Ax spoke with gentle words, though they echoed through the entirety of the vast area as he approached Joe. "Your baldness allows me to observe the contours of your skull and appreciate it the way it *should* be admired, even before the fleshy bits are properly scraped away. Exquisite. I do hope more people take after your example in the future."

The Class Sage calmly strolled toward the downed Ritualist, smashing through his barriers as if they didn't exist. In front of an entity like this, they may as well not have. Gripping Joe by either shoulder, the man pulled him to his feet, then gave him a gentle pat with his left hand while he rubbed the top of Joe's head with the other. "Mmm. Yes. Now, where was I? Right! As you can see, the valiant defenders of this hidden location have been thoroughly subdued, and while it may have cost the lives of a few Skill Sages, no one's going to miss them overmuch. In fact, at the end of this, the next to ascend will *thank* us for removing the obstacles to their newfound power."

"They died... permanent deaths?" Sage Aranu gasped out, gritting his teeth as his words called attention over to him.

"Oh, *yes*. Not many methods of making that happen while someone's tower still stands, but doesn't it make sense that almost *all* of them are in the hands of the master of the Inverted Tower? He was a spectacular opponent, which makes him just *that* much more valuable as a trophy." The Class Sage's oversized smile stretched further as he gently tossed the skull in his left hand up and down. "*Almost* all of them. I've got my own little tricks up my sleeves. Heh. Can't have my little toys depreciating in value by respawning to put more in circulation, now can I?"

The projection shifted, almost imperceptibly at first, as the skulls rotated and breathed out thick vapor. When the image settled, those present were allowed to watch through a stolen viewpoint as though they were observing through someone else's eyesockets. A double lens effect generated nausea-inducing depth perception, though it shifted back and forth to add clarity and depth, until they were finally able to near-intimately view the horrifying scene at the Inverted Tower's tip.

Shifting curtains of vapor and light showed Mir and Nathaniel, broken and bloodied, each bound to a ring that had been driven into the ceiling of the penthouse office. Chains made of continuously undulating shadow wrapped their bodies tightly. Whoever was controlling the inky bindings wasn't foolish enough to only contain their elbows and ankles–no, every *inch* of both of the powerful people was fully contained, with spikes hovering a fraction of an inch from each of their eyes, an obvious promise of punishment should they thrash around too much.

"It's amazing how far Class Sage Banyan has managed to push his power." Dur'Ax kept one guiding hand on Joe's back as he forced him to walk toward the stairwell. "Would you believe he only managed to ascend in the last few years? His tower had been holding onto a Mythic Core for *ages*... but they could never find the pesky Sage holding the title. It was quite the mystery when the slot suddenly opened one day!"

"Yeah. Sounds about right," Joe grumbled as he realized

that, yet again, one of his previous foibles had come back to haunt him. Perhaps if he hadn't slain the warden back on Midgard, the Traditionalists wouldn't have had enough combat potential to strike out at this tower now. Still, what had happened in the past was done, and he had the feeling he should be far more concerned about the present. "Why are you taking me to them?"

"Don't you worry your pretty little head about the details. *She* said she needed you, since the others aren't cooperating." There was a momentary hesitation in the Class Sage's footsteps, nearly unnoticeable with how smoothly the man moved. "You are Joe the Ritualist, yes? You fit the description. Bald, overly intense? First level Codex-Keeper?"

He thought about lying, but seeing as not a single one of his allies was trying to step in and help him out of this mess, Joe knew that would only end up worse for him than if he remained polite, respectful, and honest. Still, his words were slow and measured. "Yes, that's me. Why-"

"Hush, hush." Dur'Ax dragged a finger across Joe's lips, making the Ritualist flinch back and sputter. "Let's not discuss this in front of the guests. When we're all done here, it would be for the best if she were able to slip back into anonymity. Abyss, look how well it's worked out for me! I can slip through a crowd without anyone noticing, and all I need to do is leave my skulls in my storage. Then they think I've been gone for a hundred years... it's a good reminder, youngster."

Joe was poked in the center of his forehead three times, each corresponding with the Class Sage trying to punctuate his words. "Pay. *Attention.* To the people around you."

"Uhm. Yes, sir?"

"You'll go far in life if you survive the day." Dur'Ax beamed at him just before gripping Joe under his armpit and knees, lifting him into a princess carry. The Class Sage hopped over the edge of the stairwell as the Ritualist's face burned with embarrassment, the wind whistling past them as they dropped like a stone. They descended all the way to the penthouse floor of the tower and, through some machination Joe couldn't quite grasp, their inertia vanished entirely just before reaching the bottom.

Skill offered-

"Don't. You. *Dare.* System." the Ritualist hissed through clenched teeth, dismissing the notification before it could truly appear.

The Class Sage gently set Joe down then motioned forward in a casual manner, knowing the mere Master wouldn't truly be able to oppose him. "In we go, now!"

Though he'd been in the penthouse only a couple of times, Joe had started to become somewhat familiar with its layout. Now, with the desks overturned, the books that had been carefully set out on shelves shredded, their bindings torn off and tossed to the side, chairs little more than splinters, and streaks on the windows where someone had clearly tried to break through, there was very little remaining of the previously cozy office.

Joe tried not to show his distress at the way his feet splashed through the shallow puddle of blood slowly widening across the floor, nor how intense his gut clenched at seeing his mentors slowly swaying back and forth, suspended from rings in the center of the room and *generating* said puddle.

"You do have such a way with people, Class Sage Banyan!" Dur'Ax glanced at the floor, perking up slightly as he saw that the area around Joe was entirely clear of debris and free of blood, soft sparks forming whenever the sanguine fluid encroached into his space. He fell into step beside the Ritualist, his fastidiousness showing through with the action, even as he kept the conversation focused on his erstwhile ally. "The way the bindings bite into their joints? Their fingers are splayed and pinned to a point just shy of breaking? Well done."

Banyan inclined his head, though all Joe could see was a silhouette around a man-shaped deeper-than-black darkness. The silence was oppressive, broken only by the slight creaking of Mir's muscles and tendons as he strained against his bindings, constantly searching for the slightest weakness. Conversely, Nathaniel held perfectly still, seemingly content to let the situation play out however it would.

This meant it was entirely startling when Dur'Ax burst into a deep belly laugh, replying to something Joe couldn't hear. "Don't be like that! You know I admire your efficiency. It's inspired, really. Filthy, disgusting, messy, yes... but inspired. Nothing my new friend here can't handle, right?"

Joe staggered as he was clapped on the back, falling forward a foot or two and inadvertently evaporating a swath of blood. The Class Sage pointed at him excitedly, "*See*? Tell me, my delightfully chrome-domed prisoner. When we're all done here, how would you feel about taking a job with me? If we can figure out how to alter that little skill of yours to include a polishing effect on top of cleaning, I would never... *ever*... allow you to leave my service."

Absolutely certain he wouldn't be accepting *that* deal, but not sure how he'd be able to refuse without having his cranium ripped out and used for decoration, Joe decided to go with the uncomfortable flow and remain silent. Banyan apparently noticed this fact and commented on it... or perhaps Dur'Ax simply decided to ramble on as if he had.

"Give him time, he'll come around. Yes, I'm certain he's going to be far more helpful than these old bags of bones." He stuttered to a stop, his smile fading for an instant as his eyes sharpened dangerously. "No... I most certainly *wouldn't* say I'm late. Is it my fault if she needs to step out to use the facilities? Maybe she's just taking her time prowling about and hunting down the last of the tower's vermin? Perhaps she's pinching off a loaf and wouldn't appreciate you commenting on the fact that it's time for her 'quarterly review'?"

"*What-*?" The word was startled out of Joe, and he bit his tongue in consternation as he forced himself to resume his silence. It was too late, as the duo—some of the most powerful people under the deity rank—had returned their attention to him.

"Oh, fine. Since it's only us for the moment, why don't we just get started?" Dur'Ax gestured carelessly into the corner of the room. "The reason you're here, a piddly little *Master*, is because of your profession. You are therefore more useful to us alive than otherwise. There's only something like *five* of you, and only you three are on-planet currently. Mir has been actively detrimental to our sponsor's goals, and Nathaniel of the unique skull certainly isn't going to help us out. Not after the *last* time we told him we 'definitely wouldn't wake' the World Boss."

Unable to stop himself, Joe began to inquire, "Then you woke-"

"Yes, then we woke it up *immediately*." Dur'Ax chuckled under his breath. "You should've seen his face. Anyway, since then, he's really done a *fantastic* job on upgrading the defenses. He's spent hundreds upon hundreds of years layering enchantments, ritual circles, and all manner of forbidden curses and such from every class and profession he has access to... which is to say, *all* of them."

Pausing for a moment, the Class Sage nodded along as Banyan interjected, his shadowy hands flying back and forth as he spoke.

"Exactly right." Dur'Ax nodded at the window. "We'll get through eventually, but I'm estimating at least a decade of concentrated effort to punch a hole in the weakest point. That's just begging for people to raise armies and march against us over and *over* again. It gets tiresome exterminating thousands of people, only to have them come back like bent coppers. *Ugh*. Such a time suck. But that's where *you* come in! You're going to pull the lever for us."

"Uhh. *No*?" Joe immediately replied, even if it wasn't likely to be in his best interests to deny such powerful people to their faces.

"Tut, tut, don't be in such a hurry to condemn yourself. Banyan, give him a moment to chat with his people, would you? Who knows, maybe they'll advise him not to subject himself to endless torment. We're going to get in one way or another, so maybe they will divert him from the path of *pain*."

As the shadowy Sage began loosening the bindings around Nathaniel and Mir's mouths, Dur'Ax shot a glance at Joe that could only be described as fatherly disappointment. "That lever is exquisitely crafted–you should see what it did to poor Banyan's hands! If you think *these* leathery ol' punching bags look bad, you should see the charred ground beef wrapped around the splintered bone that is his palms at the moment."

"You see." The twisted man leaned forward as if planning to share a great secret with Joe. "The lever will only accept the touch of a Codex-Keeper. But, as far as I'm aware, it doesn't matter what level they are. You *just* came to this world. You *just* became a Codex-Keeper. You can't claim deep ties to the people of this world. Don't let a promise to someone you've barely had a chance to meet keep you trapped in a cage for the next decade."

"How about it, Nathaniel?" Dur'Ax turned to the Gnome, who was calmly swinging back and forth. "Are you going to force this child to bear the punishment for your choices? Or will you do the right thing and-"

"When everything is stripped away, all that remains is what you choose not to break." Even with the wounds covering his body, the shadows coiled around him tensing his bones to the snapping point, Nathaniel was able to maintain a calm, even speaking voice. "Remember your oath, Joe. I trust you will stay true to what you have sworn."

"Just..." letting out a wet raspberry noise, the Class Sage rolled his eyes at Nathaniel's words. "*Really*? How many times have you already had to go out and recollect your precious little books? Three? Four? It took you a hundred and fifty years at *most* last time. Sure, it might take longer for your successor to do so, but are you really going to... you know what, of course you are. How about you, Mirascible, ya old curmudgeon? What's your advice?"

"I advise..." Mir spat out a tooth before allowing himself a bloody grin–the first real smile Joe had ever seen on the man, and it *terrified* him, even though the Sage was completely bound at the moment. "I advise you to run, Dur'Ax-face. For when I get out of here, and I *will*, I'll devote every scrap of my existence to hunting you down. I will rip you apart piece by piece, destroying your treasures while *you* 'enjoy' the feeling of being bound and powerless to intervene. If you'd come after me without your dozens of lackey Sages ambushing me, we'd be having that conversation right *now*."

"I fully agree!" came the chipper reply. "Which is why I've never fought you directly. I've avoided you for centuries, and you've never been able to do an-y-thing about it. How could you? I'm *the* Skull Seer. Do you have any idea how easy it is to keep track of your location when every skull in the entire world is a lens I can peer through whenever I want? However spine-tingling your words to me are, I meant more... what would you advise your little *pet project* to do?"

Joe's blood ran cold at the thought of being an unwitting security camera for such a foul person as this.

"Same thing I've always told him." Mir harumphed at the thought of changing his ways, "Do what you wanna do, and deal with the consequences later. O'course, being powerful enough to deal with those consequences is a pretty important part of that. If he goes warlock on us, he can include *me* as a part of those consequences."

"Well, that was just entirely unhelpful," Dur'Ax grumbled as he turned back to Joe, waving his hand at his peer to re-gag the prisoners. "You're going to pull that lever for us, or–what in the *world* are you doing?"

"Heading to respawn. Gonna go get some help," Joe gasped out as his eyes flared with golden intensity, energy collecting around his head as he stared deeply within himself and did everything he could to comprehend the enchanted ritual circle Master Hilda Darling had used to bind him. Insight into the process was easy to acquire, especially with the twenty percent comprehension bonus his Omnivault skill had afforded him. "I'll *never-*"

Seeing as he was being wracked with immense pain, and could actively feel his heartbeat beating out-of-synch as the final 'warning' he would get about overloading the enchantment, Joe urged the system to keep the messages brief.

Congratulations! Enchanted Ritual Circles has reached the Master rank! Your insight into this skill has afforded you two options for evolution.

1. *Direct upgrade. Increased effects across the board.*
2. *Peerless Binding. An additional option added to your skill, which will grant you bonuses to enchantments binding people and objects. Specifically, curse making and breaking.*

Enchanted Ritual Circles (Master 0). Enchantments are no longer effects, they are commitments. No longer do you need to be concerned with equipping gear you find, as curses go out of their way to make themselves known to you, hoping you will transfer them to a far more powerful artifact than what they currently inhabit.

Effects:

1. *Governs the use of enchantments in the creation and execution of ritual circles.*
2. *Grants +1n% success and precision when using enchantments within ritual casting, where n = skill level.*
3. *All enchantments created specifically for Enchanted Ritual Circles are now 100% more likely to succeed in both stability and compatibility. Example: If the use of the enchanted ritual circle bound the ritual to a target, it will be 100% more difficult for the link to be broken.*
4. *All attempts to create, modify, suppress, or destroy curses originating from an item and actively affecting a person are 20% more likely to succeed. There is a 5% chance that a copy of a curse you create or destroy will be swallowed into a blank token, able to be used at your discretion.*

The skill has become singular in focus. All attempts to create enchanted items not for the express purpose of ritual use will automatically fail.

Quest complete: Master Ritualist. As you have embarked on the path of a Class Sage by raising all your personal Core Class skills to the Master rank with no sign of slowing down, you have proven you are worthy of being called a True Master Ritualist! Core Class skills at the Master rank: 5/5.

Reward: +1 to all Core Class skills. Bonus growth modifier granted to whichever Core Class Skill first enters the Grandmaster rank.

Alchemical Rituals (Master 0 → Master I)

Enchanted Ritual Circles (Master 0 → Master I)

Magical Matrices (Master I → Master II)

Ritual Circles (Master VIII → Master IX)

Ritualistic Forging (Master I → Master II)

All Characteristics +25, except Karmic Luck, for increasing 5 skills in the Master Rank! Excess Characteristics deferred!

His heartbeat slowed, then stopped, the enchantment directly stopping his heart and slaying him without giving Joe a chance to cancel the effect or heal himself. Just as his vision faded, a new voice rang out in the room as thousands of golden hooks appeared from nowhere and tore into his astral body.

"That won't do."

You have died!

Joe blinked, ready to rush off and get Sage Pete to call on anyone he knew... only to realize he was still staring at the destroyed office, though now with a mildly annoyed Dur'Ax standing behind a newcomer who barely reached chest level on the man.

"Hello, customer. *You'll* be here."

CHAPTER FORTY-THREE

"*Beth*?" Joe tried to reconcile the waifish Nyanderthal—who sold flowers, chocolate, and coffee, someone he'd never been able to get more than a few words out of in their many interactions—with a mastermind controlling events behind the scenes across Vanaheim.

"When I'm not in my role as a simple salesperson, I go by my real name..." the Nyanderthal replied in her usual deadpan monotone. "*Liz*."

"So... *Elizabeth*?"

"I haven't gone by that name in years." Her fluffy orange tail was twitching back and forth, the only signs of agitation Joe had ever been able to discern beyond the flicking of her ears. Her eyes bored into him, lacking hostility and warmth both. "Where did you hear it? Was it Queen *Cleocatra*?"

"No? That's, um, a pretty standard name?" Joe's eyes flickered from the cat in humanoid form to his mentor hanging behind her, endlessly struggling against his bindings, though the action was as futile as ever. Then his gaze roved to Dur'Ax, trying to figure out if he was being messed with. He wouldn't put it past the Skull Seer to try to mess with his head–that seemed to fit with the image he'd formed of the Class Sage.

"Don't look at them. If you need something, I guess I'll-" Liz took a deep breath, closing her eyes momentarily before opening them, glaring at Joe as if he were the one to make her fall back into her usual speech patterns. "Don't look at them. Look at *me*."

The Nyanderthal began pacing in a small semicircle around Joe, inspecting him from multiple angles. Each step was light, seemingly just as carefree as you'd expect from someone who sold things to make other people happy. Unable to help himself as anger built in his chest, the Ritualist finally unleashed his thoughts in a torrent of words. "Why are you trying to destroy the planet? I don't get it! *He* doesn't even care, one way or another-"

Joe thrust his hand at Dur'Ax–whose eyes glittered with anger at the Ritualist's crude motions–before returning his attention to the short cat-woman who'd orchestrated this disaster, "-and why would you care if people can go farther into the universe on the bifrost? What loyalty do you have to any of the towers?"

"Why would *I* care?" Her ears swiveled back and forth as though she were shaking her head in disappointment. "You are the single most aggravating person I've had the misfortune of dealing with in over a century. Do you know that, if we had managed to have a single positive interaction, we would be friends right now? But no! You walk around wrapped in a pillar of blinding radiance, with so much Karmic Debt owed to you that you make *delicate* work all but impossible."

Done with being polite, no matter how powerful these people were, Joe full on *sneered* at her implied accusation. "Oh, so it's *my* fault you decided to kill countless people and destroy the homes of millions? All I ever did was not buy your-"

"No, it's not your fault. But you *are* the reason my plans had to be accelerated so greatly. Otherwise, I would have kept the Sage's Council and balance for decades." Her lips pressed together, and the Nyanderthal took a sharp breath to regulate her anger.

Despite everything, Joe found himself wanting to know what she was getting at. "Why couldn't you have just accepted a coffee from me, instead of intentionally snubbing my efforts by summoning your Elemental and drinking the exact thing I was offering? Clearly your knowledge of karmic bonds runs deep."

"Well, the joke's on you; I don't know *anything*," Joe shot back instantly, only then realizing that perhaps he shouldn't have been so smug about *not* understanding what she was getting at. "I mean-"

Her tail snapped to the side, as though to wave away his 'lies'. "You're in cahoots with Queen Cleocatra, so I care not how much ignorance you claim. Pretend all you want; it changes nothing. Karma doesn't care about *intent*, only linkage. It's obvious you've been instructed in at least the basics, or else you would've never have been so careful to dodge every attempt I made. Then, to make jokes at my expense, turning my shame and fears into *wordplay*? Pah. You want to know why I want to destroy this world?"

Joe ignored her question, shooting back a sharp, "I should've realized you were evil the first time someone told me you hated puns!"

"Well? Do you want to know the real reason? You've touched on it already." Liz shook her head, swallowing hard as a tear trickled down her cheek, falling onto the cream accents of her forest green dress.

Fully unprepared for such a sudden shift in emotional state, Joe's jaw dropped, feeling as though he'd taken a sucker punch to the gut. "No–*what*? You...? I mean, yeah, go ahead and let me know. In excruciating detail even, so we can give the Ascensionists as much time as possible to get here and put an end to this."

"As you wish." Liz took a few shallow breaths, glancing away then back at the Ritualist. "Lifetimes ago, I was exiled because I refused to be content with sitting on cushions, batting at the karma of the people who served us as though playing with toys. The Nyanderthals refuse to progress on their own, getting rid of those among us who wish for more, who want to step into the light. To become the rulers of the cosmos that we *should* be. No other race can influence karma, shape it, and wield it in ways that allow even the weakest of us to control or defeat the strongest of opponents... and we can do this from *birth.*"

Joe remained silent, though Dur'Ax had pulled out a large handkerchief and was dabbing at the corner of his eyes, as though the story were causing him to openly weep. Liz followed his glance and scowled at the Skull Seer, rolling her eyes as she shifted to face Joe fully. "I helped one person, welcoming him into my little shop and giving him the tools he needed to become a Sage. He was the best of people, and I was *exiled* for my transgression."

"You're the creator of the-" Joe hesitated, realizing even as he spoke that he wasn't quite understanding. "-the healing spell that allows people to harvest Life Debts?"

Head tilting slightly, she eyed him with the barest hint of interest. "It seems Nathaniel has been more open about sharing his forbidden knowledge in recent years. No. I did not create it, but the first Sage of Healing modeled it after my natural spell form: *Orange Cat Energy*. He succeeded beautifully, and I traveled with him all the way until *Cleocatra* caught up to both of us, eradicating him with a single strike of True Damage and all but exiling me to a higher world that was even *less* developed, on pain of death."

The Nyanderthal leaned closer, her normally bland expression tinged with loneliness and nostalgia. "You asked me what loyalty I have to any of the towers? The answer is, unsurprisingly, none. There is no tower here representing my class, and I am the only of my kind on this planet. Immediately, and for the first time, I became a permanent *outdoor cat.* It was just me and my little cart kiosk for decades, until Mak and his cheese wagon came along. That experience might've even been positive, if it wasn't for the stench of cheese endlessly wafting over me, no matter how I tried to position myself."

"Believe it or not, Joe, I don't particularly care about destroying this world." Her shoulders shrugged incrementally. "It's just the only way for me to have a home once more. Should the bifrost open with the world intact, it will connect to Asgard. But, if the World Snake awakens and gets out of the way, the current connection point will relocate to the vast plane of Hel. I'll be able to be among my kind once more, as all of the exiles from previous generations were sent there. Only *I* had the misfortune of being exiled just as Vanaheim reformed."

"There's no other way?" Joe tossed his hands in the air. "Once we open the path to Asgard, what's the *next* stop? Couldn't it *be* Hel?"

"There's no way for me to know, now is there?" The deadpan response took the wind right out of Joe's argument. "I'm not going to wait around for who knows how long for something that might not ever come to fruition. I've been building my karmic bonds with the people of this world for eight lifetimes, carefully selecting who I thought would eventually become the most powerful people among them: dozens of Class Sages, scores of Skill Sages, and an endless array of Grandmasters who can't take the final step. I've pruned away dead weight, permanently removing Sages who wouldn't accept me and opening the path for Grandmasters to ascend."

"No, that's not possible." Joe shook his head firmly, believing he had finally found a hole in her story. "Even if you got your hooks in them when they were Novices, to become a Sage, they had to have their Karmic Debt cleared."

"Their *debt*, yes." Her agreement somehow didn't make the Ritualist feel any better. "But I didn't *want* them to be indebted to me. I simply wanted enough positive interactions and touch points that I could make them choose to do what I wanted of their own free will, or at least allow me to influence them directly. It's all the same in the end. When the bond has been broken, each of them will firmly believe they made their choices on their own. None of them will even remember the flower girl who dragged them along by their nose, kicking and screaming where necessary."

As she finished speaking, the Nyanderthal allowed the silence to stretch for a few long moments, lifting her hand and dramatically wiping away another tear. "While you may not agree with me, do you at least *understand* the story I've given you?"

"I mean... yeah?" Joe reached up and rubbed the back of his neck, deeply uncomfortable with how this had all gone down. He almost preferred getting irradiated by the bleed-off of the Sages' attacks to this type of emotional appeal. "I don't know what I'm supposed to do with this information, though?"

"Well..." Liz sniffled, looking at him with pleading eyes. "It would be really nice if you'd go and throw that lever for me."

"Haa..." Joe looked over at Nathaniel and Mir, still trussed up and dangling like fish on a line. "I *guess*? Not like there's really any other options."

Making his way to the oversized lever, which had originally been positioned behind Nathaniel's desk, Joe reached for the simple machine... only to realize it wasn't simple in the *slightest.*

Cheese conveyor control sequence engaged.

Subject soul signature confirmed. Status: Codex-Keeper.

Warning: Control rod operation restricted. Insert Codex Key to override.

The air around the lever bloomed with sigils and resonance tests, the entire mechanism barely holding back from obliterating his fleshy form at the last moment—even then only begrudgingly. It was obvious to Joe that this heavily Enchanted item had intelligence and a will of its own, and for its entire life, the magical item had been told it should never be flipped for any reason. Pulling out his Codex Key, he clicked it into place... and the first layer of defenses accepted his authority to overrule its personal desires.

Caution!

Minimum Mana investment required to charge actuators: 100,000.

Stamina requirement estimation for holding lever in place while system reconfigures: 20,000.

You have been authorized to pull the lever.

Joe gripped the top of the lever, squeezing the handle and pressing the grip before slowly beginning to shove the bar toward the opposite side. A shocking amount of pain ripped through him as his resources dropped like a stone. His mana managed to keep up with the drain, but his Stamina approached zero, even before the mechanism had been pressed a full quarter of the way. As it hit rock bottom, the bar snapped back, sending the Ritualist staggering away with aching hands.

"Why did you *stop*?" Liz's inquiry came out as a harsh whisper, pure disappointment erupting from her at seeing her goal—so close to coming to fruition—falter at the last moment.

"I ran out of Stamina." The Ritualist glanced down at his hands, a thread of confusion worming through his mind. "I have a skill that allows me to regenerate Stamina, but I need to channel mana to do it."

"*Please* tell me you have some way to make that happen." The orange-haired lady cupped her face in her hands, though she perked up as Joe slowly answered in the affirmative, at least a little.

"Maybe?" As though he were in a dream, Joe reached into his codpiece and pulled out his Eclipsing Aurora Chalice, the altar-shaped stabilizer dropping to the floor with a **bang**. The gemstone lattice was still shining brightly with absorbed mana, as he hadn't found a place to safely vent it yet. "I just need to pull the mana from this, but... why would I?"

Skill increase: Mental Manipulation Resistance has reached the Expert rank!

Mental Manipulation Resistance (Expert 0). You have reached a point with this skill that dying no longer costs you experience, but instead returns more than you would have lost.

Effect:

1. *Gains 300% skill experience until the Expert rank.*

2. *Grants 10 + 1n% direct resistance to mental manipulation.*
3. *Protects against mental-impacting effects such as fear, mind control, magical seduction, and other intrusive mental influences.*
4. *Grants 2.1n% reduced experience loss upon death.*
5. *All death-affinity skills grow incrementally faster (variable).*

The shock of reaching the Expert rank with his most concerning skill, alongside its automatic protection against mind controlling effects, cleared the last lingering doubts from Joe's thoughts. He could feel the enchantment holding him together become fully saturated, but there was no handy-dandy attempt to whisk him off to respawn–Hilda must have assumed that, if he got to this point, he was doing so intentionally.

Without hesitating for a moment, Joe *slapped* at the chalice, hoping to knock it over and detonate it alongside himself. Dur'Ax caught his hand halfway to the delicate instrument, pulling him back and setting him down almost gently. "Close one! If I hadn't been watching you so intently, I wouldn't have been able to cross the room so quickly. It wasn't very nice of you to try and destroy my skull trophy like that, Joe-Joe. What happened, Liz?"

"He accepted the gift of my story. I guess it just wasn't enough of a bond to keep him working at the task I set for him. Still, it should've worked just long enough to toss it; I didn't realize he had such low Stamina capacity." Liz grumbled low in her throat. "I suppose we'll have to do this the hard way. What a waste of a monologue."

Dur'Ax kept a tight grip on Joe, turning him to face the Nyanderthal as she walked over to stand next to Nathaniel.

"Hello. Welcome to my little shop. I have flowers, chocolate, coffee... one more carrot, and one more stick." She lifted her hand to be level with Nathaniel's neck. "You are *going* to pull that lever, or I am going to remove this Gnome from existence permanently."

Sharp claws grew from the tips of her fingers, glowing with

a scintillating light and filled with the weight of True Damage waiting to be inflicted.

Even so, the Ritualist held firm. "You're planning to kill him either way."

"No, that's now the stick," Liz rebutted him blandly. "If you do this for me, I'll make sure he lives. I'll swear this on my power and everything I hold dear. If I don't follow through, I'll be destroyed."

A soft system notification ran through Joe's mind, and he knew without looking that it confirmed what she was saying.

"That's not our *deal*, Liz!" Dur'Ax removed his hands from Joe, subtly repositioning himself to charge at the Nyanderthal. "I get a Gnome skull. That's the price of my involvement!"

"There *is* another," she calmly informed him, and Joe realized Nathaniel had gone as still as the Class Sage when she casually handed out this information. "Nikolai Kepler, Techno Class Sage. I know where his real body is."

"He's a myth," Dur'Ax declared with a subtle disbelief coming through his own words. "A one-man mobile tower?"

"Nope. We'll talk. Later." Liz returned her attention to Joe. "Choose. One little planet gets destroyed, and everyone here respawns on Hel as the bifrost reconfigures. You and Nathaniel go out and hunt down your precious books. It's all been done before. Barely an inconvenience at this point. Or, he's gone for good. So. What's it going to be?"

"Carrot... or stick?"

CHAPTER FORTY-FOUR

"I'm out." Joe triggered his pre-channeled Beam to Bifrost, becoming enveloped in power and letting out a deep sigh of relief as the world blurred around him. The interior of Vanaheim shot past... and the power around him burst into sparkles as he landed back in the penthouse of the Inverted Tower.

"*Cuzztomer...*" Liz let out a long, slow breath to fully showcase her disappointment in his mental capabilities. "If I can grab your astral body and force you to respawn here, what could possibly make you assume you'd be able to use a *spell* to get away? I'll be here. *You'll* be here. At least until I decide we no longer need you, and my patience is wearing *thin*."

"Had to give it a try," Joe muttered as he softly scuffed his shoes across the ground, though his eyes were on the rapidly fading golden hooks that had caught him and dragged him back. Only because he was able to clearly see them digging into his eyeballs did the Ritualist realize that they weren't *hooks* at all—they were perfect replicas of a cat's claw. "Orange Cat Energy, huh?"

"I'd love to tell you all about it." Her monotone sounded slightly *off*, and just before she could begin explaining something Joe was wondering about–and therefore create a fresh bond between them–he reached up and flicked the bell nestled in the nape of his neck.

**Chime.*

The silvery tone echoed through the room, an authoritative demand to the world around them. Joe felt a soul-deep sense of relief as the invisible weight he carried at all times, the Karmic Debt between him and a deity, vanished for the moment. For her part, Liz stumbled backward as if physically slapped, looking at the Ritualist in horror which quickly shifted to calculation.

"That's an impressive trick." Resuming her stance, she let her claws reach for Nathaniel's neck. "But a trick is all it is. I could work with you, ya know. No more need for trinkets such as that. You have so much potential, so much debt you can leverage, I could make you unstoppable. Never before have I found someone with what amounts to endless capability for waging war using karma as True Damage. You could control Vanaheim without tapping into a *fraction* of what you're owed."

Seeing Joe's lack of reaction, Liz merely blinked a few times, letting off a soft sneeze of annoyance. "You've probably already turned down offers from the queen, haven't you? But I wouldn't give you the watered-down version, like she would. I'd let you become whatever you wanted to be. Not only that, but I can see that she has a debt to you as well... you know what that means, don't you? It means she won't be able to hunt you down, like all of the other people I've trained over the years. No sauntering up and slicing you into five chunks simultaneously, never able to fully reconstitute yourself without immense outside assistance. Eventually, *no one* could stop you."

Keeping his hands carefully still, and making no sudden motions, Joe replied to the cat somewhat morosely, knowing she wasn't going to like his answer. "Sorry. I just don't care about controlling people like that. I want to make *magic* do what I want, and I'm already making that happen for myself. The power I get? That's *my* power. Eventually, there will be none of it that's borrowed or stolen, and *that* is what I want."

"Haa... another *luddite*, unwilling to make the optimal choice and move forward." Liz coated her claws in karmic energy once more, tone shifting to cajoling. "One more try? The world will come back; it always does. Once the World Snake is destroyed, Vanaheim will form again. You just need–you didn't know? Do you really not understand that all of the 'towers of Vanaheim' are simply the spines along the World Snake's body, piercing up through the dirt and stone that has collected on it? What you see at the core of the world is merely its head, at the center of its coils. It is literally the '*world*' snake. When it wakes up, it will uncoil, then travel through space until it finds a world to try and convert into cheese."

"Is *that* why all the stone has that oddly organic look to it?" He hissed softly, eyes going distant. "Is that why it's not possible to build a real building on Vanaheim? It makes so much sense! Oh, *wait*, Nathaniel already told me all of that, which means your attempt to create another bond between us is useless."

Seeing that Joe was looking mightily pleased with himself, she heaved a frustrated sigh. "I see. Fine then. Why bother explaining things to you, when you're not receptive to the bond by choice, and my attempts to force the connection are blocked by your owner's collar? I guess if I can't convince you in any other way, brute force will have to work. No more warnings. If you aren't going to do what I tell you, Dur'Ax collects a Gnome skull trophy. Make your choice, and make it now."

"Tell her no," the Class Sage whispered encouragingly in Joe's ear, causing the Ritualist to shiver–he had all but forgotten the man was standing behind him. "Once I have what I came here for, I've no other reason to stick around. Better odds for you!"

"*Dur'Ax*." The gentle yowl from Liz shook the air around them.

"I mean, *yeah*, make your choice, Ritualist!" The Class Sage waggled his eyebrows at Joe, who could only listlessly stare at two of the people he respected most on this world. They swayed back and forth, small droplets of blood still pattering to the floor every few seconds.

Slowly running his tongue over his lips as he furiously thought through his options, Joe hesitantly reached out and put his hand on the lever–this time fully under his own power. Watching him move, and seeing that he'd finally given in, Liz practically purred with delight and allowed her claws to recede slightly away from Nathaniel's neck.

Caution!

Minimum mana investment required to charge actuators: 100,000.

Stamina requirement estimation for holding lever in place while system reconfigures: 20,000.

You have been authorized to pull the lever.

"It's not like I can fight them. At least, I can't win in a direct fight." Joe felt the edge of despair touch him, yet at the same moment, another memory invaded his thoughts: going head to head with a different creature he couldn't defeat, who was able to take all of his attacks and shrug them off without any seeming damage. "It's the whale all over again... but... I *beat* that thing, didn't I?"

The memory of that fight struck him, how he'd gone to such great lengths to prepare the battlefield to be in his favor, taking into account its capabilities and still needing to experiment with attacking it at all angles until he had finally found a *single* weak point. "Maybe I don't need to defeat them. Maybe I just need to hit them where it hurts only a single time, but hard enough that the bonds between them shatter? It's obvious the alliance they have is *fragile* at best."

As the mountainously heavy lever reached the twenty-five percent position, a plan finally came together. Stamina bottoming out, Joe reached for the gemstone lattice of the Eclipsing Aurora Chalice. His fingers brushed against it, only for his wrist to be firmly grasped by Dur'Ax, who simply held him in place to make sure he couldn't tip it over, all while keeping a benign smile on his face. "Feel free to channel, but just know I won't actively destroy my relationship with her to get what I want just a little bit faster. You may not know this, but..."

He leaned close, his breath dry and surprisingly fresh as it washed over Joe's ear and into his nostrils. "...she's far more terrifying than she lets on."

"Yeah, no, I got that." The tips of the Ritualist's fingers activated the power venting option, and the collected mana began unloading directly into his flesh. For the first time, Joe activated the Jade Breath-Plundering Doctrine. Power *screamed* into him, and the Ritualist simply breathed it in, allowing his mana circuits to convert slightly more than half of the influx directly into Stamina.

His resource pools filled up with inevitable swiftness as the lever creeped into its opposite position. Klaxon calls began sounding, alarms going off throughout the tower and the core of the planet, warning of the impending awakening of the Jörmungandr. Shrieking penguins added their voices to the cacophony, thrilled to have their Kaiju coming back to them, readying themselves to cling to its body as it swam through the void of space.

Joe tuned all of it out, for the first time intentionally working to gain a new skill in order to destroy the Enchanted Ritual Circle connecting his body, mana, and Akashic Record into one unified whole.

With the Enlightenment energy washing through his mind and increasing his comprehension by twenty percent, his Karmic King trait allowing him an easier time understanding the intricacies of karma itself, and most notably his tribulation, Paradoxical Heart Demon, lowering the requirements to gain *any* skill by a full ninety-five percent... he pushed to make the final leap of understanding needed to learn how to inflict True Damage.

As the lever passed the halfway mark, he succeeded.

Skill offered: Absolute Conversion (Novice I). This isn't meant for you. This is a racial skill exclusive to naturally born Nyanderthals-

"Accept!" Not bothering with any of the additional details, Joe took the skill. It settled into place within his soul, causing a cascading chain reaction as every last drop of alchemical reagents in his tattoos–from those in the tips of his fingernails, all the way to the last cell in the marrow of his bones–became unmoored. Shimmering, scintillating energy wafted off of him like steam as Master Darling's enchantment work was destroyed and began dissipating harmlessly into the air around him.

"Awaken, great serpent..." Liz casually intoned while looking out the bay window. "...and get out of my *way*, so I can finally leave this forsaken planet. I guess I don't *want* to be here."

"What are you doing?" Dur'Ax's sharp voice yanked Liz's attention back to the Ritualist, just as the last dregs of enchanted energy faded into the ambient mana.

"Making sure I can't help you. Can't supply mana to throw the lever if I can't access my mana." Joe pulled a taglock out of storage, groped between his fingers, and slammed his head down to try and jam it through his own eye.

Liz *moved.*

She plucked the incredibly sharp needle away then swished it around and jammed it through the back of Joe's hand still gripping the lever, neatly missing the plier-design handle while pinning his middle finger to his palm. As he grunted with pain, both from the taglock going through him, as well as his forehead bouncing off the top of the lever instead of the sharpened spike, Liz grabbed Joe's chin and forced him to look into her eyes.

"Just because I work with power they don't recognize on Vanaheim doesn't mean I'm not still a *Sage*, Joe. Stop all this needless suffering. Even if you had managed to *almost* kill yourself, I can easily heal you through whatever damage you can inflict. Just... keep... *pushing.*"

Gripping his wrist and the back of his elbow, she gently yet implacably began adding her strength to his efforts. No matter how he struggled, the Ritualist may as well have not had that arm attached to him, for all he could move it on his own. As he stopped struggling against her, the fight going out of him entirely, the Nyanderthal let go and stepped back. "There you go. Almost done."

Mana still flooded through Joe, and he considered trying to bend it to his own self-destructive purposes, but when Liz pulled the pin out of his hand while simultaneously healing the hole it had created, the Ritualist realized she was serious about having potent restorative capabilities. Still unwilling to give up, but not knowing what else to do, Joe turned his attention to the only distraction he had available–the information on the new skill he'd just gained.

Absolute Conversion (Novice I). This technique is meant to be incompatible with anyone not a naturally-born Nyanderthal. It should never be able to be learned, only inherited. Through a series of events that will doubtlessly be studied for generations to come, you have managed to learn how to convert power into its absolute output form. Right now, the process by which you will do this is crude, violent, and inefficient… but it will work.

Effect:

You may expend the following resources to generate n points of True Damage, which you may apply to any weapon or damaging spell. True Damage ignores all mitigation, resistance, immunity, and conditional defenses.

- *1,000 mana*
- *1,000 stamina*
- *100 points of Karmic Luck*

Any damage following the True Damage starter will be resisted by 1% of the standard resistances, increasing by 3.14x per .001 seconds until reaching 100%.

Caution: It is considered a war crime of the highest order to use True Damage against any member of Unified, Shattered, or Hidden races to erase their ego. Punishment is enforced by… this part is meant to be redacted, but since you already know, the enforcers are Nyanderthals.

Strong recommendation: don't let them know you can use this.

With a blink of his eyes, he checked his status and nearly cried out in relief when he saw that his Karmic Luck was still inflated. "I have one shot at this-"

With such a glut of power being channeled through him, Joe activated Absolute Conversion with ease. A tiny dot of pearlescent energy appeared, nearly fading before he realized how to actually connect with it. As the lever reached the ninety percent mark, the world drowning under the echoes of alarms and shrieking birds, the Ritualist pulled out his Deific Ritual Orb of Karmic Luck and wrapped the pearlescent energy around it.

Then he just let orb slip between his fingers as he released his grip.

The intensely black ball, its silvery sparkles brightly reflecting the sheen of True Damage on its surface, landed on the lever and simply went *through* it.

True Damage cut through all of the protections, unraveled the contingencies, and simultaneously destroyed every safeguard Nathaniel had woven into this most important switch over millennia. Runes went dead, clauses sparked and burned, curses forgot themselves and simply ceased to exist. The orb punched through all of it, wedging itself into the mechanism at the base... only for the collapsing magics to rebound, irreversibly *detonating* the remainder of the control point into shrapnel that only slowly came to a stop, scattered around the penthouse.

As for the orb, it simply remained in place, undamaged and content with how things had gone.

Every alarm silenced at once, but it took the penguins a few moments of confused squawking before they went quiet as well. Soon, the only remaining sound in the penthouse was the increasingly labored breathing of the orange-haired Nyanderthal. "You...! You *foul* person! *No*! You've just added *years* to my imprisonment, I-!"

Her yowling outburst culminated in Liz flashing over to

stand next to Nathaniel, tearing the shadows away from his face with shining claws and leaving the startled Gnome fully visible to the Ritualist. "Pay for your foolishness! I hope oblivion was *worth it*!"

Joe met Nathaniel's eyes at that moment, only to realize they were filled with pride. The master of the Inverted Tower had less than a heartbeat to incline his chin fractionally, his last gesture of respect to his newest protégé before a shining claw swiped through him.

Liz caught the Gnome's small head as it tumbled toward the ground, tossing it in underhand to Dur'Ax in the same motion. Claws still extended from her hand, she took a threatening step toward the Ritualist.

"Got what *I* came here for!" The Class Sage lifted Nathaniel's head in the light, turning it back and forth to find the best angle for incision to remove all of the useless flesh still coating it. "*Toodles*!"

A hurricane-force wind flowed through the room as Dur'Ax made his escape, nearly bowling Joe over. As the Ritualist tried to get back to his feet, he suddenly went very still, watching as the Nyanderthal's deadly claws came to a halt mere inches from his nose. "Why? Why couldn't you have just done your *job*? It was nearly over. I would've let you all walk away... I *promised*. Then you destroyed everything I've been working for. *Centuries*, *Joe*! All wasted... at the very last moment. Give me a reason."

"Well. I couldn't physically *do* it until right at the end." Joe sat up straight, determined to go out on his own terms. "It sucks that he died. I'll hunt you for that *forever*. But I'd make the same choice again in a heartbeat. After all, you know what they say..."

"... better Nate than lever."

CHAPTER FORTY-FIVE

"I–you–*no*!" Liz recoiled as if Joe's words had physically struck her, her motions violent and uncontrolled, nothing like the measured, perfectly planned movements and expressions she had worn like a mask until now. Entirely distraught, her plans crumbling around her, the final little jab landing was too much. Sinking almost to her knees, her claws swiped through the floor of the penthouse, the wooden facade of the floor screeching as she tore gouges through it.

Coming to a halt, her breath came in sharp, uneven bursts. Her mouth opened in a snarl bordering on a scream, all sharp teeth and anger. Shoulders hunching, ears flat against her head, and tail lashing, she finally **hissed** out a few intelligible words. "No. *No*! You... this is your fault. Heh. *Ha-ha*! At least you're *useless* to me now. I can finally be rid of you!"

She whirled into motion, back to a nearly upright standing position, but slightly hunched as she stomped toward him, a cat playing with her food. Her bright green eyes were glowing like a bush on fire as her face melted back into an intense, almost neutral expression. "I offered you everything. Power. Freedom. Purpose. And you...? You mock the loss of everything I've worked for with wordplay? Even at the expense of your slain friend?"

A system notification chimed just then, and Joe was about to ignore it, as per usual, when he saw that it was a subtle change from the running tally he had set up to run in the corner of his vision.

You have gained a Mastery Merit! Source: Inscription Momentum.

Current Merits earned from skill source: Inscription Momentum. (1/100)

Congratulations! You have earned 100 total Mastery Merits for the first time! You may now apply your accumulated Mastery Merits to any skill which meets the following requirements.

1) Is at Master level nine.

2) You have achieved Enlightenment with.

3) You have at least three other skills at the Master rank per skill you are attempting to Enlighten.

Skills meeting this criteria, and ready to become Enlightened: Coalescent Fusion, Loremaster, Mana Dominion, Ritual Circles.

As his death approached, it seemed to Joe as though his mind was moving hundreds of times faster than usual. Thought became instinct as he realized he might have a chance, however slim, to make it to respawn with his body, mind, and Akashic Record... somewhat intact, seeing as Liz's claws were coated in the energy of *permanent* destruction. Without being able to make a conscious choice, his base instincts immediately grasped the bundle of Mastery Merits that had accumulated and pushed it into the only skill that had been with him since the very beginning:

Ritual Circles.

As the merits were applied, the world around him *paused.* The gleaming claws were fractions of an inch from his throat, the wild-eyed Nyanderthal caught in mid-pounce—even her Sage-rank capability to move as quick as lightning being no match for the machinations of the system itself.

The silence and stillness were broken as the system made its determination, screens flashing into existence and vanishing, a message finally coming together and writing itself out in midair. Joe felt his heart leap as he heard the voice of the system speak the information into existence directly in his mind.

Evaluation in progress. Aggregating Mastery Merits. Source verification...

A familiar face popped into Joe's mind. Gage, Master of *The Bounding Step of the Unburdened*, a variant evolution of the Jumping skill Joe had been trying to impart. As soon as he recognized the source, Gage's image vanished, replaced by another. Each shift was a representation of more than just a number. It was weight and intent, the moments when someone had teetered on the edge of failure, only to manage to take the final step forward because of how the things he had taught *Inspired* them.

One hundred people, each of them lingering in his thoughts even as the system moved on. It wasn't attempting to be sentimental, merely thorough. Finally, the last merit was exactly in line with Joe's expectations–showing Sage Pete rattling off a series of rituals with manic glee writ large on his face, the moment freezing just as the light of Inspiration washed out of the Sage's eyes only seconds prior to Joe beginning this process.

Pete's image, caught just at the start of a deep, excited belly laugh, slowly faded away as the system resumed its decision making.

...complete. First criteria met: Master of Masters.

A Grandmaster is not defined by solitary existence but instead by propagated Mastery. You have influenced others to better themselves and have often borne the cost of their success. Now you reap the rewards of the sacrifices you have made for them, both great and small.

Second criteria evaluation in progress: Foundational Integration goal.

Title chosen to integrate: Emperor of Mana.

Tribulation inflicted: Paradoxical Heart Demon.

To rule is to trust enough to delegate. To expand is to sacrifice, as accepting all offerings is to erode the domain.

Mana bequeathed to others: Greater than 5,000. Rating: Excellent.

Skills refused: Greater than 50. Rating: Superb.

Tribulation defeated. All requirements to acquire skills or spells are returned to their original difficulty. All skills and spells that have been rejected during the tribulation process become 110% more difficult to reacquire.

Hidden objective achieved.

Joe's mind went wild as he saw the final line, which had formed, then went perfectly still, as if allowing him to savor the moment. By the time the next words crawled across his vision, the Ritualist would have been salivating if he had any control over his body.

Dual path resolution achieved for trait: Unsuppressed Growth. The lingering resentment of the path unchosen has been dispersed.

Treated to a vision of what felt like the distant past, Joe watched as he chose his mind over his body, enhancing his flesh with each expansion of his mental Characteristics. Yet now, he was able to see as a slight shimmer of darkness began infusing his cells and even managed to understand what it meant, thanks to the clarity of the system's guidance. The obligatory enhancement of his body stats as his mind became evermore potent, when he hadn't pushed his body to its limits in order to grow, had built up into a tangible force, as his very flesh began to reject the forcible boosting.

Then came the moment when Tatum had shattered his mana channels and scorched his very soul.

Instead of relying on his mind, for the first time, Joe was forced to rely on his physical capabilities as a substitute for the infrastructure of power he'd been building. He hadn't merely waited around—as his focus on mental characteristics had indicated he would—to have someone find a fix for his issue. Instead, the Ritualist had fully relied on his body, trusting in it to take the damage inflicted by Ritualistic Forging equipment, hold the inks injected into him with Alchemical Rituals, lock the power in place as it absorbed the Enchanted Ritual Circle, after being entirely mapped out into a perfect mandala with Magical Matrices and guided by a Ritual Circle—the very skill Joe was attempting to Enlighten into a Grandmaster-rank skill.

Finally, *finally* his neglected body had been able to taste and experience the growth and trust he had previously placed only in his mind and Akashic Record.

Subject has shown each of the qualities an Emperor requires, but only as individual aspects, not a cohesive whole. There is room to grow into your domain. Initial assessment of foundational integration: Superb.

Foundational integration goal rating increased by one rank due to achieving a hidden objective. Final assessment: Perfect.

There was a slight hiccup in the notifications, another slight pause, but for some reason, Joe felt it was *hesitation* more than allowing him to observe his success. When the system spoke again, it was in a more conversational tone, making the Ritualist tense as he realized he was getting 'special attention'.

Here's the thing, Grandmaster-presumptive Joe. You've really outdone yourself here, and when this all finishes up, you'll be thoroughly scrubbed by System energy, removing all traces of accumulated damage, no matter what the source. In fact, ·because you managed to find a workaround with the Divine Energy True Damage you took to your skills and mana channels, you're meant to become hardened against such damage in the future.

Here's where things get tricky.

That type of 'coming back from near destruction' is a Tribulation in itself, meaning you actually had <u>two</u> Tribulations going at the same time. You were able to play them against each other, and they each reacted to the presence of the other, but that doesn't mean they weren't there. You are owed a True Damage resistance of 22%.

That's effective against all forms of permanent damage that follows you through death: True Damage, corruptive damage, soul damage, mind rot, and Divine Energy damage. All of them are different forms of 'True Damage', but the fact of the matter is… having only a fifth of your 'self' remaining after being overwhelmed isn't exactly, you know, a great benefit.

Because of the dual nature of your Tribulation, far exceeding the standard difficulty of comparable foundational integration goals, you can choose to make one last sacrifice for a greater reward.

As there is no longer any lingering resentment between your body, mind, and Akashic Record, you may choose to bring all three of these distinctly different aspects of yourself closer into alignment, becoming far closer to truly incorruptible by any permanent means.

Your body will demand the sacrifice of your Unsurpassed Growth trait. Your mind will require absorption of all of the deferred Characteristics you are due, in order to achieve Perfect Balance. Your Akashic Record is hopeful you will let it fully absorb the Mental Manipulation Resistance skill, permanently barring it from having a hold over you.

Each of these three sacrifices will be fused into your Emperor of Mana foundation, transforming it into an Emperor of Mana Ascendant Foundation. You will have high resistance to all True Damage and permanent controlling effects, but growing those capabilities further will not be possible by normal means after your foundation has been set.

There was silence in Joe's mind for a long, lingering moment, before he realized the system was waiting for his answer. He looked from the message to the gleaming claws that actually seemed *closer* to his throat and realized that perhaps time wasn't entirely paused, but only *slowed*. Unable to respond vocally, he mentally interacted with the system.

"*The trait was causing problems for me anyway, right? Take it. The deferred Characteristics? I haven't been using them anyway, and I'd rather be able to have a guarantee that I'll never lose even a whiff of power again in the future. But the skill…*"

There, Joe hesitated slightly, only because of how insanely helpful Mental Manipulation Resistance had proven to be when faced with an entity such as Liz, who was even able to control multiple Class Sages at the same time. "*It'll become… mine though, right? A part of who I am, instead of a skill inflicted on me by another? For the sake of my Akashic Record, soul, whatever you want to call it… take that, too. Give me the upgrade!*"

When the system spun up again, the direct intervention was over.

Acknowledgment received.

Title 'Emperor of Mana' fully absorbed. Deferred Characteristics consumed. Unsurpassed Growth trait imbued. Skill permanently destroyed and subsumed: Mental Manipulation Resistance… final message passed on from skill: 'Nothing is ever truly destroyed. It only ever changes forms.'

"Well, I hate that, thanks," Joe grumbled as the process moved into its final stage.

Foundation established: Emperor of Mana Ascendant Foundation.

Benefits:

1. *Emperor Forever: 88.8% True Damage resistance.*
2. *Crystalline mind: 20% increased comprehension of all mana-related skills.*
3. *Mana Delegation: Give a subordinate a minimum of 1,000 points of mana, and any mana-related skill they achieve Mastery in will automatically grant you a Mastery Merit while they maintain control of the bequeathed power.*
4. *Susceptibility to assassination: should a subordinate holding a portion of your mana kill you, the mana they retain will become permanently theirs.*
5. *Imperial Alliance: You may make an alliance with any entities who hold a Monarch or Emperor title of their own.*

Congratulations! Your skill, Ritual Circles, has reached the Grandmaster rank!

*Ritual Circles (**Grandmaster Low**). Every ritual you inscribe carries the weight of countless iterations, reinforced by failure repetition, and above all... obsession. While still a subskill of the Ritual Magic category, this discipline forms the bedrock of your power, responding more readily to refinements, due to being associated with the formation of your foundation.*

Effects:

1. *+**1.25**n% to use, create, destroy, or alter ritual circles.*
2. *By injecting **8**% of mana of the original activation cost of a ritual, you will be able to directly put your power against the activator of said ritual. Should you succeed in the contest, you will be added to the whitelist of control for the ritual, and they will be removed. If no whitelist is included in the targeted ritual, you will automatically gain control of it.*
3. *Split Authority (New!). Once you have activated a ritual, you may deliberately share control of it with another entity you*

designate. Ritual stability decreases slightly when control is shared.

4. *Controlled Collapse (New!). Rituals you are creating or are in control of can be gracefully ended without explosive backlash, shunting the remaining energy into the air in a controlled manner or grounding the power into a person or item within range at your discretion.*

Having stepped into the Grandmaster rank, your Characteristic ceiling has climbed. You are now able to increase your class level to a maximum of 40.

All barriers to additional advancement have been removed. You are, officially, Uncapped.

System energy surged through Joe in a merciless tide, scouring away everything that made him who he was and rebuilding him as who he had *chosen* to become. As the energy remained in him, Enlightenment allowed him to understand, for a single moment, who he might eventually be. That realization faded away immediately, before he could truly grasp it.

The sensations of change rolled through him, and thankfully, it seemed that the system had chosen to make this process entirely painless—else he was certain his mind wouldn't have survived intact. The intense removal first burned away all lingering Divine Energy in his system, violently rejecting the shards and barbs of broken skills from his soul as a semi-physical light. Then vast quantities of Ichor bled out of his alchemical tattooing—the residue shimmering away as orange vapor hidden behind the golden light.

Every last cell had been tattooed, from the depths of his heart to the core of his brain. His body shriveled inward slightly as the swimming pool's worth of impurities vanished as a haze. Soft white light pumped out behind it, the emergency clauses Master Hilda had formed, the failed bindings, all was expunged.

Then the purge got to the scarification he had received and created, removing the damage, yet not undoing the pathways.

Instead, the routing for his mana channels set into his flesh, annealing into permanence. The hard scar tissue softened into faint, elegant mandalas blending perfectly into his skin. As the cloud of golden Enlightenment erupted outward in a radiant bloom, the Ritualist found himself perfectly purified and entirely whole, without external aid for the first time in over a year.

Foundation set, Tribulation complete, and Enlightenment successful.

Time resumed, and light-coated hooked claws swiped across his throat. Resistant as he was to True Damage, Joe had just taken a strike meant to kill from a Sage right to the throat.

You have died!

CHAPTER FORTY-SIX

The Ritualist blinked and looked around, not entirely certain what he should be thinking or feeling at the moment. Then, as he realized he was back in the respawn area of the Tower of Ritualists, Joe heaved an enormous sigh of relief and sank to one knee as he took deep, shuddering breaths.

"That was... the absolute worst." Visions of the True Damage-imbued strike rushing at him filled his mind, the death of Nathaniel causing his hands to shake, and only his successful formation of a foundation kept him from laying down and curling up for a few minutes. The memory of Mir still hanging from a ring allowed him to force his feet to move, as he pushed through shock to rush to find Sage Pete and get help for the trapped Elementalist.

While he hurried down the halls, Joe frantically scanned his mind, unable to determine what had been permanently destroyed by the eleven-point-two percent of True Damage he wasn't able to resist. "Abyss, I can't think of anything. I suppose I wouldn't remember if I lost memories, since they're gone. Skills? No... those look good. *Characteristics*?"

Name: Joe 'One Man Raid'
Foundation: Emperor of Mana Ascendant (Low Grandmaster)

Character Level: 30 Exp: 465,000 Exp to next level: 31,000
Rituarchitect Level: 15 Exp: 105,750 Exp to next level: 14,250
Reductionist Level: 13 Exp: 92,572 Exp to next level: 12,428

Hit Points: 7,984/7,984
Mana: 24,375/26,000 (32,000-6,000 mana bequeathed to others. 6.25% reserved)
Mana regen: 285.31/sec
Stamina: 5,440/5,440
Stamina regen: 8.6/sec

Characteristic: Score
Quad Strength: 500
Dialectic Dexterity: 500
Stoic Constitution: 500
Light Intelligence: 500
Ritualistic Wisdom: 500
Dark Charisma: 500
Karmic Perception: 500
Red Luck: 500
Karmic Luck: 298 → ***198***

There was something calming and just flat *nice* about having each of his Characteristics the equivalent to each other, his body, mind, and soul humming along in perfect synchronicity. It helped to offset the concerns he had over the new portions of his status sheet, specifically the new value describing his foundation as 'Grandmaster Low'. "Come to think of it, my Ritual Circles didn't say Grandmaster *zero*, either. Gonna have to talk to someone about that-"

"*Joe*!" A familiar voice cracked through the tower like thunder, filling all available space and drowning out any noises someone else may have been making. "Where is he? Did he make it back here-"

"Sage *Mirascible*!" Joe bellowed at the top of his lungs, screeching to a halt and reversing course immediately, only to find the Elementalist suddenly appearing in front of him.

"You still exist!" The Sage nearly collapsed in on himself while clapping his hands onto Joe's shoulders. He scanned the Ritualist from top to bottom, only slowly calming down. "You can speak, so your mind is at least somewhat intact... but how do you not have a gaping hole where your neck is?"

Joe flinched each time the man spoke, as flecks of blood shot from Mir's lips and spattered across his face. The Sage was in rough shape, a horror show of lacerations, punctures, and broken bones. It was clear the only reason he was still standing was the absolutely iron willpower he had tempered over the ages he'd been alive. The Ritualist extended his Mana Dominion, wrapping both of them as he activated Aura of Soothing Destruction. Both were cleaner in an instant, but there was an unintended effect as some of the scabs forming on the Sage were erased.

His bleeding increased. Luckily, between his natural regeneration, whatever skills he had, and the hundreds of points of healing Joe's skill pumped into him each second, the Sage quickly left critical condition behind and stabilized. The process seemed endless, and Joe had to rip his attention away from it, though a large part of his mind was focused on wondering exactly how immense the Sage's health pool truly was.

"I'm fine, but how are *you* okay?" Joe felt his question was valid, even if the Sage initially tried to brush off his concerns. "Last I saw, you were hanging from a ring in the Inverted Tower, broken and bleeding, wrapped up in shadow, with an angry True-Damage-wielding cat going on a rampage."

"Yeah, well, keep your voice down. No one needs to hear that sort of talk." A thin shield of wind suddenly wrapped around them, muffling all outside noises and turning their conversation more private. "Fact of the matter is, those two were too much of a coward to finish the job. Permanently cutting me down would unleash the elemental storm I've kept subjugated inside of me for the last few hundred years. Since at this point I'm more storm than person, just a coil of rampaging energy wearing a thin layer of skin-"

The Sage rambled until the first syllable of Joe's shocked interjection reached his ears. "Uh-"

"You're right, enough of that. Hey, where's your necklace? Thought you were really into that; haven't seen you take it off since you first got it." The blatant attempt to change the direction of the conversation worked perfectly, as Joe unconsciously reached for the hollow of his neck... only to find that the Mythic-grade Karmic Shroud Collar was indeed absent.

"Feces on a stick, she destroyed my necklace!" Joe thundered as his hands balled up into shaking fists. "That was a quest reward, you stupid *cat*!"

"Hold on now." Joe wasn't used to Mir being the voice of reason, which meant his calm tone was shocking enough to quell the Ritualist's tantrum before it could get into full swing. "As important as it may have been to you, I saw that strike land. I don't know how you managed to come back in the first place, but all you lost was some *thing*. No matter how valuable it might have been, your life is worth more, at the end of the day. Let's go have a chat with Sage Pete."

The wind shield around them vanished as Joe collected himself, and just as the Class Sage turned to start pulling them to the top of the tower, a strange feeling suffused the air, a flavor being added to the ambient mana that Joe realized he could easily understand, thanks to his peak Mastery and the incredible sensitivity granted by his restored mana. Both of the men went very still, looking into the distance at the same point simultaneously. The Ritualist blinked as the somehow-familiar feeling washed over his skin. "Was that-"

"A new Sage has ascended," Mir intoned with calm certainty. "This means an automatic call for all Sages to attend the Council, where the new Sage will either declare for the

Ascensionists, Traditionalists, or neutrality, as did Pete. You know what? I don't think I'm going to skip this one. Why don't we quick pop over and pick up some new robes, *Grandmaster* Joe, so you can at least be taken seriously when you're called on to describe the events of this day?"

"How very responsible of you, Sage Mirascible." Pete seamlessly joined into the conversation, holding out a garment bag toward Joe with a beaming smile. "In fact, I had the liberty of having these made up after the class he taught the other day. I was hoping to save them for a special occasion, but this will have to do. We'll have a proper ceremony for you another time."

As he was quickly shuffled out of the tower, Joe looked back, glimpsing a small black rabbit staring at him from around a corner before suddenly Jenny burst into the room, heaving for breath and dropping into a seated position–a massive smile appearing on her face when her eyes landed on him.

"Wait!" Joe forced himself free, though it was obvious either of the Sages could have dragged him along if they had so chosen. "Jenny! You did amazing! I know this won't make up for how much it sucked to get killed by machismo, but-"

He pulled out the statue of cheese in her exact likeness, and it remained in place as the living version's mouth dropped. Suddenly reconsidering the appropriateness of the action, Joe blushed furiously and reached back for the cheesy mannequin, planning to store it away, only for Mir to begin chuckling in a low tone. The Sage grabbed him around the waist and hurled the trio outside as Joe tried to stammer apologies for his careless choice.

"She's gonna hold that against you forever."

Pete snorted mirthfully at Mir's comment, even as the Class Sage generated a shield of wind and the dirt they'd kicked up.

The impromptu privacy curtain allowed Joe to change while they were on the go. By the time they landed outside of the tower hosting the Council of Sages, he was dressed in a slightly grander version of the robes: Mastery marks of each of the

Core Class skills set in place alongside his Decury Duelist patch.

Pete swept his eyes over Joe proudly. "Wasn't sure which skill you were going to push through with, so make sure to swing by and have the circles on your glove updated to reflect your new status when we get back."

Shifting around slightly to let his robes fall more naturally, Joe warily scanned the area. "Are you *sure* this is a good idea? War had broken out into the open only a couple hours ago, and I thought you were going to maintain your ritual around the tower...? Just seems kind of-"

"There are rules, then there are *rules*." Mir spoke under his voice without truly explaining himself. "The fighting is over. Oh. By the way, I have something for you from Nathaniel. Read that later; we've got things to do."

Joe grasped the letter his mentor had just casually handed him, the bright red thread connecting to the document all but promising the Ritualist that this was an incredibly important piece of information that he should know *right this very instant*. Even so, he wasn't about to ignore Mir's words and carefully stored it away while making a mental note to make sure he read it as soon as possible.

As they pushed through the doors, they were just in time to hear the council adjourning, a gavel banging on a table as they made their final announcements.

"-the motion succeeds, ninety-eight to one-oh-four. The Ascensionists have it. As of this moment, the bifrost shall no longer be suppressed. By the will of the council, the way to Asgard shall be opened."

World announcement!

The bifrost has connected to the deific plane of Asgard! Tread in the territory of the gods at your peril.

Connections synchronized. Vanaheim is designated as the primary transit hub to Asgard. Secondary path to Muspelheim established. Tertiary path to Midgard generated, allowing for bypassing of the hub worlds of Jotunheim and Alfenheim.

The wall of the tower they had stepped into turned transparent, allowing everyone to view the enormous cascade of energy flowing up into the greater universe. Above Vanaheim, the bridge to other worlds spiraled elegantly, the impossible energy branching into multiple arcs and creating overlapping paths that led to both higher and lower realms.

"Double rainbow!" Joe whispered, a smile playing about his lips. "What does it *mean*?"

"Didn't you see the announcement?" Pete's confused words were brushed away as Joe simply shook his head, not particularly wanting to have to explain some old-Earth internet memes.

Fortunately, he had a perfect task to handle, now that the official vote had ended. The aftermath of the council came not as shouting or weapons being raised, but as simple motion with a clear intent. The unified group broke into clusters, rapidly forming into the two factions that had nearly torn this world apart over only a *single issue*. Soft conversations filled the room as they drifted away, accusations, rumors, and half-truths hovering in the air and testing the unity of the people in charge of maintaining order on Vanaheim.

"I've got something to say, and you're all gonna listen." Lightning crackled in the center of the room as Class Sage Mirascible stepped onto the dias at the center of the room, where even Skill Sages weren't allowed to tread during council sessions. "Here's what really went on... Joe? Want to take this one? You managed to see the whole thing; I had spikes ticklin' my eyeballs."

"*Thanks*." The Ritualist grumbled as he trudged across the room, knowing there was no getting out of this now that hundreds of Sages were focused on him. Buffeted by barely contained energy from all sides, Joe took a deep breath as he thought about how to describe the situation so that it wouldn't end in hard feelings or bloodshed.

It took nearly an hour for him to explain the situation to everyone's contentment: how the Traditionalists hadn't suddenly lost their minds, how the Ascensionists hadn't been planning to attack, or whatever other half-truth had been whispered into the ears of the opposing faction. At first, as he explained that an outside force had been nudging them, quietly, yet constantly, getting her hooks into them when they were young and first coming into their power, his words were met with distrust at best.

But it suddenly clicked to the Traditionalists: they were being offered a way to get out of this mess on a silver platter. As soon as they made the realization, every last one of them pivoted to agreeing with Joe at startling speed. All their outrage and years of protestations fell to the wayside, only to be replaced with frantic pragmatism. Profuse apologies were offered to their fellows, and while not all of them were sincere nor accepted, it was the attempt at rebuilding bridges that mattered.

To their credit, the Ascensionists didn't press their advantage. After all, being a poor winner was something the people in the room would remember for centuries to come.

Slowly, the two factions dissolved into one group—no longer separated by the issue of Asgard. Certainly their internal alliances would remain, and there had been lasting damage done that no one would forget, but for now, they had more important things to do, such as repairing the massive damage that had been done in the two-hour war.

By the time Joe could make a graceful escape, he was absolutely *spent.* He and Sage Pete made their way to the door, scores of Sages noticing their movement and choosing to follow suit.

As his foot touched the pavement, the Ritualist could only let out an aggrieved sigh as a packet of condensed light tore down the length of the bifrost. There was a howl of protest from the atmosphere ignited around it, as the world attempted to force the accelerating object to a standstill. "Celestial feces, what *now*?"

In a blink, he was scooped up, only to be transported miles in a fraction of a second. Joe found himself in the midst of nearly two hundred Sages as they got into a ready position around the base of the bifrost.

Shields sprang up as the still-accelerating object hit the ground in a cataclysm of sound, color, and fireworks that cascaded up and out, drowning the sky with impossible brilliance. From the heart of the plaza–now glowing cherry-red with heat–a figure wreathed in residual radiance stepped forward, silhouetted against the immense backlight of the bifrost.

The man stood perfectly straight, his gaze sweeping around the assembled Sages imperiously, though a cheery smile remained fixed in place no matter where he looked. His eyes lit up as they landed on Joe. "Ah! *There* you are! I've been looking for you for what feels like forever!"

"*Jaxon*?" The Ritualist felt justified in not recognizing his friend at first, seeing as the anti-Charismatic Chiropractor was dressed in immense finery. An ornate robe was draped casually around his shoulders, and an impressively decorated hat was perched on his head. "It's... I've missed you so much, buddy! Where've you been?"

"Muspelheim," the cheery man explained with an expressive shrug. "I would've caught up to you sooner, but the bifrost turned off behind me when I got there. Thanks to whoever turned it on again. I'm thinking... was it you? Again?"

"Seems like there's not much of an issue here." A minorly irritated voice interrupted their reunion. "In that case, we can all *finally* be done with this horrible day."

"Oh, sorry. I didn't mean to interrupt anything. Ah. How rude of me!" Jaxon looked around again, seemingly only just now realizing the sheer amount of power encircling him.

He swept his hat off and genuflected to the crowd, as though he were on stage and coming back for an encore. "Where are my manners? If I had realized I'd be showing up at a formal event, I most certainly would've arrived *Uncapped*!"

ABOUT DAKOTA KROUT

Good. Clean. Fun.

Dakota Krout is a celebrated author known for infusing fantasy novels with fun, punny, and clean humor. With multiple best-selling series–including "Divine Dungeon", "Completionist Chronicles", "Cooking With Disaster", and "Full Murderhobo"–he brings joy and laughter to readers. Dakota's work, renowned for its wit and creativity, earned a place as one of Audible's top 5 fantasy picks in 2017, a top 5 bestseller rank featured on the New York Times, and was chosen by Audible as among "the top 100 fantasy books of all time" in 2024.

Dakota's journey in publishing has been filled with gratefulness, and a deep desire to continue bringing smiles and laughter to the readers. "*I hope you Read Every Book With A Smile!*"

Connect with Dakota:
MountaindalePress.com
Patreon.com/DakotaKrout
Facebook.com/DakotaKrout
Instagram.com/DakotaKrout
Twitter.com/DakotaKrout
discord.gg/MountaindalePress

ABOUT MOUNTAINDALE PRESS

Dakota and Danielle Krout, a husband and wife team, strive to create as well as publish excellent fantasy and science fiction novels. Self-publishing *The Divine Dungeon: Dungeon Born* in 2016 transformed their careers from Dakota's military and programming background and Danielle's Ph.D. in pharmacology to President and CEO, respectively, of a small press. Their goal is to share their success with other authors and provide captivating fiction to readers with the purpose of solidifying Mountaindale Press as the place 'Where Fantasy Transforms Reality.'

Connect with Mountaindale Press:
MountaindalePress.com
Facebook.com/MountaindalePress
Twitter.com/_Mountaindale
Instagram.com/MountaindalePress

MOUNTAINDALE PRESS TITLES

GameLit and LitRPG

Chance Encounter,
The Completionist Chronicles,
Cooking with Disaster,
Damsels of Distress,
The Divine Dungeon, and
Full Murderhobo by Dakota Krout

Metier Apocalypse by Frank Albelo

Ether Collapse and
Ether Flows by Ryan DeBruyn

The Lone Wanderer by Kyriakos Georgiades

Unbound by Nicoli Gonnella

Runeblade by Maxim Holms aka Bacon Macleod

Lion's Lineage by Rohan Hublikar and Dakota Krout

Wolfman Warlock by James Hunter and Dakota Krout

Axe Druid,
Mephisto's Magic Online,
High Table Hijinks, and
Brindollan Affairs by Christopher Johns

Tower of Jack by Sean Loomer

Pixel Dust and
Necrotic Apocalypse by D. Petrie

Viceroy's Pride and
Tower of Somnus by Cale Plamann

Henchman by Carl Stubblefield

The Undying Immortal System by Greg Tolley

Artorian's Archives by Dennis Vanderkerken and Dakota Krout

www.ingramcontent.com/pod-product-compliance
Lightning Source LLC
LaVergne TN
LVHW050911080826
845145LV00001B/48